LOVERS OF THE DAMNED

# DEMON'S *Heart*

## COLETTE RIVERA

Fated to a broken heart.

Edited by Abbie Nicole

Proofreading by CJ Editing

Cover design by We Got You Covered Book Design

People depicted in the cover image are models and should not be associated with the book.

Interior Illustrations by Angelika Süto, Angki.s_

ISBN

Print: 978-1-991284-08-2

Kindle: 978-1-991284-09-9

# AUTHOR'S NOTE

Dear reader,

This book deals with adult themes and is intended for mature audiences. If you wish to view a list of possible triggers, they can be found in the final paragraph of this note. Please take care and use your discretion.

*Demon's Heart* is part of a series with an overarching plot. If you haven't started the *Lovers of the Damned* series, it's recommended to begin with *Demon's Mate*. The romance in *Demon's Heart* stands alone and ends in a happily ever after, but every question you have about the external story and the world won't be answered by the end. You can expect a minor series-related cliffhanger. Each book in this series features a different couple.

A note about the sooty shearwater: While some facts about sooty shearwaters presented here are representative of the real birds, others have been changed to suit the story.

Content & Trigger Warnings: (may contain spoilers) Main character with abusive relationships in his past. The nature of the abuse is not discussed in detail. Magical and physical violence. Main character violently attacked on-page. This character later experiences on-page flashbacks to the attack. Mention of witches who worship Satan. Blood-drinking—similar to vampires. Biting kink. Sexual content: intended for mature audiences.

LOVERS OF THE DAMNED

# DEMON'S Heart

## COLETTE RIVERA

1

______

## DANTE

DANTE'S HEART STOPPED. Nothing existed except the pair of bright-hazel eyes pinning him down.

"Hey, glad you could make it." Ollie Hudson smiled, dimples cutting into his soft, pale cheeks, his tumble of blond hair surrounding him like divine light.

Dante's heart restarted, thudding so hard it reverberated through his body. The apartment around Ollie came back into focus. Dante cleared his throat. "Uh. Me too."

Ollie's lips quirked. "Want a drink or something?"

"That would be wonderful, thank you." Dante rubbed the back of his neck, butterflies rioting in his chest. Had that sounded all right or was he being too formal?

Ollie turned away, navigating around a well-worn couch and heading for the kitchen in the small apartment he shared with Harper.

Dante's gaze cut to his demon brother Ash, finding an assessing look in his eye. Dante had to get it together. He was powerful and thousands of years old. Self-control was easy. Or it would have been if not for the man eagerly returning with two beers.

Damnation, that smile. Ollie pulled off angelic beauty so naturally that it wasn't fair. Angels weren't even real.

Dante couldn't do this. He shouldn't have come to dinner.

Ash, whom he'd known for millennia, recently found his mate, Harper, the young witch living with Ollie. Ash and Harper were the first mated pair out of the Fallen. Before Ash, most demons believed they'd never find their mates.

Being around Harper and Ash breathed new life into Dante's tired soul. Seeing their bond strengthen as they doted on each other was everything Dante imagined finding your mate to be. But letting the pair drag him into Ollie's presence was complicated.

Dante ached for his mate. His heart bled. He'd never lost hope he'd find his fated love, damning him to a wait that had become more agonizing with each passing century.

His gaze cut back to Ollie, snagging on his lovely curls. They'd be soft under Dante's fingers. His skin too. Ollie's round face gave him an air of innocence, even as mischief gleamed in his green-and-brown-flecked eyes.

He was perfect.

"How do you and Ash know each other?" Ollie asked as he handed Dante a beer, his keen gaze dragging slowly down Dante's body.

Dante's blood heated, and he willed his demon fire to calm. "We've known each other since we were young. We...uh..." He paused. "We moved here together some years ago."

Ash snorted, and Harper elbowed the bulky demon in the side.

Dante couldn't tell Ollie he was a demon, or that he and Ash hadn't so much moved as fallen to Earth in search of their mates thousands of years ago. Ollie was human and unaware of the magic world. He had no idea beings other than humans existed, and with their wings, tails, and horns hidden, Dante and Ash looked like nothing more than large men.

"You picked a good place to move. I love Shearwater Landing." Ollie's dimples reappeared. "It's such a great city. Coming here for school was the best decision I ever made."

Dante shifted closer to Ollie, pulled by an invisible force strangling his heart. Ollie's subtle scent of sandalwood on a fresh early morning filled Dante's lungs, urging him to embrace Ollie and breathe him in.

It could only mean one thing.

Dante stood next to his mate. His damned demon soul screamed with the truth of it, a gut feeling so strong his whole body was electrified.

His wings itched to come out, the tattoos on his back prickling. Dante rolled his shoulders, his legs threatening to give out. What if he gave in to relief and dropped to his knees, reached for Ollie's hand, and pressed his lips to Ollie's skin?

He'd be right where he was meant to be.

After thousands of years of searching, he could finally be home.

"I can't imagine living anywhere else," Ollie went on, oblivious to the way he'd changed Dante's life.

"Me either," Harper agreed, throwing an adoring look at Ash.

Dante swallowed past the lump in his throat. He had to get his shit together. He'd freak Ollie out if he kneeled and professed his eternal devotion.

He'd suspected Ollie was his mate when they'd first met. The encounter had been brief but enough. Today confirmed he hadn't imagined it. Ollie was his.

Ollie's phone chimed on the coffee table, and he scrambled to grab it. His cheeks turned red as he swiped a notification away, then stuffed the phone in his pocket. "Stupid app." He rolled his eyes.

Harper frowned. "Is it that guy again?"

"Not that one, no." Ollie shot Harper a cryptic look and took a swig of his beer. He crossed the room and cozied up to his friend's side, saying something too quiet to hear.

Was Ollie messaging men on a dating app? A rumble started low in Dante's chest.

Ash appeared at his elbow and thumped his back. "You good?"

"Fine." Dante cleared his throat.

"You might want to stop growling," Ash muttered.

"That wasn't a growl." Dante couldn't tear his eyes from Ollie. He focused his demon sense to pick up what Ollie was saying.

"I might go for it," Ollie whispered to Harper. "He's hot..."

Ash pinched Dante's arm. "Don't eavesdrop. It's rude."

Like Ash was one to talk. Dante turned away from Ollie and narrowed his eyes at his oldest friend. "He's talking about seeing some other man."

Ash's hard brow furrowed, then his eyes widened. "So he *is* your mate."

Flutters erupted in Dante's chest. "How...how did you know?" He hadn't shared his suspicions with Ash.

Ash's lips twisted in a smug smile. "Why else would you care who he sees? I knew it. Well, I hoped he was your mate when you first met him—the way you reacted—but I didn't want to pry." Ash gripped Dante's shoulder. "Congratulations, brother. I'm so happy for you."

Dante couldn't appreciate Ash's warmth. "Congratulations are premature. He's human. How will I ever explain this to him?"

Ollie laughed at something Harper said, sending tingles down Dante's spine.

Ash seemed nonplussed, his face hard as stone once more. "I thought Harper was human when I first met him. It's not impossible to work through. Besides, you have us to help. Enjoy this moment, Dante. You fucking deserve it."

Some of Dante's tension melted away. Ash was right. He should enjoy the way Ollie overwhelmed his senses, calling to him like a siren's song as the beginning of their bond sparked between them. He'd imagined finding his mate for so long, seeing this moment as the finish line when it was actually the beginning.

There was no rush to explain anything to Ollie. Surely, he'd feel the connection too. It would all happen naturally.

Dante approached Ollie and Harper across the living room. They'd stopped whispering, a lull in their conversation. Hopefully, he wasn't interrupting.

"What did you study when you moved here for school?" Dante asked Ollie.

Ollie's attention snapped to Dante so fast he had to feel the pull between them. "I went to the city's vocational school to become a hairstylist. I gave Harper his new look. Black suits him, don't you think?"

Harper ruffled his hair.

"It looks good." Dante's gaze slid back to Ollie. "So does yours."

Ollie bit his lower lip. "Thanks. Um, so what do you do?"

What did he do? Dante couldn't exactly say he was once in Lucifer's inner circle and now a sworn enemy of the Devil. "I'm involved with looking after the local shearwater population."

"Cool, like a biologist?" Ollie stepped closer.

"Yeah, I'm a conservation biologist." It was close enough to the truth. Dante had built a magical connection to the shearwaters in the area, creating his flock of loyal birds. He'd protect them and conserve their habitat at all costs.

A crease appeared on Ollie's brow. "Are shearwaters endangered?"

His immediate concern warmed Dante's core. None of his chosen brothers understood his love for the birds. "No. The sooty shearwater is near threatened, but luckily not endangered."

Ollie's eyes widened. "Near threatened sounds ominous."

"It's not so dire. They're two classes away from officially endangered."

"Oh right. Well, that's good." Ollie gazed into Dante's eyes and seemed to lose track of his words. He shifted subtly closer, his head tilted up.

What if Dante leaned down and covered Ollie's lips with his?

"Yes, it's a good thing the birds have Dante to look after them," Ash said with a laugh, sliding past them into the kitchen.

Ollie blinked and took a step back, averting his eyes as he sipped his drink. "Do you need a hand with anything, Ash?"

"No, I'm good." Ash grinned as he tied a small apron around his massive body. "Relax and enjoy your evening."

"You don't have to tell me twice. I'm going to put my feet up." Ollie's attention returned to Dante. "Wanna join?"

"Lead the way." Dante would follow his mate anywhere. Do anything. But he'd start with getting to know him.

2

———

OLLIE

OLLIE SUNK into the couch cushions and had another sip of beer. There were worse things to do on a Saturday evening than sit around with a hottie like Dante while Harper's equally attractive boyfriend cooked dinner.

Dante sat beside Ollie. He could totally wrap Ollie up with those strong arms. All Ollie needed to do was get a little closer... He bit back the urge.

*Stick to harmless flirting, not cuddling, geez.*

"Tell me more about the shearwaters." Ollie rested a hand on Dante's forearm. He couldn't help himself. The contact sent a shiver through him, and his pulse spiked.

He withdrew his hand. Holy shit, his blood was rushing south from one little touch. He crossed his legs, doing his best to ignore the beginnings of arousal.

Dante's dark gaze lingered on Ollie's hand. He had the most gorgeous eyes. His irises were a dynamic black, deep and inky, with the darkest brown flecks. His attention was ten times more intense than anyone Ollie had met.

"The shearwater population here is unique. Most of the species migrate across the globe, but not the individuals here."

Dante ran a large hand through his curly black hair. "I could go on, though it's not always the most interesting topic." He gave a tiny, almost shy smile.

It wasn't fair for a man like Dante to be bashful. It made him more attractive, and he needed no help. Dante was at least six feet of lean muscle. His simple T-shirt stretched across his toned chest. And fuck, Ollie was picturing all the perfect brown skin and black chest hair that lay beneath.

The last time Dante had been at his and Harper's apartment, Dante hadn't been wearing a shirt. It'd been weird because Ash hadn't had a shirt on either, but that was the day Ollie had learned his roommate had escaped a satanic cult, so he'd been too distracted to ask why everyone was walking around half-dressed.

Some guys used any excuse to strip down and show off, but Ollie didn't get that impression from Dante. Or Ash.

"I think conservation is interesting," Ollie said. "How could it not be? We should care about how we impact the planet and all the animals."

Dante beamed. "I agree." He seemed so pleased Ollie was showing interest in the local seabirds.

It was fucking adorable.

Ollie's phone chimed. That stupid app, going by the sound. Damn, he should have silenced it. He didn't even want to check the notification. Hooking up with his latest match had lost all its appeal.

That guy had nothing on Dante, who had launched into an explanation of shearwater mating habits and how most flocks migrate to the Southern Hemisphere, of all places.

Dante was smart and hot. And probably not a total dick. Ash was too much of a softie to have an asshole best friend. He lived to spoil Harper, and Ollie supported it one hundred percent.

The more Ollie learned about Harper, the more he wanted to wrap the guy in bubble wrap and destroy anyone who'd been mean to him. But Ash seemed to have that covered. He was a good guy, and Ollie was only letting good people into his life from now on.

He'd had more than enough of assholes.

Too bad he couldn't always sniff out the shitty people when looking for casual hookups. The whole point was not getting to know anyone, and for short encounters, it worked. There wasn't much time to be a dick.

But fuck, some of the messages he'd gotten were rude.

Dante, on the other hand, seemed considerate. Okay, shit, it went beyond that. He looked at Ollie like he'd discovered gold, and there was nothing like a little ego boost, even if nothing would happen between them.

"I can't believe they usually fly to the other side of the world to mate," Ollie said as Dante paused in explaining the intricacies of the sooty shearwater.

Dante chuckled. "Too much effort?"

"Maybe." Ollie shrugged. Animals did go through a lot to bone.

"I don't know. I'm sure it's worth it." Dante's lips twitched, and he averted his eyes.

Why was that suggestive? Excitement fluttered in Ollie's chest, but he tamped it down.

Dante cleared his throat. "Anyway. Sorry. I'm babbling."

"Don't even worry about it." Ollie nudged Dante's arm playfully with his elbow.

Dante was too cute. If Ollie had randomly met him at a party or a bar he'd make a move, but Dante wasn't random. Harmless flirting was one thing. Hooking up with one of Harper's very committed boyfriend's friends was bound to get messy.

And that was a world of not worth it.

Dante was probably boyfriend material, all committed like Ash, and casual sex was it for Ollie. He was *not* looking for a relationship or anything remotely resembling one.

Not even with someone like Dante.

DANTE RETURNED to the couch with two more drinks, handing one to Ollie. "Where did you live before coming to Shearwater Landing?"

Ollie shifted, turning sidewise, facing Dante but putting himself farther away than before. "Not far from here. About two hours inland."

Dante seemed to take this random detail seriously, nodding like it made sense.

Ollie didn't get it.

Dante's focus hadn't wavered, even after exhausting the shearwater talk. The attention was nice, but it was starting to feel like Ollie was on a date.

Ollie hadn't considered the potential double date vibes when he'd told Harper to invite Ash's friend. Maybe he should have.

Dante smiled and took a sip of his drink. "Have you always lived that close to the city, or did you move around with your family?"

Ollie shifted, trying to get comfortable again. "I've never lived anywhere else."

"Do you have any siblings?"

"No, I'm an only child." Ollie's insides twisted. Why so many questions? This was really date-like behavior, right?

But this wasn't a date. It wasn't. Ollie wasn't okay with it turning into one and didn't want to explain that to Dante. He shouldn't have to.

"Sorry." Dante's brow furrowed. "Do you not like talking about your past or your family?"

"Um..." Ollie squirmed. "No, it's fine. It's not very interesting. I don't have family drama or anything."

"That's good. I can't say the same, but it's all old news."

Great, now they were talking about their families. Why couldn't they talk about meaningless fluff, flirt like it was nothing, and have fun? Why did this have to feel like it was turning into something?

Or was that all in Ollie's head?

He needed to stay centered. Be rational. These were all normal things to chat about. It didn't necessarily mean anything. There was no reason to freak out, but not knowing Dante's intentions twisted Ollie up inside.

It was okay for Dante to want to get to know him, as long as Dante didn't have some hidden agenda or think it was going to get him more than friendship.

Ollie could see that Dante was probably just being friendly. In which case, this was good. Ollie didn't have to be on edge. All he had to do was chill the fuck out. Act like he had when Dante first walked in the door.

Maybe a little less flirty, to be on the safe side. He hadn't meant to get so carried away, touching and looking at Dante so obviously.

Ollie's phone chimed again, and he pulled it out of his pocket. "Sorry, let me get this."

Dante sipped his drink. "Sure thing."

Ollie unlocked his phone.

There were two messages from the guy he'd been talking to that day. And...one was a dick pic. Ollie's cheeks heated. At least the phone was angled so Dante couldn't see.

The guy wanted a picture in return. Ollie paused. He had

an album of ready-to-send shots but closed the app without replying.

He silenced his phone and put it away, not sure why. He wouldn't hook up with Dante, so why not stick to his plan of lining something up for later tonight?

Swearing off relationships after his last one blew up was the right thing to do, but Ollie hadn't sworn off sex, and getting laid whenever he wanted, with whomever he wanted, had seemed like the dream. Until it hadn't.

The hookup scene kind of sucked and had left a sour taste in Ollie's mouth for a while, forcing him to realize he liked being emotionally connected to his sexual partners. But what Ollie liked wasn't good for him.

He was drawn to men who didn't want to let him go, and not in a good way. Two toxic relationships in a row and a situationship with someone who used him were enough to make him glad to be single. Even if he ended up having less sex than he wanted, it was better than the alternative.

Relationships were a breeding ground for manipulative behavior. Ollie needed to be his own person, have his own life, and not disappear into someone else's world. His stomach still cramped whenever his mind strayed to his college boyfriend.

At least he'd gotten out. He'd even started putting his life back together. But he'd still wanted a relationship and had fallen into something just as bad before he could blink.

So he wasn't falling into anything again.

Ollie set his drink on the coffee table. "I'll be right back." He jumped up and disappeared into the bathroom.

Taking out his phone, Ollie selected a picture and sent it to the guy. The shot showed the tops of his thighs, his hand fisted around his hard cock, and his tidy manscaping, with the top of the frame cutting off above his belly button.

The message went to read almost instantly. Then, a notification popped up saying the user had blocked him.

Fuck.

Ollie closed the app and gritted his teeth. He hated this.

He deleted the app from his phone and opened his favorite social media, scrolling through his feed until a post made him smile.

Screw that guy. Ollie liked how he looked. He wasn't ripped, but so what? He didn't hate his soft stomach or wish he had a different body. Fuck any guy who didn't agree. They didn't deserve to touch him.

Ollie liked a post and scrolled on.

The evening had started off so promising. Now, all he wanted to do was hide in his room.

Ollie left the bathroom and grabbed his drink from the coffee table. Harper was busy chatting with Dante, and for a second, Ollie felt like he was being pulled back to the couch by a magnet. Like he *needed* to be near Dante.

His pulse picked up.

That was a dangerous fucking reaction, and Ollie didn't trust it.

He pretended not to notice how Dante's attention found him as soon as he entered the room and slipped into the kitchen without interrupting Harper.

Ollie leaned against the counter. "What are you making?" he asked Ash.

"Stuffed mushrooms and French onion chicken." A timer beeped, and Ash added a second tray to the oven, checking the one already in there. He straightened and pulled off his oven mitts. "Oh, and a salad."

"You really like cooking, don't you?"

Ash grinned. "I like when Harper eats my food. But the

process is actually quite relaxing. I haven't found a recipe I can't conquer for him."

Ollie snorted into his drink. "Oh my god, you're so cute with Harper. It's sickening."

Ash laughed. "Don't care."

Ollie loved that Ash didn't give a fuck what anyone thought. Ollie tried to be like that, but he was mostly faking it.

He glanced back at Harper and Dante. "Harper hasn't had any more issues with that cult his family was in, right?"

"No." Ash frowned, his eyes weirdly intense. It honestly looked a little scary. "They've left him alone."

"Good." Ollie grabbed an olive off the cutting board and popped it in his mouth.

Harper and Ash's relationship had moved worryingly fast. Ollie's relationships always moved fast. He'd been consumed from the get-go, letting his boyfriends' lives overtake his until there was nothing left, too wrapped up in the honeymoon phase to see the red flags.

But Ash and Harper weren't like that. Harper hung around the apartment with Ollie as much as before, spent time with Ollie without Ash, and seemed to have plenty of independent activities. From what Ollie could see, Ash was building Harper up rather than trying to change his life or take it over.

It was proof relationships weren't always bad, but Ollie knew that already. It didn't mean he was willing to risk getting involved in something. Being his own person was more important than having a partner.

And sex was overrated anyway.

3

———

# DANTE

"I THINK I SCARED HIM OFF," Dante grumbled to Ash as they flew over Shearwater Landing, the city lights twinkling below them.

They'd left Ollie and Harper at their apartment after dinner and were headed home. It felt wrong to fly away from Ollie, every wing stroke taking extra effort. But what else could Dante do?

"Scared is a bit dramatic," Ash called over his shoulder.

Dante focused on beating his wings, not bothering to disagree. Maybe he hadn't *scared* Ollie, but something had happened. Ollie had seemed less happy at the end of the night than he had at the start.

Dante had attempted to be engaging. Was it not enough? Maybe he seemed boring to a bright young man like Ollie.

Ash and Dante landed on the deck attached to Dante's large clifftop home overlooking the city and the ocean. It sat in the middle of a nature reserve, the whole building protected by an illusion to prevent humans from discovering it and by powerful spells to keep other magical beings out.

Dante opened one of the massive sliding glass doors and walked inside, tucking his wings against his back.

His muscles relaxed as the familiar scent of wood and leather filled his nose. He loved his home. He'd had it designed to accommodate him in his full demon form, but his affection for the place was more than practical. He'd dreamed of having his mate here one day and had kept everything minimalistic so his mate could put his touch on the place.

It was a building block, ready to be molded to fit him and his mate as they made their life together. He and Ollie.

Dante wandered to the open-plan kitchen and pulled out his candy drawer, craving chocolate. He selected two of his favorite bars.

"Would you like some blood with that?" Ash asked as he opened the fridge.

Demons had to drink blood to maintain their immortality in the Human Realm. Eating human food wasn't necessary, but Dante enjoyed it, especially anything sweet.

"Sure, thanks." He ate his first chocolate bar in three bites.

Ash poured bagged blood into two mugs and popped them in the microwave.

Dante bought blood from a vampire-run organization that sourced it from donors aware of magic. It was a much easier setup than when demons had first arrived and had to hypnotize unsuspecting humans to drink from them.

Ash handed Dante a mug. "You didn't scare Ollie off."

Dante set the mug aside and had a bite of his second bar. "Then why didn't it seem like he wanted to talk to me?"

Ash's brow creased. "He was stealing glances at you all night. And you two talked plenty."

Dante finished the chocolate. "I suppose you're right. I'm probably overthinking it, but it's hard not to when all I want to do is pull him close and never let him go."

Ash gripped Dante's shoulder. "I know. I felt that way too. At least you aren't in denial about your feelings."

"Maybe my feelings are the problem. What if Ollie doesn't sense the connection?" At first, it seemed like he had, then by the end of the night, Dante wondered if he'd imagined Ollie's interest.

"It's harder to feel the bond when you don't know mates exist," Ash reminded him. "These things are more subtle for humans, but the way Ollie looked at you tells me he felt something. Did you get his phone number? You can take him out on a date and let the connection grow."

Dante's cheeks heated. "I didn't get his number, but even if I had, it's not like I know how to date."

He'd never participated in modern dating. A century ago, he'd given up all physical intimacy to wait for his mate, no longer interested in satisfying his carnal desires with more than his hand.

"Spend time with him. Dating isn't much more complicated than that." Ash patted Dante's shoulder, then drained his mug. "He seemed interested to me. Maybe hesitant, but that's not bad. Harper hated me after our one-night stand. If we figured it out, so will you."

Dante pushed away fantasies of finding his mate and instantly having a cemented bond. No one but a demon would want to move that fast.

Ash and Harper's bond had grown naturally. There wasn't an on-off switch. The connection—magical and emotional—would build over time.

Dante could be patient as his and Ollie's bond blossomed. What was a little more waiting? Besides, this was a journey for him and Ollie to go on together. Why skip to fully bonded when they could enjoy getting there?

What did Ollie like? What did he dream about? What made him sad, and what brought him joy? Dante had to know it all.

He pulled a third candy bar out of the drawer.

"Drink your blood." Ash slid the mug closer to him. "Don't let your senses overwhelm you around Ollie. The last thing you need is to drop your fangs if he gets a little too friendly."

"Yeah, okay." Dante sipped the blood, hoping the mug hid the renewed flame in his cheeks. His insides twisted, skin heating until moisture prickled at the back of his neck.

He imagined Ollie touching him, kissing him, or—*damnation*—having sex with him, their bodies twined together.

Dante wanted it all now.

He was ready. But Ollie wasn't, and that was more important than indulging his baser instincts.

"I'm going to check on the birds." Dante set his empty mug in the sink. "Want to come?"

"Sure." Ash flexed his white-tipped black wings and untied his shirt from his belt, discarding it on the counter.

Dante did the same. There was no point in bringing needless clothes when flying around invisible.

It was a beautiful summer night, a sea breeze cutting through the warm air as crickets sang. Dante and Ash took to the air from the deck, flying around the cliff. They hugged the side of the sheer drop as Dante inspected the shearwaters nested for the night on their various perches.

A few untucked their beaks and opened their eyes as Dante and Ash flew passed. His birds always sensed his presence, whether he was visible or not. It was similar to how he and Ash could see each other when no one else could.

All seemed quiet around the cliff, so Dante headed north along the coast, not ready to return home.

Some of his birds had been killed recently. It might have been Lucifer. None had died since the Devil retreated to the

Realm of the Damned, but Dante was keeping an eye on things. How the birds died was still a mystery, and killing them didn't fit with Luc's other activities, no matter how Dante tried to parse Luc's motivations.

Dante, Ash, and Onyx—Lucifer's younger brother—escaped the Realm of the Damned two hundred years ago, and when Luc finally followed them to the Human Realm last month, they'd been prepared for him to try and drag them back. But he hadn't gone straight for an attack as expected.

Capturing his Hounds had to be Luc's goal. But why had Luc stalked Ash and Harper around the city? Dante hated to admit it, but Luc had had the upper hand. Why waste it?

That wasn't like him.

Missing their chance to imprison the backstabbing swine was a blow, but not when weighed against saving Harper. They'd get Luc. He'd come back to the Human Realm, and now that Dante knew Luc could disguise himself in the magic he'd stolen from him, Ash, and Onyx, Luc wouldn't be able to use the same trick twice.

But there was no ignoring the unease of not knowing what the Devil would do next.

## 4

## OLLIE

OLLIE WOKE up Sunday morning with a half-hard cock and a sinking disappointment crushing his chest.

What the...? Had he been having some sort of weird dream? He closed his eyes, and Dante's magnetic stare popped into his head.

Nope. He was not lying around longing for some guy he'd met twice. He wasn't disappointed about Dante. How could he be when he didn't want anything from the guy?

Ollie had everything he needed. No man necessary. Even not getting laid last night wasn't a big deal. Whatever was going on with his sad boner was nothing but a weird fluke.

Ollie ignored his cock until his erection deflated. He had brunch plans to get ready for.

An hour later, his best friend Dex buzzed to be let into the building.

Ollie already had a fan going. The apartment had never cooled down last night, and he almost couldn't bring himself to preheat the oven.

A knock came from the front door, and Ollie hurried down the hall.

"I've got cinnamon rolls." Dex lifted a familiar canvas bag, grinning like a dork.

"Thank god." Ollie pulled him inside. "They're the only thing worth heating this place up for."

More Sundays than not, Dex came over for brunch, bringing day-old treats from the bakery on the ground floor of his building. They'd started the tradition years ago when they were both still studying and couldn't afford to go out. The bakery owner often gave Dex stuff for free back then, after everything that had happened with Dex's parents, but now Dex insisted on paying.

Dex headed straight for the kitchen. "The cinnamon rolls are fresh, by the way. They'd still be hot if it didn't take so long to walk here."

Ollie flipped on the coffee maker. "But we're supposed to get day-old stuff. It's tradition."

Dex unpacked the cinnamon rolls. "Screw tradition. Look at these."

Three large cinnamon rolls sat in a tray, smothered with icing. "Fuck yeah. Okay, they look better than sex."

Dex snorted. "I'm guessing you stayed in last night." His teasing smile fell. "Or was he an ass?"

"No. I stayed in." Ollie turned away and got out the mugs. "I'm over hookups."

"For real?"

"Yeah." Ollie leaned against the counter and crossed his arms. "I spend more time getting rejected and scrolling than having fun. I deleted the app."

"If it's not making you feel good, that's probably the right thing to do." Dex bumped his shoulder into Ollie's encouragingly.

"I've grown so much, figuring out how to do what's right for me," Ollie muttered.

"You have," Dex said, apparently ignoring Ollie's sarcasm as he put the cinnamon rolls in the oven.

Ollie bit back a smile.

He fucking loved Dex in a non-romantic way.

Dex had helped him get away from his abusive college boyfriend, Brayden, even after Ollie had been a terrible friend and ignored Dex for months. He used to think he didn't deserve Dex, but that wasn't true. He deserved a good friend as much as Dex did and hadn't flaked on Dex once since he'd left that asshole.

Ollie pulled a few containers of fruit out of the fridge and began washing them.

Across the living room, the bathroom door swung open. "Hey, I'll be back out in a minute," Harper called as he hurried to his room, wrapped in a towel.

Ollie smiled. Harper always seemed excited to join him and Dex, no matter what they were doing.

"How was dinner with his boyfriend last night?" Dex asked after Harper disappeared.

Ollie placed the fruit on a cutting board and grabbed a knife. "It was good."

Dex paused with a stack of plates in his hand. "But..."

Ollie narrowed his eyes. "I didn't say there was a but."

Dex set the plates down, brows raised. "I'll wait."

He gave the best—or was it the worst—knowing looks. Dex had these cool gray eyes that made him seem intense even when he didn't mean to be. Kind of like Dante's stare, but Dex had never made Ollie's insides melt.

Ollie might as well give in. Dex could stand there all day. "Ash brought his hot friend, and I may have flirted a little too much right off the bat. I think he likes me." He grimaced.

"Oh, the horror." Dex pressed his hand to his chest, his face blank and tone criminally dry.

Ollie pushed him. Dex didn't budge. "You know I hate turning down guys who want to date me."

"Did he ask you out?"

"No." Ollie turned back to the fruit. "But I got a vibe."

Dex grabbed Ollie's shoulder and shifted him back around. "You know I love teasing you, but if him liking you makes you uncomfortable, there's nothing to feel bad about in turning him down."

"I know." Ollie puffed out a tired breath. "But I hate the whole...you know, confrontation. Especially when they aren't dicks about it."

Turning down kind, considerate guys was harder than turning down guys who got defensive. People who got mad about your rejection weren't people you wanted to date, but knowing someone was a decent person still wasn't enough to tempt Ollie into a relationship.

It wasn't only about fear of finding himself in an abusive or unhealthy situation again. Not dating was about being true to himself and not defaulting to someone else. It was a bad habit Ollie fell into, and it could happen even with the most respectful partner.

He wasn't living for other people anymore. Not at the expense of himself.

"Maybe you should lay out your boundaries before he asks you out. Be upfront so there's no confusion," Dex suggested.

That wasn't a bad idea. "Maybe. I guess there's nothing wrong with being clear where I'm at. But I don't know when I'll hang out with him again, so I'll worry about it later."

Harper reappeared in the living room, wearing cut-off shorts and a crop top.

"Look at you." Ollie grinned. He'd never seen Harper in a crop top.

Harper's cheeks turned pink, and he ran a hand over his shirt. "Does it look okay?"

"It looks great."

Harper smiled, his cheeks fading to their usual color. He'd confided in Ollie that he'd never been allowed to dress the way he wanted growing up. Seeing Harper flourish now that he was free of his family and their cult gave Ollie all sorts of proud, warm tingles.

How cool was it that he got to be part of Harper exploring new things and getting to know himself better?

They all fixed their coffees and plated the cinnamon rolls and fruit, taking everything to the living room. The small apartment didn't have a dining table, but Ollie never missed it. Other than last night, it wasn't like he hosted dinner parties.

Ollie turned on the TV and his PlayStation before sitting on the couch between Dex and Harper. "What are we feeling today?" He set his plate on the coffee table and grabbed a controller to scroll through his loaded games.

Harper took a bite of cinnamon roll, shaking his head. "I won't play."

"Are you not into gaming?" Dex asked like he couldn't understand how someone would pass it up.

Harper shrugged. "I've never played."

"Really?" Ollie was sure Harper hadn't mentioned that before.

"I never had a chance. We didn't have anything like this where I grew up. It wasn't the kind of thing my family wanted me doing." Dark emotion flashed across Harper's face before disappearing as he turned back to his food.

"You should give it a try," Dex offered. He didn't know the details of Harper's family situation but always opted to encourage people. "We can do a racing game and take turns playing the winner."

Ollie nudged Harper. "Go on. Plus, when you lose, you can eat your cinnamon roll while you wait for another turn, and is that really losing?"

Harper set his plate aside. "All right, good point. But this might be painful to watch. I won't even know what buttons to push."

It was more hilarious than painful. Harper couldn't seem to stop waving his arms and moving his whole body when he turned. Ollie's stomach ached from laughing.

"There's too many barriers," Harper whined as he smashed into a wall.

Dex's car shot past him. "Look how much fun you're having."

Harper laughed as he rear-ended another car. "Yeah, but I need a lot of practice. I don't even know how to drive in real life."

Ollie polished off the last of his cinnamon roll. "I don't think it would help. I haven't driven in at least a year, and I'm great at this game."

He borrowed his parents' car when he was home to visit, but there was no way he'd keep a vehicle in the city.

At the end of the race, Harper forfeited the controller to Ollie.

"Speaking of, I think I'm going to sell my parents' car," Dex said way too casually. "That way, I can rent out the parking spot."

Ollie put the controller down and faced him. "Are you sure?"

Dex averted his gaze. "I don't use it, so there's no point keeping it. I figured it was time."

Ollie's chest pinched. Dex holding on to the car had always been more sentimental than practical. "You ready for that?"

Dex cleared his throat. "Yeah. I am. I dunno. I might sell the condo too."

Ollie's eyes widened.

"Not right now," Dex hurried to say before focusing on the controller in his hands. "I've changed my mind on the whole thing. I wish I'd made this decision a year ago and moved in with you. Then you'd never have met Kirt."

Ollie wrinkled his nose. "That would have been nice, but I refused to move in with you first. So Kirt is on me. Besides, we wouldn't have met Harper if that whole thing hadn't left me with a room to fill."

Dex lived in his late parents' condo and had offered Ollie a room for free the last time he'd been looking. They'd lived together after Ollie left Brayden years ago, but Ollie hadn't wanted to move in with Dex again.

They were best friends, but Ollie still needed space. Independence helped him feel like his own person. Not that Dex ever tried to change him. But he couldn't move in with Dex just because Dex wanted him to, and Dex understood why Ollie didn't do it.

Too bad that particular shot at independence had turned into Ollie latching onto his roommate Kirt, sleeping with him, and ending up with another guy who used him.

But that was over. And the months between Kirt moving out and Harper moving in had been a good adjustment. Even if it had been lonely as fuck living by himself.

"I still can't believe how lucky I was, moving in with you," Harper said.

"Yeah, it must have been fate or something." Ollie laughed.

Harper cocked his head like he was seriously considering fate playing a role. Who knew? Maybe Harper believed in fate. Ollie hadn't asked for details about what his family's cult believed or what mystical things Harper might still subscribe to, even if he'd clearly left all the Satan worship behind.

Harper's phone dinged and he shook himself out of his thoughts. A tiny smile appeared on his lips as he read the message. "Do you guys want to go to an art show this Friday?"

Dex's face lit up. "Yeah, totally. What kind of art?"

"Paintings, I think." Harper typed out a message. "Ash's friend runs a gallery."

"Which gallery?" Dex had gone to school for art and sold pottery alongside his job at Seaside Coffee.

"Gallery Four?" Harper said it like a question, frowning slightly at the phone. "I've never been there."

Dex's eyes widened. "Wait, your boyfriend's friend runs *Gallery Four*?"

Harper nodded.

"You know it?" Ollie had never heard of it.

"Yeah, I've told you about it. It's, like, the most prestigious gallery in the city."

"Oh, that one. Sorry, I forgot the name." Ollie turned to Harper. "I guess we'll be there for sure."

"Nice." Harper beamed, typing away on his phone.

This could be a great opportunity for Dex, but Ollie's stomach swooped. "Will, uh, Dante be there?"

Harper's eyes snapped up. "Yeah. That okay?"

"Sure." Ollie forced his face to stay neutral as the swooping turned into full-on butterflies.

Feeling this drawn to someone was nothing but a recipe for disaster. Ollie had to put a stop to whatever Dante was doing to him before it started clouding his judgment.

5

———

## DANTE

Dante took off from the deck and made his rounds of the shearwater nests. For a species that avoided land most of the year, his birds had taken to Shearwater Landing well.

Some of the birds sat on their perches that afternoon while most were out flying or fishing. Dante ensured they were well-fed in the winter and spring when they'd normally migrate away from this area, but they were generally fine on their own during the summer and autumn.

Onyx once asked why Dante hadn't enchanted a bird species that didn't migrate if all he wanted were watchful eyes around the city. But that wasn't all Dante wanted.

When he, Ash, and Onyx first escaped the Realm of the Damned, Dante couldn't sit still. Ash and Onyx settled into human society, learning what had changed since they'd been gone, but Dante was overwhelmed by the world after nearly a thousand years away. The open air had called to him. He'd needed to fly.

He'd followed a flock of shearwaters across the Pacific without another soul around, except his birds. Dante loved the shearwaters, and they'd seemed to accept him into their flock.

Maybe they liked that his wings matched their sooty coloring, or maybe it was Dante's magic.

Even if he'd wanted to, Dante couldn't stay away from people entirely. The need for blood had forced him to interact with humans from time to time. He'd slowly adjusted until he found himself spending more time with people than out at sea.

But he'd missed his birds. They lived relatively long lives and Dante was always pleased to recognize individuals after a long time apart. He'd started keeping track of them with his magic, and when he'd settled on the new city being built on the West Coast of North America—where his soul insisted he'd find his mate—he'd asked some of the birds to stay.

The birds he had now were several generations removed from the original flock. He'd increased his magical connection to them over the past century until they had the almost hive mind they did now.

Dante couldn't imagine ever leaving his shearwaters. When Ash had suggested they hide after Lucifer followed them to the Human Realm, and complained that Dante's connection to the birds was giving him away, Dante realized what a poor job he'd done of explaining what the birds meant to him.

He would always have his chosen brothers, but Ash and Onyx couldn't be all Dante had. He needed connections, tethers to ground him, and while the birds didn't live as long as humans, the constant nature of his flock gave him a sense of stability human friends couldn't.

Dante might have befriended a few vampires for long-term companionship, but he could never forgive the originals— witches who slayed the demon Andras and stole the immortal magic from his blood to create their own never-ending lives—it was natural to hold a grudge against the lot of them.

The Eternal Realm had never retaliated against those demon slayers, even though killing an Eternal being was considered the most heinous crime. Some believed the Eternals and ruling council had completely forsaken the Fallen, not caring if they lived or died. Others thought it was the council allowing mortals payback since demons and magic were never supposed to exist on Earth and mortals weren't subject to the council's judgment.

Either way, Andras's death was never far from Dante's mind when it came to vampires, even if the species wasn't responsible for their forebearers' sins.

His birds were infinitely better.

Dante reached the final group of nests on the north side of the cliff, outside the nature reserve. He'd set up the reserve to give his flock a sanctuary unmarred by human development, other than his house. The large area was completely protected by magic, but he didn't force the birds to nest there if they preferred to be farther from the city.

Dante flew over empty nests, typical for this time of day, but unease slithered down his spine. He doubled back, cutting lower to get a better look.

Magic buzzed around the nests and on the rocks surrounding them. Dante frowned.

The power was unfamiliar. No way it belonged to Ash, Onyx, or even Lucifer. How was that possible?

The outcropping—halfway down the cliff face—was inaccessible unless you were an expert rock climber. Or had wings. A rock-climbing witch didn't seem likely, and the longer he looked, the clearer it became that the magic was too strong to belong to a witch.

Dante landed on a large rock beside the nests and pulled out his phone. Ash picked up on the second ring. "We have a problem."

"Where are you?" Ash asked without hesitation.

Dante relayed his location and hung up. As he waited, he

tapped into his flock's collective mind, scanning quickly through their eyes. Everyone was hunting, flying, sleeping, or playing. Nothing out of the ordinary.

Most of the time, he left the birds to their own devices. Since Luc fled the Human Realm, he hadn't asked them to monitor the city as closely, so most of the birds had kept to the sea.

Dante delved into their memory, looking for the birds that nested here.

Images of dozens and dozens of other nests flashed through his mind. His heart sank. Where were these birds? Had they been killed?

There! Dante caught a flash of the outcropping from a bird's point of view. He watched the memory of the bird landing. Others followed suit, and Dante jumped into their minds, seeing their perspectives.

The birds that nested here were all still alive.

He let out a breath, his tail twitching as he relaxed.

Carefully sorting through their memories, he paid close attention to any time the birds were perched at the outcropping. They should have seen whoever left their magic behind. His birds were trained to detect magical power, especially anything this strong.

Nothing jumped out.

The woosh of large wings beating signaled Ash's arrival. Dante pulled himself from the flock's memory and his vision cleared.

Ash landed beside him, folding his wings tight against his back, hiding most of the white feathers from view. His eyes narrowed as he inspected the area with his demon sense. "It feels like demon magic," he said at last.

"But whose could it be?" Dante let his own power sweep over

the residual magic. "It's not Luc, and I can't sense any cloaking like he used before. Now that we know how he was hiding, we'd be able to break through it if he tried that trick again."

"I agree. But if it isn't him..." Ash frowned. "The birds didn't see anything?"

"No."

"Whoever it was had to have been here when the nests were empty."

Dante had considered that. "Possibly. But the birds should have noticed the magic when they returned and told me."

"Hm. Check the last time they were here."

Dante slid back into the flock's mind. He found the right birds and called up memories from this morning, scanning all their senses. "Nothing. The magic wasn't here when they took off earlier today." Had another demon really been here a few hours ago, so close to his home?

Refocusing his vision, Dante found Ash scratching his right horn. His curved back along his head while Dante's curved up, flaring out slightly at the tips.

"I can't figure out what the spell is meant to do," Ash muttered, sounding like half his mind was focused on inspecting. "It's almost like it was wiped away, but not well enough."

So whoever it was wasn't good at covering their tracks. "But how can another demon be in this realm?"

"I don't know." Ash cut a serious look at Dante. "I'd sense if anyone broke through the spell Luc has trapping everyone in the Realm of the Damned."

Luc had used magic he'd stolen from Ash, Dante, and Onyx to trap demonkind, linking them to the prison and giving Ash in particular this advantage.

"If you haven't felt anything, does that mean someone else came through with Luc last month?"

Ash huffed. "It must. But was it someone he was working with or someone who escaped on his coattails?"

"Someone couldn't sneak out without Luc knowing. How is that possible?" It had to be someone Lucifer brought on purpose. Having an accomplice was entirely possible since they had no idea what Luc had been up to—sneaking around the city —other than stalking Ash.

"I'm not sure how someone could get through undetected. But if this demon is working with Luc, he wouldn't have left them here when he fled back to the Realm of the Damned. That would mean giving up control, and we know Luc doesn't do that."

"Maybe not, but Luc's plan didn't exactly work out." Dante grinned. "He left in a hurry."

Ash's lips twitched. "Yes, but do we really think he'd trust anyone enough to leave them here on their own for weeks?"

"Probably not." Dante scanned the nests once more, the sea breeze ruffling his feathers. Could they really have a random demon on their hands? "If someone else got free, what are they doing sniffing around my birds if they aren't working with Luc?"

"I don't know. If it were me, I'd be as far from Shearwater Landing as possible. Whoever escaped had to know Luc was coming here. It can't be a coincidence. Why risk getting discovered?"

Exactly. "They must be working together."

Ash crossed his arms. "Or they're after us too."

A heavy feeling settled over Dante's chest. "Fuck. In that case, we'll have to find them first. Tracking them shouldn't be hard now that you've sensed their magic."

"I'll get on it." Ash stooped, picked up a small rock buzzing with power, and placed it in his pocket. "See you back at the house. We don't have long until Onyx's *art* thing." He said art like the concept was ridiculous. "At least we'll be able to pin Onyx down and update him."

"I'm sure Onyx will find a way to slip out of dealing with this." Dante gestured to the nests. "He's been avoiding me."

Ash cocked his head. "Haven't you been seeing a lot of him lately?"

"No, I've been out flying with the birds. Onyx keeps brushing me off. That's why I insisted we go to the show tonight."

"It wasn't because you wanted to see Ollie?" Ash's eyes flamed and he pumped his eyebrows.

Dante's insides burned. "Wanting to see Ollie is why I suggested you invite Harper."

"Good call, brother." Ash grinned and launched into the air, hovering for a moment. "Don't linger too long. You've got to get ready. Hopefully, I'll have a location before we go."

He flew off, leaving Dante on the outcropping.

Get ready, how? He couldn't dress up for Ollie. Wouldn't that seem weird? From what Dante had read online, modern dating was very informal.

Dante's tail flicked restlessly, mouth dry at the prospect of seeing Ollie again. At least his heart wasn't aching. Yet.

DANTE PASSED on a message to his flock, telling all the birds to nest within the reserve for their safety, and asked them to be on the lookout for the new magic he'd sensed but not actively search for it. Risking his birds was unnecessary when he and Ash could hunt the demon down.

Returning home, Dante showered and got dressed. Since he and Ash were flying to the gallery, he hadn't planned to put his shirt on until they were there, but that left him stuck, staring at options.

Did Ollie like red? Did Dante even look good in red? What about green? Would carrying the shirt wrinkle it too much? Shit, it'd be ruined, and he'd look scruffy, even by casual standards.

Ash stuck his head through the bedroom doorway. "I've got a location."

Dante turned away from the shirts. "Already?"

"They aren't doing a lot to mask their location. I've picked up something near the waterfront."

"Should we check it out now?" Dante ran a hand through his hair. He had his horns away so it wouldn't dry funny around his forehead where they poked out.

"Let's talk to Onyx first. I don't want to make a move without him again. Unless it's an emergency."

"Okay. I'll tell the birds. Unless you want eyes on the location, it might be best for them to stay away."

Ash nodded. "We don't want to give away that we've found whoever this is, so it'd be best for the birds to steer clear. I'll keep half a mind on their location while we're out in case they head off somewhere."

"Great." Dante grabbed the dark-red button-down off his bed. "You better hurry and get dressed."

"I'm good to go."

Dante eyed Ash's jeans and the T-shirt tied to his belt.

"What?" Ash ruffled his feathers. "There wasn't a dress code."

"Fine. Let's go." Dante shooed him out of the doorway.

The sun set as they flew over the city, bathing the buildings in orange light. Hopefully, it would be a good night, as soft and warm as the departing sun. Maybe Dante's first date with Ollie could be at sunset. Dinner at a rooftop restaurant. Surely, Onyx could recommend somewhere. It seemed like the kind of thing he'd know.

Landing on top of the gallery, Dante and Ash retracted their wings, which melded into full-back tattoos, and put their shirts on. Dante's wrinkles weren't too bad, at least not compared to Ash's.

A ladder led down the side of the building to one of Onyx's office's windows. Dante had come in this way last week, much to Onyx's annoyance, but it was easier than finding a deserted side street to land in.

Despite his previous grumbling, Onyx hadn't locked Dante or Ash out. The gallery was protected, but like Dante's house, the spells had been crafted to allow all three of them free access.

Dante slid through the window into an empty office.

Ash followed. "There's no way these are large enough to fit through by chance. Onyx must fly in and out too."

"That's what I thought." But Dante couldn't remember the last time he'd seen Onyx's wings. Why go through the trouble of hiding them when he must fly around the city as much as they did?

Ash closed the window. "Do you know where Onyx lives?"

"No." Dante readjusted the cuffs of his shirt. "He's never offered any details."

"Maybe I should track him."

"Or you could ask." Dante led the way out of the room, not hopeful Onyx would provide an answer if they did start prying.

They exited the hall into the second-story gallery space, which had a balcony open to the floor below. Chattering voices drifted upward, echoing off the walls, the lofted ceilings adding a pleasant openness to the building.

Dante and Ash descended the stairs, finding the ground floor filled with people. Soft music played while servers slipped through the crowd with drinks. Paintings Dante hadn't seen before hung on the walls, and the sculptures that usually occupied plinths around the room were nowhere in sight.

"Nice," Ash grunted like he couldn't care less. "Oh look. There's Harper."

Across the room, Ollie stood next to Harper, each man clutching a glass of wine.

Dante's pulse quickened and warmth flooded him. A smile tugged at his lips. He followed Ash through the people, eyes trained on his mate.

Ollie's posture seemed relaxed as he talked to Harper. He smiled easily, dimples flashing with each upturn of his lips. Ollie wore all black—slim-cut jeans paired with a loose-fit V-neck tee and a silver chain around his neck.

Turning, Ollie's gaze traveled over the crowd until it landed on Dante. His cheeks tinged pink and he quickly looked away.

A rumble started deep in Dante's chest, and he cleared his throat to cover it. No growling or purring. He needed to approach Ollie as if he were human and not let his demon nature get in the way. He was a man approaching someone he liked. Simple. Easy.

Dante shook out his hands and ignored the tingling in the tattoo of his hidden tail.

"Hey, isn't this place great?" Harper beamed at Ash as he and Dante approached. "It's so fancy."

Ash wrapped an arm around Harper's waist. "It is, sweet. Are you enjoying yourself?"

"Yeah, I've never been to an art gallery before." Harper's eyes darted around the room like he didn't know where to look first.

Dante's gaze slid to Ollie, who was staring at him, cheeks still slightly flushed. "How've you been, Ollie?"

"Good." The word came out breathless. Ollie sipped his

drink and cleared his throat. "You know, work and all that. Can't complain."

Dante took half a step closer. "Did you have a lot of clients today?"

Ollie shrugged, breaking eye contact. "My morning was solid, and I had some walk-ins this afternoon. Tomorrow will be busy though. Can't stay out too late."

"Me either. Ash and I have someone to catch up with after this."

Harper cocked his head at Dante's words. Ash pulled him away, whispering in his ear, no doubt filling him in on the rogue demon news.

Ollie's attention lingered on Harper and Ash, a slight frown pulling on his lips.

"Are you a fan of the arts?" Dante asked, not wanting Ollie to ask more about who he and Ash had to see. He shouldn't have brought it up.

Ollie's gaze snapped back to Dante. "I guess? I mean, art is cool, but I don't know much about it. I can't say these types of events are my usual scene." He laughed nervously. "Not like my friend Dex. He was so excited to come tonight. This isn't his usual scene either, but it would be if he had connections."

"Sorry, who's Dex?"

"Oh. Obviously, you don't know him." Ollie pointed across the room to a man about Ollie's height with light-brown skin and brown hair, who was talking to a group of people Dante didn't recognize. "That's Dex. He's my best friend. We met in college, though Dex went to art school, and I didn't. Which you know already. About me, I mean. Dex does pottery and made the mugs I have at home. Not that you used a mug the other night at dinner..." Ollie fidgeted with his wine glass. "Wow, I'm really rambling. Sorry."

"No need to apologize." Dante smiled warmly. Ollie's infectious energy gave Dante a giddy, almost lightheaded feeling.

"True. I'm not sorry exactly. Um. I think I'm nervous." Ollie rolled his eyes like he was exasperated with himself.

Dante's brows pinched together. "Nervous about what?"

"You."

Dante's heart banged against his chest.

"I mean, not you, but kind of?" Ollie hurried on. "I wanted to say—because I didn't last time—that I don't date. Relationships aren't my thing, you know? And I wanted to put it out there, um..." His words trailed off as a panicked look flashed across his face.

"You were nervous to tell me you don't date?" Dante's heart pounded for an entirely different reason. Why would Ollie be nervous to share that? Did people judge him? Why would they do that?

Ollie directed his attention to his glass. "It's dumb. But yeah, I was nervous to say anything. Everyone's into relationships, and I'm not. I thought...last time, I got a vibe, and I don't know. I was flirty, but I'm like that sometimes, and I didn't want you to get the wrong impression."

It wasn't what Dante hoped to hear, but the glaring revelation was how uncomfortable Ollie seemed. His mate shouldn't feel this way around him.

"So, friends?" Ollie concluded, flashing Dante a half-formed smile.

"Friends sounds great, Ollie."

Ollie ran a hand through his blond curls, dimples appearing as his smile turned more natural. "Cool. Now, can we forget how awkward that was?"

Dante's pounding heart calmed, soothed as his mate relaxed, even though something deep inside Dante scrambled, trying to catch hold of the situation.

*Friends.*

He'd agreed to be friends with the man he'd waited millennia to mate with.

Dante's demon features fought to come out, but a primal reaction wasn't helpful. Fuck his demon nature right now. Guilt strangled Dante's heart. Had he just lied to his mate?

It wouldn't be fair to cultivate a friendship with Ollie while hoping it would progress into something Ollie didn't want. He couldn't disregard Ollie like that. He had to respect his wishes.

What Dante's mate wanted was the most important thing in the world, and it seemed he wasn't interested in romantic love.

He'd said he didn't date. *Everyone's into relationships, and I'm not. It's not my thing.* Maybe Ollie didn't like the idea of anything committed at this stage in his life, and that was fine, but it didn't sound like that. It felt deeper. Why else would he be so nervous to share? Had he been afraid Dante wouldn't accept this about him?

Of course Dante would. His mate was perfect as he was.

But did this mean it was possible to be mates in a non-romantic way? Could the connection be platonic if that was what Ollie desired?

Dante had never considered that possibility. He had a picture of what mates were supposed to be in his head. But romantic lovers might not be the only pairing mates formed.

Was it possible to be something else? Shit, of course, it was possible. How could it not be? Every Eternal being had a fated mate.

Dante would be honored to stand at Ollie's side as a friend, to be part of his life, share memories and platonic affection. He loved Ash and Onyx, and the prospect of another friendship like that was a good thing.

But could they still bond and cement the mating connection? Would Ollie want that?

He might not accept. Maybe mating would seem like a relationship to a human. Would Ollie choose to grow old and die and pass into his human afterlife in the Eternal Realm, leaving Dante behind forever?

No.

Ollie would reincarnate, as human souls naturally did. Dante would find him again, and their time together wouldn't be over. Unless the Eternals held his soul back, as demons suspected they'd done to punish them, keeping their mates from being found on Earth. Then Dante would never see Ollie again.

But even if that were the case, he'd still treasure what they had.

Being someone's friend could be a powerful connection and wasn't lesser than romantic love. Dante hadn't lied to Ollie. He'd needed a minute to catch up.

"We don't have to forget about an awkward moment," Dante said, a steady calm flowing through him, so powerful that even his demon sense was accepting. "I want you to be yourself around me. If I'm making you uncomfortable, you can tell me."

Ollie blinked, his lashes fluttering. "Sure, okay. But I don't know if you made me uncomfortable. I'm pretty sure I did that all on my own. I've been overthinking this. I was so sure I gave you the wrong idea. But I didn't?"

"You mean by flirting?" Dante rubbed the back of his neck. He wanted to be honest even if he couldn't bring up their fated connection. "I felt something between us and wondered if you did too. But you've made your position clear, so if flirting isn't you coming on to me, and it's something you do with friends, well, I know that now. I won't take it any other way unless you tell me to."

"Okay." Ollie sounded almost skeptical, but he hurried on. "Want to get a drink? Then we should probably look at the art."

## 6

## OLLIE

Wow, that went better than Ollie had imagined.

He set his empty wine glass on a passing server's tray and grabbed two full ones, handing one to Dante. "The gallery host, or docent, or whatever, said to start with that painting over there and move clockwise."

Dante raised his glass. "Lead the way."

Ollie guided Dante to a painting at the front of the room.

Was Dante telling the truth when he said being friends was great? He'd accepted so easily and hadn't asked any prying questions about why Ollie didn't date. That never happened.

A hollowness settled in Ollie's chest, and he wasn't sure why. It wasn't possible to be disappointed. Even if he'd read Dante completely wrong and he hadn't been interested or about to ask Ollie out, that wasn't a bad thing. It was what Ollie wanted, or at least what he needed.

Dante stood shoulder to shoulder with Ollie, looking at the painting. "It's very dark."

A waft of fresh peppermint filled Ollie's nose. Was that Dante's cologne? Fuck, it smelled good. So soothing...

Right. Art. He had to focus on the bold black and gray brush strokes. But the butterflies in his chest hadn't calmed since saying his piece. The damn things battered his heart, and something pulled deep within him.

Was he sick?

No, it was more like Dante had him on a string, tugging on his chest and reeling him in.

Which confirmed Ollie had made the right decision. This level of attraction wasn't healthy. It was a recipe for disaster and codependency. Ollie wanted nothing more than to please Dante. He burned with it. But he wasn't a people pleaser anymore. He wasn't getting sucked in.

Ollie forced his attention back to the painting. "I feel like the artist was angry at the canvas."

Dante hummed in agreement before moving on to the next display.

Ollie followed, sipping his wine. All the paintings were black and white. He preferred a bit of color. If he were going to buy art for his apartment, this wouldn't be it.

He cut a sidelong glance at Dante. The big man frowned at the painting, shaking his head, then moved on to the next one.

Ollie suppressed a smile. At least he didn't seem to be the only one not feeling it.

"What's your usual scene?" Dante asked as he inspected the painting before them. For some reason, this canvas was much smaller than the others. "If you weren't here tonight, what would you be doing instead?"

"Probably hanging out at home with Harper. Working on Saturday mornings kind of kills my Friday nights."

Dante shifted to face him. "Do you like going out?"

Ollie shrugged. "Sure. I like dancing and letting loose. You?"

Dante's brow furrowed. "I don't really dance. I suppose clubbing hasn't appealed for quite a while."

Ollie looked Dante over. How old was he? Dante seemed older, but there couldn't be more than, say, ten years between them. He wasn't approaching silver fox territory or anything.

"No clubbing, hm? Don't tell me you won't even go out after nine p.m.," Ollie teased.

Dante grinned. "I'd need a very good reason to do something that late."

Ollie bit back a smile. "You're a Millennial, aren't you?"

Dante blinked. "A...what?"

A laugh bubbled out of Ollie. "Oh yeah, you totally are. You're like thirty-five or something, right?"

"Thirty-five. Yes, good guess." Dante sipped his drink, the crease in his brow deepening. "And you must be much younger. So, in other words, you're saying I'm old and boring?"

He sounded disappointed, and Ollie's heart sank. "No. I'm just hassling you. You're not boring. Not that I'm in a position to judge. My biggest hobby is playing PlayStation. It's not like I'm terribly interesting or original."

Dante's dark eyes seemed to spark. "You like gaming?" The hint of excitement in his voice lit Ollie up.

"I do." Ollie leaned in, voice dropping to a whisper. "Beats clubbing, if I'm honest."

Dante grinned, leaning down to whisper back. "Agreed. I love video games. They're fascinating."

A weird way to put it, but Ollie's insides buzzed like Dante's enthusiasm was contagious. "What do you play?"

Dante straightened, pulling back, and Ollie realized how close they'd been. "Anything I can. I have a whole room set up with all the different consoles."

"Nice. A whole gaming room. Perks of being old, I guess."

"Hey." Dante's eyes widened, expression adorably betrayed. "You said I wasn't old."

"No, I said you weren't boring." Ollie patted Dante's forearm, his skin temptingly warm. He quickly withdrew his hand. "It's okay to be old. I'm not holding it against you. We've each got to bring our own thing to the friendship, and don't worry, I won't try to take you clubbing."

"I'm not worried." Dante frowned, lips pouting.

"You look worried."

Dante's expression smoothed out. "Not at all." He placed a hand on Ollie's lower back. "Come on, I think we've seen enough of this painting. Let's make way for someone else."

Ollie let Dante steer him to the next piece, enjoying the touch more than he should. It wasn't a very we're-just-friends move, but Dante's hand didn't linger, so maybe he meant nothing by it.

They circled the room, examining the rest of the paintings, which became more appealing as they moved along. Ollie preferred the more friendly-looking pieces, and the final one was actually really beautiful.

A man with bright-blue hair and pale skin appeared on Dante's other side. "What do you think?"

Dante nodded, stroking his chin. "I like it. Nice progression."

The man snorted. "Thanks." He eyed the wine in Dante's hand. "Want something stronger?"

"No, this is fine." Dante turned, gesturing toward Ollie. "Onyx, meet Ollie. Harper's roommate."

Onyx's gaze flitted briefly in Ollie's direction. "Hi." He turned back to Dante. "I'm surprised you came tonight."

*Cool snub, dude.* Ollie narrowed his eyes at the guy.

"Why are you surprised?" A hint of offense bled into Dante's tone. "Haven't I come to your openings before?"

Onyx wrinkled his nose. "I suppose."

What was the deal between these two? The slight animosity practically screamed ex-boyfriend behavior. Ollie's gut twisted.

Was Onyx the kind of guy Dante was into? A burning sensation rose in his chest.

"I enjoy these events," Dante said. Of course he'd be kind and want to keep the peace. Ollie had never seen Dante be anything but considerate. "You've done a great job with this place, Onyx. It's a lovely gallery."

A different kind of jealousy swelled within Ollie. This guy was the owner? The one whom Harper had mentioned was friends with Ash? Owning Gallery Four was fucking impressive, especially since Onyx looked no older than Dante.

The real drawback of Dante being older was that people Dante's age were generally more accomplished than Ollie. How could he compare? Ollie struggled to make decisions for himself and be his own person. Meanwhile, Dante was used to friends—or boyfriends—who owned renowned galleries.

"I have done well here." Onyx's lips twitched in a smug smile, clearly pleased by Dante's compliment.

Maybe Ollie should find Harper or Dex and leave Onyx and Dante to catch up. But he didn't want to. Being near Dante felt good.

"There you are." Ash appeared next to Onyx, clapping a hand on his shoulder.

Onyx shook him off. "Oh goodie, Ash is here."

Ash gave Onyx a stern look as Harper joined them. "We need to talk to you."

Anger flashed across Onyx's delicate features. He turned an accusatory look on Dante. "Is that why you're here?"

"No." Dante sighed. "We're here because you invited us. Remember?"

"Right." Onyx turned away, scanning the room as if he'd lost interest. "I have more important people to talk to than the two of you. Don't wait up." He walked off without a backward glance, nose in the air.

A strange sound emanated from Ash, almost like a growl. "That rude little—"

"I'll go talk to him," Dante said before Ash could finish. He turned an apologetic smile on Ollie. "Excuse me for a second?"

Ollie met Dante's dark stare, stomach swooping. "Sure." Why was he even asking permission?

Dante nodded and slipped into the crowd. Ollie felt unsteady on his feet. It had to be too much wine on an empty stomach, not anything to do with Dante's departure.

Harper linked his arm with Ollie's. "You two seem to be having a good time."

"Oh." Had Harper been watching them? "Yeah, it's been fun. Nice to find someone to talk to who doesn't make me feel dumb for not knowing about art."

Harper chuckled. "I could have done that for you."

Something about the silence between them seemed expectant. Like Harper was hoping Ollie would say more about Dante. But why? Harper couldn't read Ollie's mind and detect his weird, conflicted feelings.

Needing to change the subject, Ollie gestured with his wine toward Dex, who seemed deep in conversation. "He's in his element."

"Totally. Oh! Should we introduce him to Onyx?" Harper glanced from Ollie to Ash, who shrugged.

Ollie's attention wandered to where Dante was talking to Onyx in a far corner of the room. Dante's expression was tense and slightly pleading. What were they talking about? Fuck, maybe Dante wasn't over Onyx. Nothing else would give his face that hint of desperation. Right?

He clenched a fist, pushing the nausea filling him down. "Yeah, let's introduce them. Dex doesn't do studio art, but he'd love to meet the owner."

It wasn't fair to care if Dante had something going on with

Onyx, but Ollie couldn't help it. He had to know if he was on the right track. If he was, it'd be easier to get rid of these stupid warm feelings.

His emotions got so scrambled around Dante. What he wanted and what he felt didn't match. It was like Dante had some kind of hold over him, which freaked him out. He didn't want to want Dante. It tempted him to go against his better judgment.

But Ollie wouldn't. They were friends. That was all.

7

————

## DANTE

"What do you need me for?" Onyx asked in a tight whisper. "Seems like you and Ash have it handled."

Dante ground his teeth. "We don't know who we'll find. How can you assume we'll have it handled?"

"You two always have it handled. I'm the unnecessary side-kick. There's no need to rope me into everything."

Dante stepped in front of Onyx so he couldn't avoid his stare. "I'm asking for your help."

Onyx glared, chilling even without the flash of his blue fire. "I'm not ending my night early, so if you want me to come hunting, you'll have to wait."

"Fine." Why was Onyx like this? He'd settled in Shearwater Landing, knowing Dante was here, but every time Dante came to see him about something, it was as if it were the biggest imposition.

If Onyx wanted to avoid Dante, he should have stayed out of reach.

Onyx's attention snagged on something behind Dante. "Oh great. Harper is bringing his human entourage over. Why does he think I need to meet his friends?"

"He's trying to get to know you and include you."

"He is?" Onyx sounded shocked that Harper might care.

"Yes. Try not to think the worst of everyone. You need to get over your grudge against him. He's going to be around as long as the rest of us."

Hopefully, Ollie would be too. But Dante didn't want to explain Ollie being his mate to Onyx, not after realizing their mating might take a different shape than Ash and Harper's. Onyx wouldn't get it, and Dante didn't need his negativity.

"Seeing as my grudge against Ash is as healthy as ever, I don't see why I have to be buddies with Harper," Onyx said under his breath as the man in question reached them.

"Hi, Onyx." Harper beamed like he was pleased to see the blue-haired grump. "I wanted to introduce you to my friend, Dex. He's an artist."

Dex laughed shakily. "It's so great to meet you. My work is more, um, art in everyday objects than anything you'd display here, but I've always wanted to visit your gallery. This show is phenomenal."

Onyx stuck out his hand. "Pleasure to meet you, Dex." His voice was so professional it was as if he'd been possessed. "I'm glad you're enjoying the show."

"I took Tim McKinnon's class at the university. You've shown some of his work, I think."

Onyx gave Dex a look of pleasant surprise. "I have indeed. I've always liked Tim's pieces. Do you work with ceramics?"

"You know," Ash muttered in Dante's ear. "After you realized Ollie was your mate, I half wondered if there might be something there." He nodded at Onyx and Dex.

Dante's brows shot up. "Really?"

It didn't seem like there was any spark between the two other than professional interest. Not to mention Onyx grumbling about meeting Harper's humans right before he was introduced. Surely, if Dex was his mate, Onyx would have felt it as soon as Dex walked into the room. Onyx was too composed to be speaking with his mate for the first time.

Ash hummed a disapproving sound. "It doesn't appear we're in luck, which is too bad. A mate might have made Onyx less of a pain."

Dante elbowed Ash discreetly. "He might be less of a pain if you got off his case."

Ash shifted away from Dante and slipped his arm around Harper without comment. Damn him.

Dante assessed Onyx and Dex as they spoke, trying to pick up on anything that might be there, but Onyx remained unruffled.

"Is it okay that we introduced them?" Ollie asked.

"What?" Dante shook himself and stopped staring.

Ollie's gaze flitted away from Dante's. "We didn't mean to interrupt."

"It's fine. I'm sure Onyx is glad to be done talking to me."

A slight frown tugged at Ollie's lips. "I'm sensing tension."

"You could say that." Dante suppressed a laugh. "It's what happens when you've known someone your whole life. Onyx is like a brother, and brothers don't always get along."

"We certainly bicker like siblings," Ash muttered.

"Oh, I get that." Ollie's expression brightened. "I mean, I get it in theory since I'm an only child. Half my childhood friends didn't get along with their siblings."

Did Ollie seem relieved? His babbling came out when he was nervous, but why be nervous about Onyx?

"I think Ollie and I are going to head out for some food soon," Harper said, and Ollie nodded in agreement. "Do you guys have time to come with us before you meet up with your friend?"

"No, I don't think so." Dante wanted to hang around the

gallery until Onyx was done. Otherwise, he'd slip out of coming with them. "Next time."

Ollie ran a hand through his hair. "For sure."

There was a long pause, and Dante couldn't help getting drawn into Ollie's hazel eyes. He was beautiful, friend or not.

"Maybe I should get your number?" Ollie bit his lip. "We can compare notes on what games we like. Play together sometime."

Dante could have purred. He didn't, but he could have. He pulled out his phone and cleared his throat. "That's a great idea. Here, put your number in, and I'll text you."

Ash clapped Dante on the shoulder as if he were a proud father. Damnation, could he be any more obvious?

Ollie's eyes darted to Ash's grip, then away.

Dex wrapped up his conversation with Onyx and the blue-haired demon slipped away so quickly that Dante swore he'd put on a burst of inhuman speed. Not that it was getting him out of anything.

Harper and Ollie wished him and Ash goodnight, then left with Dex in search of dinner. Dante's body begged him to follow Ollie out the door, the distance between them tugging like Ollie had a hook around his heart.

"What are you going to do for your first date?" Ash asked, jarring Dante out of his thoughts.

He stiffened. "We aren't going on a date. Ollie doesn't date. He told me he'd like to be friends."

"*Friends?*" Ash said like it was a rude word.

Dante winced.

He handed his wine glass to a passing server and crossed his arms. "Yes, friends. And I plan to respect his wishes. If he isn't interested in a romantic connection, that's all right. He's my mate, but that doesn't mean we have to be lovers. I can still be by his side."

Ash's mouth opened, but it took a few seconds for any sound to emerge. "By his side as a friend? Forever? No, you're giving up too easily, Dante. Saying he doesn't date *right now* doesn't mean he never wants a partner. Plenty of young men don't want to be tied down right away."

"True. But it could also mean romantic connections aren't for him at all. You didn't hear how he said it. It wasn't the way someone casually brushes off commitment." Dante gripped Ash's shoulder. "I have to be okay with loving Ollie like a brother. If that's what he wants, that's what I'll be."

"Dante..." Ash shook his head. "You're mates. And he's young. We've forgotten what that's like, but believe me, it makes a big difference. He'll change his mind once he gets to know you. I'm sure of it."

"That's fine if he does, but I won't ask him to." The distinction was important. Couldn't Ash see that? "I can't be the friend he needs if all I'm doing is holding out for a romantic relationship. Please don't push this. As his mate, I must be attuned to his needs, and I have to do what feels right for both of us, not only me."

Ash's expression softened. "I'm sorry. I won't tell you what to do. I just can't imagine not bonding with Harper."

Dante's heart gave a painful jolt. "Maybe we can still bond. I don't know. The connection doesn't necessarily have to come from a romantic place."

Dante and Ollie were fated mates. There must be a way to bond on their terms. If Ollie chose to accept.

Would the mating spell work without physical intimacy? Dante wouldn't be able to have sex with Ollie without it carrying a romantic attachment. But perhaps sex wasn't as vital to the mating ritual as blood exchange or the incantation. He'd always assumed it was, but that didn't mean he was correct.

Ash scratched his head where his horns would be. "I've never considered a platonic mating bond."

"Me either, but maybe we should. My feelings for Ollie are still so new. I assumed they'd grow in a romantic direction, but that doesn't mean they will. I don't know Ollie yet. All I know is that I'm drawn to him and will do anything for him. I have to wait and see. Be open to different possibilities."

"Of course you'll do anything for him." Ash smiled, and Dante felt warmth radiating off him. "It already sounds like you know what your mate needs. So, what are you and Ollie going to do together when you call him? He doesn't play that silly game, does he?"

Dante huffed. "*World's End* isn't silly. It's critically acclaimed, and since Ollie likes gaming, I'm sure he won't think it's silly either." It was Dante's favorite game, and he wasn't alone. Millions of people played *World's End* online.

"Sorry." Ash rolled his eyes. "I don't know how you can play that crap."

"*Crap?* Like you can talk. I don't know how you played hunter in the woods for decades. Talk about ridiculous."

"At least I was an actual hunter. Not *pretending* to hunt on a computer screen."

"If thinking that makes you feel better, then sure, Ash." Dante shook his head, smiling.

Ash grinned back, and they fell into a companionable silence. Ash's hassling never bothered Dante. They'd always be there for each other. No matter what. And sometimes Dante needed to be reminded he took things too seriously.

The night went on around them, and eventually, the gallery cleared out.

"There's an after-party," Onyx said as he closed the door behind the last guest.

Ash crossed his arms. "Not tonight. I want to confront this demon before they make another move."

Onyx dropped his head back like a petulant child. "Fine. Spoilsport."

Ash turned and headed up the stairs.

Dante grabbed Onyx's wrist as he walked by. "Thank you."

"Yeah, like I have a choice." Onyx stomped after Ash, and Dante followed.

They exited Onyx's office window and climbed to the roof. Dante unbuttoned his shirt and shrugged it off his shoulders, freeing his wings. Ash did the same, adjusting his waistband as his tail unwound from his hips. He and Dante turned in unison to face Onyx.

He glared. "Do you have to stare at me?"

"We haven't seen your wings in a while," Ash said without his usual Onyx-induced annoyance.

"As I've said, I don't need to go around shirtless for no reason like you two." Onyx unbuttoned his shirt and slid it off, baring his slim body.

The nipple piercings were new. Onyx's eyes flashed with blue fire and wings erupted from his back, feathers a deep midnight blue at his shoulders, fading to light blue at his wingtips.

Onyx flexed his wings, ruffling his feathers, then cracked his neck. "Ready?"

"Let's go." Dante suppressed a smile, gesturing for Ash to lead the way.

Ash leaped into the air, and Dante and Onyx followed. Onyx left his horns and tail hidden, but so had Dante. It was uncomfortable flying with pants on and your tail out.

A sudden longing for the clothes in the Eternal Realm, designed to accommodate their tails, hit Dante in the chest.

Shirts had never been common among Eternals so their wings hadn't been an issue. Neither had human modesty, which was why Onyx's comments about his and Ash's lack of shirts didn't make sense. Bare chests were normal for their kind, even in the Realm of the Damned.

"What did you think of Dex?" Ash called over his shoulder as they flew across the city toward the waterfront, made invisible to any onlookers by their illusions.

Onyx didn't respond right away. He cut a confused look at Dante, then back at Ash. "You're asking me?"

Dante shook his head. "Yes, Onyx, he's asking you."

"Uh..." Onyx paused for a few wingbeats. "I liked his take on handmade objects and imperfect art. His stuff wouldn't fit at the gallery, but I'm interested in checking it out. Apparently, Dex works at a coffee shop and sells his pieces there. The shop also displays and sells other local art. I figured I'd stop by. Sounds like the kind of community space I enjoy."

Dante was stunned into silence.

Onyx never let on that he cared about anything and had never mentioned community before. It had always seemed like his interest in art was about prestige rather than anything else.

"You're interested in Dex's art?" Dante asked, unable to conceal his surprise.

"Yeah, so?" Onyx snapped back to his usual self. "Art is why he was introduced. What else would I think of him?"

"Maybe that you like him *personally*," Ash said, putting too much emphasis on the word.

"*Personally?*" Onyx shook his head and his nose wrinkled. "You mean, like him as in attracted? No. He's so not my type."

"Not at all?" Ash pressed.

"Not even a little." Onyx sped up until he was level with Ash. "Why do you suddenly care who I'm into?"

"I thought he might be your mate."

"*My mate?*" Onyx screeched, wing beats faltering and throwing him off balance.

Dante sputtered, trying and failing to swallow his laughter.

Onyx shot him a death glare. "What the fuck made you think Dex was my *mate*, Ash? Shit, imagine. If he was, fate's crueler than the council."

"No need to be rude," Ash scolded, sounding defensive about being so far off base. "It was a fair guess. Fate was clearly involved in bringing Harper and Ollie together, so maybe Dex completed our third pair."

"Dex is Ollie's friend, not Harper's," Dante pointed out. "Even if some magic brought Harper and Ollie together, it doesn't quite follow on to Dex."

Ash sighed, sounding surprisingly disappointed. Had he really been that set on Onyx finding his mate? Maybe it shouldn't have come as a surprise. Ash didn't hate Onyx as much as he pretended to.

"Wait." Onyx flipped around, hovering in Dante's path.

Dante pulled up short. "Wait, what?"

"Is Ollie your mate?" Onyx's eyes widened, his lips twitching before he covered the smile with a scowl.

"He is." Dante's cheeks flamed. "But he has no idea, so please don't say anything strange to him."

Onyx rolled his eyes. "Like I'm ever going to talk to him."

Ash circled back and pulled up beside them. "Are you seriously planning on spending eternity ignoring Ollie and Harper? What is your problem?"

Onyx whined in frustration. "No, Ash, I'm not planning on ignoring them. Fucking hell. I meant, why would I talk to a random human and give anything away? Once Ollie knows about mates and is all bonded and clinging to Dante like you and Harper, I'm sure I'll talk to him plenty. Harper too, when I'm not busy."

"Whatever. We don't cling," Ash grumbled before flying off.

Dante followed, unwilling to explain—again—not pursuing Ollie romantically. There was no reason to this early on. He had no idea how things would progress with his mate. They'd settle into something comfortable, and everything would fall into place as it was meant to.

Onyx caught up to Dante a moment later. "Well, congratulations or whatever."

"Thanks." Warmth filled Dante. For Onyx, that was as close to a heartfelt sentiment as he'd get.

"How did you know?" Onyx asked more quietly, a hint of something vulnerable cutting through his usual snark. "Could you tell right away?"

"Pretty much. As soon as I saw him, something pulled me in his direction. Nothing else existed, and my demon senses flared into full-on primal mode. And his smell..." Dante cleared his throat. "It would have been impossible to miss."

"If that's what it's like, Dex definitely isn't my mate."

Was that sorrow in Onyx's tone? He'd spoken of finding his mate the least, but that didn't mean his longing was any less.

"He's out there, Onyx," Dante assured him. "I know it."

"Maybe. It doesn't really matter." Onyx sighed, turning his face away. "Let's hurry up and find this demon."

They flew the rest of the way in silence.

The waterfront was almost as busy now as it was during the day. Bars and restaurants passed below, light spilling onto the promenade, and people milling about.

A seawall held the walkway back from the sand and rocks, with stairs to access the beach when the tide was low. The most popular spot for humans to gather was on the southern end of the beach, closer to the port and river, where all the white sand piled up. The northern end turned rocky as the land rose into the cliffs flanking the city, where Dante's home perched.

It was an odd place for a demon to hide. There would be plenty of people and relatively easy feeding, but why not fly here as needed and hold up somewhere more private?

Dante and Onyx followed Ash along the shore until they'd almost reached the end of the beach.

Ash turned inland, flying for another minute before landing on top of an older building with dark windows. "They're inside."

Onyx landed beside him. "So what's the plan?"

"We could stake out the place and see who comes out," Dante suggested.

"That will take too long. Next." Onyx turned to Ash.

Ash frowned at Onyx. "Not that we're in a rush, but I'd rather not wait around. If we confront them inside, we won't have human eyes on us and won't have to worry about hiding magic."

That was a good point. "Then let's search the place. I don't feel any protective spells, which is odd."

"Think it's a trap?" Onyx asked.

Dante closed his eyes and sharpened his demon sense, focusing on the interior sounds of the building. He filtered out all the other noise until he was sure. "I only hear one heartbeat. If it's a trap, it's not very good, leaving them three against one." Maybe they'd expected Dante to come alone, but still.

When Dante opened his eyes, Onyx's wings were gone.

"What?" Onyx put his shirt back on. "I'm not sneaking around with my wings out. This place looks like it has narrow hallways."

Ash walked to the edge of the roof. "We're going to have to enter on the ground floor. Doesn't look like there's roof access."

They jumped down the two stories to the street. Onyx landed deftly in a crouch, even without his wings to steady him.

The ground floor of the building housed a closed boutique, but a door to the side was numbered separately, possibly leading to a residence above the shop.

"Let's start here." Dante gripped the door handle. There was no protective spell, but the residual tingle of magic pricked his palm. "Seems like they've used a spell to break or fix the lock. Feels like the same essence as the magic at the nests."

Dante turned the handle, breaking the lock, and opened the door. Ash and Onyx followed him into a narrow stairwell. Dante retracted his wings, ignoring Onyx's pointed sniff.

He could hear movement ahead.

At the top of the staircase stood a closed door. Dante, Ash, and Onyx crowded on the landing, a faint humming reaching their ears. From the smell of it, whoever was inside was cooking.

Again, the door was locked but not protected. Dante shouldered it open, cracking the frame.

He burst inside, the others at his heels.

"Oh fuck!" a woman shouted as a pan clattered to the floor. Not exactly a violent ambush. She whirled around to face them, surprise fading from her fine features. "All three Hounds. My, my."

Dante growled at the offensive nickname. He was no one's dog, least of all Lucifer's. "And who are you?"

He didn't recognize the demon. Her wavy brown hair, light skin, high cheekbones, and dark eyes sparked no immediate memories, but she wasn't suppressing her power, so even with her demonic features hidden, there was no mistaking her for human.

Hundreds of Eternals fell to Earth with Lucifer to look for their mates. After the fall, they spread out across the globe, and in the Realm of the Damned, Dante, Ash, and Onyx had been isolated from the general population by Lucifer, so it wasn't surprising not to recognize this demon.

Her eyes flashed silver flames. "My name is Ren. I'd say it's a pleasure, but your faces tell me otherwise."

"Our faces?" Dante's blood heated, his voice dropping to a growl. "Attacking my flock is what's made this meeting a displeasure."

Ren's hardened expression cracked, her brows lifting. "What do you mean attack? I've done no such thing."

"So you haven't been sniffing around my birds?"

"Sniffing, yes. Attacking, no."

"What are you doing here?" Ash rumbled. He'd left his wings out and flexed them, filling the small living space.

Ren's spine straightened. "Looking for you. Your escape was a well-kept secret for a long time, but once we found out you betrayed Lucifer and were gone, everything changed. Best news I'd heard in an age."

"Best news?" Dante cocked his head. "So you're saying you don't support Lucifer?"

"That's exactly what I'm saying."

"Then why kill my shearwaters?" Dante growled.

"I haven't killed any birds. It must have been someone else."

"Are there more demons in this realm?" Ash asked, betraying a hint of alarm.

Ren's eyes darted between them all. "I don't know. I came by myself."

"How?" Dante trusted her less and less. She'd been too easy to find. Pretending to be against Luc might be a ploy to win their trust.

"I heard rumors of Lucifer's plans to come to this realm and followed when he broke the containment spell. Who knows if others did the same. I wasn't the only one who knew what was happening."

"Okay," Dante hedged. He'd see where this was going. "If you aren't killing my birds, then why were you looking for us? Revenge?"

Many demons blamed Dante, Ash, and Onyx for their imprisonment in the Realm of the Damned as much as they blamed Lucifer. Everyone assumed the Hounds had supported Lucifer freely the entire time rather than being under his control.

"Revenge for what? You escaping?" Ren scoffed. "Hardly. We're all jealous you got one over on that bastard. No one's punishing you for that. You rebelled first. It was a good thing."

"You don't seek revenge for imprisoning you?" Ash asked, his suspicions mirroring Dante's.

"Ah." Ren's eyes flashed. "I'll let it slide. Let's go with the enemy of my enemy is my friend. As long as I don't get dragged back, I don't need anything else from demonkind. Even you three. Go live your lives."

Onyx shouldered past Dante. "Great, thank you so much for your permission. But if you're so Zen, why bother looking for us at all?" He sounded nothing but annoyed to be there.

"I wanted you to know I was in the city." Ren bent to pick up the saucepan. "I'm not with Lucifer and figured giving you a heads-up was common courtesy, so there were no surprises down the road. And this way, we can help each other when Lucifer starts rounding demons up."

"Oh, so that's how it is," Onyx huffed.

"You want protection?" Ash clicked his tongue. "That's a big ask."

Ren pursed her lips. "Wouldn't you rather I allied with you? I let you find me, left myself unprotected as a show of peace." She turned to Dante, cutting him off like she sensed his argument coming. "All I did to the birds was leave magic at a few nests so you'd know I was here. I've been waiting for you all day. I didn't kill anything. That's not peaceful."

"So it was another demon?" That might be the worst possibility. Multiple demons slipping into this world independent of one another was much messier than Ren being part of a group or Luc bringing allies with him.

"Was my magic on the dead birds?" Ren asked, a hand on her hip. She glanced between them. "I'll take your silence as a no. Look, assess me all you want. I'm not the most powerful among us. I've never been great at masking my spells. If I'd killed anything, you'd be able to tell."

Ash *hmphed*. "So you say."

"I do say. Come on, I'll prove I don't have any ill will toward you. You can call on me for assistance, and I'll fight by your side."

"Fight?" Onyx cut a sidelong look at Dante. "Fight who? Lucifer? Or is there more we should know about what's going on in the Realm of the Damned?"

"And who says we need you to fight with us? If you're lacking power, you don't exactly sound like an asset." Ash really could put his foot in it sometimes.

Ren's jaw muscle ticked. "Four is better than three, no matter how you cut it."

"Okay," Dante said before things got out of hand. "Ren, you need to prove what you're saying beyond offering help in a hypothetical fight that may never come. Someone killed my birds. If it wasn't you, help us find the demon who did it."

"Have you considered Lucifer?" Ren asked as if the three of them were dense.

"Yes." Dante called on his patience. "He's been here and gone back to Hell. We had a little scuffle, but him attacking my flock doesn't fit."

Her eyes widened momentarily. "Then I'll be on the lookout."

Dante forced a smile. "Would you be willing to do a little more? Maybe reach out and see if you can find any other demons who supposedly escaped? If we know who's here, we can take care of the rest."

A flicker of fear passed over Ren's face. "I don't know. If I tried, would you protect me?"

"That depends."

It wasn't good that she assumed other demons would harm her. What had been going on in the Realm of the Damned? If Ren wasn't allied with Luc, others who escaped him shouldn't wish her ill. Unless they didn't escape and were Luc's minions, deliberately placed here.

"Did anyone come here with Lucifer? At his side?" Dante asked.

"Not as far as I know, but I'm not exactly in his confidence." Ren rubbed her brow, looking tired. "You can keep tabs on me if that makes you feel better. I won't try to block your tracking. Eventually, you'll realize I'm not the problem. But I'll see what I can do about finding any others who escaped. Not that I'm known for tracking." She shot a pointed look at Ash.

Ash ignored it. "If you give away to these supposed other demons that you've spoken to us—or that all three of us are in the city—consider any potential alliance void."

Ren bowed her head. "Fine. You have a deal."

Dante, Ash, and Onyx left Ren to her ruined dinner.

"What do we think?" Ash asked as Dante shut the door to the street.

Onyx threw a narrow-eyed look toward the apartment. "We aren't trusting anyone who crawls out of that damned place."

"No," Dante agreed, freeing his wings. "But little as I like to admit, she could be telling the truth about not hurting my birds.

Whoever killed them covered their tracks expertly, like they didn't want to be found. She was sitting here waiting for me to show up. Why cover up her kills and then change her mind and give herself away?"

"I don't know." Ash's brow creased. "But how many others could've escaped?"

There was no way to know, but having more demons in this realm was bound to be trouble.

8

———

## OLLIE

OLLIE's last client of the day rescheduled. A slight disappointment, but she'd still be coming in that week, so no biggie. After cleaning his station and checking no one else needed a hand, he said goodbye to his coworkers and headed home.

It had been almost a week since the art show. He hadn't heard from Dante and had to admit he'd hoped they'd have caught up by now.

Not that he'd initiated anything.

As friends, there was no rule about texting too soon, but it wasn't good to come off too eager. Ollie let his life go on as normal. Meeting Dante didn't change anything. He was still the same person and wasn't rearranging everything for a new friend.

Harper wasn't at the apartment when Ollie got home. Which...damn.

Ollie opened the windows as far as they would go—not more than a few inches—to try and get some air into the place, and plopped on the couch.

He pulled out his phone.

Should he redownload that hookup app? He'd kill to feel someone's hands on him and get off with another person.

No. He scrolled to his social media apps and opened one instead.

Ollie had a bit of a problem. He wanted Dante's hands on him. Dante's body against his as they came, all sweaty and out of breath, and every time Ollie let himself imagine it, his chest ached, butterflies twisting him up inside.

Dante had taken over Ollie's thoughts, and they were hardly even friends. It was the biggest red flag and exactly why it was the right decision not to get involved. Ollie could see himself disappearing into that man's life, and like hell was that ever happening.

But fuck, Ollie liked Dante's hot-sweet combo like nothing else. Even if he hadn't been so over hookups, he wouldn't have bothered with anyone else right now.

*Ugh.*

He scrolled, smiling at a cute cat meme, and sent it to Dex. Really, he should be showering and figuring out what he had in the fridge for dinner.

Dex sent back a video of a cat intimidating a giant dog, and Ollie chuckled.

His phone buzzed and a text notification flashed at the top of his screen. Ollie clicked it automatically, sitting up straighter. It was from Dante.

DANTE:

Hey. Want to help me pick a game to play tonight?

It was exactly what a friend would say. Straight to the gaming chat. No fluffing around. Good.

OLLIE:

Sure. What are you into?

DANTE:

World's End is my favorite. But I always play that.

OLLIE:

That game is so fun! I play a dragon shifter. Humanity doesn't stand a chance. *devil emoji*

DANTE:

You play the invading side?

OLLIE:

It's the only side. Don't tell me you play a human.

DANTE:

I'm a fire mage.

OLLIE:

Mages switch sides all the time. I bet you totally side with the invaders.

DANTE:

I'm a lone wolf. I haven't picked a side.

That was a tricky way to play the game. You usually needed an alliance to get anywhere.

OLLIE:

Really? You don't have a band you run with?

DANTE:

No, but it might be fun for our characters to meet.

Ollie smiled, his insides churning as if Dante had suggested something far more illicit.

OLLIE:

> We're definitely meeting up. I'm recruiting you to my cause.

DANTE:

We'll see about that.

OLLIE:

> But you said you wanted to play something different tonight?

The three dots appeared, telling Ollie that Dante was typing, only for them to disappear and reappear. Ollie waited, grinning until the message came through.

DANTE:

Yeah, maybe there's something else we can play together?

If you're free. Sorry, I didn't ask if you were busy.

Ollie bit his lip, trying to temper his smile.

OLLIE:

> I'm not busy. I got off work early. How about Spacewalk?

It was another popular online game that boiled down to warring between space stations as aliens took over.

DANTE:

Let's do it. I haven't played that one in ages.

Ollie got up and turned on his PlayStation. He grabbed his headset and controller, then detoured to the kitchen for chips and a soda.

He settled on the couch, stomach flipping. It was weird as fuck that he had butterflies over this. He wasn't even meeting

Dante in real life. But the happy fluttering inside him hadn't stopped since Dante's first message.

These really weren't friend feelings, but whatever. Ollie's emotions didn't rule him.

Logging in, Ollie created a new mission and invited Dante to join. It'd be better for them to play against the game rather than join a bigger group in one of the battles. That way, Ollie could talk to Dante without anyone else around.

He texted Dante the details and checked his weapons.

"Hello?" Dante's tentative voice called through Ollie's headphones.

"Hey, Dante. Welcome to my raid."

Dante chuckled. "Glad to be here to assist. I'll follow your lead."

Having Dante's voice in his head did nothing to quell the fluttering plaguing Ollie's insides. "You ready?"

"Let's kill some aliens."

Their first raid ended in a bloody mess, but once they got the hang of it, they started making progress. The game was cool but not Ollie's favorite. At least not until he played with Dante's commentary in his ear.

"What in damnation is that thing?" Dante made a disgusted sound. "A spider with an elephant trunk? I'm going to have nightmares."

He sounded delightfully offended by everything that happened. But Ollie's favorite Dante comment had to be: "That radioactive blob looks like a dick. It even has balls. Tell me I'm not hallucinating."

Ollie had died laughing. Dante hadn't been hallucinating.

He gasped literally any time something jumped out. Could he be more adorable? Ollie's stomach hurt. Dante wasn't afraid to have fun, and Ollie loved it. They played round after round.

"The dick is back," Dante warned. "Oh shit, it jizzed on me."

*Failed Mission* flashed across the screen.

"Did you get dicked to death?" Ollie asked between snorts of laughter.

"Its cum was toxic. I can't believe that happened. We can't tell Ash about this. He already thinks gaming is silly. I'll never hear the end of it."

"Your secret is safe with me," Ollie assured him. "Ready for another?"

"I could do this all night."

So could Ollie. He hadn't smiled this much in years.

THE NEXT NIGHT, Ollie and Dante played *World's End*.

"Holy shit, your character is powerful," Ollie said as Dante appeared at his portal, fire dancing at his character's fingertips.

"I play a lot," Dante admitted, almost sheepishly.

"I think I'll follow your lead on this one." Ollie shifted his character into dragon form. "Are you willing to make a temporary alliance if you're in charge?"

Dante accepted the offer on-screen. "Yes, but we'll be a team. I don't think I'd make a good leader. I'm not after power. That's partly why I stay away from both sides. I don't need to worry about others' rankings, and it's not like I'm going to trust anyone."

Something oddly serious in the way Dante spoke made Ollie wonder if he was half talking about something else, but what could he possibly be referring to? It wasn't like real life was about alliances and betrayals in a battle for dominance on Earth.

Reality wasn't that epic.

"Are you saying I need to watch my back around you?" Ollie asked.

"What?" Dante sounded adorably shocked. "No, I didn't mean I wouldn't trust you. I was talking about everyone else."

"So it's us against the word?"

"Yes," Dante replied, voice whisper-soft.

Ollie swore he felt Dante's breath on his neck, sending chills down his spine as heat unfurled deep inside him. *Fuuuck.*

Ollie readjusted his headphones. "Perfect. Let's find a quest."

Dante kicked ass at this game. He had these cool fire spells Ollie had never seen anyone cast before. At one point, he even conjured a fire demon.

"This game is way more fun with you," Ollie said as he and Dante killed an ice monster Ollie wouldn't have stood a chance against by himself.

"I agree. I like having you in my head."

Something pinched in Ollie's chest. "My commentary is that good, huh?"

"The best," Dante said, seemingly without sarcasm.

Ollie had been joking. He wasn't that entertaining. "I love how different you are playing this game than *Spacewalk*. I was dying of laughter last night."

"I don't know how to play that one without laughing," Dante admitted. "The story's not that deep, and there's not as much of a sense of duty in *Spacewalk*. Not like *World's End*. But that's why *Spacewalk* is good. Sometimes you want to switch off and shoot alien dicks."

"Words to live by."

Dante snorted.

Harper appeared in Ollie's peripheral vision like a phantom, and Ollie jumped, letting out an involuntary squeak.

"What was that?" Dante asked.

"Harper startled me. I didn't hear him come in with my headphones on. What time is it?" Ollie flipped his phone over. "Wow, I had no idea it was this late."

"Do you need to go?"

Ollie didn't let the disappointment in Dante's tone change his mind. "Yeah. I'm supposed to cook tonight."

"I should probably eat too. Catch you later?"

"For sure." Ollie exited the game, finding Harper watching him with an intrigued little smile. "Want to play while I cook?"

"No." Harper shook his head vehemently, eyeing the controller like it might bite him.

Ollie took pity on him. "You don't have to try this game."

"True. Maybe I should practice racing before Sunday." Harper took the controller from Ollie, still weary. "You don't need help cooking?"

"Na. Sorry I didn't get anything going earlier." It was already eight o'clock, and now that Ollie wasn't distracted, he realized how hungry he was.

"Don't worry about it." Harper paused. "You having fun gaming with Dante?"

"Yeah." Ollie's cheeks heated. He hurried off the couch so Harper wouldn't notice. "He's more of a gamer than I'd have guessed."

"It surprised me too. I never thought Ash or the other...of his friends would be into games."

Ollie's brow crinkled at Harper's odd phrasing. "I mean, nerds can be ripped too."

Harper choked on a laugh. "True."

"But Dante's not a casual *World's End* player, he's like expert level. People would totally watch him stream if he was into that." Ollie could easily see Dante being a popular streamer. He was funny, hot, and his character had to be one of the highest levels anyone could achieve.

Would Dante be interested in streaming? Part of Ollie wanted to keep Dante's game commentary all to himself.

It wasn't wrong to want a small piece of Dante to be only his, even as a friend, right?

GAMING TOGETHER BECAME A REGULAR OCCURRENCE. Not every night. Ollie had boundaries and all that. But he looked forward to meeting up with Dante and his fire mage and didn't end up doomscrolling on nights they played together.

Almost two weeks later, Ollie was curled up in the armchair watching a movie with Harper and Ash, who were snuggled on the couch so sweetly it made Ollie's heart hurt.

He didn't begrudge Harper for having a boyfriend. He wished he could have someone too.

Maybe one day he'd be able to balance a healthy relationship with his independence, but that felt so far off. He didn't trust himself to not fall into the same bad patterns and still didn't want a relationship enough to risk it.

The movie was a little slow and Ollie couldn't help scrolling on his phone as it played. He came across a *World's End* meme and sent it to Dante.

As soon as the message sent, Ollie frowned at his phone.

Was it weird to send that after declining Dante's offer to play tonight? Probably not. They were friends, so sending memes was normal. But they hadn't texted much outside of organizing when to meet online.

Dante sent back a laughing emoji, and Ollie relaxed. It was like any other interaction with Dex or his work bestie Ellie.

But instead of flipping back to the meme thread he'd been scrolling, Ollie stayed on the text screen, staring at the emoji. Should he meet up with Dante in person? He kept thinking about it. The only reason he hadn't committed was not knowing how to ask. Everything sounded too date-like in his head.

Making a new friend had never been this hard before, but then, Ollie didn't usually have massive crushes on his friends. Maybe he should have avoided Dante rather than try to hang out with him and suppress his feelings. All the butterflies and sweet tingles didn't seem to be going away. If anything, Ollie's attraction to Dante had grown.

He was hopeless. Why else would he be staring at their text thread like this?

Was this bad?

Did it mean his friendship with Dante was going somewhere unhealthy? Ollie was fixated on Dante, and that wasn't good. Why couldn't he get Dante out of his head? Dante consuming his thoughts could be the first step to consuming his life.

Ollie's stomach twisted. He took a long breath, and the discomfort faded. Maybe he was creating problems that weren't there. He hadn't blown off Harper or Dex to hang out with Dante, and there was nothing wrong with thinking about Dante if it didn't get in the way of anything else.

Ollie turned back to the movie. What were the characters even saying? He'd missed something important but couldn't bring himself to ask Harper to rewind it. He turned back to his phone.

Having a normal conversation with Dante might stop the worries banging around in his head. He could talk to Dante without turning his world upside down, just like he could with anyone else, and he'd prove it.

OLLIE:

How was work today?

They'd chatted about Dante's conservation work a few

times. Ollie couldn't help bringing it up when Dante was so passionate about it.

Dante's reply came through quickly. Maybe Ollie wasn't the only one keeping his phone close.

DANTE:

The birds are all doing well. Settled into their nests for the night. Things have been a bit slow with the project I'm working on, but I shouldn't complain.

How about you?

OLLIE:

Glad the birds are all happy and tucked in. It's so cool you work in the reserve.

My day was booked solid. So glad it's Sunday tomorrow.

The salon was closed on Sunday and Monday, and Saturday was always their busiest day. Ollie had fun at work— the Ollie and Ellie team was unstoppable—and wouldn't change his job for the world, but by the end of the week, he was tired.

He rubbed his stiff neck. How good would a massage be right now? Especially a massage from Dante.

Nope. Not going there. That was the last thing he needed to imagine.

DANTE:

You're off work tomorrow, right?

OLLIE:

Yep.

A light feeling of anticipation filled him.

DANTE:

Would you like to see the birds?

Ollie's heart skipped. How easy was that? Dante also wanted to hang out in person and managed to ask without sounding like a date.

It was everything Ollie needed.

OLLIE:

OMG, yes!

DANTE:

Love your enthusiasm.

Ollie stared at the word love. No, Dante didn't mean it like that. Obviously. Ollie's cheeks still heated. So much for this chat being the same as with any other friend.

DANTE:

I can't take you onto the reserve, but there's a good spot near the waterfront to watch the shearwaters coming in for the night. We could also watch them fly out in the morning, but you'd have to be there before sunrise.

OLLIE:

Let's do tomorrow night. I have plans to sleep in.

DANTE:

Perfect.

Birds had never interested Ollie before encountering Dante's infectious enthusiasm for the sooty shearwater, but Ollie's changed opinion wasn't about pleasing Dante or adopting Dante's likes as his own. New people were allowed to broaden your horizons. Ollie wasn't pretending to like birds to endear himself to Dante. He hadn't realized the creatures were so interesting and was glad Dante had shown him something new.

He'd love to go to the nature reserve, but it was off-limits to the public. Protecting the shearwater habitat was important, and Ollie could live with not seeing the nests up close. He wouldn't want to disturb anything.

Ollie put his phone on the coffee table and returned to the movie.

He felt strangely settled, his muscles relaxed and his head clear. He might worry too much, but in the end, he was doing what was right for him. He'd come a long way, and deep down, he knew his friendship with Dante was a good thing.

He'd figure this out. Little freak-outs along the way were fine. He could add Dante to his life without losing anything.

He'd stay true to himself—no matter what.

9
———

DANTE

DANTE ARRIVED at the beach early. It was inevitable after itching with anticipation all day. Ollie was meeting him half an hour before sunset, and it couldn't come soon enough.

It was too bad he couldn't take Ollie into the reserve. The birds would be happy to let him get close. Dante's enchantment made them more accustomed to interacting with humans than normal seabirds. But Dante couldn't take Ollie to the clifftop and reveal his house. No one was supposed to live up there.

One day, he'd be able to show Ollie his home. When they'd been friends long enough, Dante would reveal magic to Ollie and tell him who he really was. Then he could fly Ollie to the clifftop and show him the home he'd built for them.

Would Ollie ever want to live there with Dante? Ash lived with him, so maybe Ollie would too, regardless of how their bond grew.

"Hey," a familiar voice called from down the beach.

A grin spread across Dante's face as he spotted Ollie. "You're early."

"So are you." Ollie walked along the sand until he reached Dante. "It's such a nice day that I came for a walk."

They stood at the north end of the shore, right before it turned rocky. Ollie looked out at the ocean, shielding his eyes against the low sun. He wore a sleeveless top and shorts and held sandals in his other hand. The sunlight warmed his pale skin, giving him a golden sun-kissed glow. Freckles dusted his shoulders and Dante's fingers tingled with the urge to brush them.

Ollie tilted his face skyward. "I've kept my eyes out, but I think all the birds I've spotted are seagulls."

"You're probably right. It's a bit soon for the shearwaters to be heading in." Dante could call the birds home at any time but didn't want their behavior to seem unnatural to Ollie.

The sea breeze carried Ollie's fresh sandalwood scent, bathing Dante in a wave of pure bliss. He breathed deeply. Bonding with his mate over the past two weeks had felt right, even when they hadn't been physically together.

Being near Ollie now, taking this next step, made their connection stronger.

"I should come out to the beach more." Ollie dug his toes into the sand. "It feels good getting outside, like I'm buzzing with energy."

"Me too." It was probably their bond rather than the beach, but the setting didn't hurt. "I don't come down here as often as I should. With all my time spent on the cliffs, I forget other outdoor places exist."

"Then let's explore. Think there's any tidepools over there?" Ollie pointed toward the rocks.

"I'd say so. The tide is going out."

"Perfect. Come on." Ollie set his sandals on a rock. Climbing onto the one beside it, he headed toward the waterline.

Dante followed.

The water glittered before them, shining all around Ollie.

Dante drank in the sight. His mate lit his world, shining with curiosity and bringing joy to everything he and Dante did together.

"Here's one," Ollie called with an almost childlike excitement.

Dante came to stand beside him. "What have we got?"

"A few anemones, but not much else." Ollie carefully walked around the tidepool, avoiding patches of seaweed and barnacles clinging to the rocks. "Looks like there's a bigger one over there." He pointed up the rocky beach.

"Seems promising."

Dante walked beside Ollie as he navigated the rocks. He could have easily run along the uneven surface with super-human speed, but Ollie was taking measured steps, clearly concentrating on maintaining his balance.

Ollie glanced sideways at Dante. "I feel like climbing on rocks was easier when I was a kid."

"It probably was—"

Ollie suddenly lost his balance, his foot slipping. Dante caught Ollie around the waist, steadying him before he fell. Ollie leaned into him.

"Saved you," Dante teased.

Ollie swatted his arm. "So chivalrous." He rolled his eyes, his hand lingering on Dante's skin, heat radiating from the spot. Ollie cleared his throat. "But really, thank you. I don't need a sprained ankle. I totally jinxed myself."

"You're most welcome. I don't want you getting hurt when I can't heal you by sharing my health."

"Dork." Ollie shook with laughter, nothing but affection in his eyes.

Dante gave Ollie a quick squeeze and released him at the same time Ollie pulled away. Pink stained Ollie's cheeks. Fuck, he looked so lovely in the golden light, blond hair and hazel eyes shining as bright as the glittering water.

Dante could have kissed him. He cleared his throat. "Is there anything in particular you're hoping to see in the tidepools?"

Ollie blinked like the question shook him out of a daze. "A starfish would be sweet. Come on, we better hurry before the sun sets."

Dante let Ollie walk ahead, pretending he needed to go slower to navigate the rocks so he could put some distance between them.

Being Ollie's friend made him happy—it felt right—but kissing and sex had always been tied to Dante's romantic feelings, and he shouldn't let his thoughts stray in that direction unless Ollie said that was what he wanted.

This was still so new. Adjusting to a potentially platonic mate and shaking off old assumptions would take time, but it would work out.

Dante had to remain open to all possibilities and see where fate took them.

A ways ahead, Ollie stooped to examine the tide pool. "Wow, this anemone is huge!"

His vibrant energy was contagious, filling Dante to the brim. "Any starfish?"

"No." Ollie didn't sound disappointed. "There's a bunch of little hermit crabs or snails or something. They've got little pointy shells. Come see."

A crack like thunder ripped through the air, stopping Dante in his tracks. The space behind Ollie shimmered, the view distorting, and a figured appeared out of nowhere.

A tall, familiar figure with curling red horns and dark-red wings.

Dante's demon blood ran cold.

Ollie flinched. "What was that sound?"

As he rose from his crouched position, Lucifer grabbed Ollie's hair and forced him back down. Ollie's knees hit the rocks lining the pool, and he thrashed, fear lining his face as he grabbed at Lucifer, trying to pull himself free.

"*Dante!*"

"*Ollie!*" Dante's chest seized. He shot forward at an inhuman speed.

"Stop," Lucifer warned, his tone calm, reminding Dante of pain and darkness. "Don't come any closer, or I'll crush his skull."

There was no doubt Luc would. Dante stopped even though everything in him screamed not to. He was still too far away.

Ollie whimpered, his frightened gaze locked on Dante.

"Luc, what are you doing here?" Dante's demon features screamed to come out, wings burning his back and tail strangling his waist.

His mate was in danger.

He had to get to Ollie, but Lucifer could kill Ollie with magic or his bare hands faster than Dante could reach him. Inhuman speed wasn't an advantage if your enemy possessed it too.

*Fuck. Fuck. Fuck.*

Why was this happening?

Dante's phone buzzed in his pocket, probably Ash warning him he'd felt Luc leave the Realm of the Damned.

"I hope this goes better than our last meeting," Lucifer drawled, suddenly casual. Dante didn't buy the change in mood. "What's this I've found?" He shook Ollie by the hair until Ollie made a sound of protest.

Lucifer yanked Ollie to standing and pulled him close,

Ollie's back flush against his chest. "Have we a human plaything?"

Ollie's eyes left Dante as he strained to see over his shoulder. "What's going on? Who are you? Please. I'll do what you want if you let me go."

Lucifer laughed, cruelty rolling through the air.

Could a lightning spell take out Luc without hitting Ollie? No. What a dumb idea. Any energy would flow through Luc and kill him. *Fuck.* How had this happened? Dante never should have left Ollie's side.

The distance between them felt unfathomable.

All had been quiet. No one had hurt his birds, no news of any other demons, and no sign of Luc. Dante had become complacent.

"Luc, what are you doing? I'm happy to talk. No tricks this time. Your quarrel isn't with Ollie. Let him leave, and we can deal with things between us."

Ollie's gaze slid back to Dante, a tremble wracking his body. What did he think was going on? Had he glimpsed Lucifer's wings or horns? He must be so scared.

Dante's heart burned. This couldn't be happening. He needed to get to Ollie, but Luc didn't make idle threats. If Dante came closer, Luc wouldn't hesitate to kill him.

"I don't want to let him go," Luc whined. "If I do, you'll shock me and try to capture me again. I need a shield. You made me take this pretty boy hostage to ensure you'd cooperate."

Fucking asshole. "What do you want?" Dante ground out, clenching his fists.

Luc narrowed his eyes, glancing from Dante to Ollie. His eyes flashed red and a smirk twisted his lips. "Don't tell me you're obsessed with this one like Ash was with that other boy?"

"Harper is Ash's mate," Dante spat. It didn't matter that

Ollie was hearing things he didn't understand. He'd explain later. It would all be okay once Luc let Ollie go.

Dante took a step closer and Luc yanked Ollie's head back, exposing his neck, warning flashing in Luc's eyes. Dante's limbs went numb, and he froze. Sweat broke out on his neck as his gut twisted, sending pain through his core. He had to protect Ollie. Why hadn't he stayed glued to his side?

Luc laid a hand on Ollie's throat, and Ollie's Adam's apple bobbed. "Stop lying about mates, Dante," Lucifer hissed. "Ash was talking shit, and I didn't fall for it. You think all you have to do is say *mate*, and it will be true. Like I'd believe any of you. You're all deluded."

Dante raised his arms in surrender. Luc needed to get his hands the fuck off Ollie, but one wrong move and Luc could crush Ollie's windpipe.

"Ash wasn't lying about Harper. We aren't deluded. Listen to me, Luc. You should want to hear this more than anyone. Finding our mates is possible. Ollie is my mate. Now, let him go, or I will kill you. I swear it."

Ollie released a low, strangled sound that cut Dante to the depths of his damned soul.

"I don't believe you." Luc's eyes glowed red and he beat his wings, fingers flexing against the pale skin of Ollie's neck. "We will never find our mates. We've known that for well over a thousand years. Yet, you expect me to believe you and Ash have suddenly found yours?"

"Yes. It's true. I don't know how they're here after so long..." Dante's fingertips tingled and his mouth went dry. Ollie looked at him like he'd been betrayed, cutting Dante deeper than anything. He took an unsteady breath. "You're holding my mate by the throat, Luc. It's a crime to act like this. The highest offense. You know this. Please, let him go. Even after all this time, you know the bond is sacred. You can't come between us."

Luc pressed his lips to Ollie's ear, whispering too low for Dante to hear over the waves crashing on the rocks behind them. Ollie's wide eyes filled with tears.

"Luc! Stop!" Dante yelled as the tears spilled down Ollie's cheeks.

The Devil's fire-red eyes fixed on Dante. "There is no bond between you two. If there was, you wouldn't be pissing yourself right now. If you were bonded, I wouldn't be able to kill him so easily." The nails on Luc's hand lengthened into lethal points, pricking Ollie's throat. Luc's face twisted as if something pleasing occurred to him. "There is one way to know for sure if you're telling the truth."

"*No!*" Dante screamed, launching forward at full speed, wings erupting from his back.

But he wasn't fast enough. He couldn't cross the rocks faster than Luc could flick his wrist.

Lucifer dragged his nails across Ollie's throat, cutting so deep his fingers disappeared into Ollie's flesh. Blood burst from the gash, Ollie's eyes popping wide in horror as he choked and grabbed at his neck, his body dissolving into convulsions as blood poured over his fingers.

Luc tossed Ollie away as Dante reached him. He caught his mate, holding tight. Instantly, Ollie's blood coated Dante's arms and chest. There was so much. Everywhere but where it needed to be, safe inside his mate.

Everything in Dante's body screamed. He shook as he clutched Ollie. *No. Not this. Not Ollie. He can't die. Not yet, and not like this.*

Dante may never see his mate again if he passed into the Eternal Realm. His soul could be held captive. Dante wouldn't risk it. He had to save him. But would the bond be enough? It was too soon.

Dante ripped his trembling wrist open with his teeth and

pressed it to Ollie's slack mouth as he bent and licked some of the blood from Ollie's chest.

Tears filled Dante's eyes and spilled down his cheeks. No sound reached his ears except the horrible gurgling coming from Ollie's throat. He tasted nothing—felt nothing but emptiness—as he swallowed his mate's blood and began the incantation to bind their souls together forever.

If cemented properly, the mating bond would give Ollie Dante's demon healing powers. It was the only way to save him from a fatal wound, as long as the wound didn't kill him before Dante finished the spell.

Magic flared around Dante, grating on his frayed nerves like acid on his skin. Cold seawater chilled his legs, and he realized he'd fallen to his knees in the tidepool. The water was red with blood, dark and desolate, Ollie's life force staining the rocks.

Ollie turned cold in Dante's arms, his eyes glassy and chest barely moving as horrible sounds ripped from his mangled throat.

Dante chanted the mating spell with everything he had, pouring magic and thousands of years' worth of longing into the ritual. *Anything for Ollie. Please don't let it be too late.*

As Dante's chant faded, the spell complete, he rested his forehead against Ollie's, tears falling onto Ollie's clammy skin.

Ollie's heartbeat was so faint Dante could barely make it out over his own. The rhythm slowed, then stopped. Dante's stopped too, his muscles locking up. It was as if his body no longer belonged to him, but he'd rather die than come away from this without Ollie.

With a shudder that went down to his toes, Dante's heart restarted, and when it did, so did Ollie's, stronger now, beating in sync with Dante's.

The connection between them flared. Magic raced through Dante's veins, pulling power out of him and toward Ollie in a blinding pain so sharp it drowned everything out, stealing Dante's vision in a flash of light.

Everything hurt, Dante's body screaming in silent agony.

He welcomed Ollie's pain. He called it to him, taking it away from Ollie. Dante's throat felt ripped open, his lungs heavy like he was drowning, but it was okay. Dante would take any pain if it meant Ollie was still here.

Ollie remained limp in Dante's arms. Why was it taking so long? Maybe it was a mercy Ollie wasn't conscious and had been spared the pain, but he'd wake eventually, right? *Please.* It had worked, hadn't it?

At last, through the agony, Dante felt Ollie's body healing, stitching back together.

Dante's heavy lungs cleared and he drew in a choked breath. The numbness in his limbs faded and the weight of Ollie in his arms became solid. Dante brushed Ollie's hair from his forehead, leaving a smear of blood behind.

The sight made Dante's battered throat close. Ollie's whole body, from the neck down, was drenched in blood. Flecks of red marred his cheeks. Dante wiped them away, but his hands were so bloody he made it worse.

Irrational anger at dirtying his mate's face burned inside him. *This wasn't right.*

Ollie's body was healing, but Dante's mind wasn't. It broke over the rocks and sand. Red filled his vision, burning his eyes. He'd crumble into nothing.

Dante brushed the healing gash on Ollie's throat. His world had been bled dry. He couldn't do this. It wasn't fair.

But Ollie needed him to get through this.

Dante focused on their shared heartbeats, letting the sound hold him steady. Ollie would wake. He would be okay.

"Is he really...?" A choked sound cut through the thudding of Dante's and Ollie's twin heartbeats. "He...he...?"

Dante looked up, surprised to find Lucifer standing before him, splattered with his mate's blood.

He hadn't fled? The Devil's miserable face had the audacity to twist in horror as he gazed down at Ollie like he hadn't been the one to do this.

"*I will kill you,*" Dante vowed, so much venom in his tone he didn't recognize his own voice.

Lucifer turned a hollow gaze on Dante. He opened his mouth as if to speak, then blinked out of existence.

Fine. Dante could wait. There was nowhere Luc could go to be safe now. Dante would hunt Luc to the ends of the known universe. He would punish Luc for this, but he was fucking busy right now. He had Ollie to take care of. His mate was more important than vengeance. More important than anything.

And after today, nothing would ever be the same.

10

———

OLLIE

OLLIE CHOKED. Pain tore through him like glass, severing his throat. He screamed, but no sound came. Everything was black —agony—his whole body pulsing. This couldn't be real.

The throbbing in his neck grew, turning into a loud rhythmic beat.

Ollie's eyes flew open to a light so blinding he couldn't see. His head spun. Was he falling? Was he moving at all?

The pain faded, replaced by a hollow sensation as memories assaulted him.

The beach.

That...*man*.

Ollie's hands flew to his throat. It had been ripped out. A whimper fell from his lips as phantom fingers dug into his neck, pulling him apart.

He gagged, nerves crawling at the gross violation, but the skin beneath his fingers was smooth, not torn open.

Ollie's vision cleared. The beach was gone. There was no sky overhead. He was inside somewhere. Where the fuck was he? His heart clattered against his sternum, sweat coating his body. What happened?

"Ollie," a soft, broken whisper reached him.

Ollie swung his head around. Dante kneeled beside him. Ollie's hand shot out of its own accord, grabbing for Dante like he could save him. From what, Ollie didn't even know.

Dante's hand closed around his. "I'm here, Ollie. You're okay."

Ollie choked on the air in his lungs. Air. He'd been dying for air, choking on his own blood. How was he not dead?

Or was he?

Ollie looked closer at Dante. He had dark-gray wings protruding from his back and silver-gray horns sticking out of his hair. Ollie trembled. The other man had wings and horns too. The man who'd killed him.

"Ollie, talk to me," Dante begged, his face twisted in a way that hurt to look at.

"B-blood," Ollie managed.

He looked down at himself. He was covered. So was Dante. Wait, was he on a couch? Did the afterlife have couches? Why wasn't the blood gone if his neck was put back together?

"I'm so sorry, Ollie." Dante choked out a sob, squeezing Ollie's hand. "I'm sorry I let him hurt you."

"I...I died." Ollie pulled his hand away, sitting up and rubbing his throat. "W-what are you?"

Dante shifted until he was as close to Ollie as he could be without touching him. "You didn't die, Ollie. I saved you—"

"How?" Ollie asked before Dante finished. His clothes were heavy with blood, sticking to his skin in challenge to Dante's statement. "There's no way I... Not with... This is my blood." His stomach turned and he gagged, doubling over, head between blood-soaked knees.

"Let's clean you up, and I'll explain."

"No, explain now." Ollie's hands shook as he straightened. They were sticky. Fuck, the smell of copper was everywhere.

"Why do you have wings? What the fuck, Dante? I know I'm dead. Just admit it." Ollie buried his head in his hands as a sob tore from his abused throat.

Dante pulled Ollie's hands from his face, encasing them in his. "You aren't dead. We're still on Earth. I saved you with magic. I've always had wings, but I kept them hidden before. I'm sorry. I tried to put them away so it wouldn't alarm you when you woke, but I'm too worked up. I was too worried about you. Here, let me try again."

Ollie stared transfixed as the dark-gray feathers at Dante's back ruffled, then disappeared, his horns along with them. It didn't convince Ollie he wasn't dead. Maybe this was some strange misfire in his brain, happening as everything shut down.

"See?" Dante twisted to show his back, where a large tattoo of folded wings covered his smooth brown skin. "You've seen my tattoos before. That first time at your apartment with Harper, remember?"

"When you didn't have a shirt." Ollie hadn't thought about the tattoos since, but the memory must be where this hallucination had come from. "Why weren't you and Ash dressed that day?"

Dante turned back around. "We'd been flying and didn't have shirts with us."

"You expect me to believe Ash has wings too? You're like angels or something?" Ollie wasn't that gullible. But if this wasn't real, what did it matter? Or if it was real, he was one hundred percent dead. Either way, nothing mattered.

Dante ran a dirty hand through his hair. "We aren't angels. I'm a demon, Ollie, but it's not what you think."

Well, that made no sense, but for some reason, Dante looked deathly serious. What the fuck? Dante was an agent of Hell?

Ollie shivered, suddenly freezing. Was this shock? Could he be in shock if he was dead?

Could this be real?

Dante cupped Ollie's cheeks, wiping away tears Ollie hadn't felt fall. "Come, let's clean you up. You'll feel better, and then we can talk."

Ollie allowed Dante to pull him from the couch and guide him through the large modern house. It felt like a dream, floaty and distorted. Even the proportions of the hallway and doors weren't right. Ollie's whole body felt wrong, like he'd lost more than blood. He was fading away and weighed down at the same time, and something deep in his chest clawed at him.

He had to put himself right—get rid of this feeling—but he didn't know what was happening. Was this what being dead felt like?

Dante led him to an enormous bathroom with the largest tiled shower Ollie had ever seen. They both fit with room for several more people. Something had to be wrong with Ollie's brain. It was like he'd forgotten what normal houses looked like and instead was imagining *this*.

He stood shivering as Dante turned on all three rainfall-style showerheads. The water heated quickly, steam hitting Ollie's face. He stepped under the spray and pulled off his ruined shirt.

Ollie glanced down to undo his shorts, finding dark-red water circling the drain. It swirled around his toes, but no matter how much water drained, it didn't run clear.

The heat of the shower disappeared. Ollie shook, his hands numb. He couldn't get the button undone. He couldn't get his shorts off. They were soaked with so much blood the water couldn't wash it away.

Ollie was bleeding again. He had to be. This was his blood, and it was supposed to be inside him. He was dying. Dead.

Strong arms wrapped around him, and Ollie laid his head

against Dante's chest without hesitation. Ollie's trembling hands stilled, and he wrapped them around Dante.

He was no longer floating away.

"I don't know what's wrong," Ollie whispered, unable to stop his shivers. "It's like something's happened inside me, and it's not right."

A whine escaped Dante, sounding more like a hurt animal than a man. "I'm sorry, Ollie. There was only one way to save you. That's why you feel this way, but we should be able to fix it. It won't feel like this forever."

Ollie buried his face against Dante's bare chest. He didn't know what Dante meant, yet Dante's minty scent tingled his senses, and after a few deep breaths, Ollie's tremors stilled.

Dante stroked Ollie's wet hair. "Can I wash you?"

Ollie nodded into Dante's chest. God, he hoped he'd feel better when the blood was gone.

Dante helped Ollie out of his shorts and underwear and tossed the soiled clothes aside, along with his bloody jeans, leaving them both completely naked.

Ollie registered their nudity in passing like he noticed the shower's grout was darker than the tiles. His body felt foreign and wrong. He needed Dante, but not in the way he normally would have while in a shower with no clothes on.

Neither of them spoke. Ollie wasn't sure he could have. There was a lump in his throat he was afraid to dislodge, not knowing what might come out.

He held on to Dante's shoulders as the bigger man washed him with sweet-scented soap and a soft cloth. Dante's careful touch felt like heaven, and slowly, the lump in Ollie's throat dissolved.

Eventually, the water running off them turned clear, save for the suds. Ollie felt more whole than he had since opening his eyes and, for some reason, didn't want to let Dante go.

"Where are we?" Ollie asked when Dante had finished washing them both and he'd reluctantly released Dante's shoulders.

Dante stood frozen for a moment too long before turning off the water. "This is my house."

Ollie turned, ignoring the emptiness growing inside him once again, and reinspected the ridiculously large shower, realization hitting him like a smack in the face. "It's because of your wings. That's why it's all so...large."

"Exactly," Dante said as if Ollie had made a clever discovery and not the most obvious observation on the planet.

Dante stepped around a tiled wall—there was no door closing the shower—heading into the rest of the bathroom. There was another tattoo around Dante's hips, like a rope or a...tail?

Ollie stood rooted to the spot. He was beginning to suspect this wasn't a hallucination, which wasn't comforting. A hollow void bubbled inside him, growing like something sick and painful was coming.

Dante reappeared, towel around his waist and another held out for Ollie.

When Ollie didn't reach for it, Dante wrapped it around him. It was no surprise the towel was enormous and engulfed Ollie like a blanket.

Dante pulled Ollie against his chest and held him tight, and the sick feeling roiling inside Ollie faded.

"If you're a demon, why did you save me?" Ollie whispered, lying his head against Dante's shoulder.

Dante sighed, almost sounding content as he rested a hand on the back of Ollie's head. "Demons aren't evil. We aren't what Christianity or any other human beliefs make us out to be."

"Then why call yourself a demon if that's not what you are?"

"That's a good point." Dante paused, running his hand through Ollie's hair. "I'm a Fallen Eternal—an immortal being who possesses magic, banned from the Eternal Realm."

So maybe saying he was a demon was better than that. Ollie had no clue what any of that was supposed to mean. "If you saved me with magic, why do I feel so...broken inside?"

Dante pulled Ollie tighter against him. "I feel it too."

The strange sense that something wasn't right intensified, broadening and filling Ollie with an unfamiliar, painful regret.

Ollie gasped, clutching his chest. "What is that?"

Dante pulled back, looking down at Ollie, his eyes red-rimmed and sad. "To save you, I had to link us. It's called a mating bond. But I couldn't complete the ritual like we would have if you were conscious."

"Mating bond?" Snippets from the beach came back to Ollie. "You said I was your mate. You were talking about Harper. That man said..." Ollie's chest tightened as whispered words filled his mind.

*"You think he loves you, but he doesn't. He's lying. You're nothing but a little plaything to him, and now he's going to watch you die, and it won't even matter."*

Dread stole the residual warmth of the shower from Ollie's body. Claws dug into his neck. He snapped his eyes shut. What the hell had that evil man—being, demon, whatever—been saying? Dante didn't love Ollie. Why did that murderous shithead think so?

Why try to kill him because of it?

"Who was that?" Ollie managed, his voice sounding small and afraid.

Dante tilted Ollie's chin up until their eyes met. "That was Lucifer. Ash, Onyx, and I escaped him many years ago, and he's trying to hunt us down."

Ollie's stomach dropped like he was falling. The Devil was

real? Ollie's legs turned to jelly, and if it weren't for Dante holding him, he'd have crumpled to the tile floor. Everything he wanted to say stuck in his throat.

Dante held him close, whispering. "It's all right. You're safe now. I won't let him hurt you again."

Ollie pulled himself together, forcing his knees to do their job and hold him up. He nodded into Dante's chest even though he wasn't sure Dante could promise safety.

"I'm sorry you got pulled into this," Dante continued. "If I'd known there was any risk Luc would be back so soon or that he'd come to the beach, I never would have taken you somewhere so exposed."

At last, Ollie found his voice. "You said demons aren't what I thought. But the Devil is real? You're scaring me, Dante."

Another small whine escaped Dante. "I'm sorry. Ollie, I'm so sorry."

Ollie could feel how much Dante meant it. It was strange, almost like he could read Dante's mind. Not his exact thoughts, but his intentions, his emotions. Ollie sensed a regret so deep it was hard to breathe.

"It's okay." Ollie wrapped his arms around Dante, the desire to comfort overriding everything else. "You saved me. Tell me how you saved me."

Dante's tense muscles relaxed beneath Ollie's hands. "I linked us through a mating bond. As my mate, you have my healing powers and immortality. Once we were linked, you saved yourself with your newfound power, healing the wound Luc inflicted."

Hold the fucking phone. "*Immortality?*" Ollie croaked.

"Yes." Dante nodded, solemn as ever. "Your life will now be as long as mine."

Ollie's mind rebelled. That wasn't possible. But neither was recovering from having his throat gouged open. He trembled. How was he supposed to accept any of this?

That feeling of wrongness reared its ugly head, carving out Ollie's insides. Maybe Dante was wrong. "You said the bond wasn't complete. What does that mean?"

"To form a mating bond, we both need to accept the connection, but you were unconscious." A shadow passed over Dante's face. "I did as much as I could, but without you accepting, the bond will remain incomplete. That's what we're feeling."

"Can we break it, get rid of it now that I'm healed?" Then Ollie could be a normal, mortal person again and wouldn't have to try to understand any of this.

Dante flinched like Ollie had hit him. "No, we can't." His voice was painfully soft. "It's irreversible. We're mates. There's no going back from this type of magic."

Ollie's pulse raced, a heaviness settling over him. "Okay. We're mates."

What the fuck did that mean? He wouldn't have chosen to be Dante's mate if he'd been asked. Mates sounded intense. So did being immortal. But it wasn't like he'd have chosen death over this. He trusted Dante. And Dante had done something unfathomable to save him.

"If I accept the bond, will I feel better? Like myself again?"

There was no way Ollie could live with this itchy hollowness inside him. If he focused on the feeling too hard, he'd start crying again.

Dante adjusted the towel around Ollie's shoulders, studying Ollie's face closely. "Yes, if you accept, you'll feel like yourself again."

"Then, I accept." Ollie waited, but the pit inside him seemed to grow.

Dante guided Ollie out of the shower, through the bathroom, and into the adjoining bedroom. "Saying you accept isn't enough. I think we need to go through the ritual again, with you actively participating."

Ollie pulled away. "Wait, you mean a mating ritual? Like sex?"

"It's a mating ritual by definition, but it doesn't have to be sexual," Dante said in a hurry. He sat on a couch beside a large window, putting distance between them, and braced his hands on his towel-covered knees. "All I did to save you was cast the mating spell, give you my blood, and take some of yours. If we repeat that with your consent and intent to form a bond with me, everything should be fine."

Ollie stepped forward slowly and perched on the couch beside Dante, a whole new set of feelings sparking in his veins. "Is the ritual usually sexual?"

Dante swallowed audibly. "Yes, but I'm not asking that of you. We're mates, but that doesn't mean we have to physically mate. Sex isn't essential to the magic working. If it was, I wouldn't have been able to save you."

"I don't get what being your mate means, Dante. Does it mean to complete the bond and get this deep *ick* out of my chest, I have to be in a relationship?" Ollie's heart jolted. Dante said the mating bond was irreversible. Ollie had never said he was okay with being someone's mate. It sounded like a boyfriend or partner, and Ollie didn't want that, but he couldn't live feeling half-wrong and incomplete either.

He didn't really have a choice.

Dante gripped Ollie's hands. "We don't have to be in a romantic relationship. We don't have to change anything between us. But we are bonded. We will always be connected. I know I shouldn't have done this without your consent, but I couldn't let you die."

That threw perspective back in Ollie's face. "Hey. Of course you didn't want me to die. And I'm glad you saved me. Fuck, I don't think I've ever been more grateful in my life. I'm just trying to figure out what this is. There's no doubt I'd rather be bonded to you than dead."

Dante had made a huge sacrifice for him. He wasn't even asking Ollie to commit to anything romantic when a mating bond sounded like it should be marriage or something.

"I'm glad you don't regret me doing this," Dante said, relief softening his face. "And I promise, the bond can be whatever we want it to be."

"Of course I don't regret it." A smile tugged at Ollie's lips, warmth filling his insides for the first time in what felt like years. "Let's redo the ritual, and I'll accept. It feels right."

And it did. Somehow, nothing had ever felt so right in Ollie's life. His doubts faded and he became even more sure. The need to accept Dante's bond pulled on the center of his chest, reaching every deep piece of his soul.

Dante pulled Ollie into an embrace. "Thank you, Ollie."

Relief radiated off Dante. The strangeness that had coated everything since Ollie woke up faded and something good took over.

"I think I can feel you," Ollie murmured, no matter how strange it sounded.

Dante pulled back. "You can. I can feel you too."

"Wait, really?" Ollie patted his towel-covered chest, the pull on his heart turning into an ache. "You know how I feel?"

Dante smiled his bashful little smile. "It's the bond. Our connection."

"So, some things *are* going to change between us." Friends couldn't sense each other's emotions. Ollie didn't know what to think of that kind of intimacy, no matter how right this felt.

"We can learn to control what we share," Dante said as if this was all normal, though to him, it probably was. "I'll respect your boundaries, Ollie."

But how? There was no real way for Ollie to get his head around any of this. He'd have to trust Dante.

And that didn't seem as hard as it should have been.

One thing shone brightly among all the confusion, and it pointed toward Dante.

Ollie followed the light, guided by that right feeling flowing through him. It pulled him onto Dante's lap. Ollie straddled Dante, his towel falling from his shoulders and pooling around his hips.

Ollie placed his hands on Dante's shoulders. "Make me feel better, Dante. Please?"

## 11

## OLLIE

Ollie's pulse pounded, Dante's breath catching as Ollie's grip tightened on his shoulders. He wouldn't normally get in this position with a friend, but it felt so fucking right.

Ollie would do anything for the hollowness inside him to go away, to forget this day ever happened, and sitting in Dante's lap felt healing. It was like their nearness changed something in Ollie's chemical makeup. His worries faded. He might not know exactly what mates were, but it felt right to be Dante's.

"I've got you, Ollie," Dante whispered, his hands resting gently on Ollie's towel-covered thighs. "I promise to be a good mate to you. I won't let this hurt you anymore."

Ollie nodded, voice escaping him.

Dante rested his forehead against Ollie's and began to chant strange, rhythmic sounds. With each puff of Dante's breath, something familiar washed over Ollie. Did he recognize the spell from the first time Dante uttered it, even though he'd been unconscious?

Dante's chants tickled Ollie's skin, leaving him feeling infinitely more cleansed than the shower. Warmth flooded

Ollie's bones. Their breath mingled, and Dante's peppermint scent filled Ollie's nose.

Surrounded by Dante, Ollie believed he'd be okay, even in the face of everything that had happened.

Electricity buzzed up and down Ollie's spine, even after Dante finished the spell. The silence felt alive. Ollie shivered, not ready to let go of the sensation. It was weird and kind of wonderful.

Ollie found himself smiling.

When Dante pulled back, Ollie missed the press of their foreheads together. It was like he'd gotten attached to the small physical connection and didn't know what to do without it.

Dante gave him a tender look of understanding. Fuck, Ollie had never felt so seen.

"Are you ready to exchange blood?" Dante asked.

Ollie hesitated, even with all the good feelings buzzing around him. "Is it safe?"

Dante nodded. "Yes, we're immortal. Diseases and infections can't affect us."

"Okay." Ollie blushed. If they had sex, there'd be no need for a condom. Fuck, why was he thinking that?

Dante took one of Ollie's hands in his and massaged it. "We only need a small amount. A sip each. It won't hurt, but I'll go first and give you my blood, all right?"

Ollie nodded. This was the most bizarre thing he'd ever done, or it should have been. Intellectually speaking, drinking blood was creepy. Except it wasn't. He felt nothing but calm.

He needed this.

Dante brought his wrist to his lips. He bared his teeth, canines lengthening into fangs, and bit down.

Ollie expected the sight of blood to turn his stomach. He braced himself, but as Dante pulled back, red on his teeth and dripping from his wrist, Ollie's mouth watered, desire tugging behind his navel.

He reached for Dante, bringing Dante's wounded wrist to his lips, and lapped at it with his tongue. It wasn't enough. Ollie covered the wound with his mouth and sucked, blood coating his tongue as a low groan rumbled deep in Dante's chest.

Dante tasted like fresh peppermint and warm sun on salty skin. Nothing had ever been so good.

Pleasure spiked along Ollie's spine, his cock thickening unexpectedly. Holy shit. Ollie needed more. He sucked harder, his pleasure building until his cock was fully erect.

A soft, almost purring sound emanated from Dante's throat and his cock hardened against Ollie. Was it in response to Ollie's erection or Ollie drinking Dante's blood? Ollie wished they weren't separated by towels. He needed skin on skin.

Oh god, did Ollie have a blood kink? Did Dante?

It was so good Ollie almost didn't care. He drank deeper, Dante's other hand tightening on Ollie's thigh. Dante's breaths came out soft and panting—desperate—but he didn't roll his hips or pull Ollie closer.

Ollie wished he would. He wanted to mate in every sense of the word, with Dante's bare cock in his ass. Too bad they'd agreed not to have sex. To be friends. To mate but not be together. And it was the right choice, no matter how good this felt.

Ollie pulled back before he did something he'd regret, licking his lips like he'd had ice cream, not blood.

Dante's face was flushed deep red, his eyes hooded. He cleared his throat, his voice rough like gravel. "Was that okay?"

"Better than okay," Ollie breathed, forcing himself not to squirm on Dante's lap. "Is it my turn?"

Dante nodded, delicately clutching Ollie's wrist.

Pleasure tightened deep inside Ollie. It was kind of fucked

up that he was hard over this after what happened on the beach, but he couldn't focus on anything bad right now. It was impossible.

"You're doing so well, Ollie. We're almost there," Dante murmured before his lips closed over Ollie's wrist and sharp teeth punctured Ollie's flesh.

Pleasure zinged along Ollie's nerves.

His head dropped back, mouth open on a moan. Dante sucked, and Ollie swore his wrist and cock were connected. Tingles wound down his spine. His balls ached. He groaned and rolled his hips, unable to hold back.

No wonder this was usually sexual.

But Dante didn't respond to Ollie's rocking hips. He remained painfully still, except for the bobbing of his throat as he sucked on Ollie's wrist. Even his eyes were closed.

Ollie forced himself to stop moving. He couldn't hump Dante like a horny animal.

But it didn't help. The lack of friction didn't stop the pleasure winding tight inside him. Dante's still hands felt like fire on his skin.

"Dante," Ollie whispered in warning. Or was he begging for more? He wasn't sure. Much longer, and it wouldn't matter if Ollie was rubbing against Dante or not. His balls drew tight.

How was he about to come from Dante drinking his blood?

Dante released Ollie's wrist, and the bite closed so fast that Ollie's brows flew up, knocking him out of his lust-induced daze. Part of Ollie still couldn't believe magic was real or that Dante had healed him, but seeing his wound disappear banished his uncertainty.

Soft pants brought Ollie's attention back to Dante, who gave him a shy, unsteady smile. "We're mates."

"We are." Ollie grinned back. He could feel the change inside him. All the uncanniness had dissolved, leaving no doubt this was all real. He hadn't died. He felt more alive than he ever had.

He wanted to rip the towels away and beg Dante to fuck him, then fuck Dante in turn until they were both dripping with cum.

But that wasn't what friends did. Under normal circumstances, Ollie wouldn't even be sitting on Dante's lap. The lines he'd drawn weren't arbitrary.

Ollie's erection deflated as all the reasons he'd kept Dante at a distance crashed through him. He needed space. Needed to remember he was his own person, with his own priorities. But was he? He was linked to Dante. Via magic. How had he not realized what that meant until now?

A connection like this could consume Ollie. It already had. His feelings weren't his own. His urges confused him. Who was he? He didn't get horny over blood play. How could he live like this and not get lost in Dante's world?

"Hey." Dante shifted Ollie off his lap and onto the couch. "It's all right."

Oh shit, Dante could tell Ollie was freaking out. He could feel Ollie's emotions. Practically read his mind. Dante could influence him without even trying.

"The bond is what we make it, Ollie." Dante repeated his earlier words much more firmly. "I'm not asking any more of you than I did this morning."

Fuck, he could tell exactly where Ollie's thoughts had gone. "You might not be asking, but this isn't something that happens between normal friends, Dante. You know what I'm thinking."

"We'll learn to close off that part of the connection. Think of it like meditating or clearing your mind. We'll practice, and it'll become second nature. You won't have to share more than you want to." Dante seemed one hundred percent confident it was that simple, his conviction lending calm to the situation.

Ollie needed to relax. Take this one step at a time.

He took a deep, shuddering breath to clear his head, but it didn't work. None of this worked. Dante's calming presence dulled Ollie's worry but couldn't banish it. "Are you sure it's okay for me to be your mate even though I don't date or do relationships?"

"Yes," Dante said vehemently, looking unblinking into Ollie's eyes. "Our bond can be platonic. It's ours. It suits us, not the other way around."

"You won't regret bonding with me?" What would happen if Dante met someone he'd rather be mates with? This wasn't like marriage. There was no divorce.

Shit, he was more than married. To Dante. As friends.

"I won't regret this." Dante sounded so sure Ollie almost believed him. "How could I? I'd never let you die."

"Okay." Ollie tried for a light smile like his pulse wasn't pounding. How was Dante this understanding and accommodating? "Don't tell Dex, but you might be my best friend now."

Dante returned his smile. "He can still be your best friend. Being mated doesn't change your other relationships."

Ollie supposed he couldn't tell Dex any of this regardless. None of his friends would believe him. Except, apparently, Harper. Which reminded him. "What were you saying about Harper? With...Lucifer?" The name tasted bad on his tongue, sending a jolt of fear through him.

Dante's smile faded. "There's a lot to tell you. Harper is a witch—a person who possesses magic. He's Ash's mate."

"They mated? Like did the bond?" Harper's relationship had gone even faster than Ollie had realized.

"Yes. Harper knew Ash was a demon and chose to mate with him. It was different for Harper to learn all this. He already knew demons and vampires existed."

"Right, sure, vampires." Ollie felt like he'd stepped through the looking glass. "Of course there's vampires. What about werewolves?"

"No." Dante bit back a smile. "No shifters. Demons, witches, and vampires are the only magical beings."

"But you said there were Eternals? And Lucifer, is he a demon?" He seemed evil enough, which didn't make sense, given Dante said demons weren't evil.

Again, Dante sensed exactly where Ollie's mind had gone. "The real Lucifer's story isn't the one in the Bible. There is no Heaven and Hell, though we do refer to the Realm of the Damned as Hell sometimes."

"That's not confusing," Ollie grumbled.

Dante let out a short laugh. "To make a long story short, a group of Eternals, led by Lucifer, fell from the Eternal Realm—the afterlife where human souls go to reincarnate—and things didn't go as we'd planned. We came to Earth without permission and will never be allowed back home. Lucifer let magic seep into humanity, giving rise to witches. That wasn't supposed to happen. The Realm of the Damned was created for witch souls after death because they can't reincarnate. It's not a Hell to punish sinners, and 'Heaven' isn't for the righteous. It's about magic, mortality, and the cycle of human life."

Ollie narrowed his eyes. "Right." So, apparently, reincarnation was a thing. Way to drop that bombshell so casually. Ollie shook his head. "So if Hell isn't for sinners, why is Lucifer evil?"

Dante seemed at a loss for words. He turned and gazed out the window for a long moment. "He isn't evil. Or no more evil than any person who decides to do terrible things. It's not innate. Lucifer was once like a brother to Ash, Onyx, and me, but he betrayed us. I don't know what's brought on his recent changes, but he's gotten worse. Even after everything he did to us over the years, I thought there was a line he wouldn't cross. I was wrong."

Ollie's head spun. He would have to sleep on this, but there was one more thing he had to ask. "How long ago was the fall? You were there with Lucifer? Ash too?"

Dante nodded. "It was around two thousand years ago, give or take a few centuries. Eternal beings don't generally keep track of age in years, so if you're about to ask how old I am, let's say I was in the Eternal Realm for a similar length of time before falling."

"Huh." Ollie let that wash over him.

He was tied to an Eternal being. An immortal from another realm who had witnessed history and wielded magic. How was Ollie ever going to keep his independence? He was no one in the face of who Dante was. In a sense, they were one, and Ollie could see everything in him yielding to Dante.

If Ollie could have seen this coming, he'd have said a mating bond was ten—no, a million—times worse than taking the risk of getting into a relationship. But he hadn't seen it coming and hadn't had a choice.

## 12

## DANTE

THROUGH THE BOND, Dante felt a numbness growing in Ollie. His poor mate had been through too much.

If only Dante could hold Ollie close and whisper sweet words in his ear, tell him he would be treasured for the rest of time, that he'd always have Dante, and that Dante would devote his life to keeping him safe and happy. But he couldn't.

How did he express himself without it being too much for Ollie? This horrible day didn't need to be any harder to get his head around.

Maybe they needed to do something simple, find a way to connect that had nothing to do with the mating bond.

"Why don't we have dinner?" Dante offered.

Ollie looked at him as if he'd never heard of dinner and didn't know how to respond to such a silly question.

Was Ollie even more overwhelmed than Dante thought?

Even if he was, they had to do something. It was impossible to keep sitting here without clothes on, resisting the urge to hold his mate and never let go.

Having Ollie on his lap had been sweet torture. Everything in Dante begged him to claim his mate and be claimed in return.

To be close to Ollie, as intimate as two beings could be. But no primal urge was enough for Dante to cross that line. He'd never take advantage of Ollie. There were too many new sensations flowing between them for Dante to think that if Ollie had said yes to sex, he'd have meant it as much as he would have without the bond.

Ollie had been clear with what he wanted. A friend. Nothing romantic. And even if sex and romance weren't connected for Ollie, they were for Dante.

He should approach Ollie more like he would Ash, no matter what his body was trying to tell him. "We can have something to eat and keep talking. I'm not trying to brush you off. You must be hungry."

Ollie's baffled expression faded. "I am a bit, now that I think about it."

"Let's get dressed." Dante stood, but Ollie didn't move. "I can grab something from Harper's closet for you to wear. It'll fit better than anything of mine."

Ollie glanced around the room. "Harper has a closet at your house?"

"Ash lives with me and wanted Harper to have everything he needed when he stayed over." Dante didn't add that Ash routinely ruined Harper's clothes and a second wardrobe was pretty much essential. At least Ash kept on top of the laundry.

Ollie glanced at his lap, his fingers twisting together. "Sure. I'll take something of Harper's."

Dante left the room, moving at inhuman speed as soon as he was out of Ollie's sight. He didn't want to be away long. He needed a little distance from Ollie, but not enough to make him feel abandoned.

The new bond begged for closeness. Now that it was no longer distorted by Ollie's lack of participation in the ritual, it was growing stronger, begging Dante and Ollie to connect.

It dug deep like it was burrowing into Dante's soul. His skin tingled. *Closer.*

Dante focused on his breathing and the feel of Harper's clothes beneath his fingers as he selected a shirt and shorts. He centered his mind on his physical self, the way his wings itched to come out and his heart beat too fast, and used those sensations to block Ollie out, turning his mate's emotions down like the volume on a TV.

A low growl escaped Dante's throat without permission. His primal side didn't want to push his mate away, but Ollie seemed frightened of sharing his emotions. Dante hated that any of this scared him, but he couldn't stop himself from responding to Ollie's unspoken needs if he could feel them, so the only way to put Ollie at ease was to block him out.

Closing down this part of the connection was best for Ollie, and with that reminder, Dante's primal side got on board. Even his baser instincts would never desire something his mate didn't.

Returning with the clothes, Dante found Ollie hadn't moved an inch. This wasn't good. Dante wasn't doing enough to help Ollie through this, but what else could he do?

Ollie jumped the second he noticed Dante like he'd been woken from a trance. "I'll change in the bathroom."

He took the clothes and disappeared, leaving Dante to pull on the first thing he found.

Ollie reappeared, his arms crossed over his chest, voice shaky. "What if Lucifer comes back?"

Shit, Dante had been so wrapped up in the bond that he'd left Ollie worrying about Luc this whole time.

"Lucifer isn't coming back, at least not right away. He ran back to the Realm of the Damned after I saved you. It's what he did last time he was here, when we almost captured him. Ash will know the moment he returns to this realm, but until he does, he can't possibly reach you."

Ollie frowned, fear dulling his usually bright eyes. "He snuck up on us at the beach and Ash didn't warn you. What if he comes for me again?"

Dante closed the gap between them, gripping Ollie by the shoulders. "I'll protect you, Ollie. I know I failed today, but it won't happen again. I swear."

"You can't be with me twenty-four-seven," Ollie said like he was scared Dante might insist on it.

He wanted to. Dante would be content to never leave Ollie's side.

"No, I can't be with you all the time," he made himself say since it was clearly what his mate wanted. "But that doesn't mean you're unsafe. You have my immortality and my healing power. You are about as hard to kill as a demon. You'll survive anything short of decapitation or the complete removal of your blood, which can't be done without magic."

Ollie's cheeks paled.

Fuck, Dante sucked at this. "Not that I think anyone will try to do either of those things to you. I was trying to give you an idea of what possessing my healing ability means." Ollie still looked deeply uncomfortable, so Dante barreled on. "Luc realized he made a grave mistake after he saw me bond with you. He acted rashly, trying to kill you, and he won't do it again now that he knows we're mates."

Luc's attempt to kill Ollie had been for sport, to fuck with Dante, and prove him wrong about finding his mate. He hadn't believed Ollie was Dante's, but he believed it now. There had been fear in Luc's eyes before he'd disappeared.

Good. He should be afraid.

You didn't harm someone's mate. It was one of the ultimate rules. Seeing Dante with his mate had to change everything for Lucifer. Mates were why they fell, and Luc wouldn't try to destroy what they'd been seeking. Right?

Dante shook himself. What did it matter? He'd kill Luc soon enough, and the problem would be solved.

"How can you trust him not to try again?" Ollie asked. "And why are you calling him Luc, like you're buddies?"

Dante suppressed a bitter laugh. "We were as close as family for thousands of years. It's hard to drop the nickname, even now. Even when I hate him. And I don't trust him. I *know* him. Even Luc isn't so far gone that he'd harm my bonded mate."

Ollie looked skeptical.

"Regardless, his days are numbered. I don't think he'll try to hurt you again, but Ash, Onyx, and I will hunt him down for what he did to you. We'll keep you safe, Ollie."

Ollie bit his lip like he was considering challenging Dante. "Okay," he said instead. "I don't quite get how you're so sure it'll be okay, but I trust you. I can't seem to help it. With all this magic stuff, there isn't anything to do but trust you."

Damnation, Ollie sounded hopeless, like he was resigned to relying on Dante but didn't like it.

"I'll always be here for you, Ollie—I won't take your trust for granted—but don't forget, you have Harper too. He's a powerful witch."

Ollie uncrossed his arms, his face softening. "It's so cool that Harper is a witch. Uh, I mean, it's cool you're immortal and have wings too. But it's weird to think my sweet, innocent roommate has this hidden magic side."

Dante smiled. "I won't be offended if you're more impressed with Harper than me." And he wasn't. He wanted Ollie to be comfortable with the magic world, no matter what it took.

He didn't want Ollie to feel stuck with him. Dante would be here when Ollie chose to turn to him, but he wouldn't force it by presenting himself as the only option.

"Let's get something to eat. It'll help you feel better." He led

Ollie to the kitchen and pulled out a barstool at the counter. Ollie perched on it tentatively as Dante considered their options. "Do you like chocolate?"

Ollie nodded, damp blond curls falling across his forehead. "Of course I like chocolate."

Dante pulled open his candy drawer and selected several different chocolate bars, lining them up in front of Ollie. "Start with these, and I'll make you a sandwich."

Ollie glanced between the candy and Dante, a smile tugging at his lips. "I can't eat all of these."

Dante's heart fluttered, caught on that lovely grin. "Why not?"

"Because that would be seven chocolate bars." Ollie laughed like it was a ridiculous prospect.

Dante didn't see the problem. "That's never stopped me from eating this many—if not more—in one sitting."

Ollie picked up a chocolate. "Says the immortal. Do you even need to eat?"

"Not exactly." Dante hurried to grab sandwich fixings from the fridge, wishing he didn't have to explain drinking blood. Would this be the thing that pushed Ollie irrevocably far away?

He turned back to Ollie, arms full of food. "Demons need to drink blood to maintain their immortality in the Human Realm. We don't need food, but I like eating anyway."

Ollie's brows pulled together. "Do I need to drink blood now too? Since you said I have your immortality?"

Dante paused, his brow furrowing. "Harper hasn't needed blood since mating with Ash. It seems that trait doesn't pass on."

He hadn't considered whether their mates would need to drink blood. It made sense, given vampires—the only other immortals in the Human Realm—did, but for some reason, demons' mates seemed to be an exception.

It must have to do with the mating bond. Dante was happy

to drink blood for Ollie as well as himself and maintain them both through their magical connection. He'd have to ask Ash if he'd noticed needing more now that he was bonded to Harper.

"Well, I guess that's good." Ollie opened a chocolate bar, averting his gaze. He sounded disappointed.

Did Ollie want to drink blood? What a surprise. But maybe it shouldn't have been after Ollie's reaction during the mating ritual.

Dante busied himself preparing Ollie's sandwich. Drinking from Ollie's wrist had opened Dante to a new longing. He craved the closeness of sharing their essence.

Before the fall, Eternals only ever shared blood with their mates.

"No tomatoes, please," Ollie said, pulling Dante back into the moment.

He put the tomatoes to one side. "Anything else you prefer?"

"No, I'm not picky."

Dante wanted to tell Ollie it wasn't about being picky. He'd give Ollie nothing but his favorite things. But they didn't need to get through everything in one day. There was time to learn Ollie's preferences.

Ollie ate his sandwich while Dante finished off the candy bars. When they were gone, he opened his drawer to grab a bag of sour gummies, popped a handful into his mouth, and then offered the bag to Ollie.

He took a couple, a bemused look on his face. "You really like sweets."

"Guilty."

Ollie shook his head. "I'm more of a savory treat person."

"Noted." Dante would organize a treat drawer for Ollie next to his and fill it with everything tasty he could find at the store.

"I like how normal this is." Ollie gestured between them and the food before reaching for another gummy. "I didn't think I'd ever feel normal again, so thank you."

Dante's spine straightened and his hidden tail tingled. He hadn't totally failed Ollie. "You're welcome. It'll all get easier, I promise."

There was still so much to tell Ollie, like the fact that they were fated to be together. Dante had let it seem like the mating bond was something he could do with anyone, and while he hated being dishonest, it would have been too much to reveal being destined for each other. Dante had a bad feeling Ollie wouldn't want to hear that.

This wasn't how his and Ollie's bond should have formed. Ollie should have had a choice. Hell, Dante should have had a choice. Lucifer had taken something from Dante and Ollie they could never get back, and all Dante could do was try to repair the damage.

"I'm sure it'll get easier," Ollie agreed with a heavy sigh. He patted his pockets and then seemed to remember he was wearing Harper's clothes. "Where's my phone? I should probably head home."

Dante's heart sank. *Don't go.*

He held the words in. "It's over here with mine." He retrieved their phones from the coffee table, ignoring the bloody couch. He'd have to dispose of it when Ollie left.

The phones weren't clean either. Dante grabbed a cloth and wiped them down before handing Ollie's over.

Dante unlocked his phone, finding about a hundred missed calls from Ash. Fuck. Knowing he had to share what happened with Ash and Onyx ripped his heart open all over again.

"I'm going to book a rideshare," Ollie said as he tapped on his phone.

Dante placed his device on the counter. "No, you can't do that."

"What?" Ollie snapped, eyes narrowing like Dante had said something unacceptable.

"Cars can't get to my house," Dante explained, unsure why Ollie had reacted with so much venom. "We're in the reserve. The whole hill is shielded by magic and there's no road access."

"Oh." Ollie's cheeks pinkened and he lowered his phone. "I guess it makes sense for you to have a secret magic hideout."

Dante had never seen it as a hideout, though he supposed it was. "I can fly you home. It's no trouble."

"Fly?" Ollie choked on the word. "No, it's okay. I'll go meet a car at the nearest street."

Dante's gut twisted. Was Ollie that eager to get away from him? "The nearest road is all the way down the hill. Please, let me take you there, at least."

Ollie bit his lip. "Sure, that's fine." He stood from the stool. "Why do you live in the reserve anyway? Wait. Do you even work in conservation?"

"Not strictly speaking. I have a magical connection to the shearwaters. I'll tell you all about it sometime, and we can still go see the birds if you want. I live up here to be close to their nests. This area is protected for them, not just me."

Ollie seemed to like that, his skeptical expression softening. "I'd still love to see the birds, but not today. Not after..." His words faded.

Dante rounded the counter. "I know. I'm sorry our evening was ruined."

Ollie looked up from beneath his lashes. "You don't have to be sorry. What happened isn't your fault."

Dante appreciated that, but it was his fault, and he'd spend forever trying to make up for it.

"It wasn't," Ollie said more sternly. "You aren't responsible for someone else's actions, no matter what history you and Lucifer have."

"I'll still always be sorry this happened to you, Ollie. It was because of me you were at the beach. I wish I could take it back." The sight of Ollie covered in blood, limp in his arms, filled Dante's mind, and grief cut him open.

"Me too," Ollie whispered. "I wish this never happened, but it did. And it'll get easier, remember? We'll be okay. Best friends forever." He squeezed Dante's hand, his touch fleeting.

Dante's throat thickened. Would they be okay? He didn't want to part from Ollie so soon but felt unable to ask him to stay.

Clearing his throat, Dante asked for all he felt he could. "If you need anything, will you call me? Please?"

Ollie hesitated. "Yeah, sure. I'll let you know."

Dante couldn't help thinking he wouldn't. Ollie was holding back, and while Dante understood, he worried it would hurt them both.

They hadn't been ready for their bond, and having it formed anyway made things harder between them. Dante should have had time to become close to Ollie before closeness was thrust on them.

He didn't know if Ollie would ever embrace their bond when it would always be something he hadn't chosen.

"I think I need to sleep and wake up on a day that isn't today," Ollie said. "Let's play *World's End* tomorrow night, okay?"

Yes, that was a good idea. They'd go back to building their friendship as they had been. Dante would block out Ollie's emotions, and maybe the bond could sit there, patiently waiting for them to be ready. Whatever he had to do, Dante would deal with this and make it work.

"I'll look forward to it. There's a few missions I'd like to bring you on. I could use your dragon."

"Perfect." Ollie glanced out the sliding glass door. "So, how do we get off the reserve? Is there a path down to the road?"

Dante grabbed his phone and slipped it into his pocket. "No. I'll have to fly you down the hill."

Ollie swallowed, his throat bobbing. "There's no other way?"

"It'd be a very long walk, especially through the underbrush without a path." Dante tensed, something cold pooling in his gut. "Do my wings make you uncomfortable?"

Ollie shook his head, worry flashing across his features. "No, you don't make me uncomfortable. It's not your wings. I, um, don't really like heights."

At least Ollie didn't detest his true form. Dante wasn't sure he could handle that. "We won't fly high, barely above the trees, and I've carried much bigger beings than you. I won't let you fall."

Ollie studied him for a moment. "Okay. I trust you."

Dante tamped down the urge to preen as he led Ollie out of the house. Every shred of Ollie's trust made Dante feel like he could take care of his mate—even after failing so miserably—and made it seem possible to get from here to a place where their bond reflected their closeness rather than forced it.

Outside, Dante removed his shirt and let his wings and horns loose. He flexed, shaking out his feathers, muscles singing at the freedom of movement.

"Wow," Ollie breathed, gaze sweeping over Dante. "Is it rude to ask to touch your feathers?"

Dante smiled, feathers tingling at the prospect. "Not at all." He stretched out his wings, displaying his full wingspan for his mate's inspection.

Ollie stepped closer, a tentative hand reaching out, and stroked Dante's left wing. "Your feathers are warm. So soft. And some of them sparkle."

Dante swallowed a purr. Ollie's fingertips felt divine, sending shivers down every last one of his nerve endings. Ollie was being so delicate, touching Dante like he was fragile or precious. "It's my fire. It makes all demons—and Eternals—run warm. And my heat sometimes gives me a glow, or as you say, sparkle."

Ollie stroked Dante's wing back and forth, his movements growing more confident. "Fire...like your mage in the game. You have so many secrets."

Dante ruffled the wing Ollie was petting, and Ollie giggled. "They aren't secrets now. You can ask me anything."

Ollie's assessing gaze swept over Dante like he was ready to take up the challenge, and Dante shivered. "Don't you have a tail?"

Dante's face heated. "I wasn't sure if you noticed that tattoo." Ollie hadn't been himself in the shower and Dante wouldn't have been surprised if the whole scene hadn't registered.

"I noticed." Ollie looked toward Dante's rear, his cheeks flushing. "Where is it?"

Heat spread through Dante's body. "I didn't free my tail, so it's still a tattoo. I wasn't sure if it would be too strange."

Ollie's brow furrowed. "You aren't strange. None of you, not your tail, or magic, or anything. You don't have to hide yourself from me, Dante."

Relief released a tightness Dante hadn't realized was growing in his chest. "You aren't bothered that I'm not human?"

Ollie shrugged. "No. I never saw this coming, but I don't mind that we're different. It's kind of cool."

Cool. Dante would take it.

"I don't usually free my tail when I fly," he admitted. "It's annoying having it out with jeans on."

"I can see that. You can show me another time." The flush

on Ollie's cheeks spread down his neck, but his tone remained casual. "If you want," he hurried to add.

"Another time." Dante tried not to get excited about Ollie's interest in his body. It was curiosity, not necessarily attraction. "Let's get you home. You're sure you don't want me to fly you all the way?"

"Yeah, I'm sure," Ollie said, his tone stiffening. "I can get there myself."

For whatever reason, it seemed important to Ollie that he make his own way, so Dante didn't argue. Maybe it was his fear of heights, or maybe there was more to it, but it didn't feel like the right time to ask.

Dante opened his arms, gesturing for Ollie to come closer. "Wrap yourself around me like a koala."

Ollie snorted and covered his mouth. "Can't you pick me up?" He moved directly in front of Dante, leaving hardly any space between them.

"Sure." Dante grinned, scooping Ollie into a bridal carry. "This okay?"

Ollie wrapped his arms around Dante's neck and squeezed tight. "Yeah, but I'm closing my eyes. Don't drop me."

"I won't." Dante held Ollie tight as he launched into the air.

Ollie squeaked, voice reaching a surprisingly high pitch, and gripped Dante tighter.

"You're okay," Dante murmured, lips next to Ollie's ear, his nose in Ollie's hair, his sandalwood scent going straight to his head. "We'll be back on the ground in two minutes. I promise."

Ollie nodded but didn't speak as a spike of fear traveled down the bond despite Dante blocking most of Ollie's emotions.

Dante flew as fast and as smoothly as he could, and soon, they were landing among the tall trees lining the base of the reserve.

Ollie didn't release Dante right away, staying curled against his chest. "Are we on the ground?"

"Yes, Ollie." Dante chuckled warmly.

Ollie's eyes popped open to glare at Dante. "Don't laugh. That was like being on a roller coaster. I hate those things."

Dante set Ollie on the ground. "Sounds like I'll have to figure out a better way to get you to and from my house."

Ollie seemed surprised. "Will I be coming over again?"

"If you want." Dante rubbed the back of his neck. "You could check out my game room next time."

Gaming was the furthest thing from Dante's mind. He imagined cooking for Ollie, showing him the shearwaters, and snuggling together on one of his huge armchairs, even though snuggling probably wasn't on the table.

At the mention of gaming, Ollie grinned. "Oh, definitely. I want to see all of your old consoles. I can't believe you have so many vintage games." Ollie pulled his phone from his pocket. "I'd almost be okay with flying to see that."

"Almost." Dante nudged Ollie's arm, and Ollie rolled his eyes.

At least Ollie wanted to keep hanging out.

Dante waited as Ollie requested a rideshare, the two of them walking out to the road and lingering on the sidewalk until the car arrived. When it did, Ollie disappeared into the back seat with a wave.

A tether tugged on Dante's heart, urging him to follow. He gritted his teeth and stayed where he was. When the car was out of sight, Dante recast his illusion of invisibility and freed his wings, launching into the sky.

He dialed Ash. They had Lucifer's demise to plan.

13

———

OLLIE

OLLIE HEADED STRAIGHT for the couch as soon as he got home and sank into the cushions. They weren't as comfortable as he swore they'd been that morning. Harper didn't appear to be home, so Ollie pulled out his phone.

He stared at it blankly, not even waking the screen.

The sensation of unreality he'd had when he woke in Dante's living room was gone, but something else had nagged at him the whole car ride across the city.

He rubbed the center of his chest, his eyes stinging. Fuck. He closed them tight, willing the gathering moisture to disappear.

He wanted to go back to Dante's, crawl into his lap, and not feel alone.

Why was he being like this? He didn't need Dante. Too many things had changed, and he wanted to go back to this morning or earlier that evening before he and Dante went to look at the tidepools.

But he couldn't go back.

He opened his eyes and unlocked his phone, scrolling through his favorite social media. The posts rolled by, blurry through his unshed tears. Ollie scrolled and scrolled. Everything he read dragged him down. People were mean, saying stupid things. Others were insufferably happy, everything too perfect to be believable. He hated all of it.

The apartment door banged open and shut. "Ollie?" Harper's frantic voice called.

Ollie looked up in time to see Harper rush into the living room.

"Ollie!" Harper dropped onto the couch beside him and engulfed Ollie in his arms. "Are you okay?"

"I don't know." Ollie wrapped his arms around Harper, afraid to let go. He was a total mess and didn't want Harper to see, even though he must have already.

"I was out with Ash. Dante told him what happened, and I got home as soon as I could."

"Oh." Ollie swallowed. Phantom hands tightened on his neck, and he lost the will to speak.

Harper pulled back, and Ollie wiped his eyes, looking at his lap. "What can I do?" Harper asked.

"Magic me back to this morning?" Ollie cut Harper a look and forced a smile, but it felt all wrong.

Harper's face crumpled. "I can't. But I can make you something to help you sleep."

Ollie sat up a little straighter. "Like a magic sleeping pill?"

"More like a potion. They're kind of my thing." He shrugged, a hint of something bashful in the motion. "Brewing and selling potions is my actual job."

"You sell potions?" That was fascinating and much more distracting than Ollie's phone. "How? Where? I have so many questions."

Harper's face lit up. "The shop I work at is an apothecary. It's run by a witch, and we cater to the magic community more than humans. It's not a novelty shop like I told you it was. That's why I was so vague about its location and who I worked with. I didn't want you to get too interested and stop by. Sorry I lied."

Ollie couldn't have cared less. "How could you not lie? I'd have said you were full of shit if you'd claimed you could do magic."

"True." Harper's lips twitched. "I was planning on telling you about being a witch eventually. After we'd been friends longer. Not that I doubted our friendship would last, but since we haven't known each other long, it seemed best to wait before revealing something so big." Harper's face creased with concern. "I want you to know I wouldn't have lied to you forever."

Ollie's chest warmed. "It's really okay, Harper. Honestly, I'd rather have waited and found out that way."

A shadow passed over Harper's face, his features twisting in anger like Ollie had never seen. "Of course you didn't want to find out this way. I can't believe Lucifer tried to kill you."

Lucifer's whispered words filled Ollie's mind and tears prickled at the corners of his eyes. The warm feeling in his chest vanished. "I don't get why he even cared about me enough to hurt me. If he's after Dante and Ash, the whole thing on the beach makes no sense."

Why would Lucifer think Dante loved him? They'd been hanging out, not even standing close together. Why try to kill him because of love?

As he ran through the events, something snagged his attention that he hadn't considered before. Dante had called Ollie his mate before he'd needed to save Ollie. He'd screamed it at Lucifer.

It didn't make sense. Ollie hadn't been Dante's mate yet. But was that why Lucifer had whispered in his ear and ripped him apart? If so, why did Dante think Lucifer seeing them become mates after the attack would make him leave Ollie alone?

The sensation of blood spilling from his gouged-out throat cut through Ollie. He shuddered. "I don't want to think about what happened at the beach ever again."

Harper squeezed Ollie's hand. "We don't have to talk about it if you don't want to."

At least Harper had already heard what happened and Ollie didn't have to explain.

"Are we safe?" Ollie asked. It wasn't that he didn't trust Dante. He did more than he should. But he needed an outside perspective. Harper was a much better judge of the situation than Ollie was. "What if Lucifer tries to come get me again?"

Harper gripped Ollie tighter. "You're perfectly safe in the apartment. I've been protecting it with magic since I first signed the lease."

"You have?"

Harper nodded. "I cast a protective spell before I moved in and was enhancing it regularly the first few weeks I lived here. My family isn't in a cult. They're a coven who worships the Devil, and I finally escaped their control the day I came to live here. Hiding from them took a lot of powerful magic."

"Oh my god." Ollie gaped at Harper.

"I can tell you the whole story some other time. The reason I brought it up is because my spell is still protecting the apartment, even though my coven has been dealt with. And Ash cast an even more powerful protection on the whole building. The other demons strengthened it too."

Ollie glanced around the room as if he might be able to see magic now that he knew it was there. "So Lucifer can't get us at home?"

Harper shook his head. "He'd have to break the demons' spell first, and Ash would sense if someone were trying to do that. But I don't think Lucifer will go after you again."

"Why not?" Why was everyone so sure of that?

"He's hunting Ash, Dante, and Onyx for betraying him and escaping Hell. Lucifer doesn't care about witches or humans, as far as I know."

"Then why did he hurt me?" Ollie hated how his voice broke on the question. How could this all happen for no reason?

"He hurt you to hurt Dante," Harper said like he hated to admit it. Like he worried it would upset Ollie.

"But why would Dante care? I mean, he's a good guy and would care about anyone getting hurt, but it's not like I'm his boyfriend."

Harper's brow furrowed. "You're Dante's mate. Lucifer must have noticed something about you two like he did with Ash and me. He was stalking Ash and kidnapped me to see why Ash was so obsessed with me. Lucifer didn't care about me personally either. It was all about Ash."

"Dante isn't obsessed with me." Ollie's heart rate spiked. The situations weren't the same. He and Dante were friends.

"No, he's not obsessed, but it sounds like Lucifer is trying to figure out what Ash and Dante are doing with us. He didn't believe I was Ash's mate when I told him and didn't believe Ash when he backed me up. It sounds like Lucifer didn't believe Dante either, but Dante said Lucifer knows it's all true now that he witnessed your bond."

Ollie still didn't get it. He hadn't been Dante's mate until after Lucifer attacked.

"You're safe, Ollie. That's the most important thing. Lucifer knows we aren't lying about our mates. He isn't going to attack us the same way now that he understands the reality of the situation. And Ash and Dante will go after him. He won't win." As if Harper could tell Ollie was as lost now as when they started talking, he added, "Why don't I show you how I strengthen my protection spell and explain how the protective magic works?"

That might actually help Ollie feel more secure. He could

worry about understanding the details of the conflict with Lucifer later. "Okay, but what about when I'm not at home?"

Harper gave him a reassuring look. "Dante can find you through your bond. He'll know if you're in trouble like Ash can with me, so even if you aren't shielded everywhere you go, Dante will always know if you need him."

"He can track me?" Ollie's heart climbed into his throat. "He didn't tell me that."

"All I'm saying is, in an emergency, you won't have to worry."

Ollie got that, but it didn't make Dante tracking him okay. That was creepy stalker shit. The exact kind of thing Ollie needed to stay the hell away from if he wanted his independence.

"Hey." Harper bumped his knee against Ollie's. "I know this happened way too fast, and you and Dante weren't together before, but having a mate is amazing. I'm so happy for you two."

"Thanks, but Dante and I still aren't together. We aren't a happy couple to congratulate. We're friends. He did this to save me. It's not the same as you and Ash."

Harper's eyes widened. "Oh, um, sorry. I didn't realize... Do you not like Dante like that?"

Ollie ran a hand through his hair. He hadn't told Harper about his relationship issues or what happened with his exes, and now didn't feel like the time to bring it up. "I like Dante— I've been crushing on him—but we're friends. I told Dante more wasn't an option weeks ago. He gets it and said it was fine."

Harper looked momentarily confused before recovering. "If Dante gets it, that's all that matters."

Ollie couldn't help feeling like he was missing something.

It was probably that he hadn't known about magic and all this crap until a few hours ago, yet it was all normal to Harper.

Ollie would probably feel like he was missing a lot until he figured out all the rules in this weird new world.

He forced his face to relax until it wasn't all scrunched up with worry. "Come on, show me your protection spell and the sleeping potion. I want to see some magic."

Harper's face lit up. "Yeah, okay. But I should warn you, potions are pretty awesome. Are you sure you're ready for me to blow your mind?"

Ollie returned his smile. "Couldn't be more ready. Go on, amaze me."

Harper looked like Ollie had made his day. At least magic wasn't all bad.

Harper said he had the day off on Monday and stayed home with Ollie. It was a little suspect since Harper had work every other Monday—maybe he was pulling a sickie—but Ollie didn't pry. He was grateful for the company.

By Monday night, Ollie felt more like his old self. Everything wasn't terrible. Magic with Harper was fascinating, and Dante didn't even message Ollie until the evening when they were due to meet online. It was like the week before in so many ways.

As they played *World's End*, Dante didn't ask prying questions or say anything about the beach. He didn't mention meeting up in person. By all appearances, Dante wasn't letting what happened change their friendship.

It took Ollie most of the day to realize it, but he couldn't feel any of Dante's emotions through the bond. He asked Harper if physical distance affected the emotional connection, but Harper said it didn't. He and Ash often communicated through their shared emotions and detected shifts in each other no matter how close or far apart they were.

Ollie hadn't attempted closing his mind, so not feeling anything had to be Dante blocking the connection. If he was respecting Ollie's privacy, maybe Ollie didn't have to worry so much about the invasive nature of the bond or Dante stalking him and taking over his life.

On Tuesday, Ollie had a late start at work. It was his day to see clients in the afternoon and evenings, and he always liked arriving at the salon when it was in full swing.

"Hey, Ellie," he called as he passed the front counter where she was ringing someone up.

"Hey. You've had a few last-minute bookings today."

He turned around and joined her behind the counter, peering at the schedule over her shoulder. It was going to be a busy day. Thank goodness. Having too many gaps between clients was annoying, and full days meant more tips.

Ollie left Ellie to rebook her client in peace and slipped into the back room, saying hi to everyone as he went. He put his lunch away and noticed the dryer was done, so he unloaded it and rolled towels until he had a nice, neat pile.

On his way back out, Ollie dropped the towels off by the sinks.

"Thanks." Marie, the salon assistant, smiled appreciatively as she swapped out some of the empty shampoo bottles. "I was going to get to those in a minute."

"No problem." Ollie checked his station and glanced toward the front to see if his client was early.

She was, as usual, which suited him fine. He headed over. "Hi, Manuela, come on over with me." As she stood, he asked, "Can I get you a drink?"

"An herbal tea would really hit the spot."

Ollie showed her to his chair. "You got it." He found Marie

and let her know, then returned to his station. "Are we after our usual freshen-up today?"

"Always, I'm very predictable." Manuela smiled.

"Hey, if you're still feeling it, why mess with a good thing?"

"Exactly."

Ollie ran his hands through her long hair and examined the ends, confirming exactly how much he'd be taking off before getting Manuela ready and bringing her over to the sinks.

They chatted about her kids' swimming lessons and other summer activities as Ollie rinsed her hair. He pumped shampoo into his palm. Manuela's long brown hair swirled in the running water. Ollie tangled his hands in her hair, massaging her scalp as he lathered the shampoo.

Suddenly, the sight of hair wrapped around Ollie's fingers sent a jolt up his arm. Ollie's scalp prickled and burned, phantom hands pulling at his hair. The smell of blood and seawater drowned out the floral shampoo and Ollie's throat clogged.

His chest tightened and his lungs burned. Hands closed around his throat. Sweat broke out on the back of his neck, his pulse thundering in his ears. *No.*

"Ollie?" A soft hand rested on his shoulder.

He jolted, Ellie's concerned face filling his vision. Shit. He let go of Manuela's hair, not knowing how long he'd stood there frozen. "S-sorry," he muttered.

"I'll finish up here if you don't mind getting the extra conditioner out back? I can never reach that shelf." Ellie nudged him out of the way and seamlessly took up washing and rinsing his client's hair.

Ollie hurried out of the way. What the fuck was that?

He'd been feeling great all morning. No one had even touched him, and he'd completely lost it.

In the back room, he filled a cup with water from the cooler and took a long sip, absently rubbing his neck. His nerves tingled as he remembered the pain. The blood. He shut his eyes. He couldn't think about this now.

"You okay?" Ellie asked from behind him.

Ollie spun around. Was that the fastest hair wash, or had he been here that long? "Yeah, I'm fine. Thanks." He gave her a weak smile.

"Manuela's good to go, sipping her tea waiting for you." Ellie paused. "Do you need someone to take over?"

"No, it's fine. I...I wasn't standing there that long, was I?"

"Not at all. I bet your client didn't even notice." Ellie's soft features shifted in concern. "It was more the look on your face."

Fuck. "I spaced out for a second. I'm fine. Uh, had a bad weekend, but really it's nothing. Thanks for giving me a minute to get my shit together."

"Anytime." Her perfectly manicured brows pinched together.

"I'm fine, really," Ollie said before she could pry. "I need to get back out there. We'll catch up later."

"Okay." Ellie followed him out to the salon floor. "Take care of yourself, Ollie."

THE REST of the day went by without incident. Ollie washed the rest of his clients' hair without flashing back to tight, evil hands on his neck.

Ellie seemed satisfied he was okay and didn't press for more details about his weekend. Ollie smiled and chatted and was almost certain no one else noticed anything wrong. But he no longer felt good. He wasn't his old self, and Lucifer's claws slicing his neck were never far from his mind. He wasn't okay.

By the time his last client of the evening was due to arrive, only two other stylists were still working. Ollie leaned against the front counter, looking through his schedule for tomorrow as he waited for his new client. Hopefully, they weren't going to be much later. He was ready to be done.

The front door opened and Ollie looked up from the computer. "Oh, hi."

Onyx grinned, blue eyes shining. "Hello to you." He sauntered up to the counter. "I have an appointment."

The booking in Ollie's schedule said Mr. Black. "Your name is Onyx Black?"

"No." Onyx shrugged. His voice dropped to a whisper as he gave Ollie a significant look. "*We* don't have last names."

Right. Another demon thing. Good to know. "Um, I've got you in for a trim, is that right?"

Onyx nodded. His blue hair was impeccable, appearing effortlessly messy in a way that was clearly styled.

"Right this way." Ollie gestured toward the stations.

Why was Onyx here? His hair didn't look in particular need of attention, and he must have a salon he went to regularly. Did Dante know Onyx was here? Had Dante sent Onyx to check up on him? How possessive and sneaky.

Ollie's chest pinched.

He eyed Onyx as he pulled out the chair for him. The demon was about his height and looked like any other well-dressed human. He might not have guessed Onyx's true nature if Dante hadn't said he was a demon.

Onyx sat in the chair and inspected himself in the mirror, scowling at his perfect reflection.

"Your dye job is amazing." Ollie draped a towel over Onyx's shoulders before covering him with a cape and snapping it closed behind his neck. "I love the blue, and the hints of lavender are gorgeous."

"I did it myself." Onyx smirked at Ollie in the mirror. "I have a *magic* touch."

Ollie almost laughed. "I bet you do. So then, what are you doing here?"

"Didn't I say I needed a trim? My bangs are getting in my eyes."

Ollie ran his hands through Onyx's fine hair, pushing his bangs in his face. "I see. Shall we take, say, this much off the top?" He captured Onyx's hair between his fingers to demonstrate.

"Not that much. A small trim. Maybe half that." It didn't sound like Onyx wanted his hair cut, but if he was going to insist, Ollie wouldn't argue.

"Okay. We can do that. Would you like anything to drink? Tea, coffee, water?"

Onyx wrinkled his nose. "No, I'm good."

Did Onyx not enjoy eating like Dante? Maybe he only drank blood.

Ollie led Onyx to the sinks. "How'd you know where I worked?" Ollie hadn't told Dante the name of his salon. Had Dante tracked him down? Stalked him online? Through the bond?

"I asked Harper," Onyx grumbled like he'd wished he hadn't had to go through the trouble. He sat at the sink and laid back.

"Right." Ollie didn't bother asking why Onyx sounded put out. He'd been totally wrong. Dante hadn't sent Onyx. He wasn't even involved. Maybe Onyx was curious about what happened at the beach.

Since Ollie didn't want to talk about that, he took over the questioning before Onyx had the chance. He glanced toward his colleagues and their clients on the other side of the salon before whispering, "Do you have a mate?"

Onyx sat up from the sink and twisted around, looking at Ollie like he'd asked the world's dumbest question. "No. Only Dante and Ash have mates."

"You never wanted one?" Ollie couldn't keep the defensive note from his tone. How was he supposed to know Onyx didn't have a mate?

Onyx narrowed his eyes like he was reassessing Ollie. "You don't really know what mates are, do you?"

Ollie's cheeks heated. "No, not really. But how the hell am I supposed to know?" It occurred to him how strange it was that Ash and Dante were both older than dirt and had only recently mated.

Wouldn't they have wanted a partner long before now?

If mates were forever, and you only had one, why had they waited? How did Ash know Harper was the right choice? How could Dante not regret mating with Ollie to save him?

"You aren't supposed to know," Onyx said more kindly. "Don't worry, Dante will take care of you."

"I don't need to be taken care of," Ollie muttered, even though warmth spread from his core to his fingertips. "Why are you really here?"

Onyx laid back in his seat, resting his head on the sink. He waved his hand as if requesting Ollie get on with washing his hair. "I wanted to check you out after Dante told me what happened."

Ollie bit his cheek and turned on the water, testing the temperature. *Don't ask about the beach. Don't ask about the beach.*

"I'm sorry my brother is such a fucking asshole," Onyx went on. "Not believing Ash and Harper were a bonded pair was no excuse for doing what he did."

"What do you mean, your brother? Like actual brother?"

Dante had said Lucifer was like family for thousands of years, but not actual family.

"Yes, Luc is my *actual* brother." Onyx made a humming sound. "What do you think is worse, being the Devil's sibling or the spawn of Satan?"

"Um..." How was Ollie supposed to answer that?

"That's Harper, by the way. *Supposedly.* My brother's spawn, many generations removed."

Ollie cringed. Did Harper know? "That's fucking weird."

Onyx choked on a laugh, tilting his head back to get another look at Ollie. "You're not bad," he said like he was reluctant to admit it and surprised at the same time.

"Thanks?" Ollie ran the water over Onyx's hair, tilting his head gently to guide him back into the right position. "How's this temperature?"

"Meh." Onyx waved his hand again. "Make it as hot as you can stand. Everything feels lukewarm when you have internal fire."

Ollie turned up the hot water and washed Onyx's hair.

The demon remained quiet. What kind of small talk were you supposed to engage in with an immortal? Ollie could ask about Onyx's work like he did with everyone else, but it felt strange to talk about art and the gallery after talking about the Devil.

Back at Ollie's station, Onyx eyed Ollie through the mirror. "You seem to be taking all this well."

Ollie scoffed. "You should have seen me this morning."

Onyx's brow furrowed. "What happened this morning?"

"Nothing. It seems having my throat ripped out is going to leave some lasting damage." It just wasn't physical.

"Of course it will." Onyx shook his head like he was exasperated. "It's a good thing you've got eternity to get over it."

Ollie grabbed a hair brush. Eternity. His stomach dropped

and he almost tripped over his feet. He knew he was going to live forever—Dante had mentioned it—but he hadn't actually thought about it.

He'd never have a normal human life. He probably wouldn't age. How long until people noticed? He'd have to go into hiding like a vampire out of a teen movie.

How could he hide and have a life?

What if one day, far in the future—assuming he got over his relationship issues—he wanted a partner or kids? Did he not get any of that now? He might have worried he'd never be ready for a relationship, but the potential had always been there.

Ollie said he wanted to remain friends with Dante, but forever was a long time to ignore his feelings. Would Ollie's attraction to Dante fade? What if it didn't? Would Dante ever want him back?

Would Dante want romance and a family with someone else?

Onyx spun his chair around. "You're freaking out."

"No, I'm not," Ollie snapped.

Onyx pointed a finger. "Yes, you are. You're panicking. I can see it in your eyes."

"How am I supposed to be fine with living forever all of a sudden?" Ollie hissed so no one else could hear. "I had the loosest hold on what I wanted my mortal life to be, and now what? That's all irrelevant? And it goes on forever?"

Ollie didn't want his life to change unless he chose it. He hadn't asked for this.

Onyx shook his head. "Your plans aren't irrelevant. Just think bigger. If anything, you'll get more than you ever wanted. Besides, you get to be my friend now. Things are looking up for you already."

Ollie rolled his eyes. He appreciated Onyx making light.

"We're friends? I hadn't realized. Wait. Is that why you're here? To buddy up with me?"

Onyx scowled. "I'm here because I was rude to you at the gallery, but I didn't know you were anyone special, so it's not like I did it on purpose. I want a do-over. I kind of fucked up meeting Harper and don't need a total repeat."

Onyx was so sulky. Ollie wanted to laugh. "You did come off pretty pretentious at the gallery."

Onyx glared.

"But Dex loved meeting you, so I suppose I'll forgive you. We can be friends if it means that much to you."

Onyx settled back in his seat, looking put out. "Good, but don't invite me to anything boring. I only do fun. And I don't like hanging out with Ash, so unless you and Harper leave your mates behind, don't bother calling."

"What about Dante?" A flare of irritation filled Ollie. Did Onyx not like spending time with him either?

"Dante's...fine," Onyx said as if he were admitting something he usually kept to himself, and Ollie relaxed. "I'm hoping he'll be a lot less hopeless now that he's got you."

14

___

OLLIE

Ollie tossed and turned, his bed infuriatingly uncomfortable. Every position he twisted his body into was worse than the last. He should have asked Harper for another sleeping potion but didn't want to start relying on them.

As soon as Onyx had left the salon, dread settled over Ollie. He was lost and didn't know what to do. It had weighed on him the whole way home.

Harper had been a good distraction, but it had been hours since they'd gone to bed. Ollie's skin crawled. He was cold under his blankets, and every time he closed his eyes, clawed fingers closed around his neck.

He was afraid of the dreams he'd have if he ever fell asleep. The sticky sweat on his skin might as well have been blood. Ollie swore he could smell it. He felt small and insignificant, and more than anything, he wanted to undo it all.

Ollie couldn't rewind and get his old life back. His heart raced. He couldn't do this forever. He didn't want to.

He threw back the covers and got out of bed, pulling a hoodie over his T-shirt and sleep pants. The apartment was stuffy. He shouldn't need this many layers or have been cold at all. Was he sick? Wait, no. He couldn't get sick anymore.

Did being immortal mean he'd never even get a cold? What about headaches?

He didn't understand his own body. His own feelings. There was a pit inside him. Ollie had never felt this alone or helpless. How was he supposed to get over this and move on?

He grabbed his phone and went to the living room, settling on the couch and selecting a mindless game. Maybe if he played long enough, he'd pass out, but he kept fucking up and having to start over.

Frustration added to everything piled on top of him, and Ollie whined pitifully.

Harper's door creaked open and Ollie whipped his head around. Had Harper heard that mortifying noise?

"Hey," Harper said softly. "Can't sleep?"

"Not really. Did I wake you up?"

Harper shook his head. "I've never slept well. I was awake already."

Ollie's brow furrowed. "Why don't you sleep well?"

Harper sat on the opposite end of the couch. "I grew up in a pretty bad situation. My father drained my blood for the magic in it, to use for himself, and when I tried to resist, he'd hurt me. Tie me down. Do all sorts of shit. I couldn't sleep living in the same house as him. Now my body doesn't know what to do at night." He shrugged.

"Fuck, Harper. That's awful." Ollie's heart broke for him. "And here I am being traumatized after having my blood spilled once by a random attacker."

"What happened to you was horrible, Ollie, no matter what happened to me or anyone else."

The pit inside Ollie grew. He felt even more alone sitting

next to Harper than he had before. "Maybe I need another sleep potion. I'm afraid to close my eyes."

"I can make one if you want, but as soon as you stop taking them, you'll be back here, needing to process what happened."

Harper was right. His days would get worse the longer he ignored his feelings at night. He'd rather panic or have flashbacks in his apartment than at work.

"Have you thought about calling Dante?" Harper asked.

"What?" More sweat prickled along Ollie's skin. His heart swelled, filling some of the void inside him.

"He's your mate," Harper said gently. "He can help. I'll always be here to talk to you, do whatever I can, but Dante can be here for you too. He can give you things I can't."

But why? Because of their bond? Ollie wanted to resist Dante. He could accept Harper's help because he didn't have conflicted feelings for Harper. Reaching out to Dante felt like opening himself up to a world of things he didn't trust.

But that didn't mean he didn't want to call Dante. Imagining Dante with him in the dark living room settled Ollie in a way he hadn't experienced all day.

"Okay, I'll call him." Ollie looked down at his phone and butterflies erupted in his chest, chasing away the darkness eating at him.

"Good. I really think it'll help. He'll be glad you called." Harper stood and headed back to his room, squeezing Ollie's shoulder as he went.

Ollie found Dante's contact and pressed call. Normally, he'd never do anything except text. Calling was needy, and calling in the middle of the night was borderline alarming, but he couldn't handle texting and sitting around waiting for a response.

He needed Dante, even if it scared him.

"Ollie?" Dante answered after a couple rings, sounding groggy. "Hi. Are you all right?"

A soft prickle washed over Ollie from head to toe. "I'm..." He was about to say fine, but he wasn't fine. It was the whole reason he called. "I'm not feeling great. I can't sleep. Sorry, are you busy?"

Ollie cringed. Every one of his words had sounded impossibly dumb. Why would Dante be busy at two in the morning? Ollie wanted Dante so badly now that he'd heard his voice, but he shouldn't. It was too much. Relying on someone like this was a recipe for an unhealthy relationship.

"I'm not busy," Dante replied. "Would you like me to come over?"

"Yes," Ollie breathed into the phone, hating the relief washing over him. Maybe he was the obsessed, stalkery one of the two of them.

"I'll be right over."

"Okay, thanks. It's not a big deal. But I can't stop thinking about the beach and all these weird things I don't understand." Hell, he was making it worse. Shut up.

"We can talk about it, and I'll explain anything you want," Dante said like he wasn't freaked out by Ollie at all. "Thank you for calling."

"Yeah. See you soon." Ollie lowered the phone and ended the call.

He tapped his fingers against the back of the phone. How long would it take Dante to get here? What was Ollie going to say when he arrived? His cheeks burned, heart pounding, but it wasn't like when he'd been in bed. He wasn't hopeless.

Not long later, he got a text from Dante saying he was at Ollie's front door. He jumped up from the couch and went to let him in.

"How'd you get in the building?" Ollie asked as he opened the door. He should have had to buzz Dante in.

"I came from the roof." Dante stepped inside and reached for Ollie, then dropped his hands like he'd changed his mind.

Ollie wished Dante wouldn't hold back. He wanted Dante to touch him, hold him, care for him. He wanted Dante as something other than a friend. It had never been more glaring than it was right then, but Ollie was afraid of what he wanted, especially in the face of everything he didn't understand about mates and immortality.

Ollie shifted unsteadily on his feet. "Thanks for coming so quick."

Dante quietly shut the door. "Anytime, Ollie. Like I said, you can always call. It's good to see you."

"It's good to see you too." Ollie reached out and squeezed Dante's hand. He could get lost in Dante's deep-brown eyes. His gaze was grounding, tethering Ollie to the moment and keeping him from getting lost in the memory of hands on his throat.

Ollie dropped Dante's hand and turned away. Dante wasn't wearing a shirt, and Ollie would ravage him with his eyes if he didn't get himself together.

He led Dante to the living room. "You flew here?"

"I fly pretty much everywhere. Would you like me to put my shirt back on?" Dante sat on the couch, gesturing to where a shirt was tied to his belt.

Ollie shook his head. "Do whatever's most comfortable for you. You can take your wings back out if you want."

Dante smiled so tenderly that Ollie's heart skipped. "I prefer having my wings out, but space is a little tight here."

That was disappointing, even if it shouldn't be. "I didn't think of that." Ollie sat beside Dante, much closer than he'd been to Harper.

Dante ran a hand through his black curls and his horns appeared, dark gray shimmering in the low light. "How's this?"

Ollie resisted the urge to reach out and touch them. "Good." He liked seeing Dante as he truly was.

Dante's expression shifted from pleased to concerned, more lines appearing around his eyes. "How have you been, Ollie? Tell me what's bothering you."

Ollie twisted his hands in his lap. "I keep thinking about the beach and feeling his hands on me. I'm so overwhelmed. I don't get what's happening. Why did you say we were mates before you needed to save me?"

Dante didn't immediately respond, and the urge to explain himself got the better of Ollie.

"I feel like I'm missing something. What does being your mate mean? I know I have to deal with the trauma of the attack, and I'm not going to be okay with what happened and forget it immediately, but all this other stuff is worse. I don't know what's happening with my life—my future—now that I'll live forever. What if you don't want me as your mate anymore?"

Ollie bit his lip, forcing himself to be quiet. Fuck, he shouldn't have let that last worry out.

Creases appeared around Dante's mouth, bringing a sense of deep sadness to his expression. "You don't have to worry about me not wanting to be your mate. I've always wanted to be your mate. You're right. You're still missing a few things. I didn't tell you everything."

Ollie scooted closer. "Why not?"

"I didn't know how to tell you that demon mates are destined. That I couldn't have bonded with anyone, only with you. I did it to save you, but the bond isn't something I could have done to save anyone else. The bond is for you and me, Ollie. We're fated mates. Our connection was always meant to form. We were meant to be, but it wasn't supposed to happen this way."

Ollie's eyes widened and his breath caught in his throat. "How was it supposed to happen?"

Dante raised a shoulder. "I don't know exactly. Being destined for each other doesn't mean I could see our future. Mated pairs are fated, but we don't know who our mates are until we meet them."

"So you're saying I have to be in a romantic relationship with you? Because of fate?" Ollie wanted a relationship with Dante, but he wasn't ready and didn't want it because he was destined for it. If it wasn't a choice, he didn't want it at all.

"No, Ollie. We're destined to be mates, but the bond is still ours. Most mates are romantic partners, but that doesn't mean we have to be. If Luc hadn't shown up on that beach, we would have grown closer over time and built a unique bond that suited us. We'd have had time to figure it out. Being close to each other —whatever that looked like—would have naturally led into creating the mating bond. It would have made sense and felt right."

But it had felt right, even if Ollie hadn't known why.

"This is why I didn't say anything right away. It's too much to go from not knowing these things exist to accepting that something special was always meant to grow between us."

"But how do you know? What if you're wrong, and there isn't anything between us but magic?" Ollie hated that idea, but Dante was right. It was hard to accept without a doubt that they would have had this beautiful connection when they hadn't gotten there yet.

Dante smiled sadly. "If there wasn't anything between us, I wouldn't have been able to save you."

"Oh." Ollie's heart ached. "But are my feelings all because of the magic?"

Dante shook his head. "Your feelings are your own. The magic of the bond affirms them. It predicted them but didn't create them."

Ollie found it hard to see the difference. If it was meant to be, how did he know his feelings were his choice and within his control?

"This doesn't change anything," Dante went on. "There's no pressure on us to be any certain way. All it means is that our friendship will grow into something special. We can still let it happen naturally even though we're already connected."

Their friendship. Ollie was the one to insist they be friends, but it wasn't what he really wanted.

Was a friendship all Dante desired, or was he letting Ollie define their connection? Did Ollie have a choice in what happened next? Could he even trust that he genuinely wanted something romantic with Dante, or was it magic dictating a predetermined future? Dante said it wasn't, but how did he know?

Ollie was getting lost in this. He didn't know what he wanted, what was magic, or what Dante wanted. He couldn't admit he'd never wanted Dante like a friend. Not if it meant getting swept up in the mating bond and losing himself.

If they stayed friends, maybe Ollie could sort out his emotions over time. If he could be sure he wanted Dante and it wasn't fate influencing everything, maybe he could feel secure in wanting more.

"So nothing has to change?" Ollie asked, needing to be sure of at least one thing.

"No. We'll get to know each other. Play *World's End* like before. But you can always turn to me. I'll always be here. I care about you, Ollie, more than I would for any other new friend. That's all the bond means at this stage. That, and I'm here to stay."

Ollie wanted Dante to care, but was it real? It sounded like fate made him care. It wasn't Dante choosing to care. Ollie could have been anyone, and Dante would have felt the same if fate had told him to.

Ollie's heart cracked at that. He wanted Dante to want *him*. But how could Dante when he barely knew him?

Unfortunately, all these doubts didn't cancel out Ollie's desire for comfort. He needed Dante. Maybe it was magic dictating his needs, but the ache was still there.

"Will you stay with me tonight?" Ollie asked.

"Of course. Does having me here help you feel better?"

"I'm still overwhelmed," Ollie admitted. "But I don't want you to go."

It was clingy. Codependent. Not behavior Ollie should accept in a relationship or friendship. Ollie was surrounded by red flags and still didn't want Dante to leave.

He couldn't do this alone. It was too much.

Ollie shifted closer to Dante and lay on the couch, resting his head on Dante's thigh. He melted, instantly comfortable, and yawned. "This okay?"

"Yes," Dante murmured, placing a hand briefly on Ollie's head. "You can sleep like this if it helps."

"What about you?" Ollie yawned again. Dante's peppermint scent surrounded him like soothing aromatherapy. "Won't you get tired sitting there?"

"No, I'm good. I'll watch over you."

Ollie shouldn't like hearing that. He didn't need watching over. He'd never wanted it before. But at the moment, he didn't care if it was truly what he wanted or the bond's influence. He was sleepy and safe, and Dante smelled good.

Ollie turned his head and pressed his nose to Dante's thigh, breathing him in through his jeans. "Hmm," Ollie hummed, eyes closed.

Dante's hand returned to his hair. "Did you just smell me?"

Ollie's eyes popped open. "No." His cheeks burned. He couldn't believe he'd done that.

Dante's hand shifted and his nose pressed against Ollie's head. He breathed in, nose nuzzling before pulling back. "You smell good too, Ollie."

Ollie's whole body heated and his heart fluttered. It should have been weird, not the most comforting thing in his life, but he drifted off to sleep with a smile.

15

--------

## DANTE

OLLIE NESTLED against Dante's thigh and barely stirred once he fell asleep. His breathing evened into soft snores, leaving Dante free to watch him all night.

Dante swelled with pride, knowing his presence comforted Ollie. He wasn't completely incapable of taking care of his mate.

He'd hated being away from Ollie the past two days, and when his phone had first rung, Dante had feared the worst. He didn't think Ollie would call for anything short of physical danger. He'd been wrong.

If only every night could be like this, snuggled together. But that's not what friends did. Well, maybe some. Would Ollie like to be that kind of friend? Could Dante be physically affectionate without letting romantic attachment creep in? Had it already crept in?

Ollie slept through to the morning when an alarm sounded on his phone. He jolted up, glancing around like he didn't know where he was.

Dante grabbed the phone from between the couch cushions and handed it to him. "Sleep well?"

Ollie silenced the alarm and rubbed his face. "Yeah. I swear

I blinked, and it was morning. Were you up all night?" Concern creased his brow.

"It's fine. One sleepless night isn't going to bother me."

Ollie frowned, lips pouting. "Are demons like vampires and don't need sleep?"

Dante chuckled. "Both demons and vampires need sleep. All beings need to rest, but immortals can go longer than humans without it."

"In that case, I won't keep you up two nights in a row." Ollie tossed his phone on the coffee table and pulled off his hoodie, his shirt riding up and exposing his belly.

Dante looked away, unable to suppress the tingle of pleasure at seeing his mate's bare skin.

"Aww, don't look disappointed." Ollie nudged his shoulder. Dante met Ollie's gaze, and Ollie hesitated before adding, "Did you like keeping me company last night?"

Dante's body heated as his fire flared. "Yes. I like spending time with you, no matter what we're doing, and I'm glad I was able to help you rest."

"Me too," Ollie said barely above a whisper. "Um...I should get ready for work. I've got a full morning booked."

"Can I make you breakfast?"

Ollie's cheeks pinkened. "You don't have to do that."

But Dante wanted to. Maybe it was too much, especially considering the romantic direction his thoughts were heading. He shouldn't indulge them. Ollie liked space. "Should I leave you to get ready as usual?"

Ollie opened his mouth as if to say something, then closed it with a small nod.

Dante stood and stretched. "Have a good morning at work."

Ollie fisted the hoodie in his hands. "You too. Have a good morning, I mean, not at work since you don't really work. Uh...I'll text you later. After work. Maybe we can do a few missions tonight." He looked up at Dante through his lashes.

Like Dante would ever say no. "Sounds good. It'll be a while before we run out of things to do with the new expansion coming."

"For sure." Ollie's smile carried a hint of relief. "So, I'm not a dick for kicking you out after comforting me all night?"

Dante clasped Ollie's shoulder. "No. Don't worry. Go get ready for work and have a good day."

Ollie's cheeks turned from pink to red, eyes shining. "Okay. Bye, Dante." He turned and hurried into the bathroom.

Was that longing in Ollie's eyes, or was Dante seeing what he wanted? Even if it was, Ollie could be longing for the way things had been before, not for Dante. Maybe Ollie wished he hadn't needed Dante by his side last night.

It probably wasn't romantic longing.

Dante couldn't afford to hope Ollie might want something other than what he'd said. That was a dangerous game Dante couldn't play with his ancient heart. He might not survive it.

He left the apartment and went to the roof, freeing his wings and flexing his muscles. His phone buzzed in his pocket. Dante pulled it out and read the message.

ASH:

Where are you?

DANTE:

At Ollie and Harper's. I'm heading home now. Why? Is something wrong?

ASH:

You could have left a note. I'd ask if Harper and Ollie are okay, but I've already checked in with Harper.

Ash could mean through their bond or via a phone call.

Dante didn't ask. He launched into the air, aiming for the reserve across the city.

If Dante had been in tune with Ollie's emotions, he'd have known Ollie was having a bad night. But knowing Ollie was struggling and Ollie not asking for help would have been painful, so Dante continued to block Ollie, keeping that part of their bond suppressed.

At home, he landed on the deck, finding Ash waiting, arms crossed and scowling.

"What? You're that pissed about waking up alone one time after living in the woods by yourself for decades?"

Ash grunted. "I don't care about being alone. I was worried. Something might have happened to Ollie."

Dante's demon fire flared and he ruffled his wings. If anything else happened to Ollie, he'd rip the world apart. Ollie might not be in danger of losing his life as easily as before, but he wasn't allowed to suffer. Dante had to protect him better from now on.

Having Ollie limp in his arms once had been too much. Dante didn't think he'd ever forget that moment, no matter how much time passed.

"I take it Ollie is fine?" Ash pressed.

"As much as he can be. He couldn't sleep. Luc left his psychological wounds, as usual."

Ash growled.

"Come on. Let's do the rounds and see if we can get any further hunting whoever killed my birds, and I want to know what's been going on in the Realm of the Damned for the last two hundred years. See if we can figure out why Luc is taking out his anger on innocents when we're right here."

"Figuring Luc out is an impossible task." Ash launched into the sky alongside Dante. "You still think hunting him in his own territory is the best idea?"

Dante ground his teeth. "I'm not waiting for him to come back when it suits him. I'm done with defense."

"Fine, agreed, but we can't go back to the Realm of the Damned without Onyx. I need to know I can get us out again, even if we get trapped, and I can't break the confinement magic without both of you."

"I know." Dante hated that he couldn't blaze into the Realm of the Damned, fire at his fingertips, and take his vengeance. He'd have done it days ago.

But he hadn't told Onyx his plan to hunt Lucifer in Hell and wasn't looking forward to convincing him to get on board. Onyx hadn't even wanted to help Dante and Ash track down the other potentially escaped demons after talking to Ren. Onyx kept insisting he wasn't needed, but that wasn't true.

The three of them had to stand together.

Dante circled the reserve, checking all the birds' nests. Most were empty this late in the morning, so he scanned his flock's minds, checking for anything out of the ordinary.

Other than Ren leaving her magic, none of the trouble had occurred around the shearwater nests. The murdered birds had been found farther down the coast, and as with the last several weeks, nothing was out of the ordinary today.

Since the deaths, Dante had instructed his birds to stay in a large flock and not venture off in smaller groups. He disliked altering their behavior this much but couldn't risk more dying.

Too bad his safety measures meant they were getting nowhere. It didn't seem like the attacker would target the large flock, and Ash had no way of tracking them without a sense of their magic. Hopefully, Ren found something soon.

After scouring the coastline again and finding nothing, Dante turned to Ash. "Shall we head to the gallery?"

"Yeah, let's make Onyx's day."

Dante suppressed a sigh. "Try not to piss him off on purpose. You need his help, remember?"

Ash veered off toward the city without responding.

After a quick flight, they landed on the gallery's roof. Dante paused. "Maybe we should give him a call before barging in."

"So he can slink away? Not a chance. If he wanted to keep us out, he'd have woven it into his protective spells." Ash walked to the edge of the roof and climbed down the ladder.

Dante followed through the window into Onyx's empty office. Voices echoed in the hallway beyond, followed by footsteps.

Onyx opened the office door, his pleasant smile dropping at the sight of them. "Oh goodie."

Ash ruffled his feathers, tail flicking. "Good morning to you too, Onyx."

Onyx curled his lip. "Can you put those things away? There are humans around." He gestured to Ash's wings.

"I don't see any humans." Ash made a show of inspecting the room. "And even if there were, they wouldn't be able to see me. I only allow you two past my illusions, which you know I haven't dropped yet."

Dante wanted to smack Ash upside the head. This was exactly what he'd asked him not to do. "We aren't staying long," he assured Onyx.

"Then spit it out. Why are you bothering me at all?"

"It's about Ollie—" Dante began.

Ash cut him off. "I hear you were asking about Ollie. Harper told me you wanted to know where he worked."

Onyx opened and closed his mouth. "Of course he told you. Super."

Ash arched a brow. "Was it supposed to be a secret?"

"No." Onyx stalked around Ash to his desk and flopped into his chair, attention turning to Dante. "I went by Ollie's salon yesterday and had my hair trimmed. Thanks for noticing, by the way."

"Your hair looks impeccable, as always." Dante couldn't actually spot the difference.

Onyx put his nose in the air. "Thank you. All I did was reintroduce myself. It wasn't a big deal. Ollie didn't seem to mind. I had to make sure he had my number since you all insisted Harper needed it. Got to keep all the mates on the same page. Maybe we need a group chat."

Warmth spread through Dante. He shouldn't have been surprised Onyx took the initiative with Ollie. He wasn't as uncaring as he liked to act. Though it had been a while since Dante had seen evidence of Onyx's softer side.

"So what about Ollie?" Onyx asked. "Have you got him up to speed on mates? He seemed a bit clueless, asking if I have one like mates grow on trees to be picked at will."

Dante scrubbed a hand over his face. "I'm getting there. He knows we're fated, but I haven't burdened him with the saga of failing to find our mates for thousands of years."

"And you're still 'friends?'" Onyx made quotations with his fingers.

"Yes, Onyx. I explained this already. Please don't make me repeat myself."

Onyx pointed a slender finger at Dante. "You're the one who came to see me about Ollie. All I'm saying is he clearly *likes* you. He's probably hung up on something human and therefore trivial and doesn't know what he wants."

Dante's face heated and he flexed his wings. "Ollie's concerns aren't trivial. I'm not going to disregard what he tells me and assume I know better. That's not the kind of mate I am."

"Did I say you were? Whatever. I'll be here saying I told you so in"—Onyx looked at his wrist as if he had a watch—"a month tops."

"I'll look forward to it. And since you're so supportive of Ollie and me, you'll be happy to help avenge him. Won't you?"

Onyx opened his mouth and then snapped it shut, eyes narrowing.

Ash stepped up to Onyx's desk. "We're hunting Luc down. This time, he's gone too far. He can't keep hurting our mates and escaping."

Onyx's eyes widened and he leaned forward in his chair, posture no longer relaxed. "What are you planning to do? What do you mean hunt him? You can't kill him."

"He almost killed Ollie," Dante growled.

"But he didn't." Onyx leveled a piercing stare in Dante's direction. "Ollie lived. Killing an Eternal—or demon—is punishable by death."

Ash huffed. "And who's going to punish us? The council?"

"Yes, the council. That's literally the point of their existence. They may have damned us, but they haven't written us off so far that they'll let us break the ultimate rule." Onyx turned from Ash to Dante. "I know what Luc did is unforgivable, so let's trap him alone in a prison like we planned. Isn't that worse than death?"

Isolation would be torture, but Dante shook his head. It wasn't enough. Why not torture, then kill the swine? "Killing an Eternal's or demon's mate is also punishable by death. He has to pay."

"But Ollie didn't die," Onyx said as if he were trying to explain something to a small child. "We can't cross this line. Even after everything, some rules shouldn't be broken."

"I know he's your brother," Ash began.

"Fuck off, he's my brother." Onyx snarled, standing abruptly. "He's dead to me, but I'm not killing him."

"Why, so you can see if he's changed in another thousand years?" Ash scoffed.

Onyx's cheeks reddened and a hint of smoke tinged the air. In one fluid motion, he grabbed a paperweight from the desk and threw it against the wall, glass shattering.

Dante growled. Fuck, he wanted to throw things too. Trash this pretty office. Tear the building apart until nothing was left. Luc deserved to die. He needed to feel what it was like to be ripped apart.

But Onyx had a point.

Dante wanted righteous anger to blind him. If he'd been able to act the moment Ollie rode away in that car, he'd have killed Luc, consequences be damned, and lost his own life as a result. But he couldn't go to Hell and back without the others. He'd waited to act because he wanted to come back.

Ash supported him. Luc had almost killed Harper. But fuck, Onyx had logic on his side. Attempted murder wasn't the same as murder. And just because the council looked the other way at Andras's death didn't mean they'd do the same if the Fallen started killing each other.

Dante gripped the desk and shoved it to the side, sending it crashing into the wall. Onyx's eyes widened, nothing standing between him and Dante.

Dante closed his eyes. "He's right, Ash. Damn this stupid world. He's right. If we kill Luc, we'll be the ones committing the unforgivable offense."

Ash swore, his spiced smoke mingling with Onyx's, heating the air.

Dante opened his eyes.

"You can't take care of your mates if the council kills you," Onyx said, and the growing tension snapped.

"No," Dante agreed, bitterness so thick in his veins that his blood probably tasted foul. "But we're still hunting Luc. We'll go to the Realm of the Damned and punish him, even if he gets to keep his miserable life."

Ash rumbled in agreement.

"Nope. I'm not going." Onyx shook his head. "Next plan."

Ash stalked forward until he and Onyx were chest to chest. "We can't keep sitting around, letting Luc's actions go without response. Who knows what he'll do when he decides to turn up next. Your mate could be his next victim."

Onyx blinked rapidly, stepping back and bumping the wall. "I don't have a mate. You can drag me into whatever shit you're planning in this realm, but I'm not leaving. I'm never going back. Now get out of my fucking office."

Dante grabbed Ash's arm, pulling him away. It was best to leave. There'd be no changing Onyx's mind today.

Fire burned in Onyx's eyes as he shooed them out the window.

# 16

## OLLIE

"I can't believe I died." Dante's whine tickled Ollie's ears.

He snorted with laughter. "That rogue portal really snuck up on you. Too bad a bunch of crawlers popped out and ate you."

Dante huffed. "It wasn't a fair fight. Where was my backup?"

"Guarding you from above, taking out that dragon. You're welcome, by the way. You'd be doubly dead if I didn't have the sky covered."

Dante made a sound of reluctant agreement. "We almost had it. Do you have time for another mission? We can try again."

Ollie adjusted his headphones, staring at Dante's fire mage on-screen. "I should probably go to bed." It was already an hour later than he usually stayed up, and last night, he'd only had a few hours of sleep between Dante coming over and his alarm going off. "You should get some sleep too."

"I will," Dante promised. "But if you need me again, we can figure something out where we can both rest."

Like lying in bed together, Dante's arms wrapped around

him. Ollie shook himself. "I'll text if I have another bad night, but I'm hoping I can relax on my own."

As much as he wanted to, Ollie couldn't rely on Dante like that. It wouldn't be good for him.

"Okay. Try meditating before bed if your thoughts stray to places you don't like."

"Yeah, sure," Ollie lied. He had something else in mind.

They said goodnight and logged off, Ollie's heart in his throat.

Dante had been on his mind all day. His fresh peppermint scent deepened by the hint of musk. The way his hard thigh had been the best pillow in Ollie's life, even though that made no sense. Dante's soft, understanding smile, and the way he'd shown up for Ollie like it was the most natural thing to do.

Were all these things so alluring because of the bond? Was magic influencing Ollie? Did he care?

Right now, he didn't.

Ollie slipped into his room and shut the door. He closed his eyes, leaning back against the cool wood. Ollie wanted Dante's hard body pressed against his. He wanted to get lost, licking every inch of Dante, touching him, indulging every one of his urges, and then he wanted to let Dante use him any way he saw fit.

Dante's lips on Ollie's neck. Hands on his hips, his ass, cradling his back. Dante's teeth piercing Ollie's skin.

Ollie hissed and palmed his cock through his shorts. He was already half-hard. Fuck.

He stripped out of his shorts and underwear, leaving them pooled by the door. His shirt landed across the room, near his hamper. Ollie beelined for his bedside table and opened the drawer, tossing lube and a vibrating butt plug on his bed.

Standing in the darkened room, Ollie stroked his cock until he was completely hard.

Dante's firm grip would feel so much better than his. But he couldn't have Dante if they were friends. He could only pretend.

Ollie closed his eyes, imagining Dante coming up behind him and bracketing his body, hot skin pressing against Ollie's back. Dante's demon fire would keep Ollie warm, his wings surrounding them as his lips pressed against the crook of Ollie's neck.

He stroked himself faster and his heart rate climbed as his whole body flashed hot. Heat and sharp desire rolled through him before fading into something softer.

Dante held Ollie like he was precious. No one's arms were like Dante's, and he wasn't even here with Ollie. How could Ollie feel so secure in an embrace that wasn't really happening?

Ollie wanted Dante so much, but he was afraid of being with him for real. Shouldn't the bond's potential to take over his life and erase him as an individual kill his arousal and make Dante completely unappealing? Those fears usually did. But something in Ollie told him he was safe. He wasn't ready to trust it, not fully, but tonight, he could imagine he and Dante were mates in every sense of the word.

He wanted to fuck Dante as much as he wanted Dante to fuck him, but tonight, if he was pretending, Dante was going to own his ass. Ollie could save the other fantasy for another night. He was under no illusion that once would be enough.

Ollie climbed on the bed and opened the lube, coating his fingers. He lay back and hiked up his legs, spreading them. A tightness tugged at his chest and his breath stuttered.

Fuck, he wished Dante were here. But no, this was better. Less complicated.

Ollie breached himself with two fingers, wincing at the intrusion. He should take his time, but he burned for release. Waiting seemed like the end of the world.

"Dante," he murmured as he worked his fingers deeper. "Oh, Dante."

The scent of peppermint filled Ollie's nose and his skin prickled. Pleasure zipped down his spine, lighting him up and stealing his breath.

Ollie pulled his fingers out. Holy shit, he'd almost come. How was that possible?

He took a slow breath, trying to collect himself, then lubed the plug in a hurry. He aligned it with his entrance and swore he could feel Dante looming over him.

"Fuck me," Ollie pleaded.

Dante's breath ghosted his skin as if he were really there, whispering against his neck, and Ollie's insides burst with butterflies.

He pushed the toy in, bearing down. It was Dante's bare cock, ready to fill him with cum. Dante's muscles flexed above him, his feathers rustling, and Ollie moaned.

Across the room, Ollie's phone buzzed. His eyes popped open. Fuck, way to kill the mood and remind him he was alone.

He ignored the phone, pressing the plug in until it was fully seated. Ollie pushed the base, shifting the plug until it pegged his sweet spot.

"Oh fuck, right there."

The phone buzzed relentlessly, starting up again a moment after stopping. Seriously, was there some emergency? Who was calling this late?

With a grumble, Ollie stood, the plug shifting and pulling a groan from him. He grabbed a tissue, wiped his hands, and fished the phone out of his shorts, finding Dante's name lighting up the screen.

Ollie froze.

The call went to voicemail and Dante immediately called again. Was something wrong?

He couldn't know what Ollie was doing, right?

"Fuck." Ollie raised the phone to his ear and accepted the call. "Hi," he said as smoothly as he could, proud his voice didn't waver.

A harsh pant hit Ollie's ears. "What are you doing?" Dante demanded.

Double fuck. "Nothing?" This time, it came out like a question, and Ollie cringed.

"Ollie," Dante breathed. "You're projecting your emotions. I can feel them."

Fuck, fuck, fuck. "*What?* No, I'm not. I wasn't projecting anything."

"Ollie," Dante said his name like a plea.

He swallowed. "Are you saying that you know I was...?" He couldn't finish. It was mortifying. Ollie's skin burned uncomfortably hot.

"I'm sorry, Ollie. I've been blocking you, but I can't stay shielded when you're focusing on me like that. I didn't know what else to do."

A pitiful whine slipped from Ollie's lips. He still had the plug in his ass. He was hard and needy, and Dante could feel it through the bond. Dante knew Ollie had been thinking about him, lusting after him.

"What am I supposed to do? Not jerk off?"

Dante groaned. "I don't know. I'm not telling you what to do, but I couldn't let you keep going when you didn't know I was, um, aware."

Ollie appreciated that. He'd have felt violated if Dante had sat back and essentially watched him get off without his consent.

Sweat prickled Ollie's brow. "Could you tell what I was thinking about?"

"Not exactly." Dante let out a measured breath. "The bond

doesn't project images or direct thoughts. But if you hadn't been focused on me, your feelings wouldn't have broken through my shield."

Fuck. Humiliation should have killed Ollie's arousal by now, but as embarrassing as this was, part of Ollie was relieved Dante knew. His dick hardened further, his insides twisting themselves in tantalizing knots as his face burned.

He didn't hate the feeling at all.

"So you know I was thinking about you? While I touched myself?"

"Yes," Dante whispered like it was the hardest thing he'd said in his life.

A wave of lust hit Ollie in the chest, followed by a longing so potent he couldn't breathe. Were those Dante's feelings?

"Fuck." Ollie groaned. "Dante. What are you doing?"

"I'm sorry." Some of the lust faded. "I can't help it."

Ollie gripped the phone tight, more needy than he'd ever been in his life. Needy and hopeful. He burned with longing so sweet it ached. He might be making a mistake, but he had to know. "Do you want me?"

Lust overwhelmed Ollie once more, his cock leaking with it.

"Yes, I want you, Ollie. You can feel it. I know you can, just like I can feel you."

Ollie whimpered at the naked desire in Dante's tone. He stumbled back to the bed and lay down, heart in his throat. "Then stay."

"W-what?" Through the bond, Ollie felt Dante's fragile hesitation and the hint of hope it brought with it.

Ollie's own hopefulness flared. He wanted Dante, and Dante wanted him. They needed each other. Neither of them was alone.

He ran a hand down his stomach. "I don't want to stop what I've started. I won't unless you tell me to. You're going to feel me come, so why not stay on the phone with me while I do?"

"*Uhh,*" Dante whined. "Are you sure? That isn't why I called."

Ollie wished it was why. "Maybe not, but I like having you with me. And you want me too. We can't hide it."

A shiver ran down Ollie's spine. He'd never have asked Dante for phone sex. That wasn't a friend thing, and it was probably a huge mistake. But now that they were here, nothing had ever felt so right. It was like being in Dante's lap with Dante's lips on his wrist all over again.

Ollie didn't want Dante like a friend. He never had.

The mating bond was consuming him. It forced him to confront his true desires and ignore his boundaries. That should have felt wrong, but Ollie couldn't remember why.

Why couldn't he have this?

"You want me to listen to you get yourself off?" Dante confirmed like he had to be extra sure.

"No." Ollie fisted his cock. "I want you to get off with me so I can hear you too. Would you like that?"

A growl rumbled down the phone line. "Yes, Ollie. So much. C-can we do that? *Please?*"

Chills coursed through Ollie from head to toe. Dante sounded like Ollie held the keys to his salvation. "Fuck yeah, Dante. We can do that."

Dante groaned so deeply that Ollie felt it in his chest.

He switched his phone to speaker and set it by his ear before grabbing the lube. "I've got a plug in my ass. Do you like knowing that?"

"*Ngh,*" Dante grunted, rustling coming down the line like he was getting his clothes out of the way. "Is that what you were doing before? Opening yourself?"

"Yeah, opening for your cock." Ollie squirted lube in his

palm and began stroking himself. "Should I turn the vibrator on?"

"Yes, please." Dante panted, more rustling sounds in the background.

"Tell me what you're doing first."

"Oh...um..." Dante paused. "I'm jerking off."

A frisson of uncertainty radiated through the bond like Dante was out of his depth. Ollie went tender and mushy all over. Maybe Dante had never had phone sex. Ollie hadn't either, but he was happy to take the lead. He'd started it after all.

"Are you naked?" he asked, voice low. "I'm naked. On my back in bed. I'm turning the plug on now...oh yeah, goddamn, that's it." Vibrations rocked through his core, hitting his bundle of nerves, his toes curling.

"Fuck." Dante's breathing came heavier. "You're so enthusiastic, so open. I...I'm not totally naked. My pants are around my ankles. I'm stroking myself, but it's not enough. My tail is out. I need you to touch it, Ollie. Please."

Dante sounded desperate. Hell, Ollie could feel his desperation. It flooded the bond and would have knocked Ollie off his feet if he'd been standing. Dante had this frantic edge to him like he couldn't handle the magnitude of his lust, even as it grew stronger.

Ollie stroked himself. He wouldn't last long. Not when every sensation was heightened. Not when he knew with absolute certainty how Dante felt about him and how good he made Dante feel.

"You want me to touch your tail?" Ollie crooned, jerking himself harder as he felt Dante melt in response to his words. "Tell me how you like it. Where should I touch it?"

"The base," Dante panted. "It's sensitive, like my cock."

"I've got you." Ollie reveled in Dante's responding whine.

"Does that feel good? Me jacking your tail? You could fuck my throat while I touched it. On my knees, your hands in my hair."

"*Ugh,*" Dante moaned. "Ollie, fuck, you'll undo me."

"That's exactly what I want. Touch your tail, Dante. I want to feel how good it is for you."

"*Uh-h,*" Dante groaned. "Ollie, please. I'm touching it. I'm touching my tail for you."

"You're so good, Dante. You feel so good." Ollie's back arched. He'd never felt anything like this. His spine tingled right above his ass, where a tail would be if he had one. Every last one of his nerves sang with pleasure.

"Bite me, Dante. Bite me. I'm gonna come."

Dante's strangled cry filled Ollie's ears, his orgasm electrifying the bond. Ollie forgot the plug in his ass and his hand on his cock. All he felt was Dante coming inside him. Dante's cock and his cum might not be present, but Dante was *in* Ollie. Filling his whole body. His soul.

Pleasure exploded through Ollie. His dick jerked and cum flooded his stomach. "Dante," he moaned, head thrown back.

Heavy breathing emanated from the phone. "Ollie, my mate. Oh, Ollie."

Ollie's chest expanded, filled to the brim. This was the best moment of his life. Connected to Dante so thoroughly that he couldn't tell where either ended or began, and the only thing between them was pleasure. He basked in it for as long as he could.

Eventually, the vibrations in his ass became uncomfortable, and he turned off the plug before pulling it out with a wince.

"You okay?" Dante asked.

Ollie's heart skipped. Dante's knowledge of his every feeling was far more jarring now than it'd been a minute ago. "I'm good. Probably should have done a bit more prep, that's all."

"Oh...um..." Confusion swirled around them, and Ollie couldn't tell who it was coming from.

Shit. He needed to close his mind but had no idea how.

"I hope you enjoyed that," Dante said quietly.

The feelings between them faded like Dante was dampening their connection, but not before a flash of hurt hit Ollie in the gut.

"I did. That was the most spectacular thing that's ever happened to me."

Dante snorted, the sound seeming to catch him by surprise as he stifled it.

"I'm serious. It was. I'm not ready to share all of me all the time, but I don't regret what happened." And he didn't, right? Part of him wanted to do it all over again and let Dante in completely. But he was scared. What did all this mean?

"I don't regret it either," Dante said, something warm brushing against Ollie like Dante had sent it down the bond. "Now get some sleep. You should be able to rest well after that."

Ollie wiped up with some tissues and discarded them and the plug on his side table. He closed his eyes. "Yeah. You too, Dante. Goodnight."

"Goodnight, Ollie," he said with almost painful delicacy and ended the call.

17

---

## DANTE

Dante jolted upright in bed, drenched in a cold sweat.

Where was Ollie? Was he okay?

Dante glanced around his room. He swore Ollie had been in his arms, slipping away, and Dante hadn't been able to save him. But, of course, Ollie wasn't there.

It must have been a dream.

He scrubbed a hand over his face, tempted to reach out through the bond and check on Ollie. But he couldn't. Ollie had soured on their connection as soon as they'd had their pleasure. He didn't want Dante to see that much of him.

After getting up and pulling on underwear, Dante went to the kitchen. It was blessedly empty. Ash must still be asleep. Dante opened his drawer and took out a chocolate. He was running low.

A flash of Ollie, blood-soaked and unmoving, cut across Dante's mind, the feel of Ollie's blood suddenly coating his hands.

Dante rolled his shoulders, wings rustling. Everything was fine. It was only a memory.

He ate the whole chocolate bar while heating a mug of blood. He brought the hot drink and two more chocolates back to his room. The hollow feeling of doom that had jolted him awake lingered.

Even if he couldn't feel Ollie through the bond, Dante could still check on him.

He forced the mug of blood down his throat, then picked up his phone and called his mate.

"Hey, Dante. What's up?" Ollie's voice was strained.

Damnation, did he not want Dante to call? It probably wasn't cool to call so soon after a hookup or whatever the hell had happened between them.

"Hi, Ollie. Sorry to bother you. I, um…wanted to check you were okay."

"About last night?" Ollie sounded even more tense.

"No. I mean, yes. I'd want to know if anything changed there, but that's not why I called. I had a bad dream." Dante's words died and his face burned.

Would death from the known universe be all that bad? It couldn't be worse than this.

"Oh no. I'm sorry." Concern replaced Ollie's hesitance. "I'm perfectly fine, promise."

"Thank you." Dante cleared his throat, examining the candy in his hand. "I couldn't stop from checking, even though I knew nothing would be wrong."

"That's okay."

No one spoke for longer than was comfortable.

"Can I see you?" Dante asked, all but crushing the candy. "I know you have work, but can I see you later today?"

"I'm meeting Dex after work."

Dante's heart sank. He needed his mate. Even with no regrets about last night, Dante was shaken. Everything seemed different now that he'd held Ollie so close to his heart.

"I'll be home after dinner," Ollie continued. "We could meet then."

"Yes, that would be great." Dante sat on the bed, legs weak. "I'll meet you at your apartment."

"I'll text you." Ollie paused and Dante hung on the silence. "Are you okay to wait? I want to be there for you too. We could talk more now if your dream is still bothering you. Or something else?"

"Thank you, Ollie. I'm all right. See you tonight."

He needed to have this conversation in person when Ollie wasn't worried about rushing off to work. But Ollie's offer mattered.

His mate wanted to take care of him. Dante clung to the knowledge all day.

DANTE LANDED on Ollie's roof, his insides fluttering more than his wings.

He couldn't afford to hope anything had changed between him and Ollie. Being intimate over the phone was something they'd stumbled into. It might not mean anything. Ollie could feel lust and longing for Dante and still not desire anything romantic.

But Dante had to know for sure. One day of uncertainty had him at his limit.

He should have gone to see Ren and checked on her progress. He should have worked on convincing Onyx to go on the offensive against Luc. Instead, he'd done nothing but eat chocolate and sugary cereal. Then gone to the store to restock his drawer and fill another with a savory treat stash for Ollie.

At least Ash had been occupied with Harper, so no one had witnessed Dante's hopelessness.

He paced the roof until Ollie texted to let Dante know he was home.

Dante shoved his phone back in his pocket. Did he wait a little longer to go down? That way, Ollie wouldn't know he'd been sitting up here, darkening the roof like an impatient gargoyle.

No. Dante wasn't playing games or hiding things. He and Ollie needed to work this out with all their cards on the table.

Dante went inside and knocked on Ollie's door. A moment later, it swung open, revealing his wide-eyed mate.

"That was fast. Were you already here?"

Dante cleared his throat. "I was waiting on the roof."

Ollie's brow furrowed. "Come on in. Let's go to my room."

Dante followed him through the apartment, nodding to Ash and Harper in the living room. He entered Ollie's bedroom and Ollie closed the door. His sandalwood scent was everywhere, the space small and furniture arranged close together with every surface covered in one thing or another.

Dante smiled.

Ollie sat on the bed, his eyes darting around. "Sorry, there's nowhere else to sit."

Dante perched next to him. "This is perfectly fine."

He glanced at the rumpled bedspread and the sounds Ollie had made last night filled his mind. Dante's insides went molten. Ollie had lain here and touched himself thinking of Dante. Fuck. Last night seemed even more real now that he could imagine every last detail.

There was no doubt he'd revisit the memory, especially when it might be as close to Ollie as he'd ever get.

The heat in Dante's core cooled.

"I need to talk about what happened last night."

Ollie's cheeks bloomed red. "Was it not okay? It doesn't have to be a big deal or change anything."

Dante swallowed the lump forming in his throat. "I'm not saying what happened wasn't okay. I wanted it as much as you did. And it's fine if it isn't a big deal for you. But..." Dante's chest tightened. He had to admit what last night meant to him, even if it opened him up to rejection that would break his heart.

His fire burned and sweat tickled his palms. "I'm happy to be your friend. No, I'm honored to be close to you as a friend. But if we're going to have a platonic bond, I can't add intimacy to the equation. I can't have sex with you without it feeding my romantic desires. If we're going to remain friends, it can't happen again."

Ollie stared at Dante for a long moment, eyes wide and unblinking. Dante's fire raged inside him and the air between them seemed to pull tight.

At last, Ollie spoke, his voice shaking slightly. "When I said it didn't have to be a big deal, I...I didn't mean it meant nothing to me." He looked at his lap. "Having you as a friend feels safer."

Dante's heart clenched, not sure why Ollie felt that way. "I want you to feel safe and friends is what we agreed on. I'm not asking to change that. We just can't blur the lines."

Ollie looked up. "That's fair. I wouldn't want to hurt you."

"I know. And you haven't." Ollie shouldn't feel guilty. Dante wouldn't trade last night for anything, even if clearing things up strangled something inside him. "Relationships aren't for you, I know that. I'm not expecting you to change who you are because I have feelings about last night."

Ollie bit his bottom lip, worrying it between his teeth. "Change who I am? What do you mean? Wait. I'm not aromantic. I didn't mean relationships aren't for me in that way."

He wasn't? Dante had known that was a possibility, but it had seemed equally possible that Ollie was aromantic.

"Oh, okay," was all Dante managed to say. Opening up to

more than one type of bond wasn't a bad thing in any way he looked at it. He could only work with what Ollie told him.

Ollie cringed as if he were embarrassed. "Sorry."

"No, don't be. There's nothing to apologize for. I tried not to assume." Dante faltered. "Can I ask why you aren't interested in relationships?"

"It's not that I'm not interested." Ollie chewed the fingernail of his ring finger, his other arm folded protectively across his body as he seemed to come to some decision.

He straightened. "I'm scared. I've been in abusive relationships that took over my whole life, and I'm afraid of getting attached and losing myself and my independence in an *us*. Especially with our bond. I have feelings for you, Dante, but I need to know I'll still be me. I need to choose. Being a fated mate is this huge thing, and it scares me that I like you because the bond is everything I shouldn't want."

Ollie had chosen friendship as his safe space, and everything that had happened since the beach had been testing him.

Dante reached for Ollie, and Ollie held out his hand. Dante clasped it and held it tight, his heart breaking. "I'm so sorry your past partners didn't treat you right."

Ollie looked away, a heavy air of discomfort settling over him. "I don't want to get into it."

"We don't have to." Dante wished he could take Ollie's pain away and wrap him in safe feelings.

Ollie's hand tightened around Dante's. "Thank you. I'm sure I'll want to talk about it one day, but not now." His gaze slid back to Dante and held firm, their eyes locked.

Dante smiled softly. "I'll be here for you when you do."

"I like knowing that," Ollie whispered, voice thick. "I can count on you."

Fuck if that didn't feel like the most important thing. Ollie's trust was a gift Dante would never get tired of.

Ollie cleared his throat. "I've always wanted to be open to relationships again—one day—but it's hard. I don't know what I need to feel safe. Getting involved is always going to be a risk. But I wish I could figure it out because I want you, Dante, like a boyfriend, a partner, a mate."

Dante's breath caught. "What if we could find a way for you to feel safe together?"

Ollie's face brightened. "Do you think we could?"

"Why not?"

"I don't know. I never thought I'd trust anyone enough to get through this with me. But with you..." He gave his head a little shake. "If we could figure it out, I'd take these feelings and run. As long as I can trust them, knowing magic is a part of it all."

Dante gave Ollie another squeeze. "You can trust your feelings. I promise magic isn't the driving force."

The brief flare of hope in Ollie's eyes faded. "How can it not be when fate said I'm the one for you? Like it's already done."

"Nothing is already done—"

"But we're already mated," Ollie said before Dante could finish.

"We are." Dante tried to give Ollie a reassuring smile. "But that's only because I chose to save you. Fate can't tell us what to do. We still get to shape our bond. We can let things progress however we want. I don't want you to think you have to do anything. This is still a choice. If you aren't ready, we can stay friends. Being mated doesn't change that."

"Okay, but I don't know how to stay friends after admitting I like you. It's not what I want." Ollie glanced away sheepishly. "Is it possible to date as if we aren't bonded?"

"Of course." Dante couldn't help smiling. "We'll get to know each other and see how our lives fit together just like any other couple. Being bonded doesn't negate any of that."

"You're sure?"

"Yes." If only Luc had never shown up on the beach, Ollie might not have been so afraid to follow his heart. He was already dealing with enough, given his past.

"Okay." Ollie shifted closer, his hand still in Dante's. "I want to try and figure this out. Despite everything, I want to date you."

"I want to figure this out too, Ollie. More than anything. But we have to be open."

Ollie's smile fell.

Dante rubbed his thumb over the back of Ollie's hand. "I don't mean sharing emotions through the bond. I mean communicating."

"Oh." Ollie's lips turned up nervously.

"Tell me if you're uncomfortable or worried. I never want being with me to change who you are. Bonded or not, you're still you. And if there's anything you need, ask."

"But I don't know what I need to feel comfortable. That's part of the problem." Ollie's face fell and he pulled his hand from Dante's.

He didn't need to have all the answers. Doing this together was the only way. "We'll work it out," Dante promised. "As long as we talk, we can address anything concerning you."

Ollie gave a tiny nod. "And you'll do the same? Tell me what you need?"

"Yes. That's why I'm here now. I couldn't hide how I felt and didn't want to."

"I don't want to hide things from you either." Ollie paused, frowning. "Actually, that's not true. I did before. But I feel so much better now. It's silly. I didn't think I could tell you I wanted a relationship unless I overcame my fears first. But you're saying you'll help me figure this out, and that's so relieving. Everything feels safe with you, Dante, and as long as it's real and not magic or fate dictating the outcome, then I want this."

Dante could understand Ollie being hung up on fate and wasn't sure if anything other than time would show him that destined didn't mean dictated.

"Everything between us is real, Ollie. Magic isn't making you feel safe or making you want me. The magic of our bond is created between us by being together. It's ours. It's not a force that influences us. That would be an illusion, which is entirely different."

Ollie took a breath. "Okay, good...because I don't want to keep resisting you."

Dante could have laughed with relief. "I thought I was the only one."

Ollie's dimples flashed. "Guess you're onto something with this whole being open thing. We'd never have figured this out otherwise."

Dante shrugged. "Maybe not, but it's hard to be vulnerable. It's normal to be scared to open up."

Ollie's smile seemed to grow. "It's easier with you. I promise I'll tell you when I'm freaking out."

Dante's chest swelled. "And I'll do the same."

Ollie shifted closer. "So, last night meant something to you?" A hint of teasing crept into his tone, even as his expression radiated nothing but tenderness.

Dante swallowed. "Last night meant a lot to me. I loved being close to you, feeling you, sharing pleasure with you. I haven't had sex in a long time, but it was more than that. I was so excited to connect with you."

Ollie's cheeks bloomed with color, his blush tinging the tops of his ears. He pulled his bottom lip between his teeth, but unlike earlier, there was no hint of nervousness.

"I liked being close to you too. I missed you today." Ollie's eyes flashed like he hadn't planned on saying that. He rushed on. "So, how long are we talking since you last got laid? Have you not been feeling it lately?"

Should Dante say he'd been waiting for Ollie? It might be too much too soon.

But he had to be open.

"It's been about a hundred years since I've had any desire for sex without connection, and without my mate, sex would only ever be physical."

"A hundred years?" Ollie ran a hand through his hair. "You've been waiting for me that long?"

"No." Dante cupped Ollie's cheeks. "I've been waiting for a lot longer. But back then, I believed I was close to finding you. I knew you'd be in this city. So I waited."

A low whine slipped from Ollie. "You can't say things like that."

Dante's stomach dropped. It was too much. "Does it make you uncomfortable?"

"No, it makes my heart explode. I want to kiss you so fucking much right now."

Dante pressed their foreheads together. "I'm feeling something similar."

Ollie rubbed his nose against Dante's. "I'm still scared of wanting this. Part of me wants to resist the bond—I don't trust it —but I also want to enjoy it."

Dante pulled back. "You can trust your feelings, Ollie."

Ollie dropped his head back, letting out a petulant sound. "You keep saying that, and I'm sorry I'm stuck on this. Maybe I should do what feels right, and then I'll believe it."

That was one way to go about it. "What feels right to you now?"

Ollie grabbed Dante by the shoulders and climbed onto his

lap, straddling him. "This. I want to be close to you. Don't let this consume me. Okay?"

"I won't," Dante promised.

Ollie clung to him. "Can I kiss you?"

Dante had never wanted anything more. His voice dropped to a low, raspy whine. "Yes. *Please?*"

Ollie leaned in, hazel eyes sparking as his face softened with affection. "Don't worry, I won't make you wait any longer."

18

———

## DANTE

Ollie's lips brushed Dante's, and Dante shivered. The touch was sweet and exactly what Dante craved. He snaked his hands around Ollie's hips and pulled him closer.

His mate tasted fresh, like sun shining on bare skin. Dante breathed in sandalwood and smells of home. He parted his lips, allowing Ollie to lick into his mouth. Dante kissed him like he could do it for the rest of his life.

Ollie groaned, lips working more urgently. Dante met every caress, his hunger growing. He'd never get enough of Ollie's scent, his taste, his weight on top of him.

Ollie's hands delved into Dante's hair, tugging Dante tighter against him. He rocked forward, hands tightening, as Dante pressed his tongue into Ollie's mouth.

A wave of lust crashed through the barrier Dante had erected between them, lighting up their bond as Ollie focused everything he had on Dante.

Dante pulled back. "You're projecting again. I can feel you."

"That's all right." Ollie chased Dante's lips, speaking between kisses. "I like sharing during sex. I want to feel you too."

"Oh...okay." Dante's heart thudded, chest aching. Ollie craved the same closeness he did. He let his guard down, throwing the doors wide on their connection.

He laid himself bare for Ollie. How could he not when his mate was willing to trust and take risks for him?

"You're so tender and sweet," Ollie gasped as Dante's emotions overwhelmed the bond. "You want me so much."

Dante's face flamed. "It's not only physical desire."

"I know," Ollie breathed. "It's so wild that I know that. It should be impossible to feel it, but it's not. Your affection runs so deep."

"I can't help my intensity." Dante kissed along Ollie's jaw. "Not when I'm an immortal who's found his mate. Not when you've told me you want me the way I want you."

Ollie whined. "You need me, don't you, Dante? You need to be close to me now that we're here?"

"Yes," Dante breathed. He burned for it, fire eating his insides. He'd take anything Ollie gave him, and the idea that Ollie would give him everything he'd ever wanted was almost too much.

"Fuck." Ollie's cock stiffened against Dante's already firm erection. "It's like I can feel you begging for me without words."

He was right. Every cell in his being yearned for Ollie.

"We need to get naked," Ollie panted. "I'm gonna take care of you, okay?"

Dante whined. "Please, Ollie."

Ollie pulled back, his face and neck flushed, dimples framing his lust-laden grin. "Love it when you beg."

Dante could tell. His words set Ollie alight. They made Ollie feel powerful and fed a need to be wanted that thrummed deep within him.

Experiencing Ollie's reactions firsthand was enough to make Dante beg all day, but that wasn't why he did it. His desire for Ollie to take care of him was engrained in his soul. Dante needed Ollie to see and accept every facet of him, not just the demon he showed the world.

And Ollie wanted to see it. The bond made it clear. Ollie was in awe that Dante chose to share himself and held the vulnerable pieces of Dante's heart tenderly.

They fit together perfectly.

"Ollie, please. Tell me what to do for you."

Ollie rose from Dante's lap and stood between his spread thighs. "Take off your pants and let all your demon features out."

Dante bit back another whine. "And will you strip for me?"

"Of course. I know you need it."

Dante let his horns emerge from his hair. He unbuttoned his pants, and Ollie stepped back so he could stand and pull them off, along with his underwear. It didn't take much to bare himself for his mate when he'd never bothered with a shirt.

He unfurled his tail from around his hips. Ollie's eyes tracked the movement. Dante's fire sparked, lust pooling inside him as he felt Ollie's longing to touch it pulse between them.

Ollie stepped up to Dante, pressing their chests together, Dante's bare cock poking Ollie's stomach. "Your tail is so sleek. The same pretty silver as your wings and horns."

Dante curled his tail around Ollie's hip. "Mm. Do you like it?" Dante could feel the answer through the bond but wanted to hear it from Ollie's lips.

"Yes," he crooned. "It's beautiful. You're beautiful, Dante. I want to touch you everywhere."

Dante released his wings, unable to hold them back a second longer.

"Your eyes," Ollie whispered, peering at Dante from beneath fluttering lashes.

Dante blinked. "Are they glowing?"

"Yeah." Ollie reached out and caressed Dante's cheek. "I didn't know they could. It's like dark fire. Were they glowing last night when you touched yourself?"

Pleasurable embarrassment wound through Dante. "I'd say so. I didn't look in the mirror to check."

Ollie spread his hands over Dante's chest. "Is it because you're turned on?"

He swallowed. "Partly. My inner fire is intertwined with my emotions."

"I like it. I like every new thing I learn about you."

Dante stood taller. He'd pleased his mate in a way he'd never expected. It was thrilling. Dante was addicted and needed more. "Will you take off your clothes so I can see you too?"

Ollie's lips twisted in a mischievous smile. "I don't know, will you beg for it?"

He'd do anything. "Please, Ollie. Please take off your clothes so I can see your naked body. Show me all of you and you can have anything you want from me."

"Oh fuck," Ollie gasped, fingers digging into Dante's pecs. "Yeah, Dante. Baby, I'll give you what you need. Don't worry."

He stepped back and pulled his shirt over his head. Excitement sizzled between them. Dante itched to touch Ollie, but Ollie was already moving on, undoing his pants and shoving them off his hips.

Ollie's cock tented his boxer briefs, drawing Dante's gaze. He traced the trail of light hair from Ollie's waistband to his belly button and caressed Ollie's soft stomach. He cupped Ollie's hips, his skin erupting in goosebumps beneath his fingertips.

"That tingles." Ollie shivered. "Your hands are so warm. And I'm already burning up."

"Mm." Dante mapped Ollie's hips and stomach, gaze traveling to Ollie's heated cheeks. His hand followed, tangling in

Ollie's blond curls. "I love the way you're flushed red for me. You're beautiful."

Ollie bit his lower lip. "So are you. Though, I said that already." He chuckled, soft and almost nervous.

Dante's hand trembled as he stroked Ollie's cheek. He could drown in Ollie's bright eyes. "I can't believe I'm touching you," he whispered.

Damnation, Ollie wasn't even completely naked. How much more would that undo him?

Ollie covered Dante's hand with his. "Is this okay? Not too fast?"

Dante tightened his tail around Ollie. He'd waited long enough. "No, it's perfect. As long as it's not too fast for you."

"Nah, like you said, it's perfect. I want to do what feels right." Ollie hooked his thumbs in his waistband and pulled his underwear down.

He straightened and his cock brushed Dante's thigh. They both groaned and surged closer, arms tangling around each other.

Ollie pulled Dante into a kiss. His confidence made Dante want to fall to his knees.

Dante tightened his arms and tail around Ollie. His heart swelled and an ocean of feeling opened inside him.

He sensed Ollie's desire to be even closer, tugging on Dante like a physical tether. Dante grabbed Ollie's ass and hoisted him up, their cocks brushing as Ollie wound his legs around Dante's hips.

"Dante," Ollie moaned. He grabbed hold of one of Dante's horns and rolled his hips, back arching.

Dante growled and Ollie swallowed the sound in a kiss. "Please, I need to feel you."

Not that he wasn't already, but he was greedy for more. He

would never get enough of Ollie, not now that he was finally getting to know him after thousands of years.

"On the bed," Ollie panted. "Get on top of me."

Dante tossed Ollie onto the mattress and followed him down, settling between his spread thighs. He flexed his wings to the edge of the bed.

Ollie stroked Dante's feathers, humming in satisfaction. "I love this. Love your wings and tail."

Dante rumbled at Ollie's praise, swelling with pride.

"Can I touch it?" Ollie's gaze fell to Dante's tail caressing his stomach.

"Yes." Dante shifted his wings so they wouldn't obstruct Ollie's access to his rear.

Ollie ran his fingers along Dante's tail, starting at the tip. Slowly, he trailed his fingers up, reaching around Dante's back to touch the base.

Dante hissed and rolled his hips, rubbing his erection against Ollie's.

"Oh, you really like that." Ollie's other hand tangled in Dante's hair. "Your eyes flashed."

"Touch me again, Ollie. I need you," Dante moaned.

Ollie exploded with affection, sending hot emotion down the bond. "I've got you." He grasped the base of Dante's tail and stroked.

Dante dropped forward, pressing his forehead against Ollie's. He rolled his hips, moving in time with Ollie's strokes. The silky hardness of Ollie's cock against his was as world-shattering as Ollie's hand on his tail.

"Oh fuck, Dante." Ollie writhed beneath him. "You feel so good. I feel so good. I..." he gasped.

Their pleasure danced together, turning the bond into a live wire about to blow.

"Please," Dante begged. "Need you."

Ollie's pleasure heightened as Dante begged, coiling around Dante. He panted, mouth hovering above Ollie's, too lust-drunk to get their lips to meet in a kiss.

Dante wanted this to go on forever, but there was no way he'd last. He'd imagined sex with his bonded mate countless times, but his musings never came close.

Dante needed to come. He needed Ollie to come. Hell, was there even a difference when they were entwined?

"Yeah, Dante, I need it too," Ollie groaned as he jacked Dante's trail harder.

Ollie's scent flared and Dante ground their hips together. His fangs ached, descending to their full length.

"Fuck yes." Ollie's gaze locked on Dante's fangs, pupils blown wide. He arched his neck, exposing his throat to Dante, his hand faltering on Dante's tail. "Bite me."

Dante growled, lowering his mouth to Ollie's neck. His fangs brushed Ollie's skin, and Ollie whimpered, his hand jerking Dante's tail with renewed urgency.

Licking Ollie's sweet skin, Dante murmured, "My mate," and Ollie convulsed below him, his whole body shuddering as desperate whimpers left his lips.

Ollie squeezed Dante's tail tight. Everything in Ollie longed for Dante's fangs to pierce his skin. It pulled on the bond, showing Dante how deep Ollie's need to be claimed went.

It ran as deep as Dante's.

He sank his fangs into Ollie's neck, and Ollie cried out, bucking beneath Dante, his hand falling from his tail to grab Dante's hip. Dante drank deeply, reveling in Ollie's essence. He groaned, accepting Ollie's pleasure and sending his back.

"Dante, Dante," Ollie panted, working his hips frantically, their cocks slick with precum, sliding against each other.

Dante took another deep pull, gulping Ollie down, his heart bursting. Ollie gripped him tight, going rigid as hot cum spilled between them, pleasure overwhelming the bond from all sides. Dante came too, so connected with Ollie he could hardly tell their orgasms apart.

Dante shivered, groaning, and withdrew his fangs from Ollie's neck. As the punctures closed, he licked the last drops of blood from his mate's skin.

Ollie's eyes were glassy, his lids at half-mast. He was fucked out and satisfied, a perfect reflection of how Dante felt.

Dante retracted his wings and lay back, pulling Ollie against him and wrapping his tail around Ollie's thigh.

Basking in the afterglow of their orgasms, it felt like everything had worked out. Dante had reached a moment he'd dreamed of for far too long.

But that wasn't quite true. The finality was premature. He'd promised Ollie they wouldn't rush. Building a relationship was much more involved than blowing each other's minds.

Dante closed the connection between them, silencing Ollie's satisfied, sleepy emotions. They weren't all the way there yet, but this in itself was exciting.

19

---

## OLLIE

For the first time since Ollie could remember, he dreaded Sunday brunch with Dex.

Hanging out the other night had already felt off. Ollie itched to tell his best friend everything, but there was no way to talk about Dante and all his conflicted feelings without mentioning magic.

The other thing throwing Ollie for a loop was that keeping things from Dex should have been a red flag. Secrecy had been a huge part of his abusive relationships, and he'd always told himself that if he found himself hiding things from Dex, he needed to stop and really look at the situation he was in.

Things with Dante weren't like that. Magic existing wasn't something you blurted out and had people believe, but Ollie was uncomfortable keeping secrets, and he worried the more he hung out with Dex, the more Dex would pick up on his discomfort and assume the worst.

"You all right?" Harper asked from the kitchen doorway.

Ollie shook himself and took a sip of his coffee. He hadn't heard Harper coming. "Yeah. I wish I could tell Dex about Dante. Like, really tell him."

Harper frowned. "We can tell him everything. Nothing is stopping us from showing Dex magic. Some humans know vampires and witches exist and are part of the magic community."

Ollie hesitated. He needed to be able to talk to Dex, but he also worried about rushing into this. Learning about magic would put a lot on Dex. It was kind of freaky to realize the world wasn't what you'd been led to believe and that mystical things were real.

"Wait." Ollie's stomach dropped as everything Dante had said when first explaining demons came rushing back. "There's an afterlife, right?"

"Yeah." Harper shrugged as if confirming continued consciousness after death was no big deal.

Ollie scrubbed a hand over his face. How had he not given this more thought? "Dex's parents died a few years ago. If we tell him magic exists, and so does an afterlife, that will be a huge emotional revelation for him."

"Oh." Harper paused while getting a mug from the cupboard. "He's going to have lots of questions."

"Fuck." Ollie couldn't trigger all of Dex's grief because he wanted to talk about the wild new relationship he was getting into. He had to give Dex this kind of life-changing information when it was best for Dex, not himself.

Ollie played it out in his mind. "I don't know anything about the afterlife except that reincarnation is a thing and witches can't be reborn. I can't talk to Dex until I know more. He'll want to know if he'll see his parents again."

"We could try not mentioning the Eternal Realm?" Harper suggested with a cringe.

"Yeah, no. I'll bet you the first thing Dex asks after he realizes we aren't full of shit is if Heaven exists. That, or if there's a way to use magic to undo what happened to his parents."

"Okay. So we need to table telling Dex for now."

Ollie took a long sip of coffee, unable to stop himself from asking, "Will Dex see his parents again?"

Harper shifted and folded his arms across his chest. "He's human, so he'll go to the Eternal Realm when he dies, and his parents will be there since they were human, but I don't really know what it's like there. Are human souls essentially ghosts with memories of their most recent lives? Do they have memories of all their lives? Or are they something less recognizable and more abstract, given reincarnation implies humans can change vastly while maintaining an essential essence?"

Harper paused, and Ollie mulled it over. These were way bigger questions than he'd planned to contend with that morning.

Harper continued, "Even though witch souls are different, they could give us an idea of what happens to humans. I've always been told Hell is full of witches walking around as recognizable versions of themselves, but that could be wrong. I haven't exactly talked to any witch who's been there. Only Ash, Dante, or Onyx could answer these kinds of questions."

"You haven't asked Ash?"

Harper helped himself to coffee. "No. To me, the afterlife has always been as real as anything else. It was the next stage. I've never viewed it as mystical, like humans do. I was always going to end up in the Realm of the Damned, and now that I won't, I'm not that curious." His eyes darted to Ollie. "Does that sound bad?"

Ollie laughed. "No, not at all. It's not like you'll ever have to go there now that you're mated."

"Exactly." Harper sipped his coffee and set it down. "Besides, it's not like I'm torn up about never seeing the witches I grew up with again. My father is in the Realm of the Damned, and that's reason enough to skip the afterlife."

Ollie's brows raised. "He died?"

Harper winced. "I haven't told you the whole story about escaping my coven. Ash killed him."

Ollie choked on his coffee, but as Harper told Ollie exactly why Ash killed his father, Ollie found himself wishing the Realm of the Damned actually was a fiery Hell designed to punish people like Arthur Nightingale.

They finished their coffee and left the apartment together. Before Harper turned toward the apothecary, he said, "Do you want to come by the shop after work this afternoon?"

Ollie had a lighter schedule that day and would finish early unless he got slammed with last-minute bookings. "Yeah. Why not?"

"Cool. I was thinking you could meet Nico. My boss."

"Um, sure. Why?"

"To get to know more people in the magic community. You've got me and the demons, obviously, but it might be nice to see the more typical side of things."

Ollie loved that a witch's apothecary was typical for Harper. "That's actually a great idea. If we're going to tell Dex eventually, it'd probably pay for me to have a better idea of what the magic community actually is."

"True." With a wave, Harper headed in the opposite direction.

Ollie went to work. Life was weird. Who'd have thought he'd be chatting about the afterlife over coffee and making plans to meet witches after spending a mind-blowing evening with his mate.

Last night reset Ollie's world. He wanted all the hope and safe feelings he had around Dante to be real and to be the one Dante turned to. To be equals. Partners.

He still wasn't sure how to accept his future as an immortal, but knowing death had never been the end he'd believed it to be

—that he'd have gone to an afterlife and been surrounded by magic like he'd never fathomed—put things in perspective.

Regardless of Dante and their bond, Ollie would always come up against things he hadn't seen coming and didn't understand. So would every other human. That didn't make the unknown magical side of the universe bad or suspicious.

Maybe that applied to the mating bond too.

20

———

DANTE

Dante and Ash knocked on Ren's door.

"I see Onyx slipped out of helping," Ash muttered.

"He said we didn't need him for this, and he's right."

"But he always says that."

Dante willed himself to be patient. Ash and Onyx's animosity was exhausting at the best of times. "I'd rather let him out of helping today and focus on getting him on board with going to the Realm of the Damned. Or are you okay to venture down there and hunt Luc without him?"

Ash rumbled something unintelligible.

"That's what I thought."

Mercifully, the door opened, revealing Ren. "Oh hey. I guess I should invite you up." She turned and walked up the stairs to her apartment without waiting for a reply.

"It's like she's not glad to see us."

"Is anyone other than Harper ever happy to see you, Ash?"

"You are. Or do I need to be offended?"

Dante chuckled.

Ren turned to face them as they entered the living room. "I haven't had any luck."

"Shocking." Ash crossed his arms. "What have you done to look for these supposed other demons?"

"Not *supposed*. Someone else has to be here. I didn't hurt your birds." She turned to Dante. "I've been leaving my magic around the city. Trying to tempt them into tracking me down. Either they're not in Shearwater Landing anymore, or they aren't interested in me."

"What if a witch or vampire picks up on your magic?" Ash asked. "We don't need the wider community knowing demons are all over the place."

"Yes, because me in the city equals demons everywhere." Ren rolled her eyes. "They'll think I'm a powerful witch. No one's jumping straight to demon. But if you're that worried, why'd you ask me to help? What else am I supposed to do, look them up in the super-secret directory of escaped demons and give them a call?"

"We appreciate you trying," Dante said before Ash could respond. "It's good to know they aren't interested in contacting you. My flock has been fine, so perhaps they've moved on." Or maybe the measures Dante had taken to protect his birds were the only difference.

"That's certainly possible." Ren glanced at the door like she hoped they might be ready to leave.

Dante didn't budge. "I actually wanted to ask you what's been going on in the Realm of the Damned?"

Ren's expression darkened. "What do you care?"

Ash growled and Dante shot him a glare.

Ren turned away and grabbed a bag of chips from the kitchen. "All I mean is, you've been gone, you aren't going back, what does it matter?"

"If demons are escaping when Lucifer travels between realms, it'd be good to know what's going on down there." Dante wasn't revealing his plan to go to the Realm of the Damned. He doubted Ren was working against him but wasn't trusting her completely.

She ate a chip, studying him closely. "So you'll take my word for it if I tell you and not continue doubting everything I say? Does that mean I've passed your trustworthiness test? Can I have your protection if it comes to getting dragged back?"

Dante briefly caught Ash's eye. "If you're going to help us, we'll help you, but there's no blanket protection. If you turn on us, all bets are off."

Ren ate another chip. "Obviously. I'm not naïve."

Dante and Ash waited for Ren to finish her snack. Was she choosing her words carefully or stalling, perhaps crafting a lie?

"Things have been rocky," she said at last. "Demons are getting restless."

Ash's expression darkened. "Like they weren't before."

Ren glared. "It's gotten worse. And the witches aren't super pleased either. Lucifer's been hiding and people are acting out the more he stays away."

If Luc was losing control of his masses, that must be why he'd finally come for his Hounds. Dragging the three of them back would have been a strong display of power. Maybe enough to get people to fall in line and kill any hope of escape.

Once his, Ash, and Onyx's escape had become widely known, Dante was sure hope of getting out of the Realm of the Damned started to brew. Maybe it took two hundred years for it to reach boiling.

Then why wasn't Luc trying harder to get them back? Why mess around stalking Ash and Harper, then attack Ollie?

Not that this changed anything. Dante was still going to hunt Luc down. The Devil wanted them back. Learning he might be getting desperate was important but not a surprise.

Ren pulled out a phone, apparently bored of their conversation.

Dante eyed the device. "You seem to have taken to technology well."

He'd hated adapting after nine hundred years away from Earth. How was Ren coping? At least two hundred years ago, there'd been no internet.

"Lucifer's done a better job keeping us up to date." Ren smiled at something on the phone. "Modern witch souls have helped make the Realm of the Damned more reflective of Earth. Though, I suspect a lot of this"—she shook the phone—"isn't run on magic up here. I couldn't tell you how this thing works. And the internet here has completely different sites. Can't figure out which I prefer."

Ash's brows shot up, seemingly as surprised as Dante.

Unrest in the Realm of the Damned had always been inevitable. Luc trying to make the place more like Earth was strange.

Why would it matter? None of the demons trapped in the Realm of the Damned would ever have to adjust to life in the modern world, and witch souls—like human souls—prioritized different things after death. It wasn't like they showed up in the afterlife demanding what they'd left behind.

Ren knowing about smartphones before she even escaped the Realm of the Damned didn't sit right.

21
———

OLLIE

THAT AFTERNOON, Ollie headed through the Banks toward The Herb Emporium.

As he neared the address Harper had given him, Ollie couldn't help thinking that the street felt very Harper. Ollie peered in a window of a boutique. This had to be where Harper bought his trippy quilted throw pillows. Ollie hadn't seen décor quite like that anywhere else.

He checked his phone. Dante hadn't texted all day.

Part of Ollie had expected to be bombarded with messages. He'd braced himself to have to force space between them, though it seemed that wasn't necessary.

It was true that, as a rule, Dante didn't reach out much, especially outside coordinating meeting online. Dante had also said being bonded didn't mean everything was decided. Their relationship could progress naturally and in a way that wouldn't overwhelm Ollie's life.

So why was Ollie doubting Dante's word and expecting Dante to blow up his phone? Dante keeping his promise wasn't a surprise.

It was as if, despite trusting Dante and knowing what kind

of man he was, Ollie still expected everyone to lie and break boundaries.

That wasn't true and he'd have to work on remembering that. Even if he and Dante were in this together, Ollie still had things to figure out for himself. He had to go slow and steady for this to work.

Could he really do that with the bond tying them together? It was hard to imagine, no matter how hard he tried. Magic and the bond might not be inherently suspicious, but he still couldn't be sure they weren't influencing his decisions.

Was it inevitable he and Dante would end up a couple? If it was—and they both knew it—how could they be anything other than committed from the get-go?

On the other hand, Dante had shown Ollie they could do this without rushing. He wasn't acting like they'd reached some inevitable conclusion.

It all made Ollie's head hurt.

He was glad when he reached The Herb Emporium. He needed to give his brain a break.

The apothecary definitely had a weird vibe, even from outside. Ollie wouldn't usually go into a shop with candles and dried herbs in the windows.

He entered and was assaulted by earthy smells.

"Hey," Harper called from behind the counter. He grinned. "Isn't this place great?"

"Like nothing I've ever seen."

Harper laughed. "I'll go get Nico." He disappeared behind a curtain.

Ollie kept his hands in his pockets, wary of touching anything. What if a spell got him? He didn't know anything about magic other than what Harper had shown him. The place was crowded with items and plants. Who knew what any of it did.

A man maybe ten years older than them appeared with Harper. "Hi, Ollie. I'm Nico."

Ollie gave him a nod. "Hey."

Nico was as tall as Harper and wore a worn apron over jeans and a dark T-shirt. He fixed a friendly stare on Ollie, his expression open, as he stepped out from behind the counter.

"Harper tells me you're new to the magic community. I know it can be hard finding out about all this, especially if your first look at magic is through someone hurting you, but there are a lot of great things about being a human in our world."

Did Nico know he'd been attacked? Ollie glanced at Harper.

"Nico helped me when I first escaped," Harper explained as if he thought that's what had Ollie confused. "Not that I wanted to let him. Maybe we could all get coffee or something. Nico knows a different side of witchery than I do. One that's less Satan-worshipy and more morally sound."

"Yeah, for sure." Ollie shifted on his feet. "I think hearing about other witches will help me adjust. Otherwise, all I'll know is what happened to you, Harper, and being bound by fate to a demon after Lucifer ripped my throat out."

Ollie's stomach turned as soon the words were out. Shit, he couldn't act like the attack was another event in his past. Not when phantom fingers scraped his neck. He swallowed. Why had he even said that?

Whatever. Nico already knew. There was no need to dance around the details. A positive witch story would do him good. Except Nico and Harper were staring at him with wide eyes.

What?

Nico turned toward Harper, who went from looking shocked to guilty. "How does Ollie know about demons?"

Ollie's brow furrowed. How could he not? They were all over the city. Right?

Harper's gaze darted between Nico and Ollie.

It was like Ollie had fucked up somehow. "What's going on?"

"Um." Harper ran a hand through his hair.

"Harper," Nico said, his voice much softer. "It's all right. You don't have to lie to me. I'm on your side. You're working on trust, remember? I said I'd look out for you if you ever needed it. But surely this has nothing to do with *demons*."

Why say that like it was the most ridiculous thing? It was how Dex should react, not a witch.

"It doesn't have to do with demons," Harper said quickly. "Ollie's confused. That's why I brought him here."

Nico raised a brow. Yeah, he didn't buy that at all, and Ollie couldn't blame him. Lying wasn't Harper's strongest skill.

"Okay." Harper held up his hands. He faced Ollie. "It looks like we may have forgotten to tell you that demons aren't common in the Human Realm, and demons living in Shearwater Landing is a secret most witches and vampires aren't privy to. Their identities and whereabouts have been hidden for hundreds of years."

Ollie's stomach churned. "So I blew Da—their big secret? Why did no one tell me?"

"Hey." Nico spread his arms in a calming gesture. "It's fine. Harper, you know any secret is safe with me."

"But this wasn't mine to reveal." Harper's voice dropped to a whine. "I have to call Ash."

"Your boyfriend?" Nico's brows flew upward. "*He's a demon?*"

Harper cringed. "Yeah."

Some of the color drained from Nico's face. "Oh great. I told a demon I'd be watching him. No big deal."

"What? Why?" Harper asked.

"In case he wasn't good to you."

Harper's face flushed. "You really don't have to worry about that."

"Maybe not." Nico turned a piercing gaze on Ollie. "But there's more than one demon? You said you were bound. What does that mean?"

"Uh…" Ollie was guessing Nico didn't know about mates. Was that another secret? He was keeping his mouth shut from now on.

Nico clasped Harper's shoulder. "Harper, if Ollie needs help, you can count on me. Even against demons. I have powerful friends. We can figure something out."

"No, no." Harper shook Nico off. "I've fucked this all up. Ollie is fine. I'm fine. The demons aren't a problem."

"Then tell me Ollie didn't casually mention Lucifer as if he'd actually run up against him."

Harper fisted his hands in his hair. "I need to make a call." He pulled out his phone and dialed. "I'm so sorry, Ollie. I figured Dante would have told you."

Ollie stood in heavy silence with Nico as Harper scurried to the other side of the shop and whispered into the phone. Why were demons such a secret?

"Do you want to tell me what happened?" Nico asked in a low voice.

Ollie shook his head. "Seems I've said too much already."

Nico studied him. "Fine, but I meant what I said. Regardless of what happens when Harper gets off the phone."

"Uh, thanks." Ollie was taken aback by Nico's willingness to help. "I'll keep it in mind." Not that he needed to.

Even with all his doubts about the bond, Ollie was safe with Dante. Harper was right. Dante and Ash weren't the problem.

Hopefully he hadn't caused a major headache for the demons.

Harper hung up and rejoined them by the counter. "They're coming."

Nico's face hardened. "Great. We better close up."

DANTE AND ASH arrived at the apothecary a short time later.

Harper rushed forward, his expression tense. "I'm sorry."

Ash cupped Harper's cheeks. "It's all right, sweet. Don't worry."

Harper melted into Ash and Ollie looked away. The big demon's tender tone gave the moment a private edge that felt intrusive to witness.

Dante hesitated near the door, giving Ollie a small smile.

Ollie's chest erupted with butterflies. Before he knew it, he'd navigated the crowded shop and pulled Dante into a hug. "I'm the one who messed up, not Harper. You should have told me your existence was a big secret."

They pulled away from each other, Dante's hand lingering on Ollie's lower back. "I should have, but I was worried about overwhelming you with information and honestly didn't think you'd ever be in a situation to reveal us."

That was fair, and Ollie didn't think Dante was mad. Maybe this wasn't as big a deal as Harper had made it seem.

Nico cleared his throat. "Not to be the fifth wheel, but we are in my shop." He leaned against the counter and crossed his arms.

Ash stepped forward. "Fine, witch." He made a show of considering Nico. "You've been good to Harper, and he likes you. I trust his judge of character, so you can't be that bad."

"Gee, thanks," Nico said so dryly Ollie's skin itched.

Ash continued as if Nico hadn't spoken. "Who we are is a

secret that doesn't leave this room, and if you don't keep quiet, you won't like the consequences. Don't betray Harper's trust."

"Ash," Harper hissed, elbowing him.

Nico seemed unfazed. His sharp eyes left Ash briefly to inspect Dante before returning. "I won't tell a soul that I've met demons. But I'd like to know what you're doing with Harper and Ollie. If there's any trickery going on here, I'll do everything I can to get them away from you."

Trickery? What did that mean? Nico was way off base.

Dante stepped forward. "There's no trickery. We're dealing with a precarious situation at the moment, so the fewer people who know who we are, the better."

Nico pursed his lips. "Precarious, how?"

"That doesn't concern you." Ash dismissed him with a flick of his hand. "We'll deal with the demon problems and the rest of the community can stay blissfully ignorant."

"Fine, don't explain. But I'd like to know what's happening with Harper and Ollie. Ollie said he was attacked by Lucifer."

Everyone looked at Ollie.

His heart thudded. "I didn't know it was a secret."

"It's all right." Dante's hand returned to Ollie's back and his tension leaked away. To Nico, he said, "I assume you know the legends about the fall to Earth and demons giving rise to witches. But the reason we fell didn't survive the passing of time. We fell to find our mates. Ollie and Harper are my and Ash's fated other halves. No one will look after them better than we will."

Ollie swayed like the floor had slipped out from under him. What did Dante mean they fell to Earth to find their mates? That was how it all started? It had been about mates all along. Dante said he'd waited for Ollie a long time, but had Dante been waiting for Ollie for *thousands* of years?

Dante was ancient, but Ollie hadn't known so much of his

life had been shaped by mates. Mating seemed like a part of his existence, not the driving force or the thing that kicked off bringing magic to Earth.

Ollie closed his eyes. How was he even supposed to process this?

"I've never heard of fated mates," Nico muttered, giving the impression the jury was still out on whether he believed Dante. "According to legend, you must be the demons—the Hounds—who escaped Hell. Was it to find your mates? Will you drag Harper and Ollie back to the Realm of the Damned with you?"

"Back to the Realm of the Damned?" Ash scoffed. "We aren't going back. Harper and Ollie will never see that cursed place. It's not like the demons there are living happily with their mates."

"Where are their mates?" Ollie asked.

Dante gently gripped the back of Ollie's neck, turning him so they were face-to-face. "No one but Ash and I have found our mates. Most demons considered the search hopeless a long time ago."

A chill ran down Ollie's spine. "Only you and Ash?"

"Yes, Ollie. And I'm so, so grateful."

Ollie's throat thickened at the intensity in Dante's dark, flame-flecked gaze. This went so far beyond the two of them.

"Why did Lucifer attack? Is he still here?" Nico cut in. "Is that the precarious situation you're dealing with?"

"So many questions." Ash sighed. "Look, Nico. We aren't sharing all our secrets because one got out. I'm sure history told you Lucifer was displeased by his Hounds' escape. But the details don't concern you."

"Maybe not." Nico's back straightened. "But it concerns Harper and Ollie. I'll always stick up for people on the short end of a power imbalance, even if legends are going to walk into my shop and throw their weight around. I'm on their side no matter what, and if what you say is true and you'll protect Harper and Ollie from Lucifer and any other trouble, then I'm on your side too. If you ever need me, count me in, even if you don't trust me enough to explain what's actually going on."

"*Hmm,*" Ash hummed as if he were impressed despite himself.

"Thank you," Dante said much more graciously.

"Yes, and we thank you to not send hunters after us," Ash added.

Nico raised a brow. "Treat your mates right, and I won't have to."

Ash gave Nico a chilling grin, orange fire flashing in his eyes. "Don't worry about us. We'll treat our mates like kings, and if you're on Harper and Ollie's side as much as you say, and you keep our secret, there won't be any issues from us. It's Onyx you'll have to worry about."

"Who's Onyx?"

"The third Hound. He won't forgive you if you give us away, and he doesn't have a mate to keep him in check."

"I won't talk." The first hint of fear filled Nico's face. "Now, can we be done with all the threats? You could actually get to know me instead of wasting time with intimidation. Then you might trust me."

"Why don't we all get coffee?" Harper seized the opportunity to change the subject. "We can put our fangs away and relax"—he threw an arm around Ash—"more friends is a good thing. I mean, if you trust my judgment, you know I'm right."

Ash grunted in affirmation, his gaze turning soft.

"That's an excellent idea," Dante agreed. "Isn't there a coffee shop you like nearby?"

"We aren't going to Seaside Coffee," Ollie blurted out. "Dex can't get involved in any of this." There was no need to screw up anything else today, and bringing demons to Dex's work felt like tempting fate.

Nico checked the time on a clock hanging behind the counter. "I don't know about you, but I could use something stronger than coffee. The Breeze should be open. It's not far."

"Is that the bar you told me about?" Harper turned excitedly to Ash. "Yeah, let's go. Come on." He threw Ollie a grin as he tugged on Ash's arm.

Ollie forced a return smile. "I think I could use a drink too."

It might not help him process being the impossibly rare exception to an ancient demon's near-failed, two-thousand-year-long search for his fated mate, but it sure as hell couldn't hurt.

22

———

## DANTE

Dante carried drinks to a booth at the back of the bar. The Breeze was dark and cool for a summer evening, the décor dated and seeming largely unchanged from thirty years ago, but the shady atmosphere was refreshing rather than unpleasant.

He passed a few people clustered around tables, some playing cards. Nico seemed familiar with the bar staff and a few of the customers, like he came here often.

"I've got two beers and a bourbon." Dante set the drinks on the table, passing the beers to Ollie and Harper.

Nico reached for the bourbon. "Thank you."

Dante gave him a nod as he scooted in next to Ollie.

"You don't want a drink?" his mate asked.

"I don't enjoy the taste of alcohol." Dante caught Ash's eye. "And it has no effect on the likes of us."

Ollie's brow furrowed. "But it still affects me, even though I'm immortal?"

Nico choked on his bourbon, and Harper patted his back. "Sorry, don't mind me." Nico cleared his throat, muttering *immortal.*

Ollie sipped his beer, squirming in his seat.

Dante wished they were alone so he could check in. He didn't need to feel Ollie through the bond to know he was getting overwhelmed.

"It's not immortality that makes demons immune to alcohol. It's the strong magic in our blood. The bond didn't turn you into a demon, even though it gave you some of my abilities. We aren't quite the same."

"Makes sense when you put it that way." Ollie had another swig of his drink.

"Yes, but you're telling me you two are immortal? Without becoming vampires?" Nico's eyes bounced between Harper beside him and Ollie across the table.

Ash pointed a menacing finger. "Hey, don't get any ideas."

"No ideas." Nico's mouth thinned, eyes raised like he was praying for patience. "I'm not after immortality. Just looking for clarity. I don't know anything about mates, remember?"

"Well, there's only two of us in this realm, so that makes sense," Harper said kindly. "And we definitely aren't vampires. No drinking blood here."

Ollie's cheeks flushed and he hastily had another sip of beer.

Dante slipped an arm around his shoulders and tugged him closer. Ollie seemed to have a thing for biting, vampire or not. It was adorable.

Ollie pressed against Dante's side, closing the last bit of distance between them. Dante barely resisted purring out loud. He loved being able to touch Ollie and indulge his urges to physically comfort his mate.

Ash eyed them from across the table, a wide grin appearing. Dante hadn't mentioned the shift in his and Ollie's relationship, though Ash and Harper's convenient disappearance from the apartment last night likely meant Ash overheard enough to put it together.

"Do you know many vampires?" Harper asked Nico. "I can't say I've met a whole lot."

"A few." Nico shrugged, spinning his glass in circles on the table. "I'm close with one of the city's older vampire covens. And a couple of my friends are in a hybrid coven."

"Hybrid?" Harper leaned forward. "Witches and vampires don't always form separate covens? I mean, my experience of witches has been pretty limited to certain factions, but still. I've never heard that."

"You're not totally off base. Hybrid covens are rare," Nico agreed.

Eventually, the conversation strayed away from magic, most of the back and forth staying between Harper and Nico, with the occasional comment from Ash. Ollie was uncharacteristically quiet. He didn't even speak up when Nico started talking about the arcade that used to be next door and how he got into gaming because of it.

"Come up to the bar with me to get another round?" Dante muttered in Ollie's ear.

He nodded and followed Dante out of the booth, bringing the remainder of his drink.

Dante leaned against the bar in the corner farthest from the register and the bartender, hovering near a few seated customers. "Would you like to get out of here?"

Ollie perched on a stool. "No. It feels mean to abandon Nico with Ash. I know he's got Harper, but still."

Dante chuckled. "Ash likes Nico plenty. He told me on the way over. They'll be fine."

"If you say so." Ollie ran a hand through his hair, attention traveling from Nico to Dante. "I'm really sorry I blew it with the secret thing."

"Don't be. It was my fault, and I doubt there's anything to worry about with Nico." If anyone had to find out, he seemed like the safest option. Ash wouldn't trust him for no reason, and neither would Harper.

Ollie didn't seem in a hurry to agree. Dante laid a hand on his shoulder. "Is not knowing demons were a secret what's bothering you?"

"A bit. I wish I hadn't been blindsided, but I get why you didn't mention it. You can't tell me everything at once."

"I'll still keep you better informed. It's been hard to know what to share and when. I never wanted any of this introduced to you this way."

"I know." Ollie squeezed the hand covering his shoulder.

"There's something else."

Ollie's lips twitched in a smile. "You're getting good at reading me."

Warmth radiated from Dante's core. "It comes with getting to know you."

Ollie's dimples flashed, then disappeared. "I'm having trouble getting my head around everything. Hearing you talk about mates in The Herb Emporium freaked me out. You came here to find your mate—to find me—and then waited *forever*. It's so much bigger than I realized."

"I know, and I let it seem less daunting for a reason. The weight attached to finding my mate has always been there. I'm used to it. I didn't want a long history to put pressure on you. Finding you is a miracle, not only for me but for other demons too. It means our search isn't a lost cause. But finding you is also the most natural thing. The significance doesn't have to weigh us down."

Ollie hunched over the bar, leaning on his elbows, and turned to look at Dante from beneath his lashes. He was silent for a long moment. "I'm glad you didn't tell me everything right away. I'd have run scared. Maybe it seems like I did anyway, but it would have been worse."

"I don't think you ran scared at all."

"But I didn't exactly get on board either."

"I never expected you to. Not with the way everything was thrust on you." Dante paused. Ollie was taking this final revelation better than he'd expected. "Does hearing all this now scare you?"

"No, not so much." Ollie pushed off the bar, twisting around so he faced Dante fully. "I think I get what you're saying." He laughed, shaking his head.

Dante shifted closer. "What do you mean?"

"I finally get it." Ollie's brow wrinkled. "You're saying something having a larger impact on the magic world doesn't have to impact us. Me—your mate—existing is this big thing, but *to me*, existing isn't a big deal at all. It's just my life. Both realities are true. And me being a big deal to a bunch of demons doesn't change who I am."

"Exactly, Ollie. Finding you is big, and we will have something special between us, but it's also you and me. Doing ordinary things, unaffected by the weight of it all."

Ollie broke into a grin. "I like that. It's big and small. Even if it's guaranteed, it's not all predetermined. Even if we know it'll work out, we don't know how. I think I can live with that. I'd choose to sit here with you even if we weren't bonded. I know I would. And I'm still choosing even though we are."

Dante squeezed Ollie's shoulder. "Yes, more than one thing can be true at once without canceling the other out. We can be fated and choose this at the same time."

"Big and small," Ollie repeated, a tiny smile twitching his lips.

Dante leaned down and kissed the top of his head. "You got it, darling. We're whatever we want to be."

Ollie raised his drink, cheeks flushed. "Cheers to that."

Dante's demon fire flared. He signaled the bartender and ordered a Coke and another beer for Ollie. "Cheers."

They clinked glasses.

"So, can this be our first date?" Ollie asked.

"Certainly." Dante ran a hand through his hair. "Drinks is a common first date, or so I've heard." He'd read a bunch of dating advice online before the art show. He could finally put it to use.

Ollie's expression turned sheepish. "I was so worried you thought dinner at my place with Harper and Ash was a double date."

Dante set his soda down. "Worried? Why?"

Ollie picked at his beer bottle. "No relationship was worth the risk. Even good people couldn't protect me from my bad habits, like wanting to please others over staying true to myself. And since I was so against anything, it freaked me out that you might have thought it was a date when I hadn't agreed to that."

"I'd wondered if something happened that night." Dante's face heated. "I confess, I'd hoped to ask you out when I saw you again."

"But then you were so accepting of being friends," Ollie said like he didn't understand.

"It's what you wanted, and that was more important than my preconceived notions of what mating bonds looked like. I had to open my mind a little, but I trusted that whatever we'd have would be right for us. Friends or lovers, or anything else we dreamed up."

"You trusted fate. Huh." Ollie seemed to mull this over like it meant a lot to him.

"I suppose I did."

Dante had trusted fate, hadn't he? Even after all this time. Maybe that's why he never gave up. He'd never have put it that way if asked, but it fit. And it seemed Ollie was starting to trust fate too.

"Oh, I almost forgot." Dante flagged the bartender down. "Do you have cocktail cherries?"

She smiled indulgently. "We sure do."

"Can I have...?" He considered the size of his drink. "Eight cherries, please?"

The woman bit her lip. "Sure, love. Be right back."

Dante beamed at Ollie, who giggled. "What?"

"That's a lot of cherries."

"This soda isn't exactly small." Dante lifted his pint glass.

"No, it's fine. Good to know how many cherries you need for when I take you out next time."

Dante grinned.

The bartender returned, dropping off a small bowl of cherries.

"See." Dante pointed. "Why have the perfect bowl if it's too many cherries?"

"I'm pretty sure that's meant for nuts or pretzels." Ollie popped a cherry in his mouth. "Yum. This might actually be the superior snack option."

Dante leaned in and kissed the sweetness from his lips. "Then it's a good thing I ordered enough to share with my mate."

## 23

## OLLIE

Ollie glanced over his shoulder and caught Harper's eye as he and Ash stood from the booth. Harper pointed to the door, and Ollie threw him a wave.

"I think everyone is leaving."

Dante followed his gaze. "Would you like to head home with Harper?"

Ollie placed a hand on Dante's chest. "I was actually hoping you'd take me home."

"Of course I'll walk you home."

"No, take me home. To your place."

Dante's eyes widened. "Oh."

"You're getting lucky on this date. You played all your cards right."

A new perspective on fate and their bond changed everything. It all lined up, and Ollie needed to give in to the bubbly feeling coursing through him.

This thing with Dante was going to work out. It wasn't a trap. Fate didn't rob him of choice. It was a guarantee. A safety net. Ollie could take all the risks he'd been afraid of, and the bond would protect him, give him the security to make the right choices. He'd figure out how to be with Dante without losing himself because, in the end, they were meant to be.

Maybe it wouldn't always be smooth sailing, but what was?

When Ollie cleared his mind of worries about magic, he saw how right Dante was for him. Dante was dependable and consistent. When he said something, he followed through. His values and actions aligned. There was no hidden agenda or two-faced switch coming. He was the kind of person it was safe to take risks with.

Ollie could trust himself with Dante, something he hadn't done with anyone since that first toxic relationship. He'd been too afraid to give himself credit, but when he stopped doubting himself, he could admit he already knew how to do the right things.

He'd been doing them already. Taking space, being intentional, not aiming to please at the expense of himself, taking things slow. It wasn't only that the bond guaranteed a good outcome. It reminded Ollie he could do this. The bond was his. It came from him rather than influenced him. He could do this.

"I played my cards right?" Dante's brow wrinkled and his lips curved in a crooked smile. "Enough for you to brave flying?"

"Let's say my desire to explore that giant bed of yours is enough to brave flying."

With what sounded like a growl, Dante took Ollie's hand and pulled him toward the door. They left without looking back and wandered the streets until they found a deserted back lot.

"Are you sure you don't mind flying?" Dante asked after casting his invisibility illusion. "I was going to create a harness to strap you to me so you'd feel more secure if we did this again. But I haven't made it yet."

Ollie covered his mouth. "A harness? That's so kinky of you, Dante."

His cheeks darkened. "Is it?"

"You're adorable." Ollie glanced at the sky. "I appreciate you trying to help me with my fear of heights, but if you don't do any unnecessary swooping, I think it'll be okay. I'm not quite as scared as I let you believe."

Dante pulled off his shirt and released his wings, gray feathers shimmering in the streetlight. "Why didn't you want me flying you before if you aren't scared of heights?"

"After everything that happened, I needed to do things myself and not rely on you. Not do something just because you told me to. Not let everything change if I didn't want it to." Ollie's gut twisted. "I was being stubborn, and seeing everything through the lens of having my boundaries broken."

Understanding crossed Dante's face. "You were taking back control."

It sounded silly now. But at the time, it had felt hugely important. "Getting myself home was all I could do that day. And I am a little scared of heights, so it wasn't a total lie."

Dante opened his arms. "Then I won't fly higher than I need to."

Ollie stepped into his mate's embrace. "This time, I will wrap around you like a koala."

Dante hummed and picked him up, holding on tight. Ollie wound his arms and legs around Dante, burying his fingers in Dante's hair.

Dante squeezed Ollie's ass, and he yelped, dissolving into giggles.

"I can distract you along the way," Dante murmured in his ear.

Ollie sobered. "That sounds like a recipe for dropping me."

"I'd never." Dante shimmied his hips, jostling Ollie's legs as he readjusted.

Something tickled Ollie's lower back.

"What's that?"

"My tail." Dante smiled slyly as his tail crept under Ollie's shirt, sliding over his stomach.

Ollie leaned in and bit lightly at Dante's earlobe. "Okay, you have a deal. Distract me."

A low rumble reverberated from Dante's chest, the vibrations thrumming through Ollie. Dante's tail snaked upward and flicked one of Ollie's nipples. Ollie gasped, a jolt of pleasure lighting him up, and Dante launched into the air.

Ollie snapped his eyes shut. "Hey, that was sneaky. You didn't warn—*oh*." He shivered as Dante's tail flicked back and forth, arms holding Ollie so tight he'd never know they were off the ground.

Okay. The wind rushing past was a giveaway. But he wouldn't look. He wanted to enjoy this.

Ollie pressed his lips to Dante's neck, breathing in his peppermint scent as it mixed with the night air, the two melding like Dante belonged out here in the dark sky.

He sucked on Dante's neck, scraping his teeth over the spot. Fuck, he wanted to mark Dante. He tasted so good. So fresh. If Ollie had fangs, he'd latch on.

Dante squeezed his rear. "You're getting hard."

"Mm," Ollie hummed. His cock strained against his jeans and Dante's stomach. "We better be home soon. I've got ideas."

Dante's wingbeats sped up and they swooped. Ollie's stomach dropped, and he yelped as he clung on.

"We're here," Dante murmured. "One last drop."

They landed, and Ollie's eyes flew open. He inspected Dante's neck. "Aww. There's no hickey."

Dante laughed, carrying Ollie toward the open sliding doors. "You sound disappointed."

"I am. It's your demon healing, isn't it?"

"Afraid so. You'd be the same if I tried to mark you now that we're bonded."

Ollie squirmed against Dante as they entered the house. He didn't really mind. He wasn't that into wearing or giving marks. "What about biting?"

In the living room, Dante tumbled Ollie onto the couch, flicking his wrist to turn on the surrounding floor lamps. His fangs descend partially. "What about it?"

Ollie swallowed. He ached for Dante's fangs to pierce his skin, but that wasn't all he wanted. "Can I bite you too?"

Dante groaned, bracing his arms on the back of the couch on either side of Ollie's head. "You most definitely can."

A wall of desperate need hit Ollie in the chest. For once, he wasn't the one breaking through the barrier between them.

"I felt that," he teased, and Dante's eyes flashed with black fire, his face and neck flushing. "Let me in. I want to see how undone you are before we've even started."

Dante's eyes glowed and he dropped the barrier, revealing a need so strong it was like a magnet pulling Ollie toward his mate. Dante's soul begged for him. If anything, he was needier than last night. The connection felt brighter too. There was no other way to describe it. Bright and happy, echoing Ollie's own happiness.

For the first time, Ollie understood what Dante meant about the magic being created between them. Now that he was no longer resigned to this but excited about what the bond could give him, he could feel something solidifying and building on itself.

Dante's fire burned, and Ollie had never been warmer. How had he ever doubted being the source of his feelings? This wasn't a trick or outside influence. Nothing had felt as personal —as him—as responding to Dante's seemingly bottomless need.

Dante pressed his forehead against Ollie's, panting slightly.

Ollie cupped the side of Dante's neck. "Me biting you sounds that good?"

He whined. "Yes, I want you to own every part of me. Show me that I'm yours."

Bringing their lips together, Ollie pulled Dante onto the couch. He came willingly, letting Ollie push him around as if he were the inhumanly strong one.

Dante spread his wings and sank back into the cushions.

Ollie straddled his lap, running his hands along Dante's feathers. "This is my favorite spot."

"Mine too." Dante cupped his hips and dragged him closer.

It was a good thing Dante hadn't put his shirt back on. Ollie caressed him, leaning down to nip at Dante's nipples. Dante hissed, rolling his hips. Body begging for more.

Ollie made his way to Dante's neck, and Dante automatically turned his head to the side, baring his throat for Ollie. Ollie's breath caught. This was his demon. He was claiming Dante, almost more than he had when they'd performed the mating ritual.

Then, Ollie hadn't understood. He'd known it was right, but there was too much pain. Too much he had the wrong way around. Now he knew. Dante was the one he'd face all his fears for. The one he could build a life with.

He'd figure it all out with his sweet demon. He chose this. How could he not? The potential of a fated mate was intoxicating.

Ollie licked a stripe up Dante's throat. "Is it going to hurt since I don't have fangs?"

Dante shook his head. "Not when I want it like this." He trembled slightly, and Ollie felt a tingle of anticipation shoot down the bond. "Have me."

Ollie growled, Dante's need sparking a raging hunger in him. He bit into the arch of Dante's neck, breaking the skin. Dante bucked his hips, crying out as warm, sweet peppermint flooded Ollie's mouth.

Dante whimpered, holding Ollie tight as he drank. Pleasure filled Ollie from within, down his spine and deep in his core. It flowed from Dante to him and back again.

Ollie met each of Dante's frantic thrusts. Fucking hell, they should have taken their clothes off.

Dante's heart thundered. Ollie felt it as he drank. How wild was that? Its rhythm matched their pleasure until Dante's thrusts faltered.

"Ollie. Fuck. *Please.* Yes. Take me. Fuck me."

Ollie's eyes rolled back. He almost came. So did Dante. But Ollie pulled away, licking the wound on Dante's neck until it disappeared. "Is that what you need, baby? My cock in you? Gotta claim you that way too?"

"Yes, you have to. Fuck, I can feel how much you like the idea."

Ollie didn't like it. He loved it. "I should have known you'd want me filling you as much as I need you inside me. You're my mate. Let me guess, you're vers too?"

Dante tangled a hand in Ollie's hair. "Yeah, but I need you this way first." Something vulnerable cut through all their pleasure, and Ollie held it like the precious piece of his mate that it was.

"Of course you do." Ollie pressed his lips to Dante's ear. "Don't worry, I'm not going anywhere. You've got me now, and I'm here for you. I'll take care of you."

His words set Dante alight. Ollie felt his demon fire flare deep within and everywhere they touched.

Ollie had never been more confident than he was with Dante. His mate brought it out in him, gave Ollie what he needed to let himself loose and be more him than he'd been with anyone.

"Have you got lube?" Ollie shifted off Dante, standing on unsteady legs. He hadn't topped in a while, and suddenly, he couldn't wait any longer. Why hadn't he thought to bring lube with him?

"I'll get it." Dante flicked his fingers, and a moment later, a bottle came zipping into the room and landed on the couch.

Ollie laughed. He pulled off his shirt. "You want it that bad, huh? Can't even get to the bedroom."

Dante swallowed, sitting patiently, hands resting on his thighs, feathers and tail completely still. "No, I can't wait. I... Please, Ollie."

He wasn't nervous. Ollie felt nothing like that coming from him, but there was something delicate there.

"Anything you want, baby. Sorry, I was teasing. I wouldn't make it to the bedroom either. Not when you're so sweet. So perfect for me. I'd never deny you." Ollie kneeled before his mate, and that felt delicate too.

He belonged. He had so much to offer Dante it felt like it would come spilling out of him. Just as he was, Ollie was everything Dante had ever wanted.

Ollie took Dante in. He could get lost in the black of his eyes, the dark, enigmatic glow. Ollie reached for Dante's waistband, his jeans already riding low on his hips. Unfastening them, he pulled them down along with Dante's briefs.

Dante lifted his hips, his tail resting over Ollie's shoulder. Ollie wrapped a hand around Dante's thick shaft, stroking as he traced the line of dark hair from Dante's belly button to his groin.

"*Ollie,*" Dante whined, muscles quivering.

"I'm right here." Ollie leaned in and took Dante's cock into his mouth, musk and peppermint hitting him hard.

Dante rumbled in appreciation. The bond went lax, almost like it was sated.

Ollie sucked until precum coated his tongue. He licked up

and down, teasing around Dante's cockhead as he tugged his balls. He could do this all night.

"You feel too good." Dante ran his hands through Ollie's hair, his tail cupping the back of Ollie's neck. "Please, I need more, Ollie. *More*, but I don't want to come until you fuck me."

The bond thrummed. Ollie's heart skipped and he ached. Dante called to him, desperate and sweet and so fucking open.

Pulling off Dante's cock, Ollie rocked back and admired his mate. "Get down here, and I'll give you what you need."

Dante ran a hand over one of his horns. He got up on slightly shaky legs and glanced around the living room. With another flick of his wrist, the coffee table shot to the side, bumping against the far wall.

He kicked off his shoes and stepped out of his jeans before getting on all fours, wings spread out on either side of him, beautiful gray feathers shimmering bright like diamonds. Dante's tail flicked as he arched his back, legs spread. He looked over his shoulder and locked his glowing gaze on Ollie, panting like he already couldn't take it, his fangs fully descended.

"Fuck. Look at you." Ollie bit his lip. No one had ever laid out for him like this. Ollie went dizzy with—he wasn't even sure —power, lust, love? "You're perfect."

"*Uh-h,*" Dante moaned and dropped his head between his shoulders.

A heaviness settled over the bond, and Ollie's stomach fluttered. He quickly got rid of his clothes and shoes and kneeled behind Dante, palms brushing Dante's firm ass. Dante shuddered, groaning, and Ollie's breath caught. So much emotion flowed from Dante into him that he couldn't breathe, couldn't think.

"Baby, I've got you," he soothed, caressing Dante's rear, his lower back, his tail. The ocean of feeling calmed, lapping at the bond. "You're so hot like this, but I want you on your back so I can see you. Will that work with your wings?"

Dante glanced over his shoulder. "I can put them away."

"You better not."

Dante grinned. He folded his wings in tight and got to his knees, turning around. He lay back, spreading his wings out as he had before, and let his thighs fall wide, giving Ollie a glimpse of his tight hole.

"I feel so vulnerable on my back," Dante said, almost breathless. "I wouldn't do this for anyone else. Having my wings trapped under me sets my demon instincts on edge. Or it would if you weren't with me. But this feels right."

Dante trusted him so much. Ollie made him feel safe. Ollie had been so caught up in his own safety that he'd forgotten it went both ways. It jolted him. He and Dante were in this equally, in a way he'd never considered.

Ollie leaned over Dante, planting his palms on the floor on either side of Dante's head. "Is this how you want me this first time? On your back and vulnerable?" Dante nodded, fangs poking out between his plush lips. Ollie leaned down and kissed him. "Good."

Dante wrapped his arms around Ollie, and Ollie deepened the kiss, licking at Dante's fangs and rolling his hips, rubbing their cocks together.

"You've found your mate, Dante. After so long, you can finally relax. I'm here now. I've got you."

Dante went limp, pliant beneath Ollie, happy relief washing over them both. Ollie might not be able to get his head around how long Dante had waited—it was still overwhelming—but being here with Dante was big. That Ollie could understand. And that huge significance was okay.

Ollie wanted all of Dante's overwhelming emotions. His

demon wasn't alone anymore. Ollie was ready to be here for him.

This was a partnership, not Ollie losing his identity in something he couldn't fathom. It was him taking this big thing and fitting it between them. Making it theirs.

Ollie grabbed two pillows, one for Dante's hips and the other for his head. "That's better." He adjusted the cushion beneath Dante's head, caressing his horns and hair, chills traveling down his spine as Dante leaned into his touch. "My sweet mate."

"I could say the same," Dante murmured, eyelids half-closed.

Ollie kissed Dante deeply, trailing his mouth down his body, swirling his tongue around his dark nipples, and following his happy trail to the dark curls at his groin. Ollie settled between Dante's legs, reached for the lube, and coated his fingers. Dante sighed, spreading wide as Ollie circled his rim, touching him like he was the most delicate thing in the world.

This time wasn't about rough, frantic fun. It was about pampering his precious demon. Giving him all the softness he deserved.

Dante's tail wrapped around Ollie's waist. He fucking loved that. It was so sleek and pretty, and something about being cradled with it melted Ollie's heart.

He pressed a slick finger into Dante, meeting little resistance. "There you go. So good opening up for me."

Dante moaned, thrusting into Ollie's touch.

Ollie massaged him, going deeper and adding another finger when Dante was ready. The bond seemed to coil, tightening and sparking every time Ollie brushed that sweet spot inside his mate. He stretched Dante, and the way their pleasure was shared, Ollie wouldn't last long. Fuck, he wasn't even touching himself, and he was on edge.

"Please, Ollie. I'm ready." Dante gripped the back of Ollie's neck. "I need you now."

"Yeah, fuck, Dante, I need you too." Ollie slicked his cock and lined himself up, hitching one of Dante's legs back beneath the knee. "Gonna make you mine, mate."

"Mate," Dante echoed, dropping his head to the pillow, horns digging into the carpet as Ollie pushed in.

Dante strangled his cock. Fucking hell, he felt good. So hot inside. Ollie gazed transfixed as Dante stretched around him. He took hold of Dante's cock and stroked, thumbing his precum-slick slit. *Ugh.* It was almost too good.

"Yes, Ollie. Please don't stop." Dante groaned, arching into it and taking Ollie deeper.

Ollie's focus shifted to Dante's flushed face. His eyes were pools of shimmering darkness, almost no whites at all. Dante bit down on his lip, and a bead of red appeared beneath his fang.

"Fuck, Dante." Ollie swiped the blood with his finger and licked it clean, the sweet drop mixing with the precum coating his hand.

Ollie wanted to stay like this for hours, caught between as their pleasure built. But he was making his mate wait, and he hadn't intended to. Ollie thrust, working his way in with shallow rocking motions of his hips.

Moans spilled from Dante's lips. "Fuck me, Ollie," he pleaded, cupping Ollie's ass as he sunk all the way in, and his tail squeezed Ollie's waist.

Ollie groaned and buried his face in Dante's neck. The scent of peppermint flared, and Ollie kissed every bit of skin he could reach, rolling his hips. "Like that, baby?"

"Yes," Dante nearly sobbed, urging Ollie on with his hands, tail coiling impossibly tighter.

Ollie hooked Dante's knees over his elbows and bent his demon in half. He rolled his hips in a steady sensual motion that had his cock dragging slowly in and out. The bond burned every time Ollie hit Dante's prostate, and Dante dissolved into a begging mess, clutching Ollie's shoulders, his wings twitching helplessly as he fell apart.

"Ollie, *uh*, yes, Ollie." Dante's glowing eyes didn't leave Ollie's face. He shuddered and came between them, setting off Ollie's orgasm.

Ollie collapsed on Dante's chest, panting and clutching his mate. "Filled you up. Now you're mine. Fuck, I like taking care of you."

Dante purred loudly, rubbing Ollie's back in slow circles, his tail still secured around Ollie's waist. "I like you taking care of me too. That was worth waiting millennia for. Thank you."

Ollie bit back a grin. It was a ridiculous statement. No way he was good enough at fucking to be worth that kind of wait. It was too big a deal to make out of it, but it also wasn't. Being worth the wait wasn't about orgasms.

"No need to thank me, silly. It wasn't a favor." Ollie's grin broke through, and Dante chuckled. "I won't make you wait that long again, promise."

"No, I don't think either of us would survive that." Dante ran his fingers through Ollie's sweat-damp hair and the emotional connection between them dimmed.

"Wait." Ollie lifted his head. "Don't go yet. I want to keep you close a little longer."

The bond opened back up, radiating an electrifying energy that gave Ollie whole body tingles.

Dante brushed Ollie's cheek with his thumb. "You got it. Anything for you, mate."

Ollie snuggled back down. He liked being mated. Who'd have thought? It wasn't a burden at all.

Dante was a gift.

24

DANTE

Eventually, Dante and Ollie made it to the bedroom, and after cleaning up in the shower, Dante brought Ollie to bed.

Ollie dove onto the large mattress and bellyflopped, his perky ass jiggling.

Dante's tail flicked. "You said you wanted to explore, but wow, you're really going for it."

Ollie giggled and rolled over, showing Dante everything he had, and damn if it wasn't the most beautiful sight. "If I didn't know better, I'd say you'd been having threesomes and more in this bed. It has to sleep at least four."

Dante snorted. "Sometimes, I lie on my stomach with my wings draped over the sides. I need the extra support."

Ollie spread his arms. "I like imagining you sleeping with your wings out. I could tuck right under one. Keep me nice and warm."

The image of Ollie snuggled in, safe and happy where nothing could harm him or tear them apart, had Dante by the throat.

Ollie crawled up the bed and settled in, pulling the covers

up to his nose. "I'll admit, this is pretty nice. But the living room floor is cutting some fierce competition."

Dante's face flamed. "I hadn't imagined using the space so, uh, creatively when I designed the room, but I'm glad I left enough space for my wingspan."

"Mm." Ollie wiggled deeper into the covers. "It was meant to be."

Dante climbed in and pulled Ollie against him.

Meant to be. It sure was, and his mate was saying it like it was a good thing, not something to fear.

Ollie settled his head against Dante's chest, letting out a soft moan, and even with their emotional connection closed off, Dante knew his mate was happy.

There was no rush to share emotions all the time, even though it would be immensely special. Doing it like this gave Dante time to appreciate connecting in other ways. How he and Ollie would have if they hadn't been forced into this.

"I have to be home early," Ollie said with a yawn. "Dex is coming over for breakfast. We get together most Sundays."

"No problem. We can fly, or I can pop you down the hill to catch a ride."

"Maybe fly? Then I can sleep in longer. It's faster than driving across the city."

Dante stroked Ollie's hair. "Flying it is."

"What are you up to tomorrow?"

Dante's hand stilled. "I've been having some problems with the shearwaters. We think there's a rogue demon in the city who escaped the Realm of the Damned when Luc came here last month. Some of my birds died, and I've been keeping them close since, but we need to find whoever's lurking around, so I'm going to set a trap."

Ollie propped himself up on Dante's chest. "Is it dangerous? For you or the birds?"

Dante would never get sick of Ollie caring about his birds. "Potentially, but I have Ash and Onyx. I'm going to let some of my birds break away from the main flock into a smaller group and stick with them, hidden by an illusion, until the demon comes sniffing around."

The birds would be safe with Dante there. Otherwise he wouldn't use them as bait.

Ollie's face creased with concern. "What if no one comes?"

"That could mean the demon left the city. But I don't think that's likely. Why make a move against me and then flee? I have a feeling they're still here. They can't have gotten what they were after. When they take the bait, Ash, Onyx, and I will capture them."

Ollie's brow furrowed. "To do what? Keep them prisoner?"

Dante needed answers and couldn't let an attack go unpunished, but he disliked the idea of having to imprison anyone. Other than Luc. "That's not our aim. We have to find out if the demon is working with Luc, and if not, why they targeted my flock. What we do depends on the answer."

Ollie caressed one of Dante's horns, serious lines around his eyes. "Be careful."

"I will," Dante promised.

Ollie had questions about the other demons being trapped in the Realm of the Damned, so Dante explained, filling in the gaps he'd left when first introducing Ollie to demonkind's long history.

As he finished the tale, a nagging thought returned. "There's another demon here, named Ren. She escaped when Luc first returned, like the demon we're trying to track down. I don't think she means any harm, but something she said has been bothering me."

"What's that?" Ollie sat up like the problem needed his full attention.

Dante grabbed his phone from the side table. "Ren said they have technology mimicking ours in the Realm of the Damned. It runs on magic, but still, she could use a smartphone easily even though she hasn't been on Earth for over a thousand years. When I escaped after nine hundred years, I struggled. And that was two centuries ago."

Ollie's eyes widened. "I see. Is technology in Hell bad?"

"On the surface, no. But I can't figure out why Luc would modernize in the exact way humans have. It's never something that's been done in the afterlife. The Eternal Realm didn't mimic Earth. They're supposed to be separate worlds." He set the phone aside.

Ollie considered for a few moments. "Maybe Lucifer wanted to know what the world was like before he hunted you down. If he hadn't been here in a thousand years, he'd have trouble when he arrived and probably didn't want it getting in the way of his plans."

"Maybe. But he could have kept knowledge of human technology to himself rather than share it." It's what Dante expected Luc to do. He'd keep any advantage he could.

"You said things are tense down there," Ollie reminded him. "Maybe he was trying to soothe the masses. Give them a little something to make not getting what they really need seem more tolerable."

"I hadn't considered that. It fits though." That sounded much more like Luc.

"Yeah?" Ollie sounded pleased, his dimples appearing.

"You have good insight." Dante smiled as Ollie blushed. "Luc wouldn't go through the effort to make demons happy, but to placate or distract them, definitely."

Ollie snuggled back into Dante. "There's been no word of him, right?"

Dante's arms tightened around his mate. "No. But once we

figure out if the demon lurking here is on Luc's side or not, we're going to hunt him down in the Realm of the Damned."

"For what he did to me?" Ollie whispered.

"Yes." Dante's whole body tightened at the hint of fear in Ollie's words. "Unless you don't want me to. I want him to pay, but it's ultimately up to you."

"Pay how?"

Dante's sated demon fire flared to life. "At first, I wanted to kill him. Wipe him from the universe. Permanent death is the punishment for killing a mate or Eternal being, but he didn't kill you. I'd have been the one wiped from the realms if I'd followed my impulse."

Ollie clutched him around the middle. "I'm glad you didn't. Don't risk yourself to make him pay. I want to be safe, but I need you with me."

Dante kissed Ollie's forehead. "I know. We aren't killing Luc. We've always planned to imprison him, so I'll stick with that. But I can't sit around waiting for him to attack again."

"You won't get trapped down there, right?" Even more fear laced Ollie's words than before.

"No. We can always break out like we did before." If Onyx got on board.

"Okay, but don't kill him," Ollie said like he feared Dante would change his mind once he faced Luc. "Not for me. In a world where life after death exists, permanent death seems like too big of a punishment."

A lightness expanded in Dante's chest. "You're right. I promise I won't make him pay the ultimate price or risk myself."

"You can kick his ass though. I don't regret our bond, and I'll never want to undo it, but it shouldn't have happened this way. I can still feel him lurking, his hands clawing at me. I hate him. He had no right. Me surviving doesn't make it okay."

"It doesn't, and he'll pay. Don't worry."

"Good." Ollie shook, sniffling quietly, and Dante held him firmly to his chest. Eventually, he settled, wiping his eyes and sighing into Dante's chest. "Thank you."

"What for?" Was Ollie surprised Dante would avenge him? Comfort him? Surely not.

"For talking to me and asking for my input even though I'm new to the magic world. It makes me feel like your partner."

"You are my partner, Ollie. Even if we're at the beginning. Having someone to confide in is something I've waited eons for, and I'm not holding back. It isn't the same with Ash or Onyx."

Dante could lean on his mate in a way he hadn't with the others. For the first time in his long life, Dante was seen, unconditionally accepted, and cared for by someone who would let Dante do all those things in return.

At its core, that's what being mated meant.

DANTE DROPPED Ollie off at his apartment in time for him to get ready for brunch, then met Ash and Onyx at the sea cliffs. He landed on a rocky outcropping, waves lapping at his feet.

"Then why not come with us?" Ash growled at Onyx. "Not standing against your brother is starting to feel a lot like supporting him."

"Not standing—not—" Onyx sputtered, his cheeks bright red. "Fuck you, Ash. I'm not supporting him. How far did you have to twist my actions to get to that? We said we'd *never* return! I'm not willingly walking back into that Hell."

Fuck, Dante should have gotten here sooner. "We know you're not supporting Luc, Onyx."

"Oh?" He rounded on Dante, blue wings catching the light off the ocean and sparkling in an echo of his fiery eyes. "Then what's Ash, hmm? A big fucking liar?"

"Ash is a pain in the ass," Dante said levelly.

"Hey!" Ash glared at Dante.

Dante had had enough. "You know Onyx isn't siding with Luc. There's no reason to say shit like that. You only do it to make him mad."

Ash gritted his teeth, jaw muscle ticking, but he didn't deny it.

"*Hmph.*" Onyx turned up his nose.

"We'll be able to escape the Realm of the Damned easily if all three of us go," Dante said. Onyx was worried, and Dante had to remind him he was safe. "We won't be trapped. You know I wouldn't risk that for any of us. And if this other demon can confirm Luc is working alone, then we'll be set. He won't be expecting us. We'll have the upper hand."

Onyx swept his bangs from his face. "How do I know you won't lose it and kill him when you see his miserable face? I'm not participating in your eternal death."

Dante held back a smile. Is that what Onyx was worried about? "I swear I won't. We're throwing Luc in that empty cell, that's all. I promised Ollie I wouldn't kill him. He doesn't want an execution in his name."

Onyx was silent for a long beat. "He doesn't?"

"No. He's hurt and scared of what Luc might do, but that doesn't stop him from being compassionate. Even if it wouldn't have meant my death, I don't think he'd have asked for Luc to be killed. It makes me doubly glad I held back."

Onyx nodded, chewing his lower lip. "There's no way you'll go against your mate's wishes. So...fine. I'll help you with this. But you fucking owe me." He jabbed a finger at Ash. "You too."

Ash rolled his eyes. "Sure, Onyx. Next time you want to go clubbing, I'll follow along. Harper might have to come though."

"If I wanted to go clubbing with anyone, it'd be Harper and Ollie, not your sorry ass."

"My ass is amazing, you prick."

"For the love of all that is damned, shut up, both of you." Dante sucked in a breath. Calm. He had to relax. He'd survived far too long with these demons to strangle them now. "I'm going to call a small group of shearwaters to me. Are you both sticking around to see how long it takes our friend to come sniffing, or are we doing shifts?"

"I'll stay," Onyx said quickly.

"Me too."

How predictable. Ash couldn't be outdone. Oh well, Dante would take it. "Then behave, or the birds will peck your eyes out. They like peace and quiet."

25

———

OLLIE

OLLIE HAD the coffee brewed by the time Dex arrived. Harper hadn't surfaced from his room, but given what he'd said about not sleeping well, Ollie wouldn't wake him.

"I've got croissants today." Dex raised his bag as he entered the apartment. "We can do breakfast sandwiches."

"Hell yeah." Ollie led him into the kitchen. "I've got eggs and everything else we need, so it's perfect."

"That's what I like to hear. I'm starving." Dex unpacked a box of croissants and a bunch of bananas.

"You work up an appetite last night?" Ollie teased.

Dex peeled a banana and took a bite, shrugging slyly. "Maybe."

Ollie waggled his eyebrows. "Anyone worth seeing again?"

"I didn't get that vibe. Or a phone number." Dex hadn't had a steady relationship or anything resembling one in years. Even his interest in hooking up seemed to come and go.

For a flash, Ollie wished Dex had a mate. He deserved that kind of partnership even more than Ollie. Someone he'd never lose, never have to worry about dying or being taken from him.

"How about you, still over hookups?" Dex asked around another bite of banana.

"Huh?" Ollie's face burned. "I mean, yeah. Something like that. I'm never redownloading that app."

"Come out with me next time. You know I'm a good wingman."

He was, but Ollie wouldn't ever need that particular help from Dex again. "I don't know, maybe. How's selling the car going?"

"Good. I've got a buyer lined up. Should be done this week. I'm going to call a realtor soon too. Selling the car made me realize it's past time to get out of the condo, you know? I probably won't even bother renting the parking space unless it looks like it'll take a long time to sell the place."

"You want to be out that soon?"

"It'd be for the best. I need a fresh start. Not that I'm leaving the city," he added quickly. "I couldn't leave everything I have. Especially you."

Ollie was hit with a rush of affection. "I couldn't leave you either. But if you wanted a bigger change, you wouldn't lose me."

A hint of sadness crept into Dex's gaze. A blink later, it was gone. "No, I wouldn't. But all I'm doing is selling the condo. I probably won't even move neighborhoods."

"Why would you? We already live in the best one." They shared a smile. "Let me know if you need help with anything. Selling the place is going to be so much work."

"You're going to regret offering."

"Ugh. Don't ask me to clean." Ollie almost regretted it. He didn't because he'd be there for Dex no matter what. But cleaning was not his favorite.

"Yep. You're helping scrub the place for sure." Dex looked

more closely at Ollie. "You seem better than the last time I saw you."

Ollie averted his eyes. "I am."

"You want to talk about it?"

Ollie had been vague when Dex asked how he was doing last time. Everything had felt unimaginable and confusing, and if he were honest, he hadn't wanted to share the worst of it.

Today was different.

"Something, um, happened at the beach last week."

Dex put his banana down. "Something like what?"

Ollie's hand found his throat of its own volition. "I was there with Dante. Hanging out. He works with seabirds. But, um, this man attacked me."

"Oh my god." Dex grabbed Ollie's shoulder. "What do you mean attacked you? How?"

Ollie scrambled for a lie. "I think he wanted to mug me, maybe? I'm okay, physically. Obviously. But he held a knife to my throat, and I keep flashing back to it. I didn't want to tell you before. I didn't know what to say. Dante saved me, which should make me feel lucky, but the whole thing shouldn't have happened. You know?"

All Ollie's fears from that day came rushing back. His fear of dying, fear of being bound to Dante, and his fear of an unknown future. He wasn't wrong about it all, was he? For a second, he doubted everything. Was he being a fool with Dante, thinking he'd ever choose this?

No. He wouldn't sink back into that mindset. He and Dante might have bonded out of a horrible situation, but that didn't cancel out what they had. They were fated. And as mindboggling as that was, it was Ollie's guarantee of something good.

"Of course it shouldn't have happened." Dex hugged Ollie close. "I'm so sorry. That's awful. But I'm so glad you weren't hurt."

If only that were true. "Seems like a miracle," Ollie mumbled.

Dex pulled back to inspect him. "Did the guy get away?"

Ollie nodded. "I think that's part of what freaked me out. Why I couldn't tell you."

"You had to process, Ollie. That's okay. I'm glad Dante was there." Dex looked heartbroken, knowing Ollie had almost been hurt. He'd experienced so much loss. This kind of thing always affected Dex deeply. He had to be running through all the worst-case scenarios in his head, and Ollie hated that.

"Me too. I didn't know what was happening, but Dante did everything he could." Ollie reached for his coffee mug. "I've been hanging out with Dante more, since then. He's been helping. Talking to me and listening. It's been nice."

Dex smiled and it warmed his cool eyes. "So he's being good to you?"

Ollie bit his lip. "Very. I shouldn't have been so worried about him. I think we're going to turn into something."

Dex's brow creased. "Something like dating?"

"Yeah. It's what I've always wanted with him."

"Oh, you're being honest with yourself now. Great."

"Shut up." Ollie shoved Dex's shoulder, then said more seriously, "I talked to Dante about my exes and told him my hang-ups. It made everything easier. I think I'm making progress and can figure this out in a way I couldn't before."

"That's so great. I knew you'd get here. Didn't I tell you?" Dex slung an arm over Ollie's shoulders. "You can trust yourself, Ollie."

"You know, Dex, I think you're right."

26

———

## DANTE

By the late afternoon, Ash and Onyx had agreed to do shifts at Dante's side. Ash left Dante and Onyx sitting on a rock not far from shore, enjoying the peaceful sea as the shearwaters dove for fish nearby.

"He can't deal with being away from his sweetie long," Onyx said once Ash was out of sight.

"Yeah. Ash won't deny it. It's funny seeing him so smitten."

Onyx narrowed his eyes at Dante like he was surprised Dante agreed. "I had no idea he could be so gooey."

"Yes, you did." Dante elbowed him. "Even if it's been eons since dreamy little Ash evolved into the broody demon we love."

"*Psh*, speak for yourself. I don't love his grumpy I'm-better-than-everyone attitude."

"He may have an attitude, but Ash doesn't think he's better than anyone." If anything, it was the opposite. At least Harper seemed to have reminded Ash he was worthy of love.

"Whatever." Onyx flicked his wrist, sending a splash of water toward the birds. "You were agreeing with me, remember? Go back to that. It was more fun."

"I was having a conversation with you, not agreeing for the sake of it. It's not like I'm opposed to teasing Ash now that he's got hearts in his eyes rather than flames."

Onyx snickered. "And how's your little mate?"

Dante nearly melted all over the rock. *His mate.* "Good. Ollie's come around to the idea of fate, and he's not so frightened of everything. He's opened up to me, and I think he's happy."

"Aww." Onyx pinched Dante's cheek.

Dante swatted him away. "What was that for?"

"You're so red. The heat coming off you is going to give me a sunburn."

Dante swiped a hand over his face. "Shut up."

"I'm guessing coming to terms with magic and all that jazz isn't all that's making your little mate happy."

Dante sniffed. "I have no idea what you're implying."

Onyx laughed, scaring a nearby bird, who flew off with a squawk. "Sex, Dante. I'm implying that sharing orgasms makes your mate very happy."

Dante mumbled something unintelligible, even to him.

Onyx tipped his head back, eyes closed. "Congrats on ending your dry spell. I'm surprised you've left the bedroom so soon."

"Mating isn't all about that." Dante's face got impossibly hotter. "I'm building a relationship with Ollie. We have a lot more to work out than my pent-up sex drive."

Onyx elbowed him. "Hey, look at me. I know. I'm just being me about it. I'm overjoyed for you, Dante. Okay? I want you to be even mushier than Ash. Fuck, I want you to get human married so I can cry at the ceremony. I gave up on mates, and being wrong is the best thing that's ever happened. Especially if it means *you* were right all along."

There was a beat of silence like they were both stunned, and then Dante wrapped a wing around Onyx and pulled him close. "Love you, brother."

Onyx ruffled his wings, folding them more tightly so he fit better in Dante's embrace. "Love you too, you big softie."

Dante wanted to tell Onyx he'd be next. His mate was out there. Would that comfort or hurt him? Renewed hope in finding their mates didn't mean Onyx's fated love was around the corner.

Hopefully, he wouldn't have to wait much longer. He needed more love in his life, someone he didn't feel the need to keep outside his walls.

"How long is this going to take?" Onyx asked abruptly, all tenderness gone. "Ash better be back first thing in the morning."

"I'm sure he will be."

"I'll enjoy the excuse to harass him if not."

THAT FIRST DAY was otherwise uneventful. Dante allowed the birds to nest in the reserve at night so they could all sleep and any demon watching wouldn't be suspicious of completely strange behavior. Onyx stayed in one of Dante's guest rooms and—much to Onyx's annoyance—didn't need to remind Ash about his shift in the morning.

Onyx returned promptly that afternoon like he was glad to help, or at least glad to spend time with Dante.

It was nice to fly and spend idle time together. Something had shifted between them, and hopefully, Dante would see more of Onyx without having to push so hard.

But after three days of nothing, Dante was restless. What if there was no rogue demon other than Ren? Or if there was, what if they'd moved on? Maybe whoever killed his birds never cared about finding him.

"That one is such a little shit." Onyx pointed at a slightly larger shearwater as he and Dante hovered next to the group. "He never does anything but prester the others."

"I think they're playing. He's mischievous and never wants to let up."

"Hmm." Onyx flew around the birds to get a better look. "Doesn't mean he isn't a little shit."

A buzzing sensation shot through Dante's temple, sending vibrations up his horns. "Damn it. Onyx, someone's trying to break one of my protective spells."

Onyx was at his side in a blur of blue wings. "The one on the reserve or Harper and Ollie's apartment?"

"The spell around the reserve."

"It has to be our mystery demon." Onyx gestured to the north. "Come on."

Dante shook himself and flew after Onyx, calling the shearwaters with him.

Had his trap been too obvious, leading the demon to believe Dante's home was exposed while he was busy bating his attacker? He wouldn't have thought so. Even if a small group of shearwaters was conspicuous after the flock had been so tightly contained, how had the demon found the spells protecting the reserve?

Dante's protections were cloaked in counterspells to prevent magical beings from realizing they were barred from the clifftop. Every witch, vampire, and demon in the city was under the illusion they were disinterested in the sanctuary, and if they got close to the protected area, they wouldn't sense even a hint of magic before they were repelled by an illusion.

But the buzzing didn't stop. Someone was breaking in.

"I'll call Ash." Onyx brought his phone to his ear.

Good. He'd meet them there.

As Dante sped up, the urge to check on Ollie reverberated through him. He'd be safe at work, and the demon couldn't attack Ollie if they were at the reserve, but fear for his mate wasn't soothed by logic.

Dante swore he felt Ollie's blood hot on his hands, the smell of copper drowning out the salt air. He clamped his eyes shut.

Could he break Ollie's trust to check on him through the bond? Would Ollie understand, or would it remind him how much there was to fear in their connection?

Dante's limbs went cold despite his burning fire. He couldn't let anything happen to his mate. But he needed to give Ollie the choice of how much to share.

He sent the small flock of shearwaters across the city instead. They'd keep an eye on Ollie, just in case.

Onyx finished his phone call and turned to Dante. "How did they get past your web of illusion? You haven't had a single trespasser since you set up the reserve."

"I don't know. Not even Luc found me." A twist of unease uncoiled within Dante. His deflections worked against his greatest enemy, but not this random birdkiller?

"Exactly." Onyx's expression darkened. "Luc heard of your birds. That's how he knew to find us in Shearwater Landing. Searching for you around their nests would be step one, but your illusions were strong enough to keep him away."

"So this demon is more powerful than Luc?"

"That, or they're working together."

But Luc couldn't be back. Ash wouldn't miss it. "Why wait to attack until now if they're working together?"

"I don't know."

Ash caught up to them over the waterfront. "Good to go?"

"No, we're hoping for a break first," Onyx snapped.

"Don't worry. We've got this," Ash said, for once seeing past Onyx's attitude to the reason he lashed out.

"*Worry?* Not likely." Onyx put on a burst of speed. "Just get your fire ready, big boy."

Ash cut a glance at Dante. "My fire is always ready."

Dante scanned the approaching cliff. Nothing looked out of place, which was no surprise. Attacking without an invisibility illusion would be foolish.

He led the way to the top of the cliff. "Revealing spells on three?"

Ash gave an affirmative grunt, positioning himself back to back with Dante, and Onyx fell in line at a right angle.

Dante pulled on the deep well of magic inside him, his fire roaring to life. Onyx and Ash flared with heat beside him. "One, two, three."

Magic surged from the trio, rolling out in all directions.

Over the cliff edge, something sparked and flickered.

"There!" Dante pointed and flew straight for it.

An unseen body collided with his and Dante scrambled for purchase, grabbing until he caught what felt like a neck.

Releasing a second revealing spell, Dante crushed the being into the rocks below. A face appeared and disappeared. Another second later, the illusion shattered.

Dante held a slim demon by the throat, his eyes burning green. Vague recognition tickled at the back of Dante's mind, but he couldn't recall this demon's name.

Fire erupted from the demon, and Dante swore as it kissed his skin. His grip loosened and the demon struggled to get up, but his wings were pinned beneath him.

Dante readjusted his hold and squeezed the demon's neck, ignoring the pain caused by the demon's fire. He summoned his own, letting it burn along his skin in a protective shield.

The demon beneath Dante clawed at him with long nails and released a bolt of lightning.

Dante's fire tempered the lightning strike. He jolted, freezing up, but his heart didn't stop. He dropped his invisibility illusion to save energy. "Who are you?"

The demon growled, shocking Dante again. "Fuck you."

Dante's teeth clenched. The lightning cut through his shield that time, leaving him momentarily exposed. He squeezed the demon tighter. "You're caught, so you might as well talk. Who are you?"

"Take your hands off him, or I'll stun you, and he'll rip your heart out," a voice called.

Dante whipped his head to the side, finding a white-winged demon hovering nearby. She bared long fangs, lightning crackling at her fingertips.

Two attackers. Was that how they got around his deflections? By combining their power?

Before the newcomer could make a move, blue lightning struck her chest. Eyes popping, she froze and dropped from the sky like a rock.

Ash caught her and Onyx was there in an instant to help.

Dante shot the other rogue with lightning and he went rigid. "Let's bring them into the trees."

Ash and Onyx flew off without a word, still invisible to their attackers.

Dante adjusted his grip on his captive. "Come on."

The demon went limp like the fight had left him. Dante dumped him next to his companion. Neither made a move, seemingly cowed by the invisible threat of Ash and Onyx.

Interesting. They'd given up more easily than Dante had expected.

"You killed my birds." Dante stood before them and spread his wings imposingly, his eyes glowing with raging fire.

The two shared a glance. "How many are with you?" the green-eyed man asked.

"It can't be more than one," the woman said. "Hitting and then catching me isn't that hard. We can still take them."

The man didn't seem to share her confidence, his eyes darting frantically around. "What if it's Lucifer?" he whispered.

Lucifer? Dante almost laughed. These demons thought *he* was on Luc's side?

"What are your aims?" he demanded. "You killed my birds, then attacked the sanctuary. Why?"

"To flush you out," the man said.

The woman grabbed his arm. "Shut up."

"We could've taken one Hound alone, not two, not one with Lucifer." He glared at her, green eyes flaring. She glared back.

"How did you escape the Realm of the Damned?" Dante asked, changing tactics.

The man swallowed. "The seal was broken briefly, and we slipped through before it closed."

"I see." At least that lined up with Ren's story. Dante pretended to consider the man's words. "Then why not run off and hide?"

"If Lucifer ever found out we escaped, we'd be hunted. You have his permission to be here and would have come after us as soon as he asked. There's no hiding forever. I'd heard one of you controlled the birds—"

"That's enough," the woman interrupted, and he fell silent.

So they'd been hoping to rid themselves of an enemy. What had they been planning to do to Dante? Surely not kill him.

He suppressed a shudder.

"Did you ever consider I might not be on Lucifer's side?"

Shock transformed their faces, the woman's stern features cracking for the first time.

"You *escaped*? He didn't send you here?" The first demon rounded on his companion. "I told you. I said Lucifer planting them here didn't make as much sense as the other rumors. How could they be looking...?" He shut his mouth, silencing himself for once.

He seemed to have heard a very different story than Ren. Had Luc spun a lie saying he sent his Hounds to Earth? It was plausible. He'd have wanted to save face. But what did this demon think Dante and the others were looking for? Surely not mates.

Lucifer had clearly given up on mates. But was there an advantage to convincing his masses all wasn't lost?

It was a mess. No one in the Realm of the Damned knew the truth. There were probably dozens more stories circulating. Confusion was certainly to Luc's benefit.

"He could be lying," the white-winged demon muttered. "Lucifer could still be hiding right behind him."

"Well, we're screwed if that's the case," the first reminded her.

At least Dante could be reasonably sure these two weren't working for Luc. His lackeys tended to go for threats and intimidation, never giving up when they thought Lucifer was in their corner.

It was lucky for Dante that Luc seemed to have no allies. All he apparently needed to get past Dante's counterspells was a little backup.

"What are your names?" Dante asked.

After a pause and a reluctant nod from his companion, the first demon said, "I'm Maxwell, and this is Lillian."

"All right, Maxwell and Lillian." Dante drew in his wings. "I might have forgiven you for thinking I was on Lucifer's side. I'm sure he worked hard to convince everyone of that. But I can't forgive you for killing my birds."

Maxwell shared an outraged look with Lillian. "They're animals."

Dante growled. "You think animals should be killed for no reason? I disagree. And what were you planning to do to me when you drew me out into the open? Have a civilized chat to figure out whose side I'm on? Let me go on my way unharmed afterward?"

Their silence was heavy with guilt.

"I didn't think so. I'll give you credit and assume you weren't planning to commit the offense of permanent death, but you've still made an enemy of me."

"Wait," Lillian held up a hand. "You're right. We should have considered the other rumors more seriously, but it seemed naïve to hope you'd escaped and were no longer in Lucifer's pocket. What else were we supposed to do?"

They would have had to risk exposing themselves. Ren's peaceful move was bolder than Dante had given her credit for. Could he really blame these two for not doing the same when they had a very different impression of where Dante's loyalty lay?

Maybe not, but he couldn't appear too forgiving and risk being taken advantage of. "If you escape again and find me without your fangs drawn, maybe we can start over."

Lillian's eyes flashed. "Escape again? No, please. Don't send us back!"

Doubt turned Dante's stomach. He couldn't let them go without a guarantee they wouldn't attack again. They could be lying or decide Dante was a risk they didn't want to leave unmitigated. He also couldn't let their actions go without consequence, but re-trapping them in Hell seemed like something Luc would do.

No, that wasn't quite true. Dante was giving them a second chance. All they had to do was follow Luc through the seal again. Because Luc would be back. He might be planning to enter the Human Realm any second.

But it was wrong for any demon to be trapped in the Realm of the Damned. Should he, Ash, and Onyx have done more for the rest of their kind over the years?

Before escaping, they'd considered freeing more than themselves but couldn't completely break the containment. Luc alone held that key. Dante, Ash, and Onyx escaped because their magic helped bind the prison together. They couldn't get anyone else out with them.

Ash dropped his invisibility, and Lillian and Maxwell's attention snapped to his massive form. "Send them back. They can escape again." He fixed burning orange eyes on the two. "While you're down there, let everyone know we aren't on Lucifer's side. Anyone else you share the secret to escaping with better come through knowing where we stand. We don't need enemies among ourselves here."

Onyx also dropped his invisibility, adding his cold glare in rare agreement with Ash.

Lillian straightened. "Understood."

"Wait." Maxwell turned frantically, glancing between them all. "Just wait."

"No." Lillian grabbed his arm. "I'm sorry, but what they're suggesting is fair. We'll earn your trust," she said to Dante. "I assume your certainty that another opportunity to escape will present itself is because Lucifer isn't in this realm anymore?"

"That's correct."

But Dante planned to hunt Luc and trap him. There was no more reason to delay with Onyx on board. Would there be another opportunity? Not if Dante acted now. But they couldn't leave everyone in the Realm of the Damned for eternity.

Fuck.

Ash stepped forward, an orange glow swirling around him.

His connection to the containment magic had always been stronger than Dante's or Onyx's, and it would allow them to send Maxwell and Lillian back.

The warm glow of power tugged on Dante's magic, and he let his join Ash's spell. Onyx followed suit, blue and black now mixing with Ash's orange.

"I hope we meet under better circumstances next time," Ash said as the swirling spell engulfed the demons.

In a blink, they were gone.

27

OLLIE

Ollie was having a great Saturday. Relief that Dante and the others had caught and banished the demons hurting his birds cured the tension he'd been carrying around all week. It was one less thing to worry about.

"We've got overlapping lunches today," he said to Ellie as he organized his station.

"I saw that." She passed him a comb she'd borrowed. "Sushi?"

"And coffee."

"Uh, totally. I'm going to need an extra-large by the afternoon. I really should stop going out on Friday nights."

Ollie laughed. "You need gaming friends. Though that might not help with the late nights." He and Dante had played *World's End* for hours last night.

Ollie had a few new clients scheduled that day, one an artist that Onyx had apparently referred. Ollie swallowed his surprise. Onyx was nothing like Ollie's first impression of him, and the artist turned out to be a generous tipper.

The morning flew by.

As Ollie stood in line getting coffee while Ellie got their

sushi, he pulled out his phone to thank the demon for the referral. A message was already waiting. Onyx had added him and Harper to a new chat. Ollie rolled his eyes at the group name, smiling.

### Your Favorite Group Chat

ONYX:

I'm taking you mates out. Let me know when you're free.

Ollie quickly replied.

OLLIE:

Where are we going?

The texting dots popped up almost immediately.

ONYX:

You pick. Exclusive club or a five-course dinner?

HARPER:

Dinner!

Wait. Why does it feel like you're taking us on a fancy date?

Ollie snorted.

ONYX:

Because you are a sweet, innocent little witch. This is not a date. You couldn't handle a date with me.

HARPER:

How would you know?

OLLIE:

Yeah, he handles Ash just fine.

ONYX:

Stop right there!

There are things I can't allow inside my brain.
Not when they'll live there for eternity, and the
details of Harper handling Ash is one of them.

Harper sent a devil emoji.

Ollie grinned, looking up in time for the barista to ask what
he wanted. He placed his order for two iced coffees, one extra-
large, and then went to wait by the cream and sugar.

OLLIE:

So does that mean you don't want to know
how Dante and I got together?

He wasn't really going to share how they'd stumbled into
phone sex, but the threat should rile Onyx up.

ONYX:

Not if it's anything other than a cute story
about Dante swooning all over you. That's my
perspective on the situation, by the way.

How unexpectedly sweet.

HARPER:

Aww

OLLIE:

Yeah, Dante is pretty cute. I'm keeping the
details to myself.

ONYX:

Dante is not cute. I'm cute.

HARPER:

Being short doesn't automatically make you
cute.

OLLIE:

Hey, don't call us short.

ONYX:

Yeah!

HARPER:

Sorry. But come on. Onyx, you were never going for cute.

ONYX:

True. I'm too sophisticated. Too sensual.

"Oh my god," Ollie muttered under his breath. The barista called out his order, and he shot off one more text before grabbing the drinks.

OLLIE:

How about next week for dinner?

They coordinated the details as Ollie added cream and sugar to his coffee and cinnamon to Ellie's. He'd loved to have invited Dex since he was way more of a foodie than Ollie, but this was clearly a demon's mate thing.

Next time Gallery Four had an opening, he'd make sure to take Dex. Maybe Onyx had contacts in the art world who sold handcrafted homeware. It would be cool to get Dex's pieces in more shops.

Ollie and Ellie took their lunches to a small park near the river. Time passed too quickly, and soon, they were hurrying back to work. Ollie would be dead after this, but it was the good kind of tired. At least it was the end of the week.

The attack at the beach seemed further away than ever. Yes, more time had passed, but it went beyond that. Ollie's doubts and fears faded with each passing day. His life had settled back into place and he felt like himself. Even things with Dante felt normal, leaving Ollie excited for the future.

Back at the salon, a poised woman with chestnut-brown hair waited for him. His last new client of the day.

"Hi, Pamala?" Ollie approached her. "I'm Ollie. I have you scheduled for an updo?"

"Yes." She beamed at him. "Thank you for taking me at such short notice. I have an important event this evening and my stylist was sick, so my friend recommended I come here."

"Happy to help." Ollie led her back to his station. "Tell me what you're thinking."

She was very organized, pulling up references on her phone and showing Ollie the dress she would wear. She walked out looking stunning and leaving Ollie with another generous tip.

"I hope she comes back," Ellie said in his ear. "She's magnetic."

Ollie swatted her playfully. "I'm not being your matchmaker."

"Good, because I don't need your help." Ellie grinned evilly before going to check the schedule. Probably to see if his client had rebooked.

As Ollie was about to turn away, Pamala returned to the salon. It seemed she'd forgotten something at the counter. Ellie handed it to her and Pamala lingered, leaning in.

Ollie finished tidying up. No, Ellie didn't need his help at all.

When Ollie got home, Harper was curled up in the armchair, struggling through a first-person shooter game.

"I died again? This sucks."

"You're getting better. Did you check if you're on easy mode?"

"Yeah, it doesn't help." Harper blinked at Ollie like he'd

been focused on the TV for too long. "I need a break anyway. The demons are coming over soon."

Ollie plopped on the couch. "All of them?"

"Even Onyx." Harper set the controller aside. "They want to discuss their plans with us."

Ollie's light mood darkened.

Dante wanted to make his move against Lucifer soon, but tonight? Hunting the Devil in Hell seemed a lot less scary—or maybe less real—when they'd been chatting about it, snuggled in bed.

"Did Ash say anything else?"

Harper shook his head.

Ollie ran a hand through his hair. Dante going to a completely different realm left him feeling like he was teetering on the edge of a cliff. He'd rather find a way to feel safe from Lucifer without Dante having to do this. Maybe they could figure out something else.

It wasn't long before there was a knock at the door.

"How did they know when I'd be home?" Ollie asked as he got up to answer. It wasn't like he shared his exact work schedule with Dante when his hours varied.

"I sent Ash a signal down our bond when you got here." Harper paused. "Was that okay? I should have told you."

"No, that's fine. It's not that different from texting." For a brief moment, jealousy strangled Ollie's insides. He wanted to communicate with Dante like it was normal to share so much.

Was he ready for that? Ollie had assumed he'd never want to blur the lines between them as individuals, but sharing didn't mean losing himself. It meant gaining something new with Dante.

Later. He'd think about it and talk to Dante later.

Ollie opened the door and let the demons in.

"Lovely home," Onyx said as he stepped inside ahead of the

other two. "You'll see that I came properly dressed out of respect for human customs."

Ash rolled his eyes, pushing past Onyx and heading straight for the living room. He and Dante were both shirtless.

"Uh, thanks, Onyx. But you can do whatever's most comfortable for you. Harper and I don't mind."

Onyx narrowed his eyes. "Angling to see me undressed, are you? Watch out, Dante. I'll steal your man."

"I think I'm safe." Dante pulled Ollie close. "How was your day?"

"Good." Ollie snuggled in, pressing against Dante's warm skin. "My friend Ellie got a hot date."

Dante rumbled softly. "I'm glad that makes you happy."

"It does, and so does seeing you again. Playing online last night wasn't enough." Being committed to relatively normal dating meant not spending every second together, and though they'd talked and met online, Ollie hadn't seen Dante since he'd spent the night in Dante's huge bed.

"Last night was fun though. Wasn't it?" Dante covered Ollie's lips with his without waiting for a reply, purring softly as they kissed.

Ollie got lost in the heat of Dante's mouth, his scent swirling around them.

Remembering why Dante was there, he pulled back. "I'm not denying it was fun. But why are you all here? Are you going after him tonight?" It was too soon.

Dante's soft expression hardened. "Let's join the others, and I'll explain."

In the living room, Ash had repositioned Harper on his lap and Onyx was perched on the back of the couch, his bare feet on the cushions. Ollie couldn't bring himself to disentangle from Dante's side and sit, so they stood by the TV.

Dante didn't seem to mind, rubbing his hand back and forth

over Ollie's lower back as he said, "We're ready to make our move against Lucifer."

Ollie's heart clenched.

Harper visibly stiffened. "Like, ready, as in now? Tonight?"

"If we all agree," Ash said, and Dante and Onyx nodded.

Everyone seemed to look at Ollie.

He only had eyes for Dante. "I know we talked about it, but are you sure it's safe? I don't need this for my sake. Not like I did before. I'd rather you stay here, in this realm. I mean, there's got to be other ways to manage my fear. I am doing better, and you've all said now that we're mated, Lucifer won't attack like that again."

Dante cupped the back of Ollie's neck, grip warm and tender. "You've done so well acclimating to all this, but nothing will be completely safe as long as Luc is free. He's hurt you and Harper, and knowing he won't kill you any more than he'd kill me isn't enough. Harm isn't only physical. And what if we do nothing, and he hurts someone else next time? How much of that will be on us? It doesn't feel right."

"But is it safe for you to go down there?" Ollie glanced around at the other demons. They could be hurt or captured. Could they still get back to this realm if Lucifer imprisoned them?

"It's as safe as it's going to be," Ash said. "Going off what we've heard, there seems to be several factions of demons standing against Luc. He doesn't seem to have allies. If he did, he wouldn't have come to the Human Realm alone, so even though we're going into his territory, we'll have the upper hand."

"We need to take advantage before he can turn the tables on us," Dante added. "Then, once Luc is imprisoned, we can try and fix the rest of his mistakes."

"Fix them how?" Ollie asked. Wasn't punishing Lucifer the end of it?

"We aren't the only demons who deserve freedom," Dante said. "We couldn't free anyone else before, but once Luc is subdued, we can steal some of his power and destroy his containment spell completely, freeing everyone."

"Everyone?" Harper caught Ollie's eye, seeming to read his mind. "Won't having so many demons in the Human Realm be dangerous?"

"Dangerous, how? Magic has already infected humankind. The greatest damage is done." Dante sounded regretful even though it had been over a thousand years and not his fault. "Demons aren't any worse than anyone else, no less moral than any other group. And I can't sit here with my mate, knowing they're all trapped and kept from theirs."

"I get that." Harper shifted to sit up straighter. "It's still going to be a huge change for the magic community."

"It will be," Onyx agreed. "But it's the right thing to do. We can't shy away from change because it's hard."

He was right. They couldn't enjoy freedom at the expense of others.

"We aren't freeing everyone tonight," Dante reminded them. "Working out how to extract Luc's magic will take time. Meaning we can prepare and get the word out that change is coming. We'll do this right."

"Yeah, we don't want to upset every single witch and vampire on Earth," Onyx said, but Ollie couldn't tell if he meant it tauntingly or not.

"Okay," Ollie said mostly to himself. He had to step back and see the situation objectively, not through the cloud of his growing unease and personal desire to keep Dante close. "So, tonight, you're going to take Luc by surprise, imprison him, and come back home?"

"Yes." Dante cupped his cheek. "And we'll keep you somewhere safe while we're gone."

"What do you mean? Shouldn't we stay at the apartment?" Harper glanced around as if he expected to see his protections broken.

Ollie didn't want to leave home any more than Harper seemed to. "We've been safe here up until now."

"Yes, but not if something goes wrong. Luc knows where you live. It's better if he's unable to find you," Dante said, and understanding dawned on Harper's face.

But something going wrong wasn't an option. They'd said the odds were good.

But they couldn't let confidence make them careless. If Dante, Ash, and Onyx didn't return, nothing would stop Lucifer from breaking into the apartment eventually.

"What about the nature reserve?" Ollie asked. He'd be comfortable waiting at Dante's house. Harper too.

Ash hummed agreeably. "That would be safer."

Dante shook his head. "Unless Maxwell and Lillian decide to tell Luc they got past my counterspells and discovered I had the whole area protected. They could trade the information for power or safety or change sides for any number of reasons. In that case, Luc will know exactly where our mates are. All he'll need to do is bring a few demons to help break in."

Harper looked dismayed. "We'd be trapped. I can't go up against multiple demons. Lucifer nulled my powers completely when he kidnapped me. It wasn't even a fight."

Onyx bounded off the couch. "How likely is it that Lillian and Maxell will suddenly see Luc as the better ally? They didn't seem much fonder of him than we are."

"But he is in charge of the world we sent them back to. We can't be completely sure," Ash grumbled.

Ash and Dante would never leave Ollie's and Harper's safety to chance, and trusting demons who attacked them would be foolish any way you looked at it.

Ollie's stomach twisted, gnawingly empty. "So if we aren't going to the reserve, where will we go?"

Harper grabbed Ash's arm. "What about Nico?"

"That's not a terrible idea," his mate agreed.

Onyx wrinkled his nose. "Who the hell is Nico?"

"My boss. He said he'd help me and Ollie. We can trust him."

"A witch?" Onyx choked like he was trying not to laugh. "What good will he be? He doesn't even know what's going on."

Dante and Ash shared a look. "He knows about us, Onyx." Dante quickly explained what happened at the apothecary.

Onyx's face was bright red by the time Dante finished. "I can't believe you didn't tell me someone learned our secret."

"Don't be mad at Ollie and Harper," Ash warned.

"Ollie and Harper? Why would I be mad at them? It's our responsibility to guard our secret, not theirs. And you didn't tell me like it wasn't important." Or more like Onyx wasn't important.

Ollie's chest pinched. "I'm sorry."

The fire burning in Onyx's eyes dimmed. "I'm not mad at you, Ollie. I don't like being kept in the dark." His attention returned to Dante and Ash. "You always ask for my help, but you don't bother treating me like I'm on your stupid little team. Then you act all offended when I don't jump the second you glance my way. I'm sick of it."

"Are you backing out?" Ash growled, shifting Harper off him so he could stand.

Onyx's fire flared. "No, I'm not because Dante is right. We need to do something about everyone being trapped, and my brother can't get away with hurting your mates. But if you want my help again, fucking act like having me around matters. Stop keeping things from me."

"We're sorry." Dante laid a hand on Onyx's shoulder, but Onyx pulled away.

Ash approached, mumbling, "Sorry."

Onyx released a long, measured breath. "Whatever. We've got shit to do tonight, and I can't deal with this too. At least you threatened this witch with my wrath. Can't have him thinking we're all like you hopeless saps."

Ash snorted. "Don't let him meet you, or he won't be scared long."

Ollie caught Harper's eye, and Harper looked at the ceiling. Yeah, his mate sucked at apologies.

"Fuck you. I'll meet Nico if I want." Onyx straightened his spine. "I'll put the fear of Hell in him. I'm much scarier than you, Ash. You're just big. It's not that impressive."

"Let's get going," Dante said before Ash could jab back. "We haven't given Nico much notice, but I'd still rather not delay."

Harper called Nico and explained that the demons had to take care of some dangerous business and that he and Ollie needed a safe place for the night. "He says we should meet him at his friend Rowan's place."

"Who?" Dante and Ash asked in unison.

Harper spoke into the phone. "Um, his vampire friend? Heads a local coven. Rowan's properties are more secure than Nico's, and Nico says Rowan will help without question. Apparently, their friendship is like that. Nico can take us somewhere guarded by the coven, so we'll have a small vampire army at the ready."

"But we don't know Rowan," Ash said like he wasn't sure if he wanted to growl or not. Likely because he was talking to Harper, not Nico directly.

"It'll still be better to hide with him." Ollie hated to admit it. Was he ready to meet vampires? "No one will have any idea where we are. None of us are connected to Rowan, and if something goes wrong, finding us at Nico's house or the apothecary shop won't be too hard."

"Lucifer probably stalked me and Ash to The Herb Emporium," Harper said.

"But—"

"Then it's settled." Onyx clapped his hands, cutting Ash off. "Mates with the vampire coven and the witch. But if any vampires find out about us, blood will be spilled."

Ollie would never feel great knowing Dante was walking into Hell, so he braced himself. He couldn't ask Dante not to do this. It wasn't all about what Lucifer did that day on the beach, even if that had spurred Dante into action.

Dante needed to focus and get back as soon as possible. If their mission was successful, it didn't matter where Ollie spent the night.

"Where are we meeting Nico and Rowan?" he asked.

Harper's cheeks turned pink. "A strip club."

28

DANTE

"This feels like a joke," Dante muttered to Ollie as they landed on the roof of an old-style building in the Business District.

Ollie gave a soft chuckle. "I know, but if I'm safe at a vampire-owned strip club, who cares."

Dante couldn't argue with that.

He reluctantly set Ollie on his feet. Ollie was trying hard not to let his nerves show, but the occasional jolt shot down the bond.

"It'll be all right. Luc won't kill any of us. We'll always be able to get back to you, even if the worst happens."

"That's not exactly comforting." Fear shone in Ollie's eyes. "I don't want the worst to happen."

"I don't either. But we've prepared for it, so you'll be safe either way." And that was the most important thing.

Ollie gripped Dante tight around the waist. "Can we share our emotions while you're gone? Will I still feel you even if you're in another realm?"

Dante's breath caught. "Yes, you should be able to feel me no matter where I am. But are you sure?"

"More than sure."

Dante hesitated. His emotions were bound to be tumultuous and physical altercations weren't out of the realm of possibility. "Luc won't go down without a fight. Feeling everything might not be reassuring until it's over."

Ollie's resolve seemed to harden. "I know this isn't going to be easy, but I'm not just looking for reassurance. I want to be there for you. Hold you through it. Give you...I don't know, inner strength."

Dante kissed Ollie. How could he not? Dante felt warm and fuzzy, and not even returning to the Realm of the Damned could dampen his joy for one bright moment.

"Thank you, Ollie. You don't know how much that means, or maybe you do. Having you with me is going to make this so much easier."

"Good." Ollie traced one of Dante's horns. "At least if I can help in some way, I won't feel like I'm sending you off to fight for me."

"You aren't sending me. I'm doing this because Lucifer hurt you but also for all the times he hurt me, Onyx, Ash, and all the demons in the Realm of the Damned. Maybe we should have done this centuries ago..."

But they hadn't been sure their escape would work until they tried. Fighting Luc and trying to crack the riddle of how to steal his power before escaping had seemed impossible. Too many things could have gone wrong and they couldn't have risked him discovering their plans.

And when they were finally free, they'd put it behind them. Maybe Dante hadn't had the strength to face turning their escape into a full-scale exodus back then. Maybe he needed Ollie to help him see a better future. He'd never stopped believing, but things had been bleak for a long time.

Now, Dante's world was bright, and he needed everyone to see it. They all deserved their mates.

Ollie took his hand. "Don't worry about the past. There's no point looking back and beating yourself up. Let me take care of you while you do this, then come home, and the other night will seem like nothing compared to what I'll do to you."

Dante let the walls guarding their bond drop and purred at the affection pouring out of Ollie. "The other night could never be nothing, but I'm sure we can build on it."

"Knew you two wouldn't be out of the bedroom long," Onyx taunted, appearing beside them.

"Don't eavesdrop." Dante flashed fiery eyes at the menace.

Onyx stuck out his tongue. "Where's this witch?" He looked around the rooftop. "I'm going to give him nightmares."

Harper shot off a text. The vampire and his coven ran the strip club on the first two floors of the building and an underground casino on the floors above that operated on an invite-only basis. Apparently, Nico was already here.

Rowan must trust Nico a great deal, allowing Nico to lead him blindly into something like this. In Dante's experience, vampires didn't usually trust witches that much.

"He'll be up in a minute," Harper said, putting his phone away.

"Excellent." Onyx gathered power around him, shedding the illusion that tricked other magical beings into thinking he had no magical power.

Even with his shirt on and demonic features away, there was no mistaking him as benign. Magic thrummed, electrifying the night air. Onyx's eyes glowed with cold fire, casting an eerie blue light on his cheeks and sharpening his brow with shadow.

Ash curled his lip in distaste.

Before Dante could comment, Nico exited a service stairwell, the door banging open.

"Everything's ready down…" Nico stopped in his tracks.

Onyx let his fangs drop and hissed, the sound so wrought with emotion chills ran down Dante's spine.

"Hi, Nico." Harper rushed forward. "Don't worry about Onyx. He's mad you found out about them, but it's fine."

Nico's eyes didn't leave Onyx, seemingly fixated on the fire crackling at Onyx's fingertips. "It doesn't look fine."

"It is. Promise. Come on, Ollie." Harper waved him over. "We don't want to hold you guys up. Get back soon, or I'll spend all my money on lap dances."

Ash rumbled and Harper gave him a sly look.

"Figured I'd pick up some tips and tricks."

The sound deepened to an appreciative growl.

Ollie covered his mouth, his mirth tickling Dante's insides through the bond.

Onyx didn't move, frozen except for his burning eyes and sparking fingers. It wasn't a bad display. They'd better get out of there before Nico changed his mind about helping.

"Thank you, Nico," Dante called. "We'll make sure he's better behaved next time. Had to let him get it out of his system."

"Right…" Nico almost looked hesitant to leave. Maybe he was afraid to put his back to Onyx. "We'll be in Rowan's office on the top floor unless Harper is serious about going to see the dancers. The building is secure either way. You won't have anything to worry about."

Ollie and Harper nudged Nico toward the stairs, and he jolted, shaking himself, and hurried to lead them away.

"Thanks, Onyx," Ash said dryly. "Do you feel better now?"

Onyx turned his fiery glare on them, panting slightly. "No. I feel like kicking my brother's ass."

DANTE HELD his tether to Ollie tightly as Ash surrounded them with his orange glow. Magic quickly obscured the view of the rooftop, and Dante's power rose to meet Ash's, joined by Onyx's.

This was it. Dante dropped his fangs. He wasn't only hunting Luc for Ollie, but he let anger fuel him. Pain still crushed him every time he remembered Ollie limp in his arms.

Lucifer's reign ended now.

Darkness engulfed Dante, pressing in as they moved between realms.

With a pop, the constriction disappeared and Ash's glow dissipated, revealing familiar stone walls.

They stood in their old quarters inside Lucifer's fortress. It was a risk to enter here, not knowing what the rooms had become since they'd left, but it was less of a risk than entering the Realm of the Damned elsewhere and having to sneak into Luc's heavily guarded lair.

Dante turned from the wall, hit with recognition and a sinking sense of déjà vu. The room was unchanged. Their old possessions crowded the space, color muted by time and dust as thick as snow.

This wasn't what Dante had expected. Forgotten despair threatened to pull him down, clawing at his insides. He took a deep breath and choked. Fuck, even the air was stale and oppressive.

Onyx picked up a tarnished goblet, a detached look in his eye, all his intensity gone. "What...?"

The sitting area was a time capsule, the curtains drawn and moldering. A picture of their old life. Was it exactly as they'd left it? Had Luc not been in here since Dante, Ash, and Onyx escaped?

"It's a fucking tomb." Ash frowned at a pile of clothes on a settee. "I remember dumping these here."

Dante's skin crawled. Why hadn't Lucifer repurposed the space? "We should go. Luc might have sensed us enter like you do in the Human Realm."

Ash grunted, turning away from his old clothes.

Dante's footsteps were muffled on the stone floor. So much dust. Centuries worth.

He led the way out through the suite's foyer. Hinges creaked as Dante pushed the door open, revealing a dim stone corridor. Early morning light filtered through the uncovered windows, doing nothing to chase away the heavy air of abandonment.

Dante stepped into the hall, greeted by more dust. Was the whole floor unused?

"Come on." Ash pulled Onyx along.

"Why the fuck is everything abandoned?" Onyx whispered.

Ash closed the door behind them. "Luc must not use this wing anymore."

Dante hurried to the stairs, finding them covered in dust. The hair stood up on the back of his neck, and he reached for Ollie's warm presence. His mate sent soothing tendrils of affection his way, but Dante's soul remained cold.

"I don't like this," he said as he headed downward.

"Look." Onyx caught his wing, pointing out the window.

Dante turned. The view was unrecognizable. He remembered fields and greenery and the city to the south. Not anymore.

Barren dirt marred the foreground, and in the distance, huge high-rises dominated the skyline, obliterating what had once been rolling hills. Lights blinked, creating colorful displays on the sides of the enormous buildings. The sprawl had a strange formation, nowhere near as dense as a human city, like it was only a few blocks deep, favoring a wide expanse.

"It almost reminds me of the Dawn Cliffs," Ash said, referring to the capital city in the Eternal Realm, built into cliff faces so high they touched the clouds.

He was right. The buildings seemed divided into two sides with a large gap between them, even though no river flowed there.

The Eternal Realm was all mountains and valleys, huge raging waterfalls and rivers. There was almost no flat land. As winged beings, it suited Eternals perfectly.

The Realm of the Damned was a stark contrast, nothing higher than a gentle slope, created as if to remind everyone of the perfect place they'd lost.

"Good for them." Onyx turned from the window. "Just because the council tried to ground us didn't mean we had to stay down here. Demons were always talking about building mountains."

But why had nothing come of those dreams until recently? For nine hundred years, the Realm of the Damned had hardly changed.

Ash followed Onyx down the stairs. "Interesting that they went with skyscrapers rather than natural formations." With magic at their disposal, building either would have been equally possible.

"They really are making it like the Human Realm." Dante turned away from the view. "I don't think we're going to find Luc here."

Every floor of the fortress seemed as deserted as their old quarters. Dust coated everything, and it appeared Lucifer had taken nothing with him when he left. Art hung on the walls.

Vases and statues marked the doorways. The courtyard was overgrown and the front gates rusted shut.

Dante looked at the sky. "I don't sense any protective spells. We can fly out and track Lucifer down."

It wasn't ideal. If Luc had sensed their arrival, he'd had plenty of time to prepare, compared to the three of them running through the fortress and bursting in on him.

Onyx shrugged off his shirt and freed his wings. "I don't think we'll have to track him. Didn't you notice one building was taller than the rest?"

"He would put himself in the highest tower." Ash launched into the air, and Dante and Onyx followed. "Strengthen your illusions. We don't need anyone seeing us coming, whether Luc knows we're here or not."

They flew over barren flatland and a slow-moving stream. A few remnants of the old city remained, even though it hadn't been long enough for the ruins to crumble away completely. It must have been dismantled. Had it been a war or a cathartic kind of destruction?

The Realm of the Damned was devoid of animals, only inhabited by demons and witch souls, another reminder they weren't in a natural realm. Dante had forgotten how much that unsettled him. No birds in the trees. Nothing grazing in the expanses of grass. Not a single creature to ever join him on his flights. He'd avoided the outdoors in an effort to forget.

But as they approached the towering cityscape, birdsong filled the air.

"Those are morning fowl." Dante scanned the sky. The rare creatures came out in the first few hours of daylight, perching on the tallest peaks of the Eternal Realm.

Ash caught an air current and drifted higher. "I don't see anything."

Dante didn't either, but no other bird sounded quite like

these. He might not have heard them in thousands of years, but it wasn't the kind of thing he'd forget.

They reached the edge of the city. Up close, the buildings looked like they were constructed of smooth gray stone. Windows of all shapes and sizes glittered and harsh neon lights flashed in every color. Signs and screens were everywhere except on the rooftops, where each building was adorned with a lush garden.

Onyx followed a string of lights from one garden to another. He hovered next to the pole securing the cord. "It's not birds at all. It's coming from here."

Dante flew over. Mounted on top of the pole was a small speaker. It looked almost like something he'd find in the Human Realm. "But how did they create the sound? It can't be a recording."

"Must be magic." Onyx gave Dante a look as if to say *come on*. "It'll be a crafty little spell. Something linked to memory, no doubt."

Ash appeared, wrinkling his nose at the speaker. "Fascinating, but we're wasting time."

Dante turned away and flew with him toward the tallest tower. A few wing beats later, he noticed Onyx hadn't followed.

"What's his problem?" Ash grumbled before doubling back.

"Being here is hard. Don't pretend it's not." Dante reached for Ollie and a hint of his sandalwood scent filled his nose. No matter what happened, he'd return to where he belonged. In the human world, at his mate's side.

Onyx didn't have a mate to tether him. Maybe that's what was wrong.

As Ash and Onyx caught up, a window opened in the next building over and a gray-and-white-winged demon leaped from the ledge, taking flight. She flew to the garden across from Dante and perched on a bench.

Ash and Onyx hovered at Dante's side. None of them moved, all eyes fixed on the demon as she stretched her wings.

A moment later, a second demon joined the first. Dante recognized him. His name was Niall or Neil. He handed his companion a drink. Wait, Dante recognized her too. Cora.

"Have you heard the Hounds are mated?" Cora asked.

Niall-Neil nodded. "Yes, but do you believe it?"

"What would be the point in lying?"

Ash dragged Dante and Onyx away, flying higher into the sky until they'd cleared the buildings by a longshot.

"How do they know?" Dante stared down at the two demons, now leaning into one another with their heads bowed. They should have stayed to listen.

Ash herded them forward. "We sent Lillian and Maxwell back with instructions to spread the truth, but they didn't know about our mates."

"So what? *Lucifer* announced our mated status?" Dante couldn't see it.

If Luc had a new trusted inner circle, he might have told them, but Niall-Neil had been vehemently against Luc for a long time, and Cora had been no friend of his. Neither would be the first to know or to hear any leaked secrets, given how they avoided anyone in Lucifer's good graces.

Unless all that had changed.

"We can wonder about it later. We've taken too long already." Ash didn't wait before flying off.

Onyx caught Dante's eye as they hurried to catch up. He didn't seem to like this development either.

Lucifer must have mentioned their mates to someone. Maybe a secret like that would travel faster than anything else, reach demons who normally avoided Luc as much as possible. It had been a couple weeks since Ollie's attack, so it wasn't unreasonable for news to have circulated.

As they approached the tallest building, windows opened on all sides and the sky filled with demons. Early rising was typical for their kind, but it seemed Dante, Onyx, and Ash weren't the only ones heading toward the ornate building towering above the rest.

What the hell were they flying into? Hiding behind illusion felt less secure than it had in centuries.

Ash led them in a circle around the tower, away from the other demons, who seemed to be congregating on one side. "It would have been better to turn up in the middle of the night."

"Could you remember where we were in the time gap between realms?" Dante hadn't thought about that difference in so long. Days didn't change length in the Realm of the Damned. There were no seasons. It was one long, unchanging existence.

The top of the tower was more glass than stone, shimmering like a polished jewel. Dante, Onyx, and Ash hovered out of sight of the crowd.

"I feel him inside," Ash muttered.

The glass reflected the rising sun at their backs, completely obscuring the interior of the building. At least their illusions held firm. Not even a shadow betrayed their presence.

Should they burst in or try to open a window quietly?

Abruptly, the birdsong cut off. Two large panes of glass in front of Dante swung open, revealing Lucifer in full demon form, his expression hard, fangs accentuating his frown.

Impossibly, his burning red eyes focused on Dante before flicking to Ash and Onyx on either side.

"Brothers, I was hoping to find you."

29

OLLIE

OLLIE FOLLOWED Harper and Nico down the service stairwell. There must've been great soundproofing because he didn't hear any music or dinging slot machines.

"Is Onyx always like that?" Nico asked, voice shaky. He had Ollie's sympathy.

"No," Harper said vehemently, looking back at Ollie for agreement.

"He's actually a decent guy. I think that was more about Ash and Dante than you." Didn't Onyx care about giving such a bad impression? It was worse than the first time Ollie had met him.

"If you say so." Nico shook his head and opened a door. "We can head down to the club if you want, but I should introduce you to Rowan first."

"Of course. We don't want to be rude." Harper dropped his voice. "I was kidding about getting a lap dance."

Nico chuckled. "No shame if you want one."

He led them down a carpeted hall to a polished wooden door and held it open. Ollie followed Harper into a large corner office. Low, moody light filled the room. There was a hint of cigar smoke and something sharp in the air, and while nothing about the room should have been threatening, Ollie wanted to leave.

Nico shut the door, addressing the man sitting at the desk by the window. "Here we are."

There was no immediate response.

Ollie half expected the vampire to be ghostly pale and wearing a cape, maybe looking like he'd recently popped out of a coffin. That was far from the case.

Rowan sat poised, eyeing them with a keen dark gaze, his skin golden brown and glowing with life.

Harper stepped up to the desk, seemingly without a care in the world for the vampire sitting behind it. Ollie willed himself to project confidence. He reached for Dante, detecting unease in his mate.

Rowan stood, buttoning the jacket of his perfectly tailored suit, and brushed his long dark hair over his shoulder. "Thank you, Nico," he said as if Nico had done him a favor. "Harper Nightingale and Ollie Hudson, it's nice to make your acquaintance. I'm Rowan Valero."

He smiled, and Ollie's neck prickled. Rowan had his fangs hidden, but somehow he looked less human than the demons, as if Ollie could sense the magic in him. Ollie averted his gaze.

Harper dipped his head. "Thanks for offering us a place for the night."

Rowan stepped—glided?—out from behind the desk. "Don't mention it. Any offer of help from Nico is an offer from me."

Well, that sounded ominous. They were sure about trusting Nico, right?

"Would you like a drink?" Rowan gestured to a small bar set out in the corner. "Bourbon? Tea? Water?"

"I wouldn't turn down a water." Harper chuckled for no reason. Maybe he was more nervous than he seemed.

"Come sit." Rowan pointed to two leather sofas separated by a glass coffee table.

Everything from the walls of books to the immaculate furniture looked expensive. Ollie imagined the kind of fancy lawyer he'd never be able to afford might have an office like this.

Nico collapsed onto the cushions like he'd finally come home after a long day.

Ollie sat on the opposite sofa, perching so close to Harper they were almost touching.

"A water for you too?" Rowan asked, piercing eyes drilling into Ollie as he handed Harper his drink and Nico a glass that seemed to be filled with bourbon.

"Yes, thank you." Ollie rubbed sweaty palms on his jeans.

Rowan turned away. "New to the magic world?"

Ollie cleared his throat. "Yeah." Fuck, it must be obvious.

"Well, you know the right people. You're both welcome at my club any time. The casino too." Rowan returned with Ollie's water and a bourbon for himself. "The stage areas are open to the public, so no mentioning magic down there, but the third floor and above are magic community and aware humans only." He focused on Harper. "Spells are forbidden on the premises."

"Understood." Harper shifted in his seat. "I've never been to a casino. Or a strip club."

Rowen's eyes flashed and his fangs lengthened enough to draw attention. "How fun."

Nico side-eyed the vampire. "Are you finished?"

Rowan pouted, expression turning alarmingly innocent as his fangs retracted. "Yes, fine." He threw back his drink and his aura shifted, some of the tension leaving the room. "I'm not so scary. You two can relax."

Ollie didn't believe him.

"We can't all be as approachable as Nico," the vampire

continued. "Too much of a friendly reputation, and you can't intimidate your enemies."

Nico raised his glass to his lips. "You do need both sides of the coin."

"We really appreciate you looking out for us tonight," Harper said, and Ollie nodded his agreement, even if he wasn't completely comfortable.

"It's what we do." Rowan shrugged like it was nothing. "I don't advertise it, so I'd appreciate it if you kept this favor between us." He waited for Ollie and Harper to nod. "I have some work to do, so I'll leave you in Nico's hands, but I'll be in the building if you need me. Feel free to call on my coven. Many of them are lurking around."

How would they know who was in Rowan's coven? Maybe Nico knew them all. Ollie didn't ask, and Rowan exited the room.

He relaxed a fraction.

At least Rowan would be busy elsewhere. It was one less thing to be unsure of. Ollie needed to project confidence and good vibes for Dante.

There was a lot of confusion and surprise coming down the bond. "How do you think they're doing?" Ollie asked Harper in a low voice even though Rowan had closed the door behind him.

"Okay. Doesn't seem like anything major has happened. Maybe it's not what they expected?" Harper's brow scrunched like he was concentrating hard.

"Yeah, but that makes sense after they've been gone so long."

Nico set his bourbon down. "Are you communicating with Ash and Dante?"

Ollie and Harper made eye contact.

"Yeah." Harper leaned forward, voice low. "There's a telepathic element to our connection."

Nico grimaced. "That seems intense."

"It can be," Ollie admitted. "I was pretty hesitant, but Dante can block it if I want, and it's good in times like this."

"Hm." Nico considered Ollie skeptically. "You're comfortable with how this turned out for you?"

"It's a work in progress, not gonna lie. But I'd have chosen this with Dante eventually. We're good together."

"Okay. I'll take your word for it. You're very understanding for a human who's new to our world." Nico picked up his drink. "I'm glad you called me tonight, Harper. Whatever those three are dealing with won't get into this building. Unless it's Lucifer." He made a sound like that was ridiculous.

Harper choked on his water, and Nico's face fell.

"You're kidding me? The dangerous situation they're dealing with is the Devil?" Nico hissed.

"He won't come after us. Don't worry," Harper hurried to say. "No one knows where we are."

Nico finished his drink. "That's a good point. Fuck, if Rowan knew I'd brought that kind of trouble here, he'd..." Nico shook his head.

"Not have wanted to help?" Ollie guessed.

"Have been impressed," Nico corrected. "Hopefully, he'll never know. Do you guys want to stay in here, or would you rather have a distraction?"

"I don't really want to sit around." Harper directed a questioning look at Ollie.

"Me either. Time's going too slow already." Feeling Dante brush up against him gave Ollie rushes of warm affection despite Dante's undercurrent of unease. Ollie wanted to send something strong back, other than his burgeoning distrust of vampires.

"Do either of you know how to play poker?" Nico asked.

Harper shook his head.

"Not enough to want to put money on it." Ollie didn't have the disposable income for gambling. "I'd rather tip strippers than lose at cards."

Harper stood and pulled Ollie up. "Why don't we start with a cocktail at the bar? I want to check out the casino at least a little. Then we can see the dancers."

Nico polished off his drink. "I'll introduce you to Leo. He makes better cocktails than should be legal."

They closed the office behind them, Nico nodding to two suited men standing in the hall. Down another flight of stairs, carpeted in red, two more suited men greeted them. They had to be security. Coven members, maybe?

Ollie didn't let his gaze linger. It was like being in a Mafia movie or something.

"Good luck." The man on the right opened the door for Nico and sound spilled into the corridor.

"I might need it," Nico said as he walked into the casino, most likely not referring to gambling.

Bright light and cool air gave Ollie a jolt. That sharp scent from Rowan's office filled the air here too, but Ollie couldn't place it.

The floor was full of people. A few slot machines lined the far wall, but most of the space was taken up by card tables. Roulette and craps were set up closer to the bar, and a live band played in the corner.

"Do you think everyone here is a witch or vampire?" Ollie asked Harper.

"No, there's plenty of humans too. Staff and guests."

"You can tell by looking?"

Harper shook his head. "It's not visual. I have to actively scan for magic. It's a habit whenever I walk into a room. Rowan was projecting his power back there, so there was no missing it, but no one here is doing that."

Ollie scanned the room again as they moved through the crowd. "I felt Rowan projecting."

Harper's brows rose. "Wow, that's unusual."

"Maybe it has to do with your connection to Dante," Nico guessed.

Ollie shrugged. He'd have to ask his mate. "So most humans wouldn't have been able to tell Rowan was something else?"

Nico leaned against the polished bar. "They'd have felt uneasy or afraid. Gotten a bad vibe or decided he was untrustworthy, but they wouldn't have known why."

Ollie supposed he'd never have assumed Rowan wasn't human a month ago. Maybe he couldn't really sense magic. He just knew what the unsettling feeling meant.

Harper picked up a cocktail menu. "Oh, these look amazing. There's a chocolate orange martini."

He and Ollie took their time reading through the drink options. Harper wanted to try them all and might have if they weren't here under such serious circumstances.

Ollie ordered a piña colada because why not. The bartender made a show of mixing their drinks, chatting with Nico about something Ollie didn't bother trying to interpret.

"Oh shit, that's good. What's in this?" Ollie groaned after his first sip.

The bartender, Leo, grinned, showing what was surely a bit of fang. "Nothing more than what it says on the menu."

"I'm guessing you haven't heard of witch-brewed rum?" Nico pulled a bottle from behind the bar, showing it to Ollie. "Gives it a special kick."

Ollie froze, halfway to taking another sip. "Like a magic kick? Is a spell going to get me?"

Leo laughed, the sound melodic. "There's no spell on what you're drinking. Magic used during the distilling and aging processes enhances flavor. That's all."

"We'd never serve it to you otherwise," Nico added. "At least without telling you what the magic would do to you first."

Harper nudged him. "Believe me, no potion would taste this good."

"That's a relief," Ollie muttered before taking another sip.

When he turned around, a third of Harper's drink was already gone. Harper's cheeks flushed red. "This martini is dangerous. I already want another. Unless I can get my hands on a piece of chocolate cake."

Ollie and Nico laughed.

Leo passed Nico a pile of chips. "Go show your boys some fun. They're too lively to darken my bar like you always do."

Nico swiped the chips with an eye roll and pushed off the bar. "You're lucky to have me."

A wave of surprise hit Ollie out of nowhere. He clutched his glass. What had Dante seen? Harper's brow furrowed like he'd sensed something too. He grabbed Ollie by the hand and pulled him after Nico.

Surprise wasn't necessarily bad. No fear followed, so at least there was that.

Nico divided the chips between Ollie and Harper. "You can thank Rowan for these."

"He's very generous. Leo too." Harper gestured to an unoccupied roulette wheel with his drink, his eyes lighting. "Let's try this one!"

"He's like a kid in a candy shop," Nico muttered to Ollie.

"Totally." He loved how much joy Harper got out of everything. His life with the Nightingale Coven had been so dark, and now that he was getting to have so many firsts, he seemed to hold nothing back.

Once Ollie and Nico explained how to play, Harper placed his bet. He was adorably dejected when he lost but immediately placed another, and his excitement flooded back.

The wheel spun, the ball circling. It bounced into a black pocket.

"Oh Satan! I won!" Harper turned to Ollie, grabbing him by the shoulders.

"Nice one, but did you say *Satan?*"

"Sorry." Harper pulled a face. "Old habit. You don't tend to swear to god when you grew up like I did."

"No, I suppose not."

Next time, Ollie placed a bet too. Another few people joined them, and Harper happened to win a few more times. Fuck, he was lucky.

Harper played until he'd lost almost all the money he'd won. He didn't seem to care, probably because they'd gotten the chips for free, but Harper wasn't ready to lose every chip he had.

He gathered the little he had left. "Let's try something else."

Nico had been pulled into a conversation with a woman at the next table, so they left him to it, though Ollie swore he felt Nico watching as they crossed the casino floor.

Shock flared down the bond, followed by a blinding anger. Ollie stopped in his tracks, rubbing his chest. Had Dante found Lucifer? Was this it? Dante's feelings became muddled and hard to follow.

What did that mean? Ollie closed his eyes, all his focus on Dante.

Harper put a hand on Ollie's shoulder. "Maybe we should sit down for a minute."

"Good call." The casino seemed to rear back to life around him, and Harper led him toward the bar.

They settled on stools away from Leo, who was chatting with other customers. The bond went quiet. Did that mean whatever upset Dante was finished? Ollie could still feel Dante like a solid presence in his chest, but not more than that.

"Maybe we should go back to the office." Suddenly, being in a crowded room didn't seem like such a good idea.

Harper discarded his empty glass. "Yeah, I'm feeling a lot less like screwing around. We can come back some other time when we can enjoy it. I'll go get Nico."

"Ollie?" a soft voice called from behind him.

He spun in his seat and came face-to-face with Pamala. "Oh hey."

"Funny seeing you here of all places." She set a glass of wine on the bar. "My hair still looks amazing, so thank you." She turned her head from side to side.

She was right, hardly a strand had come out of place. "You're welcome. Was your event here? Sorry, this is my friend Harper. Harper, this is one of my clients, Pamala."

Harper said a quick hello before disappearing to fetch Nico.

Pamala gave a cute little shrug. "The fundraiser wasn't here, but what's a night out without an after-party, right?"

"Right," Ollie agreed as a sharp stab of rage came down the bond. He pushed it away, needing to focus on the conversation until he could get away. At least an after-party explained why Pamala wasn't wearing the floor-length dress she'd shown Ollie on her phone.

"Can I get you a drink?" Pamala asked.

"Oh, thank you, but no. I was about to head out." Ollie pointed after Harper.

"Maybe some other time. I'm sure I'll be seeing you again." She dropped her voice. "Especially if things go well with your sweet coworker. Oh!" She clapped her hands together. "Before you go, can I introduce you to one person? My friend absolutely loved what you did with my hair."

Ollie wasn't sure how to say no politely. "Sure." He stood, spotting Harper and Nico, who were still talking to that same woman by the roulette wheels.

"Perfect." Pamala linked her arm with Ollie's and pulled him along.

Fuck she was tall. Ollie hadn't noticed until now that she wasn't even wearing heels. Her grip wasn't tight, but something about it drew Ollie's attention, and it dawned on him that if Pamala was in the casino, she must know about magic.

"Oh damn. I think she's gone to the restroom." Pamala led Ollie toward an open doorway with a restroom sign.

Ollie slowed. "We can wait out here until she gets back."

It was like Pamala hadn't heard. She urged him into the hall, and Ollie stopped in front of the first restroom, extracting his arm from Pamala's.

"Hey, wait."

Pamala turned to face him. She was very close. Her eyes glowed, immaculately done lips stretching in a wide smile. "Come with me," she purred.

Ollie fell back into step with her. He had to go. Certainty burned within him. This was important. He couldn't leave Pamala's side, no matter what.

Pamala opened a door at the end of the hall and Ollie followed her into the service stairwell.

Everything went black.

30

DANTE

Hot fire burned through Dante's blood. He launched himself at Lucifer, with Ash and Onyx at his wingtips.

*Brothers?* How dare Lucifer utter that word like it meant anything to him.

"Wait!" The Devil stumbled back from the open window.

Dante crashed into him and closed his hands around Lucifer's throat. Wind rushed in Dante's ears, or maybe it was the blood roaring through his veins. He didn't see Luc before him. All he saw was Ollie, bloody and lifeless.

A roar ripped from his lungs. Dante's fingers sunk into Lucifer's throat, and he clawed at him. Blood sprayed, coating his hands, the smell hitting hard. Dante choked. Luc deserved this. He deserved worse. But the hot, sticky feeling made Dante's skin crawl.

"You have to pay," Dante screamed in Lucifer's face. "You hurt him, and now you pay."

"Y-yes," Luc gurgled, blood leaking from his mouth even as his mangled neck healed.

Dante's hands stilled, his breath heaving. Luc wasn't moving. He wasn't fighting. The Devil lay there giving the impression he'd let Dante rip his head clean off without so much as lifting a finger in self-defense.

Dante blinked, his pulse drumming impossibly faster. "Fight me, you piece of shit."

Luc's eyes turned a dull brown, completely devoid of fire or emotion. "For what?"

*"For what?"* Dante bashed Luc's head into the floor. There was a crack, and Luc's gaze slid out of focus before his magic healed the damage to his brain. "For nearly killing my mate."

Luc blinked. "And why would I fight you for that? It's your motivation, not mine."

Dante roared. He couldn't take Lucifer's mind games.

The damned traitor didn't move. Dante's fire burned until his skin felt like it might start smoking, but the urge to rip and destroy faded.

A hand landed on Dante's shoulder. Ash pulled him up, glowing orange with protective fire. Onyx glowed blue beside him. Dante hadn't even protected himself. He wasn't thinking. Not that it mattered. Lucifer lay on the ground as if he'd accepted defeat.

Except Lucifer would never accept defeat.

"What are you up to?" Dante snarled.

Luc's lip curled. "Letting you purge the anger from your system. Get it out."

"My anger will never be purged. He is my mate, Luc. How could you?"

"I didn't believe you," Lucifer growled, pushing to a sitting position, grotesque splatters of blood marring his chest, face, and healed throat. "You had to be lying. Taunting me. I thought..."

"So you tested him with attempted murder?" Ash growled, his own anger rising. "You nearly strangled Harper."

"There's no excuse, Luc," Onyx said more calmly, but not without emotion.

Lucifer turned his attention to his brother. "Did I say anything about an excuse? Don't put words in my mouth. I didn't believe Ash or Dante. That's the reason I did what I did, nothing more. What was a human life in the face of confirming the lie? The boy would have reincarnated."

Dante shot lightning at Luc's face, a shielding red glow appearing in time to save him. "Oh, are you done taking it? Ready to fight?" Dante sheathed himself in a swath of protective black flame.

"No." Luc stood. "I'm sorry, Dante. Ash. I'm not arguing or fighting. I'm sorry."

"Bullshit," Onyx spat, taking the word from Dante's lips. "You've never been sorry a day in your life."

Luc's nostrils flared. "How would you know?"

"If you're sorry, kneel down." Ash pointed to the polished stone floor beneath his feet. "Take your punishment without protest."

Lucifer took a step back. "What punishment?"

Did Lucifer think all he needed to do was shed a little blood, and they'd forget about everything? Dante snorted. "The punishment you should have faced centuries ago. For everything you've done."

"No. Wait." Lucifer held up a hand, his eyes darting to the side where a strange iridescent screen glowed.

Of course he had a plan. The apology was probably part of it. Dante had given him too much of a chance already.

What was he doing in this tower? The room was bare of furniture and decoration except for the glowing screen. There didn't seem to be a door or opening leading to the lower levels. All around clear glass shone, demons gathering outside the windows.

Could they see in, or was the glittery, reflective surface enough to obscure the interior from all angles? No one seemed to be looking directly at them. Perhaps an illusion kept them hidden inside.

With a flick of his wrist, Dante closed the glass panels behind them, sealing them shut with a spell and trapping them in the odd space.

"Dante, just—" Luc's eyes flared, cut off as a tendril of Onyx's blue power encircled his neck.

"Open the prison," Onyx ground out, face contorted with the strain of forcing the spell past Luc's shield.

Ash dropped to his knees and pressed a palm to the floor, pouring power into the spell they'd crafted to open a prison that existed between realms. The magic worked best if they could tie the entrance to something physical, and the stone tiles would work fine.

Dante lent his power, murmuring along with Ash, but they needed Onyx too. Onyx grimaced as he cast a blue glow their way, still maintaining his hold on Lucifer. He needed help. Dante split his focus, gathering power for a lightning strike.

Lucifer grabbed the blue magic collaring him and pulled. The tendril snapped, and Onyx swore.

"We have to put him down first," Dante shouted, abandoning the prison spell.

Ash stood, and together, all three shot lightning at Lucifer. He disappeared, and the spells hit the windows behind him, sending crackling energy through the glass and reverberating around the room.

The light pouring in from outside intensified as if someone had flipped a switch.

"Fuck. He's gone to the Human Realm," Ash shouted at the same time Onyx said, "Why didn't the windows shatter?"

There was a thud, then Lucifer's voice. "Please, we need to talk."

They all spun around. Dante struck out with lightning. Luc

deflected with a shot of his own, the two spells colliding in midair with a thundering boom.

"Just listen for one moment," Lucifer begged, almost convincing Dante he meant it. Like he really was sorry.

But he'd never been sorry. Not in thousands of years, for anything he'd done.

"Give us control of your magic, and we'll listen to anything you have to say," Dante countered.

Lucifer's eyes flashed. "Control? Fuck that."

Dante laughed. "I knew you didn't mean it. You aren't giving up. You came to hunt us, and now that the tables have turned, you're scrambling."

"Is that so?" Lucifer sent a bolt of lightning flashing in Dante's direction.

Onyx blocked it before it collided with Dante's shield.

Shouts rose outside the tower. Demons were pointing inside, looks of rage on their faces. If they couldn't see in before, they could now.

"You must pay for what you've done to Ollie and Harper." Dante circled Luc and shot him again.

Lucifer swiftly blocked the blow. Onyx shot from the other side, but Lucifer was too quick. He blocked the second strike, his eyes burning red. "They're both fine. What is there to pay for?"

"They are not fine," Dante shouted, striking Luc again. The Devil blocked it.

"And what about everyone else?" Ash asked. "Our mates aren't the only ones you've wronged."

Dante struck exactly as Onyx and Ash did. Luc blocked Dante's hit, but the other two struck home and Luc went rigid.

Onyx was on Lucifer in a flash, pulling a potion from his pocket. "Open the prison."

Dante and Ash kneeled, starting the spell over.

Onyx yanked Luc's mouth open, shocking him again in the process, and popped the cap off the vial.

Glass exploded around them, shards flying and cutting through Dante's shield, slicing his exposed skin. He hissed, folding his wings to protect his body. Ash shouted beside him, barely audible over the sound of beating wings.

Dante's cuts healed rapidly and he lowered his wings. Demons flew in from all sides. Onyx growled as a wing knocked his hand and the potion went flying. Hands closed around Dante's throat from behind, and he reared back.

Ash blasted the attacker off and Dante flapped his wings, keeping anyone from getting close.

"Get Lucifer!" Onyx shouted. A boom sounded and something hit the floor.

Two demons shot lightning at Ash simultaneously and his shield wavered. Dante incapacitated a demon as he lunged for him, but another was right behind him.

Fuck. There had to be more than two dozen demons surrounding them. A few were recognizable as those who'd always hovered around Luc. How had he gained the support of so many others? Surely, not even the city and all its new perks could make demons forget what he'd done.

Pain erupted in Dante's back and his teeth clenched, his heart stopping. Someone had broken his shield completely, or more likely, several someones. He couldn't stave off multiple attacks indefinitely. No one could.

Lucifer rose from the chaos, fully recovered. "I did say to give me time to explain."

His taunting tone made Dante want to scream. If he had to listen to the miserable retch gloat...but Lucifer turned away.

He walked toward the iridescent screen, which had escaped damage in the blast, likely by magic.

Dante was shocked with lightning again. Ash too, and Onyx

was nowhere to be seen. Where was he? Had he fallen from one of the broken windows? There were too many bodies and wings crowding the space to be sure.

Another shock vibrated through Dante's body and he blacked out for a second. When he came to, Lucifer stood in front of the screen, which was now displaying a series of flashing runes from the Eternal Realm.

"Clear the floor." Lucifer swiped a hand across the screen and the demons crowding the destroyed room backed away from the center. "It's time to get out of here."

Lucifer pressed his palm to the flashing runes, and they flared with his red power. The ground trembled and demons shouted, more pressing in through the shattered windows.

A flare of acute fear hit Dante through the mating bond. *Ollie!*

Another shock of lightning hit him, but it hardly registered. Something was wrong with Ollie. His mate's fear grew, and a rising panic flooded Dante's emotions. Fuck, Dante couldn't think past Ollie needing him and not being there.

He had to protect Ollie. He could never be hurt again. But Lucifer was here... What was going on?

Magic sparked at the center of the room and a growing shimmer filled the air above the center of the stone floor. The shimmer grew and grew until it obscured Lucifer and the demons on the other side of the room.

Ash snarled. "He's opening—" His words cut off as someone shocked him.

There was no need for Ash to finish. A darkness opened in the middle of the room, crackling around the edges, as something pulled on Dante's chest, right behind his breastbone.

"It's true!" a demon shouted.

In a blur, demons rushed toward the shimmering gateway and disappeared into the darkness. Into the Human Realm.

Lucifer had opened a gateway between the realms. That tug on Dante's chest was the link he still bore to the confinement magic, which was now broken.

Ollie's fear flared again. "Ollie!" he called desperately as he was thrown to the ground. Whoever had been holding him was clearly more interested in escape than keeping him incapacitated.

Dante's call was lost in the chaos erupting around them. Demons flew in from all sides, shoving each other out of the way to get to the portal. Dante looked around frantically. He couldn't get up. A wall of flying demons pressed in from above.

Where was Lucifer? Where was Onyx?

Ash snarled.

Wings beat and demons cried with joy as they disappeared in droves, and all the while, Ollie's fear clawed at Dante's heart.

"We have to get back," he yelled.

"Where's Luc?" Ash shouted.

At last, the stampede thinned, revealing a nearly empty room.

Onyx was slumped near the edge of the stone floor, one arm hanging out the shattered floor-to-ceiling window. Dante rushed to his side, pulling Onyx from the ledge.

His face was a grayish color and no breath passed his lips.

"Why isn't he waking up?" Dante shook him. There were no visible wounds and Onyx's magic should have healed him from any poison or mortal death quickly.

Ash staggered toward them. "A curse. Fuck. We'll have to counteract it, but something is wrong with Harper."

Dante hoisted Onyx up. "Ollie too."

"It started before the portal opened. It can't be Luc." Ash took a breath and scanned the empty room once again. "Why would he let them out?"

It was the perfect diversion, but it couldn't have been

completely spontaneous. How long had that screen held Eternal runes? It wasn't how the containment spell was initially created. What had Luc changed?

"I don't know. We can worry about it later. Can you get us back with Onyx like this? He can't help with the spell."

Ash folded Onyx's wings, supporting him alongside Dante. "It should work since the containment is broken. It's not ideal, but I'm not flying through that portal with no idea where we'll end up."

It could deposit them anywhere on Earth, thousands of miles from their mates.

Ash began the spell, and Dante let his power loose. Ollie's fear hit him in a fresh wave.

He'd failed with Luc. Again. He wouldn't fail Ollie too.

31

———

## OLLIE

OLLIE STIRRED, darkness all around him. His face was pressed against something cold.

What the hell?

He remembered being in the casino. Pamala! She'd done something to him. Ollie's eyes flew open. He wasn't in the casino anymore. He was outside. It was dark, the air foul. He was in the street. No, an alley.

Where had Pamala gone? Ollie reached for his phone. He had to call Harper.

"Don't," said a soft voice behind him. Ollie's arm seized, muscles going rigid. "Keep your hands where I can see them."

"Okay." The tension fled, and Ollie pushed off the ground, twisting around to face Pamala. "W-what are you?"

She smiled, as lovely and unassuming as she'd been in the salon. "That doesn't matter." She stepped closer and grabbed Ollie's chin.

Ollie's skin crawled. His gut urged him to run, but it wouldn't help. She'd catch him. Magic him. Ollie had no hope against her.

With all his energy, he called down the bond. *Help!*

Pamala's eyes glowed. "Where did the demons go?"

Ollie was overwhelmed with the urge to answer. He couldn't fight it. "To the Realm of the Damned."

Pamala's eyes widened. "What did the Hounds do with Lillian and Maxwell?"

"Who?" Ollie's pulse pounded and his whole body went cold and shaky. When Pamala had used this strange power on him before he'd been calm, happily compliant. Not this time. "Somebody help me!"

Pamala's grip tightened on his chin. "Don't speak unless I ask you a question. You must tell the truth. What happened to the demons stalking the shearwaters?"

"They were sent back to the Realm of the Damned."

Pamala hissed and chills ran down Ollie's spine. "Traitors. They're as bad as Lucifer, imprisoning everyone like they're the only ones who deserve to be free. No wonder they're his dogs."

It wasn't true, but Ollie couldn't speak to object.

How did Pamala know so much? How did she even know he was connected to the demons? She must have followed him from work, but he'd been invisible when flying to Rowan's club with Dante.

"They obviously care about you, sending the birds to watch over you." Pamala turned Ollie's head from side to side like she was inspecting him. "Will they rescue you?"

"Yes," Ollie said, trying and failing to add a plea not to do this.

"Then be a good little hostage and stay close. No talking, and don't touch your phone." She released his chin and strode down the alley. "Hurry, along."

Ollie caught up against his will. His whole body tingled and his mind fogged as he fought to disobey.

*Dante!* He pushed jolts of anxiety and fear down the bond. But what if he distracted Dante, and something even worse happened? He tried to rein it in. Ollie couldn't get a good read on Dante, his own emotions overwhelming everything else.

Commotion came from the street ahead, footsteps hitting the pavement hard. Pamala stopped short, grabbing Ollie by the back of his shirt collar.

Two suited men appeared at the alley entrance. "Stop!" one shouted as they both dropped their fangs.

Pamala dragged Ollie forward, unconcerned, her eyes flaring. "Sleep," she purred, and both vampires dropped to the alley floor.

Behind Ollie, a door crashed open. He couldn't turn to see who it was. Light flared around him, and he shuddered, a sensation like cold air passing over him.

He lurched from Pamala's grasp, suddenly free of her magical hold. "Help! She has mind control."

Ollie spun away from Pamala, and Harper rushed toward him. Ollie ran and collided with his friend, almost going limp as Harper's arms wrapped around him.

Nico pushed past, muttering something unintelligible, his hands glowing.

"Nico, wait!" Harper yelled.

Pamala growled. She swiped her arm in front of her, hand flicking in an upward motion, and Nico flew back, sailing past Ollie and Harper and crashing into the back of the alley.

"Don't look in her eyes." Harper pulled Ollie against him so his face was buried in his neck. "Fuck, I don't know what spell Nico used to break her hypnosis."

"You think you can avoid my stare and that will save you?" Pamala asked. "Like I have no other powers? You can't stop me from taking Ollie. Two witches are nothing against me, so hand over your friend, and no one has to get hurt. Well, any more hurt."

No sound came from the back of the alley. Was Nico okay?

Ollie was desperate to look but couldn't risk falling under Pamala's spell.

Harper's grip on Ollie tightened. "You're a demon. What are you doing here?"

Pamala ignored the question. Footsteps sounded on the pavement. She sighed. "Looks like it's two hostages then."

Something shifted behind Harper, and Nico launched out of the dark, a broken piece of wood in his hand. There was a squelch and a grunt of exertion. Labored breathing.

Ollie couldn't take it. He looked.

Nico had run Pamala through with the wood, lodging it firmly in her chest, below her breasts, blood spreading across her shirt. She snarled and ripped the wood out, tossing it away.

Nico frantically wove his magic, hands flashing.

Something hot flared over Ollie's skin, and he jolted.

"Sorry," Harper whispered. "That heat is a shield. I don't know how it'll hold up against a demon, but it's better than nothing."

Pamala spat blood. "Missed my heart. You could have had me out for a good minute if you had better aim."

"Run," Nico called.

Ollie wanted to run, but he couldn't leave Nico behind, even if he had no magic or hope of fighting a demon.

Harper didn't flee either. Instead, he raised his arms and water from the gutter flew into the air. He said something too fast for Ollie to make out and the water rushed toward Pamala, transforming with a hiss.

Steam hit her face and she yelped, her yellow magic flaring. Nico hit her with whatever spell he'd been working, but the blow was met with another yellow glow, seeming to deflect whatever Nico was trying to do.

A shout sounded from above. In a rush of air, Dante landed beside Ollie, followed swiftly by Ash, carrying Onyx. Dante's gaze ran over Ollie, relief written all over his face, but he didn't linger. In a flash, he had Pamala in a headlock.

"Keep away from my mate," Dante growled in her ear.

"*Mate?*" Pamala squeaked, sounding scared for the first time.

"Yes, you heard me. Ollie is my bonded mate. Why are you attacking him and his companions?"

"I'm sorry." Pamala struggled, but Dante didn't let her up.

Nico retreated, grabbing Ollie and checking him over while Harper rushed to Ash's side.

Was Onyx unconscious? After what Pamala had endured, that seemed impossible. What had happened? Dante was covered in flecks of blood.

"I didn't know he was your mate. I swear," Pamala said desperately, a curtain of hair obscuring her face as it fell out of Ollie's carefully placed pins. "You sent the shearwaters to protect him the day Lillian and Maxwell disappeared. I followed the birds and figured he must be important enough for you to make a trade, but I never..."

"A trade for what?" Dante asked, his gaze finding Ollie, eyes burning.

"Your human—your mate—said you banished my friends to the Realm of the Damned. I want them back. We just want to be free. You'll never hear from us again, I promise."

To Ollie's surprise, Dante released Pamala. She straightened, brushing back her hair, but made no other move.

Dante crossed his arms. "You wanted to trade Ollie for your friends' return?"

"Yes, but I'd never have done so if I'd known he was your *mate*. A connection that sacred shouldn't be exploited. Even knowing you have a mate is... It's a miracle. After so long, it didn't even cross my mind. I thought we were doomed."

Pamala's whole demeanor seemed to change, looking between Dante and Ollie with frantic awe.

Nico took a bold step toward her. Or at least it was bold to Ollie. Pamala might have had a drastic change of heart, but she was still dangerous.

"How did you get into the casino?" Nico asked.

Pamala blinked, focusing on Nico like he'd pulled her from the depths of her mind. "It wasn't difficult. I hypnotized the bouncers into believing I was on their approved guest list."

"But they're vampires," Nico argued. "They aren't susceptible to hypnosis like the rest of us."

"They aren't susceptible to other *vampire* hypnosis," Pamala corrected. "I'm a demon. The bloodsuckers may have stolen the power from us, but they never could achieve our strength."

"How did you find me at the casino?" Ollie could see how she'd used the shearwaters to find him at work, but that didn't help her find him tonight.

Pamala's gaze flicked to Dante, and she hesitated for the briefest moment. "I want you to know I have nothing to hide." She waited for Dante to nod. "I followed Ollie home from work and waited to see if you'd visit him. I cast a spell above the building to check for invisibility illusions. I couldn't see you, but the spell detected your presence, and I followed the magic here." She straightened her shoulders. "I suppose you're going to send me back now?"

"No." Dante ran a hand roughly over his horns. "We never wanted to trap anyone. I sent Maxwell and Lillian back for killing my birds, but with the knowledge they could return. We were going to free everyone once Lucifer was subdued, but Lucifer beat us to it. You can go find your friends. They're somewhere in the Human Realm already. So is everyone else. Even if I wanted to send you back, the gateway is open."

"So I can go?" Pamala didn't sound like she believed her luck.

Dante's eyes glowed a frightening black. "Yes, if you agree to never conspire against me, Ash, or Onyx, and if I ever see you near my mate or Ash's, you'll wish you'd never met me."

"You'll never see me again," she said hastily, putting up her hands. "I only wanted Lillian and Maxwell back. It seemed you were on Lucifer's side, content to imprison us. But you're not? And you're saying you *both* have mates? How? Were you really going to release us all?"

Dante pushed past her and wrapped Ollie in a tight embrace. "I don't have the time or the desire to explain. We have to attend to Onyx."

To Ollie's surprise, Pamala nodded in understanding. Ollie expected her to make a quick exit, but she remained still as everyone turned away.

"Make sure no one comes down here," Nico said to her, almost as an afterthought.

Pamala agreed and went to guard the front of the alley.

Nico's attention settled on Onyx, concern cutting creases around his eyes. "What happened to him?"

"A curse." Ash laid Onyx on the pavement. "Between Dante and I, we should be able to counter it."

"I can help," Pamala called.

Ollie frowned at her. "Is she seriously going to act like she didn't try to kidnap me?"

"I think she's trying to prove she'd never have kidnapped you if she knew you were my mate," Dante said, simmering anger traveling through the bond despite his outward calm.

Ollie's head spun and he leaned hard against Dante, desperate to ask what the hell had happened, but not while Onyx was lying there so helpless.

Dante and Ash bowed their heads over Onyx. After a long

moment, the blue-haired demon began to glow with a mix of orange and black magic. Dante and Ash murmured in low tones, words unrecognizable. The longer it took, the more tense Ollie became.

With a sudden gasp, Onyx's eyes popped open. His gaze darted around, catching on each of them.

"*Ugh*. Too many live witches to be in Hell," he muttered dazedly. Then, like he'd remembered himself, he snapped, "Move! You're crowding me. Get out of my way." Onyx leaped from the ground and cracked his neck. "What did I miss?"

He swayed like he was drunk, and Nico caught his arm. "Careful."

"Hands off." Onyx pulled his arm away. "I don't need *your* help. Where the fuck is my miserable brother? What did he do to me?"

Dante clasped Onyx on the shoulder, steadying him, and explained how Lucifer had escaped in the rush as all the other demons flooded into the Human Realm.

Ollie's heart pounded. There were hundreds of demons on Earth. Lucifer was here.

Nico looked as pale as Ollie felt, his gaze locked on Onyx in a strange mix of emotion. "It's going to be chaos," Nico muttered, maybe not to Onyx, but it was hard to tell from the way he was staring.

"Not necessarily," Pamala butted in. She'd inched closer without anyone noticing. "Many will want to blend in—as we once did—and live their lives. Most of us never caused any problems in the first place and were imprisoned anyway. We aren't going to squander freedom."

"I don't know," Ash rumbled, sounding skeptical. "It only takes a few demons to cause chaos in the magic community."

Speaking of the magic community, Ollie noticed the ground behind Pamala was clear. "Where'd the vampires go?"

"I woke them and sent them on their way, memories wiped. Figured being attacked wasn't the best way to reveal demons were back."

"No, I'd much rather be able to discuss this with Rowan." Nico looked questioningly at Dante. "If that works for you? Because we can't keep him in the dark now. Not completely."

"Can you hold that thought for tonight?" Dante asked, sounding exhausted.

"Sure." Nico seemed almost relieved. "But let's not put off dealing with the increased demon population long."

"Well, I'll be going." Pamala pointed over her shoulder. "Sorry, Ollie. I hope there are no hard feelings. I was never going to hurt you."

"That doesn't make it okay." Ollie's cheeks flamed. Wasn't forcing him to do things against his will a form of hurting him? Or was this not a big deal to demons? Was kidnapping and hostage exchange how they operated? If that was the case, Nico was right. They couldn't put off telling everyone demons were back.

"No, it doesn't make it okay," Pamala said to Ollie's surprise. "I'm sorry. I wish I'd waited to act. Lillian and Maxwell would have come back if I'd done nothing, but I didn't know that, and I was so mad. I was afraid I'd disappear too if I didn't get the upper hand." She glanced at Ash and his arm around Harper. "Anyway, congratulations. I never dreamed I'd see another mated pair. You have no idea how much this changes things. Actually, you probably do. All the best for mated life." She gave a regal nod and was gone in a flash of inhuman speed.

"Who the fuck was she?" Onyx asked, and Ollie snorted with laughter.

"Ash and Harper can explain." Dante squeezed Ollie around the waist, warmth filling Ollie to the brim from the inside out. "Let's go home."

Ollie nestled into him. "Best idea I've heard all night."

"Me too," Harper agreed, and Nico seemed to take that as his cue to head back toward the casino.

Ollie grabbed Nico's arm, and he paused. "Thank you. I'm sorry this was such a mess."

Nico smiled. "Not a problem at all. Like I said, call on me any time. Especially now."

"We will," Ash promised.

Nico's posture slumped somewhat. "I think I'll call it a night. Leo has some witch-brewed bourbon with my name on it. Unless you need anything?" He turned to Onyx, who still seemed unsteady on his feet.

Onyx looked at Nico like he was the most baffling thing he'd ever seen. "Me? Why would I need anything from you?"

Nico shrugged and disappeared through the club's service door.

Ollie sagged into Dante. "Take me home?"

"I'd love to."

## 32

## DANTE

Relief swept over Dante as he flew Ollie home. He shouldn't have assumed Lillian and Maxwell were the only ones he had to worry about.

At least it hadn't turned out any worse. Everyone wanted to be free, and getting desperate or acting rashly was something every demon could understand.

Ollie seemed to recover from the attempted kidnapping quickly, peppering Dante with questions about the Realm of the Damned as they flew and explaining the details of his night.

Dante landed on the deck outside his home as Ollie finished his tale.

He hadn't asked Ollie if he wanted to go back to his place instead of returning to the apartment. There'd been no need. He'd felt their aligned desire to be close and undistracted by anyone else through the bond.

Sadness hit Dante in the gut as he thought of Onyx alone tonight. Ash would be with Harper, and while he had no doubt they'd offer to stay with Onyx, Onyx would likely push them away. If only Harper had found Onyx's mate like he'd found Dante's.

Ollie ran his hands through Dante's hair. "I'm so glad you're okay. You came just in time. It was nothing like what happened at the beach, but I was scared."

"I know, darling, and I'm sorry someone tried to use you to get to me." Dante held Ollie closer, having no intention of putting him down. "Let me take care of you. Show you everything is going to be all right."

"Okay, but I'm taking care of you right back."

Dante smiled and kissed him. "I'll allow it. At least I'll get one thing right tonight."

Ollie pulled back. "Hey, you're getting lots of things right. Lucifer getting away doesn't mean everything is ruined. The demons are free. It might be chaos, but it's how things are supposed to be."

"I can't argue with that."

"No, you can't. And I think I finally get what you mean about Lucifer not hurting me again after seeing Pamala flip her switch like that. I'm not afraid of Lucifer like I was that day after the beach. I hate him and don't think he should get away with everything he's done. What he did still haunts me. But I'm not terrified he's out there. At least not completely."

Determination shone in Ollie's eyes and through the bond. Dante loved it as much as he did every other aspect of his mate. "You're so much braver than me, Ollie."

"I don't know about that. I'm only brave because I have you. I'd still get heart palpitations and freeze if Lucifer snuck up on me."

"He'll be dealt with, and I'll make it my mission to ensure that doesn't happen. Who knows, maybe it'll be easier to take him down now that everyone is free. Plenty of others will still want justice." Even if freeing the demons himself would have gained Luc favor, there were thousands of years of bad blood to consider.

"Can we forget about him for the rest of the night?" Ollie nuzzled Dante's cheek. "Let's face it all in the morning."

"With you at my side, that sounds perfect. I believe you have a promise to fulfill."

Ollie's eyes flashed mischievously. "Does my needy demon want some personal attention?"

Dante nodded, heat pooling inside him.

"Then let's start with a shower." Ollie pointed toward the house, and Dante dutifully carried him inside.

Ash planned to track Luc, and if Luc was anywhere near the city, he'd call Dante, but making another move tonight didn't seem likely. Lucifer had gotten away, and Dante was sure he'd be scheming before coming for them again. He and Ollie were perfectly safe in the reserve.

Dante set Ollie down in the bathroom and froze, struck by a realization. Now that Luc had released the demons, there was no need to drag him, Ash, and Onyx back to the Realm of the Damned. Luc had abandoned his post as ruler of Hell. What did he need his dogs for now?

Would he leave them alone?

It was a strange thought, but it flew from Dante's mind the second Ollie pulled off his shirt and flung it away.

Ollie quickly shucked off his pants and underwear before reaching for Dante's belt. "Come here, sweet mate. Time to spoil you." Ollie dropped Dante's clothes to the floor and kneeled before him, Dante's cock stiffening rapidly.

"Fuck, Ollie." Dante ran both hands through Ollie's tumble of curls.

"*Mm,*" Ollie hummed as he took hold of Dante's cock. "Love giving you what you need, baby." He glanced up and guided Dante's cock to his lips, kissing the tip before opening his mouth and taking Dante in painfully slowly.

Dante breathed deep as hot suction enveloped him. He couldn't look away, not that he ever wanted to.

Ollie's cheeks bloomed a lovely crimson. His eyes burned and Dante's fire responded, sparking hot.

"You feel so good." Dante gasped as Ollie took him to the back of his throat. "Better than good. On my cock and in my heart."

Ollie whimpered, and desire flooded the bond like hot lava. Dante's chest expanded.

Tonight's loss seemed more manageable with Ollie holding him close, giving him what he needed. All wasn't forsaken. His mate had his back, and there was so much to look forward to, no matter what challenges they faced.

Whatever came, they'd conquer it together.

Ollie worked his throat, swallowing deliciously around Dante until Dante was dizzy. Sucking in desperate breaths through his nose, Ollie pulled back, grabbing Dante's ass, fingers digging in as he inched them toward Dante's tail.

"*Ugh*," Dante cried out, thrusting forward as Ollie wrapped a hand around the base of his tail. "Oh, Ollie, yes. Please. Don't stop."

Ollie groaned, bobbing his head as he worked Dante's tail, encouraging Dante to thrust with his other hand.

Dante's face burned. Tears welled in his mate's eyes as Dante thrust, stuffing his cock down Ollie's throat. He could feel Ollie craving more through the bond. Craving Dante's possession of his body. Dante gripped Ollie's hair firmly in both hands, the tip of his tail settling along the back of Ollie's neck, and fucked his mate's pretty face.

Ollie choked and squirmed, tears spilling onto his cheeks. He stroked the base of Dante's tail, tight and unfaltering as Dante used his mouth. Spit dripped down Ollie's chin, his face and neck a deep red.

"Ollie...Ollie," Dante moaned like he was pleading for his life, over and over, and every sound lit Ollie up and sent pleasure down the bond. "I'm going to come. Ollie. Oh fuck." Dante shuddered, and Ollie squeezed his tail, swallowing around his cock.

Dante came, vision blurring as the bond exploded, shooting pleasure along his spine and through his core. Ollie sputtered, scrambling to swallow as he held Dante in place by his ass. Dante thrust twice more and went lax, stroking Ollie's hair as his cock softened.

Ollie pulled back at last, panting, breath ragged and face a wreck of spit and tears. Dante hoisted him up, and Ollie wrapped his arms around Dante's neck, his legs around Dante's waist, his cock poking needily into Dante's stomach.

Dante kissed him, delving deep into Ollie's mouth and tasting his own seed. Ollie groaned, rubbing against Dante shamelessly and smearing his abs with precum.

Dante's lips trailed along Ollie's jaw to his neck. He nipped his mate's skin.

Ollie gripped him tighter, hand traveling to the back of Dante's head. "Yes, Dante. Bite me."

Dante kissed Ollie's neck and released his fangs. Ollie moaned, rutting against Dante, his sandalwood scent flooding the air. Dante sunk his teeth into his mate, and Ollie's sweet blood filled his mouth.

"Yes," Ollie moaned. "Yes, bite me. Mark me everywhere. Make me yours."

Dante released Ollie's neck and brought his lips to Ollie's ear. "You're already mine." Ollie shuddered, and Dante bit into the soft flesh behind the corner of his jaw.

Ollie gasped, thrusting harder against Dante.

Dante squeezed Ollie's rear, parting his cheeks. He withdrew his fangs, licking Ollie as he mumbled, "I want to bite this ass. Eat you everywhere."

"Yes," Ollie groaned. "Yes. Now. Or I'm gonna come."

Dante shuddered and set Ollie down, spinning him around and placing his hands to brace against the tiled wall. Ollie arched his back, ass out, and Dante kneeled, parting his cheeks and licking up his crack.

"*Dante*," Ollie wailed, legs shaking.

Dante growled, nuzzling and licking his mate's hole until Ollie sobbed with desperation. Dante cupped one of Ollie's ass cheeks in each hand, leaned in, and kissed them both before sinking his fangs into the swell of Ollie's right cheek.

Ollie cried out, shuddering from head to toe. Dante drank deep, massaging Ollie's hole with his fingers, and Ollie's orgasm crashed through him. Dante moaned as it zipped down the bond, reverberating through him as he pulled little aftershocks from his mate.

Ollie slumped against the wall. "Fuck me. Oh my god. That was... That was...fuck."

Dante stood, chest to Ollie's back, and pulled him in. Every one of his primal instincts was sated. "Tasty little mate."

Ollie huffed, melting into Dante. "Like you can talk. You taste pretty damn good too."

Dante grinned, pressing a kiss to Ollie's neck. Ollie trembled, and Dante scraped him with his fangs.

"Do it again," Ollie pleaded.

Dante bit into Ollie's neck, running his hands up and down his stomach, his chest, and over his cock and balls.

Ollie's breathing picked up, and he arched into it. "I'm going to get hard again."

"Good." Dante kissed the wound as it healed. "So am I."

Ollie shimmied his ass against Dante's burgeoning erection. "That kind of recovery time must be magic."

"Something like that." Dante cradled Ollie's hips and walked him around the tiled wall into the shower.

Ollie turned in his arms, nestling into the crook of Dante's neck as Dante turned on the water. Dante shook out his wings, and Ollie laughed, pulling Dante into a drawn-out kiss.

They washed each other slowly, taking their time as they explored each other's mouths. Once they were clean, Dante rubbed Ollie down a second time, peppering him with little bites, taking barely there sips from his neck, his shoulders, his pec above the nipple.

As he went to pull back, Ollie caught the back of his head. "A little more."

Dante flicked Ollie's nipple with his tongue, scraping it with his fangs. His tail circled Ollie's waist and held on. "Don't worry. We have a never-ending future. I'll always give you more."

33

OLLIE

Ollie caressed Dante's horns one at a time and brought their lips together. "It still doesn't feel like enough."

His body thrummed, tingling everywhere Dante's fangs had pierced him. With every bite, his desire to be consumed grew.

"Fuck me, Dante. I've been imagining it for so long."

Dante purred, so deep it might have been a growl. "Have you?"

"Pretty much since the start." Ollie gave Dante a sly smile, but he was so blissed out, it probably missed the mark. "I know we have eternity, but I want you now."

Dante rolled his hips, rubbing his erection against Ollie. "You want me inside your perfect ass? Fucking your face wasn't enough?"

Damn, Dante was stepping up his dirty talk. He was getting more comfortable letting loose, and Ollie approved.

"No, it wasn't enough," he whined, desire spiking as frustration heated his blood. He pulled from Dante's grasp and braced against the wall, sticking his ass out. "What happened to always giving me more? Fuck me."

Dante spread Ollie's cheeks and brushed his thumb briefly over his hole. "I will, don't worry. I'm enjoying the buildup. I think I like it when you beg too." His thumb returned slickened, and he pressed against Ollie's pucker.

Ollie gasped, pushing back. "Where'd the lube come from?"

Dante's breath tickled his ear. "Magic. I can't have my mate waiting when he's impatient and the lube is all the way in the other room."

"Oh, baby, you're perfect."

Dante purred, warmth flooding the bond. "So are you, Ollie. Just the way you are."

He pressed his thumb in and Ollie hissed, the stretch exactly what he needed.

"Is this what you imagined, alone in your bed?" Dante asked.

"Yes." Ollie turned his head. "But real-you is better."

Dante's glowing eyes flared completely black for a split second. He pulled out his thumb and thrust in two magically slicked fingers.

Ollie's breath punched from his lungs. Then Dante's lips were on his, kissing him with renewed desperation. The hint of copper on Dante's tongue, mixed with his peppermint scent, pushed Ollie even higher, creating a new thread between them that turned into an echo chamber, amplifying everything.

Dante fucked Ollie with his fingers until Ollie's legs trembled. When Dante finally added a third finger, he bit Ollie's lip, drawing blood.

Ollie moaned and almost came. Dante sucked his lip, curling his fingers inside him. Ollie's hand slipped on the wet tile, and he scrambled for balance.

Dante's wing was there in a flash, and Ollie held on. The other folded above them, blocking the shower spray and enveloping Ollie in a new kind of heat as Dante's demon fire burned.

Dante released Ollie's lip and nuzzled the back of his neck. "I'm so happy, Ollie. I can't wait for everything we're going to share. I can't wait to fuck you for the first time and can't wait to fuck you for the thousandth."

Ollie whimpered. He couldn't wait either.

Withdrawing his fingers, Dante replaced them with his slick cock. He rubbed it against Ollie's hole, smearing magic lube everywhere.

"I can't wait to love you, Ollie." He pushed in, girth stretching Ollie until his toes curled.

"Me too, baby," Ollie whined, vision going hazy as Dante filled him. "Me too."

Dante bottomed out and swiveled his hips against Ollie's stuffed ass. "Anything for you. Everything for you," he murmured into Ollie's hair, pulling back and snapping his hips forward.

Ollie shouted as the thrust pegged him just right. Dante fucked him like no one ever had, not giving him a moment to catch his breath. Ollie barreled toward his release, Dante's desire racing alongside his, and when Dante sank his fangs into Ollie's neck, Ollie came, his whole body exploding with pleasure.

As they came down, slowly catching their breath, Dante's chest heaving against Ollie's back, Ollie felt the first kernel of their future taking root inside him, glowing softly.

Dante was his and ahead lay something bright.

One week later.

Dante and Ash were coming over for dinner, and it was one hundred percent a double date.

"This Saturday night better go smoother than the last one," Harper muttered as a knock sounded on the door.

Ollie jumped up to get it. "I'm sure it will."

Dante swept him up in a kiss the moment he opened the door.

"Careful. Don't knock the cake." Ash shooed them to the side so he could get the many things he was carrying inside.

"If it survived the flight, I'm sure the cake will be fine," Dante said.

"Next time, I'll bake it here and save myself the trouble."

Dante's face fell. "But I like you baking at the house. It smells so good."

Ash raised a brow. "I thought it was torture because I never let you taste anything?"

Dante grumbled, "Doesn't mean I didn't like it," as Ash walked away.

"Come on." Ollie pulled him into the living room.

Harper and Ash were whispering in the kitchen doorway, so Ollie flopped onto the couch, dragging Dante along with him. It had been a long week, and all Ollie wanted to do was wrap up in his mate.

"I think we need to see each other more often. There are too many days between Saturdays."

Dante chuckled.

They'd closed off the bond again. Sharing twenty-four-seven was still too much, but Ollie was open to doing it more. Not only during sex but any time one of them needed the extra support.

"Why don't we meet for coffee in the middle of the week?" Dante suggested. "I've been looking up cafés near your work. A few bakeries too."

"That's perfect. And maybe we can get drinks with Dex one evening. He needs to meet you properly."

Dante's face broke into a wide smile. "I'd love to."

Harper joined them on the couch. "Do you guys want to go to Rowan's club after dinner? Ash and I are going to check out the dancers."

Ollie grinned at the pink staining Harper's cheeks. "You two have fun. I think Dante and I are going to play *World's End.*"

Harper shrugged. "Okay, suit yourself. I'll text Onyx and see if he'll meet us there."

Onyx had already declined to join them for dinner because "no one needed a fifth wheel," but it was worth trying again. "Good idea. Hopefully, he'll be up for that. Even with Ash."

"Hey," Ash called from the kitchen.

Ollie was disappointed Onyx wasn't coming over tonight. They'd postponed their fancy mates dinner, and hopefully, Onyx wasn't avoiding him and Harper. Ollie wished Onyx would find his mate. He cared about all his friends' love lives, but knowing how long Onyx had waited hurt Ollie's heart.

One day, Onyx would find his mate, and Ollie would be there to celebrate with him. No matter how long it took. It was one of the good things about immortality.

"Have you figured out how Luc saw through your invisibility illusion?" Harper asked Dante.

When they'd been in the Realm of the Damned, Lucifer had spotted them when they should have been invisible. Ollie had missed that part of the initial story, understandably, with how many things had been going on that night, but it had been bothering Dante ever since.

"No." Dante frowned, rubbing his horn. "It might have been a trick of the tower we found Luc in. There was at least one illusion cast on the glass, preventing anyone from seeing in. Maybe he also had a counterspell cast on the reverse side, so he could see past spells to a true view of what lay beyond."

Harper nodded like that was logical.

"It's our best guess," Ash added as he came out of the kitchen, wiping his hands on a towel.

Ash hadn't been able to track Lucifer down. He'd tried searching for Luc's magic, but instead of getting an idea of where he might be, Ash had been overwhelmed by Luc's power pinging from every direction as if there were hundreds of Lucifers.

Dante had wondered if Luc had incorporated his magic into the fabric of the portal, meaning any demon that passed through now carried his residual magic.

"I still can't believe he released everyone." Harper paused. "Are we sure witches can't come through the portal?"

Ash laid a hand on Harper's shoulder. "Once a mortal soul passes into the afterlife, reincarnation is the only way they can return to Earth. None of the witches in the Realm of the Damned will ever return to the Human Realm."

Harper was probably worried about his father, and Ollie couldn't blame him. At least Harper was safe. He seemed relieved to hear it but also like this wasn't the first time he'd asked for this particular reassurance.

"How long do you think Lucifer had been planning to release everyone?" Ollie asked.

Ash looked deeply displeased as he headed back into the kitchen, saying, "It couldn't have been long—release was never his aim—but controlling his spell with that computer screen makes me wonder. I don't know how long that took to set up."

Harper hopped up and followed his mate into the kitchen, asking something Ollie didn't understand about mixing magic and technology.

Ollie turned back to Dante. "Maybe knowing you can find

your mates changed Luc." He didn't like to give the Devil credit for anything, but it seemed to fit. Everything was about mates.

Dante clasped Ollie's hand. "Perhaps seeing our bond pushed him into action, but he hasn't completely changed. His apology was hollow. It served him in the moment, and I don't believe he's sorry."

"Maybe not for what he did to me." Ollie's gut still twisted when he thought about it, but fear didn't overwhelm him like it used to.

"Even if he's sorry for imprisoning everyone, setting demons free doesn't undo all his past wrongs. And I don't like not knowing Luc's new aims."

It was almost like Lucifer changing bothered Dante and Ash more than facing the same old enemy they'd known forever. Ollie got that. The unknown was so much harder to deal with.

Dante brought Ollie's hand to his lips and kissed his knuckles. Ollie's insides melted. He'd never get over how sweet his demon was.

"I know dealing with all this wasn't the life you wanted, Ollie. While we can still shape our relationship how we want, take things slow and date like humans, it doesn't look like we'll be settling into a completely quiet life anytime soon. I want to make sure you don't feel like you're disappearing into it all."

Ollie's chest tightened. "You're right. Demons and the Devil isn't the life I imagined. But my life can change without it changing me. This isn't the kind of taking over I was worried about. I was afraid of losing my independence, deprioritizing myself in favor of pleasing someone else. This is so far from that. You need me to help you get through this, Dante, and I want to support you. There's nothing to be lost in that."

Dante pulled Ollie onto his lap. Ollie's favorite place to be. "You're absolutely right. We've got this, mate. There's nothing we can't face together."

Ollie kissed Dante, fresh peppermint and soft lips. He couldn't agree more.

# EPILOGUE
## DANTE



Ten years later.

Dante walked down a busy street in the Arts District, heading toward the vocational school. It was a nice spring day, the trees covered in fresh blossoms. Dante could smell the change in the air signaling summer heat's early arrival. Surprise flared down the mating bond, but Ollie was doing his best to keep his emotions hidden.

Surprise could go either way. At least Dante detected no disappointment.

At last, he arrived at the school. Students milled around the courtyard, drinking coffee and looking at their phones.

As Dante contemplated entering the main building and waiting in the foyer, the doors opened and Ollie walked out, looking impeccable in his suit and tie. The sun caught on his golden curls, and he shone. Hell, he'd have been shining even in the dark. Ollie smiled so wide his dimples looked like they might etch permanently into his cheeks.

He spotted Dante and his eyes widened in delighted

surprise. Ollie rushed over, and Dante pulled him into a crushing hug.

"I got it!" Ollie said excitedly, the barrier he'd erected around their bond coming crashing down. "I got the job."

Dante spun him around. "That's wonderful, Ollie. I knew you would." He set him down, and Ollie pulled Dante into a quick kiss.

"We better get out of here before we make a scene and the dean changes his mind."

Dante laughed and pulled Ollie back the way he'd come. "Tell me everything."

"The meeting was more of an introduction than a second interview." Ollie shook his head as if exasperated with himself. "They went over the school's policies, HR stuff, and gave me a contract. I start fall semester."

Ollie had applied to teach at the Shearwater Landing Vocational School. As a senior stylist, he'd been mentoring stylists in training, and even though he was happy working at the salon all these years, Ollie had wanted more.

"Ellie said part-time will be perfect. She won't have any trouble redistributing some of my clients." Ollie threw Dante a sideways look. "I can't believe it's all working out."

"Have you texted Ellie?"

She now managed the salon, having taken over when the owner decided to step back.

"Not yet. I had to tell you first. You know that."

Dante purred softly. "Keeping me in suspense all afternoon was torture. You could have let me know instantly if you hadn't insisted on waiting to break the news."

Ollie knocked their shoulders together. "I wanted to see your face when you found out, and it was so worth it."

"I can't argue with that. I've rarely seen you so happy."

Their wedding day had blown Ollie's smile today out of the

water, of course. Waiting for Ollie at the altar had been one of the most transcendent moments of Dante's life.

While they might have mated sooner than either wanted, they got engaged at exactly the right moment. It was important for Ollie—and Dante—to take that step when they were ready, as a way to mark their commitment and promise to be each other's forever. To choose the relationship they were fated to.

Onyx had cried his eyes out at the ceremony, unwilling to contain his joy or thousands of years of heartache. Ollie's parents still asked about him and when they'd be invited to his wedding.

Ollie squeezed Dante's hand. "Where are we heading, by the way? Is there somewhere to take off around here?"

"We aren't flying home. I've got a surprise for you."

"A surprise, but no flying? Are you sure it doesn't involve whisking me away to a secluded spot so I can ravage you?"

Dante stopped in his tracks. "No, but that would have been an excellent idea. After the surprise, that's exactly what we're doing."

Ollie laughed. "We make the best plans when we work together."

Did they ever.

Dante brought Ollie to a new wine bar Onyx had discovered. Everyone and their mates were waiting inside.

Ollie had been nervous about applying for the teaching job, even after his initial interview went well. Dante knew that regardless of the outcome, Ollie would want his family around whether he'd gotten the job or not.

As they approached, Onyx and Harper waved out the window. Love flooded the bond as Ollie caught sight of them. "I've changed my mind. This is a better surprise than whisking me away for something sexy. I need both in my life."

Dante puffed out his chest. "Noted."

Ollie pulled Dante to a stop just outside the door. "I love you."

"I love you too, Ollie." Dante cupped Ollie's cheek, unable to contain his smile. "Every moment with you is one I'll treasure forever, even the hard ones. Hell, especially the hard ones. But I'm glad today is a good one where we can celebrate this life being everything you wanted."

Ollie wrapped his arms around Dante's waist. "It's turned out pretty damn good. I can't wait to see what we do when the next hundred years roll around."

Dante leaned in for a kiss. "That's when we'll get to all the things we haven't even begun to dream of."

The End

Looking for more Ollie and Dante? Don't miss *Dante & Ollie's Wedding Day*, a steamy bonus epilogue available for free to my newsletter subscribers. Join now and get a glimpse of their special day.

Will Onyx get his happily ever after? Find out in *Lovers of the Damned Book Three: Demon's Desire.*

Want to keep in touch? Join my reader group on Facebook, Colette Rivera's Coven. You can also find me on Patreon for monthly bonus ficlets, weekly WIP chapters, and behind the scenes updates.

# THANK YOU FOR READING DEMON'S HEART

I hoped you enjoyed Ollie and Dante's story.

Reviews are invaluable to authors. Please consider leaving a review for *Demon's Heart* on your favorite review site or the site where you purchased this book to help others find magical books they'll love.

# DEMON'S DESIRE

**Frustration shouldn't feel this good.**

Onyx doesn't need anyone, least of all a mate. He certainly doesn't need his demon brothers, but can't seem to get rid of them or their task of helping the magic world adjust to demonkind's return to the Human Realm.

What's worse than that? The most annoying, do-gooder witch won't leave Onyx alone.

Nico Velázquez may have discovered demons in Shearwater Landing by accident, but he's committed to ensuring a peaceful transition for everyone. Especially if it means working with Onyx.

Onyx is beautiful. Terrifying. Bratty.

Nico can't get him out of his head. Onyx needs someone to be firm with him. Someone who shows up for him, and Nico would love to break through his prickly exterior and take charge of the demon hiding beneath.

Onyx doesn't understand why Nico cares. Why does hating Nico feel so good? No one's ever captivated Onyx like Nico. It's maddening. If it weren't for all the wrong reasons, Onyx might think Nico was his mate.

Order Now

# ACKNOWLEDGMENTS

I loved Dante and Ollie's story so much! Thank you to everyone who was excited to see Dante find his mate at last. Every reader has my gratitude and thanks. You make this job amazing.

Thank you so much to Abbie Nicole for working with me on editing and proofreading Ollie and Dante's story. And thank you to Callie from CJ Editing for proofreading as well.

Molly from We Got You Covered Book Design did another fabulous cover. Thank you so much! Dante's stare is just so smoldery and perfect, and I love the shearwaters in the corner.

Thank you to Laura for chatting with me about plot as I wrote this one. You helped me see the rest of the series from this point forward, and all the pieces fell into place.

And finally, thank you to TK for your love and support, and for coming on this magical journey with me.

# ABOUT THE AUTHOR

Colette (she/they) is an author of queer paranormal romance novels living in New Zealand. Colette loves to write couples who take care of each other and show their soft sides in love, even when they're prickly in other facets of their lives. Sugar, spice, and magic are key ingredients in all of Colette's books.

Colette can be found on Instagram @colette_rivera and on Facebook under Colette Rivera Author. Colette can also be found on their website coletterivera.com where you can sign up to their newsletter for bonus epilogues and updates.

# ALSO BY COLETTE RIVERA

**Lovers of The Damned**

Demon's Mate

Demon's Desire

**Moonlight Falls**

The Fall of Elijah Gray

The Seduction of James Gray

The Cursed Sebastian Storm

The Heart of Moonlight Falls

**Love & Magic**

Give a Witch a Chance

Keep Your Witches Close

One Wicked Night

Witch Boyfriend Wanted